ENDLESS SILENT SCREAM

TONY J FORDER

A DI Bliss Novel

Copyright © 2020 Tony Forder

The right of Tony Forder to be identified as the Author of the Work has been asserted by him in accordance Copyright, Designs and Patents Act 1988.

First published in 2020 by Spare Nib Books

Apart from any use permitted under UK copyright law, this publication may only be reproduced, stored, or transmitted, in any form, or by any means, with prior permission in writing of the publisher or, in the case of reprographic production, in accordance with the terms of licences issued by the Copyright Licensing Agency.

All characters in this publication are fictitious and any resemblance to real persons, living or dead, is purely coincidental.

tonyjforder.com

tony@tonyjforder.com

Also by Tony J Forder

The DI Bliss Series
Bad to the Bone
The Scent of Guilt
If Fear Wins
The Reach of Shadows
The Death of Justice

The Mike Lynch Series
Scream Blue Murder
Cold Winter Sun

Standalone
Degrees of Darkness

For my readers, whose tireless support and friendship makes me want to be a better writer.

ONE

Bloody, bruised, battered and torn, the frail young girl with the thinnest arms Bliss had ever seen stood on a ledge six inches above the drainage gulley that ran around the edge of the hotel roof. She stared out at an unforgiving slate-grey sky, foggy puffs of breath escaping her open mouth like wraiths leaving the bodies of the recently departed. Rain beat down incessantly, plastering her long dark hair to her scalp. Her pale naked limbs visibly shivered in the frigid morning air. With legs no sturdier than her arms, it looked to Bliss as if a gust of wind might pick her up at any moment and float her out towards the oblivion she sought.

Both hands hung down by her sides. In the right she clutched a knife, her knuckles in stark white contrast to the lurid red that dripped and splashed onto the lead flashing and all over her splayed bare feet. The toes overhanging the lip of the parapet appeared incapable of bearing even this waif's inconsiderable weight for much longer. She was in trouble, and Bliss realised he needed to act.

He remained a dozen paces behind the slight figure, knowing that if she chose to step into what awaited her five storeys down, he had no chance of saving her. Increasingly terrified he might say or do the wrong thing, he inched toward what looked to him like a child in immense distress despite her still and silent exterior.

In more than thirty-five years in the job, he had never once been in this position before. It was a fine balance, he was discovering, an internal battle he struggled with as his gaze remained fixed on the girl while blinking rainwater away. If he called out, the sudden sound might cause her to stumble and fall, or panic and decide to take that final step into the void. If he continued creeping towards her, she would eventually become aware of his presence no matter how stealthy his tread. If she so much as sensed his approach, she could jump. His was an impossible situation to be in, yet it was also his to confront.

Unprepared for having his plans interrupted by a girl clearly intent on killing herself by jumping off the top of a tall city-centre building, he had no harness with which to secure himself – not that his own safety was his prime concern now that he was out on the slick wet roof with her. Having laid eyes on the girl, he could not bear the thought of her life ending in this manner. Not here. Not on a day like this. Not with him so close he was able to hear her every stuttering breath.

Rushing a suicidal individual on the edge of a roof in an attempt to grapple them to safety was for screenwriters only; Bliss knew his best chance was to engage with this young kid. To listen to what she had to say, empathise with her no matter what, then seek to establish a rapport with the intention of influencing a behavioural change that would see her step back into the safety of his embrace.

Risking another move closer, planting his feet deliberately on the slippery flat roof, Bliss's attention was snagged more by what he did not see than what he did. Previous jumpers in the city centre had for some reason been fans of multi-storey car parks, eventually leading to the Peterborough council erecting perimeter fencing of the kind that presented a barrier to all but the most determined. This girl's job had been made easier by the lack of even a single obstacle.

He had been sitting in a nearby coffee bar when the call came in, and had responded immediately. On his way up to the roof, where he eventually encountered hotel security, Bliss called in to inform the main switchboard back at Thorpe Wood police station of his attendance on scene. He left instructions for the first responding officers to clear the streets and pavements and the car park directly beneath the young girl, and to keep people as far away as they could. As unbelievable as it was to him, it was not unusual for a gathered crowd to actively encourage the potential suicide to end their life. The mere act of acknowledging this truth pained him. His final instruction was for someone better trained than himself to get there as quickly as humanly possible. Bliss had faced down the very worst kind of violent monsters during his long career, but for the first time in a long while, he felt wholly inadequate.

Reaching a decision he could no longer delay, Bliss began easing his way across to his right, angling away from the girl but maintaining an even distance from her. Rather than speak and have her react in a way that might cause her to lose her balance, he decided it would be better if he appeared in her peripheral vision. That way she would notice him gradually, and if she was capable of rational thought at this seminal moment in her life, she would realise he was making no attempt to physically interfere with her plans.

'Don't,' she said without turning her head.

Her voice took him by surprise. It was deeper than he had imagined was possible for a someone as slender and fragile as this child. Neither did the single word show any sign of wavering, let alone breaking, as she shivered and shook in the freezing rain.

'Don't what?' Bliss asked. 'I'm not coming anywhere near you. In fact, I'm walking further away from you than I was a moment or two ago. So what don't you want me to do?'

'Don't try talking me out of it.'

Bliss shook his head. 'I'm not about to do anything of the sort, sweetheart. Not a lot of point, given I reckon you've already done that yourself.'

This snagged her attention. 'Why d'you say that? You think I won't?' She shuffled her feet on the sodden ledge. It was just eighteen inches wide.

Bliss's stomach lurched. 'I don't know you well enough to say one way or the other. What I do know is that you must have been extremely determined to get this far, and yet you've been standing there now for a good fifteen or twenty minutes. It's a crappy day and you've clearly had an even crappier start to yours, but still you're with us. That tells me you're uncertain.'

'You think? Who are you, anyway?'

Telling the truth and establishing trust was textbook. Bliss's wild mind had no idea how any of what he had done so far would be judged in retrospect, but it was just him up here with this kid exposed to a cold December downpour and staring down at an ugly death. The deluge was relentless, bestowing yet more misery on an already bleak situation. The breeze had also picked up, rippling and pulling at the girl's long, baggy nightdress.

'Police,' he said. 'I'm Detective Inspector Jimmy Bliss.'

'A detective, eh? I am honoured.'

'Oh, they didn't send me, love. Don't flatter yourself. I work Major Crimes, and if you go ahead with your threat then you become just a red smudge on a wet pavement, and bugger all to do with me afterwards.'

'Cheerful fucker, ain't you?'

'Sweetheart, believe me, if my superiors had a choice they would never have sent me up first. I happened to be minding my own business nearby when word went out. Frankly, I'm the last person who should be standing here doing this.'

After a moment, the girl said, 'At least you're being honest with me, which is more than most people are.'

'I try my best. Now, you want to tell me what all this is about?'

'Not really.'

'Fair enough. Then, will you do me a small favour? Only, you look a bit wobbly and disorientated. I'm guessing you weren't exactly a champion weightlifter to begin with, but I don't suppose whatever caused all that blood and bruising all over you can have helped. You may still decide to jump when the time suits, if only to avoid listening to an old fart like me prattle on, but I don't think you want to fall by accident. Doesn't have quite the same panache about it. So how about you turn around and sit on the ledge, facing the roof? We're far enough away from each other. Even if I rushed you suddenly you could easily still propel yourself backwards and you're done. To tell the truth, you're making me very nervous standing there like that. I'm an old man, and I don't think my ticker will cope much longer.'

Quite unexpectedly, the girl did as Bliss suggested and slumped to her backside with a groan. He could tell she was exhausted and glad to be sitting. She put the knife down on the ledge beside her, the lightening rain pattering on its steel blade. Now that she was side on to him, Bliss noticed further bruising along her jawbone, puffiness beneath red, swollen eyes. Her arms and hands wore thin slashes of blood, to match one vivid streak which ran across her midriff. Though the flesh was covered, the thin, rain-soaked material of her filthy cream-coloured nightdress adhered to her body, leaving nothing much to the imagination.

'That's better,' Bliss said, happy to have established genuine contact. 'I don't suppose you fancy doing me another favour now, do you?'

She turned her head to peer at him with hollow eyes, beaten both inside and out. It was the first time that he and the girl had looked directly at each other. 'What now? You want me to lie on the floor, spread my legs for you?'

Bliss reared back, horrified. 'Christ, no. Don't even think such a thing. But what if I were to take off my jacket and toss it over there – would you put it on? Or at least wrap yourself up in it?'

'What's the catch?' she asked, tilting her head and looking him up and down.

'None at all. It's just that you look frozen.'

Her laughter hit him like a slap, emerging from her slight frame as a haunted and unappealing shriek. 'What the fuck are you on, mate? I'm about to throw myself off a building. What does it matter to you if I'm cold when I do it?'

Bliss shrugged, thinning his lips. 'I don't know. I just thought it would be better for you to be warm and comfortable instead. You know, while we wait.'

'Wait for what?' She glanced around anxiously, perhaps afraid that someone else was sneaking up on her while he caused a distraction.

'For you.' His eyes drilled into hers, demanding attention. 'This is all about you now. Waiting for you to decide what you want to do.'

He did not wait for her to respond. Instead he slipped out of his thigh-length waterproof jacket, folded it into a rough ball and lobbed it gently over to her. It landed against her ankle, where it sat for a full thirty seconds before she picked it up, unfolded it and casually eased herself inside, pulling it tight at the neck.

'Better?' he asked.

She said nothing.

His mind was racing. Before long the roof would be crowded with people attempting to reach this kid. They would undoubtedly be more effective at this than him, but Bliss was not about to wait and see. Wrong or right, he needed to keep the girl talking.

'What's your name?'

'Why d'you want to know?' She was no longer looking directly at him, but continued to steal apprehensive glances like a mistreated dog fearing abuse at the hand of a stranger.

'It's easier that way.'

'Who for?'

'Me.'

She bobbed her head a couple of times. 'I'm Molly.'

'Okay. Good. Now we're making some real progress. So, tell me how you see this ending up, Molly? You a red Rorschach pattern in the car park below and me standing where you are now, looking down? Or you having a rethink and postponing these unpleasantries for a nicer day?'

'You're shit at this,' she said, the merest hint of amusement in her voice.

'I know. You drew the short straw with me, love. But at least you won't be able to sue me if you fall backwards now.'

Molly edged forward an inch or two, away from the drop behind her. It gave him hope, although he had run out of things to say to her. The girl saved him by asking a question of her own.

'Do you have any kids, DI Bliss?'

'Call me Jimmy. And no, I don't.'

'Really? You're old enough to be a granddad. What is it – you gay or something?'

'Not that I'm aware, Molly. Just haven't had the good fortune, is all.'

'And how does your wife feel about that?'

'I'm not married.'

Molly puffed out her lips. 'You *are* gay, man.'

He chuckled. 'Not that it matters, but I'm not. Just another part of life I haven't had the best of fortunes with.'

'Don't get me started, Jimbo. If it weren't for bad luck I'd have no luck at all.'

Bliss locked eyes with her. 'You call me Jimbo again and I'll throw you off the bloody roof myself.'

Her eyes flashed. 'What kind of copper are you, man? You're demented, mate. You just, like, threatened me or something.'

Bliss shrugged and smiled to let her know he was not being serious. 'We're on our own up here for now, Molly. Whatever you claim I said or did, I'll deny it. I'll argue the facts one way, you won't be able to argue anything because you'll be the jellified mess on the ground downstairs.'

'Seriously, mate,' she said, shaking her head at him. 'You need help.'

'Yeah. Because I'm the one on a roof, half naked, rain pissing down all over me and threatening to end my own life.'

This time there was no smart-arsed response. Fractionally more subdued, she said, 'If you had kids, DI Jimmy Bliss, would you treat them properly? Would you be kind to them?'

'I like to think so. I can't see any reason why I wouldn't.'

'Even if they behaved like little shits? Even if they were vile little fuckers?'

'All kids are little shits at times. I was a complete bastard for several years in my youth.'

The girl nodded absently as if she had heard it all before. He could only imagine her story, but he assumed abandonment and abuse would feature heavily. Molly had that bleak and dispirited look shared by all kids who had given up on life.

'Seriously,' he insisted. 'I got into fights, stole cars, gave my parents such a bad time.'

After a moment she looked him and up and down, head to toe. She sniffed derisively and said, 'So, that's… what? That's you and me sharing a moment? Like we was twins or something? Like you know me, know everything I've been through?'

'Not at all, no. That was me telling you there are other shitty, vile kids in the world.' He decided to take a risk. 'So what's your real name?'

'I told you my name.'

'Yeah, but you know what? In my experience, the sort of people I have to deal with rarely give me their proper name first off.'

'Why's it so important to you? What does it matter?'

Bliss took a moment. 'Because at any moment now you might reach the point of no return and decide enough is enough. When you're gone, I'd like to know who I've had the pleasure of talking to.'

'Pleasure?' Her tone was all scoff and self-mockery. 'What's so pleasurable about me?'

'To be perfectly honest with you, I'm not sure I can answer that. I mean, you probably scrub up well enough, but you're a bit of a state right now. You've got a gob on you, too, and a rather unpleasant disregard for the police. Leaving all that aside, though, you seem bright and intelligent and you have something about you. Something I'd like to see survive this day at least. But if… if you do end up down there below us, then I'd just like to know the name of the girl who charmed me today.'

'Did you ever do drugs?' she asked. She stared hard at him, a challenge in her eyes. 'And I mean hard drugs, not just a bit of blow. Did you ever have to sell your body for a fix, or just so's you'd have a bed to crash in for the night? Did you ever steal from your own family and friends? Did you ever stab somebody?'

'Not all in the same day,' Bliss replied with an easy grin.

Hope sprang in his heart when she cackled with laughter. 'You're a freak, man. A nutjob and a freak.'

'Part of the job requirement,' Bliss told her. 'Nutjob, freak, and a love of extendable batons and CS spray.' He counted the items off on his fingers as he spoke.

Still chuckling, she said, 'You're all right, Jimmy. For a cop. Okay, then, you earned it, I guess. My name is–'

'No, no, no,' he said, holding up his hand. 'I don't want to know your real name, not really.'

'Why not?'

'Because then I'll know for sure you're going ahead with it. And I don't want that, Molly.'

The smile she gave in return was impossibly sad. It was as if in that single crooked twist of her lips she had summed up her entire existence. She got to her feet, swathed in Bliss's jacket, warm and snug. 'I'm sorry,' she muttered. 'Really, I am. I didn't mean what I said before. You've done a great job. Much better than the arseholes I'm used to dealing with.'

'It'll be no job at all if I haven't managed to persuade you not to jump.'

'That was never going to happen, Jimmy. My life is over. I'd rather go this way than in some acid attack, or worse. I'm walking dead right now, and that drop off this roof is the quickest way out for me on so many levels.'

'It's a long way down,' he pointed out.

'Yeah.' She sighed. 'But it'll be a very short scream.'

Bliss had been hunkered, moving toward her in gradual increments. It was hell on his calf muscles and thighs, and he was still much too far away to stop her going off the corner if that's what she'd decided to do.

'Fuck it!' he said, standing upright. The girl grew tense and gripped the slick rooftop with her toes. 'Come on then, Molly – or whatever your name is.'

'Come on where?'

'Let's go. Over the edge. One step. Balance teeters. Second step. Gone. Sounds good, actually.'

'What? Good? Are you fucking mental or something?'

Bliss put his head back and breathed out heavily. 'No. I'm just tired, Molly. Tired of the game we call life. Stop the world, I want to get off. Fact is, I've wondered for much of my life what it would be like to take a plunge like this. I've always been fascinated by it, wanted to know what it feels like. Those few moments between stepping out into nothing and splatting onto the ground like a sherry trifle.'

The girl was looking at him oddly. 'What do you expect it to be like?'

Bliss shook his head. He took a step closer. 'I imagine it's the nearest you ever come to genuine peace,' he said, looking ahead away into the distance. Rain lashed against his face, stinging his flesh as runnels dripped from his nose and chin. He blinked it away from his eyes one more time.

'You… you think?' she said, edging backwards.

'Yeah. Either that, or you just shit yourself in mid-air.'

This time, Molly closed her eyes as her laughter escaped. It was all Bliss needed to breach the gap between them, grab hold of his jacket and wrestle her to the ground.

TWO

By the time he arrived for his therapy session with Jennifer Howey, Bliss was twenty minutes late. Having explained away his tardiness, he was pleasantly surprised by Howey's reaction. Her manner was gentle, her voice soothing. She allowed him to compose himself gradually, acknowledging the fact that his experience that morning had exacerbated the jumble of confusion he carried around inside his head.

'Do you ever feel the need to have just one quiet day when nothing much happens?' she asked him.

Undergoing counselling was not Bliss's favourite way to pass the time. He had previously considered it entirely unnecessary, not useful at all, as he struggled to come to terms with a sequence of events dating back so many years it now felt as if he'd been born into strife. Latterly, however, he had begun to appreciate the benefits of talking to someone trained to recognise the signs of angst buried deep inside another, and he'd struck up a healthy relationship with Howey. She had come as close as anybody to understanding the forces driving him, and he now acknowledged the worth of dredging up hitherto unspoken feelings in a non-judgemental setting. Even so, there was still so much the young woman had to learn about his job.

'You'd be surprised at how many of those we have,' he said. 'My experiences over the past year have been highly unusual, and even I get bored when we're just ploughing through admin, preparing cases for the CPS, or dragging our heels through an actual trial. Believe me, struggling through the daily chore of our more run-of-the-mill investigations is mostly dull. Which pretty much describes the last few weeks prior to today.'

'Speaking of your recent experiences, that was where we left off at the end of our last session. You were telling me how relieved you were at one point to be putting your past demons behind you, and that just at the very moment when you began to think positively about the future, you suffered that great loss.'

Bliss stared into Jennifer Howey's eyes, but what he saw was a friend and colleague lying on the floor of a grubby trailer, her face having been obliterated by a shotgun blast at close range. He knew next to nothing about the technical aspects surrounding a spray of pellets, the velocity of the projectiles, nor the explosion of gunpowder. What he did know was the damage a single cartridge shell was capable of causing, and that standing in the quarry looking down at the mess of flesh, blood, bone and muscle that had been Detective Sergeant Mia Short's death mask was something he would never stop reliving.

'Other than my wife's murder, it's the hardest thing I've ever had to contend with,' he admitted with a slight lift of his shoulders. 'I honestly thought I was inured to such atrocities – that after finding my wife murdered in our own home, nothing else stood a chance of reaching inside me in quite the same way.'

'But Mia's death did.'

'Yes. She was so small, so graceful, but she was also a pocketful of dynamite. And she was blossoming when she was murdered.'

'Does the fact that she was pregnant make it worse? For you, I mean, when you think about that night?'

'Of course.' He nodded, thinking back to the moment Mia told him she and her husband were expecting their third child, neither of them knowing she had only days to live. 'How could it not?'

'You were close to Mia. Closer, perhaps, than you were with some other colleagues, with the obvious exception of Penny Chandler.'

He gave that some thought before eventually agreeing. 'I suppose I was, yes. Mia came into the team during my first posting to the city, and she wasn't one of those who suffered as a result of my final case before I was transferred out. When I returned last year, she accepted me as her boss again without any concern for how others might view her through the prism of our previous relationship. DS Chandler has been my right hand, but Mia wasn't far behind.'

'And Detective Sergeant Bishop?'

'What about him?' Bliss tilted his head, uncertain where this was going.

'You've previously referred to him as a strong, able, reliable and honest individual. You ranked him on a par with both Chandler and Short when you were discussing the merits of your team. Yet it seems to me you were closer to them than you were to him.'

'And I'm guessing you have a theory as to why that might be.'

Howey looked up from the A4 pad she was writing on. Bliss had come to realise that the majority of her sessions were conducted without their eyes connecting, but that when they did, there was a purpose behind it; an emphasis she believed was necessary.

'Do you think it's because they are both female and DS Bishop is male?'

Bliss responded immediately. 'No. Both Bishop and Short were in danger the night Mia was murdered, and I feared for them equally. If you recall, initially I thought it was Bish who had been shot, and…' His voice trailed off as his mind followed the logical path the words were taking.

'Don't finish that thought,' Howey said, edging forward in her chair. 'Instead, tell me where your head is at right this second.'

He made her wait, but eventually gave her what she was after. He cleared his throat. 'Bish is this huge bull of a man. When I thought he'd been injured or killed, I felt pain and rage. I felt sick to my stomach. But Mia, being so… tiny and slight, I admit that it somehow seemed worse. She looked like a child lying there, especially alongside Bish. My focus wasn't on their gender, more the stark differences in their stature.'

'So because of her diminutive size, you did feel more protective towards Mia?'

'Generally speaking, yes. But what are you suggesting?' Bliss asked.

'Only that the protective side of your nature tends to be the most dominant, and that it appears to extend towards females to a greater degree than males. That interests me because you have neither a younger sister nor a daughter, which is what I would expect in such cases.'

'Which means what, in your opinion?'

Howey cleared her throat before continuing, still meeting his gaze. 'There is something called the saviour complex. Essentially, it's a psychological construct which makes a person feel the need to save others. In our previous series of treatment sessions, you admitted to holding back those under your command in order for them to be spared the burden of responsibility and even accountability. You chose to shoulder that weight on their behalf. You shielded them from that particular aspect of the job. In other words, you saved them from it.'

'And look at how it worked out for Mia when I stopped,' Bliss snapped. His voice was clipped, but louder than he'd intended, fuelled by the anger he'd been bottling up inside since his colleague's death. 'You had me feeling I was wrong, that I was hurting their careers by not allowing them to take on more responsibility. Why did I listen to you? You want to ask Mia's husband – or their children, for that matter – whether they'd rather I'd carried on as I was? Because if I had, she would be alive now. She'd be Paul's wife still, mother to their twins, with a third child on the way.'

Bliss slammed his fist down on the arm of his chair, pounding it three times, each blow harder than the one before. His face twisted, he glared at Howey sitting opposite, remaining perfectly poised as she studied him. 'Look at you,' he spat. 'Does nothing move you? What the fuck does it take to shake your own self-belief, to pierce that ridiculously thick skin of yours? You can be wrong, you know. You can be… human.'

Her only reaction was to lean forward. 'Who would it help if I became emotional as well? And at the risk of making you more so, I'm going to suggest that you think about everything you just said to me. I want you to concentrate on your words, and ask yourself how true they were.'

'In what way?' Bliss heard the snarl of contempt in his voice, but he did not apologise for it.

'You suggested I made you feel you were in the wrong, that you were hurting their careers. I'd ask you to think back. Did I make you think you were wrong, or did you arrive at that conclusion on your own? You asked yourself why you listened to me, but isn't the truth of the matter somewhat different? You didn't listen to me. You listened to yourself. You listened to what you knew to be the truth.'

'So, this is all about absolving you from any blame, is it?'

'I'm not the one in treatment here, Jimmy. This is not my therapy session.'

Bliss liked that she used his given name. There were no ranks in this room. In here he was first and foremost an individual, human;

something he had just accused her of not being. He leaned back in his chair and closed his eyes. Howey was right, of course. She always was. For although she had coaxed it out of him during their sessions, he had both realised and admitted to specific failings. Wrapping his team in cotton wool was one of them. He bore the brunt of every investigative workload so that he would also take the hits for any failures – real or perceived. He didn't merely try to build a protective wall around them; he became that wall. Surrounding them, not prepared to allow attacks to find any target other than him. But in doing so, he wasn't only preventing those on the outside from piercing the barrier he presented. He was also stopping his colleagues from finding their own feet, making their own mistakes, learning by doing. From becoming better detectives.

But there were no more tears for Bliss. He was all cried out. Detective Sergeant Mia Short had not been murdered on that awful night in the early autumn because he had allowed her and DS Bishop to scout ahead on the possible location of a ruthless assassin. No. A confluence of reasons had decided her fate, including the proclivities of a deranged gunman, the late arrival of an Armed Response Vehicle and, it had to be admitted, the conscious decision made by both Mia and Bish to ignore orders. Everything conspired to create the combustible moment when an uncontrolled hostage negotiation became yet another scene of crime.

'I'm sorry for my outburst,' Bliss said when he found himself back in the room with Howey. It was a plain office without many adornments, designed to provide no stimulus other than the words spoken within. His eyes were not yet kind when they sought hers, but they were no longer filled with resentment. 'It was wrong of me to accuse you in that way. I know you're only trying to help.'

She nodded and gave him a weak smile. 'And whether you believe it or not,' she said, 'I do care. About the loss of a fine police officer, a friend, a wife and mother, daughter and sister. But today

I am here for you, as I am in each of our sessions. My job is to steer you through this, Jimmy.'

'I understand. I got caught up in the moment.'

'Which ignited shortly after I mentioned the saviour complex. Now, let me say right from the beginning that I'm not suggesting you show all the markers associated with the construct. There are many aspects to it, and my feeling is that you currently occupy a position on the edges of the condition. The reason I mention it is that, far from being a good or positive thing, it can be unhealthy – in this case, I suspect, mainly for you. Because your desire to save others is, I believe, an outlet for your focus so that you don't have to turn it inward and recognise your own problems.'

This was one of the many reasons why Bliss didn't ordinarily approve of, or even necessarily believe in, psychoanalysis. Everything was always a mask for something else in the eyes of people like Howey, yet surely there were times when things were exactly as they appeared to be. It was true that in his sessions following a major investigation in the summer, from which he had emerged physically beaten yet mentally nourished, he had found succour in emoting freely while sitting in this very same chair. He understood the benefits of being able to speak openly, and now often encouraged others to do the same. It was when the therapist started turning everything around, insisting up was down and right was left, that Bliss began drifting away again.

He scratched the back of his neck and said, 'Let's say you're right. Let's say I'm not protective because it's in my nature, but rather I act that way so as to forget my own woes. That's what you're saying, yes?'

Howey shook her head. 'Not exactly, no. I don't think you're acting. It's merely a subconscious behaviour. For whatever reason, being protective is part of your DNA. And the smaller the bundle, the more protective you are. That you take it to such extremes is not entirely natural, but neither is it an act. I would say it's more of a compulsion, one you're not even aware of. You care, you want to protect, and so you do. The tendency is exacerbated at times when you are feeling vulnerable, or perhaps even hurt by something. And rather than concentrate on the cause of how you feel, you turn to others, seeking to find ways to immerse yourself in their lives. You do this by throwing up defensive barriers way above and beyond the usual expected levels.'

'So how do we fix me?' Bliss asked.

Howey's previously timid smile became fulsome this time. Her eyebrows rose and lowered slowly as she sighed. 'That, Jimmy, is the biggest question of them all.'

THREE

SITTING IN THE SQUAD room with DS Chandler, the rest of the team busy about their work elsewhere, Bliss related his early morning experience in as much detail as he was able to recall. The therapy session had been a tempestuous one, but his mind had nevertheless strayed often to the young girl. Molly, or whatever her real name was.

'Sounds to me like some solid, virtually textbook police work,' Chandler said, regarding Bliss with a less than favourable expression. 'I mean, what could possibly have gone wrong?'

'It worked, didn't it?' Bliss gave an unapologetic shrug. 'Next time you're up on a wet roof trying to talk down a jumper, you tell me how close to any bloody textbook you come. I did what I had to do to get her to open up, for her to see me as no threat. Then I figured out what made her tick and I used it against her. Like I say, she's still with us, so you know where you can stick your textbook.'

Chandler had arrived on the hotel roof together with a uniformed officer and two paramedics in time to hear much of the exchange between Bliss and the girl; it was now the talk of the station. She mentioned this to him, finishing by saying, 'I can't wait until the new DCI gets an earful of what happened up there.'

Bliss rolled his eyes as theatrically as he was able. 'Oh, please,' he groaned. 'Just what we need around here is another fast-tracked, opinionated arsewipe Chief Inspector taking up precious oxygen while disguised as a copper.'

'I trust you don't think about all of us DCIs that way, Inspector Bliss,' came a voice they all recognised.

The team were congregated in the open-plan Major Crimes area, into which there were two entrances. Bliss turned to look at the open door to his left, grinning when he saw who stood there.

'DCI Warburton,' he said, rising to his feet. 'Very good to see you again.'

Diane Warburton ran her own team in Lincolnshire and had featured prominently in the recent cross-county task force investigation that had ultimately resulted in DS Short's murder. The DCI had proven herself to be terrific at her job, as well as trustworthy and reliable. Those were more than ticks in her favour in Bliss's book. He extended his hand, and she smiled at him as they shook. He recalled her smile as lighting her up from the inside, and he was glad to find his memory had not betrayed him.

'I'm happy to hear you say that, Inspector. I hope you mean it, too. Otherwise, this would become a very long posting indeed.'

Bliss frowned. 'Why do you say that? I'm not with you.'

'You're waiting for the arrival of a new DCI, are you not?'

'We are. But... hold on, don't tell me. You? You're the unit's new boss?'

Warburton's grin now matched the one slowly fading from his own lips. She nodded and said, 'The post came up, I was looking for a fresh challenge. I thought that knowing you all would give me a flying start. Though being described as a fast-tracked, opinionated arsewipe wasn't quite what I had in mind for my first day in the job, I have to say.'

He closed his eyes and bit down on his bottom lip. His mouth was still getting him into trouble even after all these years. 'I'm sorry about that. And I absolutely was not referring to you that way, and nor would I. Fact is, now that I'm over the immediate shock, I'm delighted.'

'Are you sure? Because if so, please tell your face. And if not, I could always ask DCI Edwards if she'd be happy to swap places with me and remain in charge of Major Crimes.'

Warburton finished speaking with a peal of gentle laughter which showed she was only having a joke at his expense. He nodded and offered his congratulations, although the appointment was a sideways move at best for her.

As a result of the investigation they had worked together, the staffing situation at Thorpe Wood had been addressed. The squad's leader, DCI Alicia Edwards, had taken the decision to also make a parallel move. More likely the brass had steered her that way, the less charitable of her colleagues suggested, though Bliss had no insight into the reasons behind the new arrangements. Detective Superintendent Fletcher had overseen a steering group which recommended expanding the leadership roles to include an additional DCI with a remit giving them overall control of Major Crimes, with sub-unit teams specialising in organised crime, drugs and sex workers, plus the Roads Policing and Dogs units. The introduction of another DCI had allowed Edwards to move across to CID. Each unit and sub-unit then had its own Detective Inspector, with a varied number of sergeants and constables attached to each, but whose flexibility of roles allowed for them to switch across to any unit struggling for numbers during peak crime periods.

That the changes had come about in the wake of the team losing a colleague to a contract killer's gun was not perceived as a reflection of Bliss's handling of the investigation. He had pushed for DS Short's promotion to acting DI, with a recommendation for the role to become permanent after a trial period, but subsequent to her murder the senior management team had made the decision to revert back to the rank levels used in Peterborough shortly prior to Bliss rejoining the unit.

He had not even remotely considered throwing his hat in the ring for the additional DCI position. Not only did he not want the job, he also knew the job did not want him. As a consequence of the proposals, the team's anticipation had been at fever pitch for weeks now. Diane Warburton's appearance had caught them all on the hop, because the new DCI had not been expected to be in post for several more days.

When she asked Bliss how things were going, the sympathetic glint in her eyes told him what she meant.

'We're doing okay, I think,' he replied with a nod. 'It's taken us a while to get back to where we were as a team, and individually we've all gradually come to terms with Mia not being here. I don't know that we'll ever accept her losing her life the way she did, but we are finally able to function. We pull together when one of us stumbles, and somehow we make it through the day.'

The words sounded glib even to his own ears. Not that Bliss didn't mean them, because they were true in so many ways. But he didn't feel them – not where it counted. His intellect accepted the loss of his DS, colleague and friend; the lack of Short's presence in and around the office was a daily reminder. But his heart refused to acknowledge it in the same way. A piece of him had been torn away on the day Mia Short was killed by a man who had previously shot and killed a number of other people, and Bliss was convinced the wound it left behind would never heal, never be covered over with scar tissue. That he would never be whole again.

Not that he had said as much to any of his colleagues. Not even to Penny Chandler, whom he considered to be his closest friend and ally. And certainly he had made no mention of his feelings to the mandated counsellor. Had he offered Howey a rare glimpse into the darkest regions of his mind, he would never have been allowed back to do the job he still loved despite all of its inherent difficulties.

'We must talk,' Warburton said, interrupting his thoughts. 'I have a meeting with the Super, then another with DCI Edwards. But let's catch up later on.'

Bliss nodded. 'As it happens, I'm not even supposed to be on duty, so officially I have nothing to do.'

'If that's the case, why are you here?'

'That… is a long story. If you've not heard all about it by the time we see each other next, I'll fill you in. Oh, and welcome aboard.'

'Thank you, Inspector. After we've had a chance to catch up, I thought I'd address the entire team.'

'I'll look forward to it.'

Chandler smiled and shook Warburton's hand before the DCI left the squad room, after which she returned to Bliss's side. 'Well, what a turn-up for the books. Diane Warburton our very own DCI. I guess that's put paid to any romantic notions you had about her.'

Bliss shot her what he hoped was his fiercest warning glare, but Chandler wasn't one to back down. It had become almost her life plan to pair him up with somebody, and when they had worked the task force with Lincolnshire, she had referred often to Warburton being his type. It did not seem to matter that the woman was married, nor that Bliss was uninterested in striking up a romance with anybody. Chandler apparently considered neither of these two things a deterrent. The DCI being their new boss had definitely put a different complexion on the issue, however.

'Surprised to see you here today, boss,' DS Bishop said as he entered the room. He took off his jacket and flapped rainwater from it, before wrapping it around the back of his chair. 'Something serious gone off?'

'Our fearless leader talked down a jumper,' Chandler said.

Bishop laughed, his large frame juddering up and down. 'Yeah, right. Course he did.'

'What's so funny about that?' Bliss demanded to know.

'Well, no offence boss, but you're not exactly the most sympathetic and touchy-feely of people.'

'Offence taken. That's you on a month of nights, Sergeant.'

'I may have been exaggerating when I said he talked her down,' Chandler admitted, barely able to conceal a grin. 'But she didn't jump, which is the main thing. The boss snatched her off the edge of the roof, no less.'

Bishop seemed impressed. 'Good on you, boss. How come you were even involved?'

Bliss had been due in court to offer evidence in the trial of Lewis Drake, a local scrapyard owner arrested by Major Crimes in connection with a people trafficking and murder case in the spring of that year. Because he was scheduled to be out of the office, he'd also rearranged his weekly session with Jennifer Howey for first thing in the morning. He was grabbing a large Americano in the city centre when the call came in about the potential suicide. Given he was no more than a couple of minutes away, Bliss had reluctantly found himself up on the roof of the hotel, fervently hoping a uniform had beaten him to it.

'So, that scumbag Drake is finally in the dock.' Bishop's face had turned grim. 'I do hope that bastard is shivved in the showers sooner rather than later. Surprised it hasn't happened already.'

'He's been in HMP Peterborough awaiting trial, so he's still one of the untouchables, on his home turf,' Chandler said. 'If he gets sent down, they'll probably ship him out to a maximum-security place, and then he won't be so comfy.'

The three were silent for a few moments as they paused to reflect upon the horrific details surrounding the murders of a local airman and a young foreign woman, and Bliss also recalled just how close a number of others had come to death with the investigation team initially unaware of their existence.

'So what's the girl's story, anyway?' Bishop asked. 'The one that wanted to top herself?'

Bliss shook his head. 'No idea. I passed her over to uniform and the paramedics. I gave my statement and then went to my session with Howey. When I came out of there, I had a message waiting for me from the CPS. They told me I wasn't wanted after all – there's been a delay.'

'Big surprise.'

'Yeah. As it happens, I felt a bit sorry for the kid on the roof. When I found her, it was obvious she was no age, standing there covered in bumps and bruises, grazes and cuts, flimsy nightdress, rain pouring down on her. She's got a bloody great carving knife in her hand, blood washing off it… quite a first impression, but she had something about her. I mean, she looked about as desperate as anyone I've ever seen, and although I don't think she wanted to jump, neither do I think she cared if she lived or died.'

When he finished speaking, Bliss noticed Bishop staring at him strangely. 'What?' he asked. 'What's up?'

Bishop was pulling his jacket back on. 'You know I was helping out on that drugs raid earlier today, over in Eastfield? Well, much to our disappointment, our dealer friend Ryan Endicott wasn't at home when we went through his front door. One of the many scrotes we did snatch up from inside the house told us Endicott had been involved in a massive barney with a courier. It happened first thing this morning. He tried it on with her and was a bit too forceful about it, so she fought him off. They think she stabbed him. Evidently, she scarpered – wearing only her nightie – and a few minutes later, Endicott got tooled up and went after her. That's the only reason we didn't catch the fucker in bed, apparently.'

'Your roof girl's a drugs courier,' Chandler said, switching her gaze to Bliss. 'Which explains a hell of a lot.'

He nodded, troubled by the revelation. 'Looks that way. Worse still, it means Endicott will do anything to get to her. Now I understand what she meant when she said about getting attacked with acid.'

'Too true. If she did stab him, he's hardly likely to let her get away with it.'

'Not only that,' Bliss said, 'but he'll also be desperate to get to her before she has a chance to talk to us.'

FOUR

WHEN THEY REACHED THE city hospital in Bretton Gate, Bliss had already requested an armed presence to watch over the girl. He and Chandler arrived first as expected, although a uniformed officer had earlier been detailed to remain with her until she was ready to be spoken to. PC Lamb met them outside the single occupant room.

'How's she doing?' Bliss asked. She had not taken kindly to his having dragged her away from the edge of the roof, her volatile reaction in complete contrast to her relatively calm demeanour during their conversation. Having subsequently heard what Bishop had to say about the drug raid, Bliss understood why Molly had not welcomed being wrestled to the ground.

'A few stitches, but there are no serious wounds, sir.'

Bliss had seen Lamb around HQ, but not enough to talk to in any deep or meaningful way. He immediately liked her directness. 'How is she emotionally?'

'Surprisingly good. She calmed down after a few minutes, and she's been perfectly pleasant since – not that she's saying a great deal. And nothing about how she came to be standing on that rooftop.'

'I think we may have something there,' Chandler said. 'Seems she was involved in an altercation not far away from where we found her. I take it you were informed that armed officers are on their way over?'

'I was, and I've been particularly vigilant since. So you think Molly is still in some danger, then?'

Bliss liked her all the more for putting the girl's safety ahead of her own.

'The ruck was with a nasty dealer by the name of Ryan Endicott,' he told Lamb. 'We believe our girl in there may have stabbed him in the process of fighting off a sexual assault, so we also have uniforms on their way to keep an eye on the Casualty department and the car parks. Endicott is unlikely to be dumb enough to come here for treatment, but I do suspect he'll want to reach out to Molly and will probably assume she'll end up in here. I'm hoping the kid's ready to tell us all about it now.'

The PC cleared her throat, looking awkward. 'Um, Inspector… I should just say that I don't think she's going to welcome you with open arms. She kept saying you'd betrayed her. Lied to her after getting her to trust you. I got the impression she doesn't put her faith in many people, so you'll find her defensive armour back in place.'

Bliss was not at all surprised. 'I'll let DS Chandler do as much of the talking as possible,' he said. 'But Molly – if that is her real name – is going to have to accept my being in there with them.'

'You want me inside the room with you, or out here?' PC Lamb asked.

'Please stay where you are. Give us a shout when the armed officers arrive – or if anyone shifty-looking starts poking around. The girl's not sedated, is she?'

'Just a mild one. Nothing that's going to mess with her thinking, though. Like I say, she's been lying there accepting all of the treatment without any fuss whatsoever. She just won't talk about what happened.'

'We'll see if we can shift her on that,' Chandler said, pushing open the door and entering the room.

'Thanks,' Bliss said to the uniform. 'When the firearms team arrive, you shoot off and get yourself some lunch. Stick around, though, just in case. If you've built up any sort of rapport with her, there's a chance we'll need you back in the room with us at some point. Oh, and one last thing: what name is she here under?'

'All she gave us was Molly, so she's in as Molly Doe.'

'Speak to somebody in charge and have that altered, will you? If anyone comes looking for her, they'll check the Doe names first. Have it changed to Smith or Jones or something. Thanks.'

The moment he entered the room to join his DS, the girl reacted. 'No!' she cried, holding out a hand, index finger raised in his direction. 'I won't deal with him! He's a lying, two-faced scumbag and I refuse to talk to him.'

'If my DI lied to you, then it was for your own good,' Chandler insisted. There was a forceful empathy in her voice that brooked no argument. 'Inspector Bliss is staying put, Molly, but you can talk to me for the time being. I'm DS Chandler. Penny.'

The girl pulled the covers up to her chin and turned her head away. 'I've got nothing to say.'

'Then you can listen instead. First of all, do you want us to carry on calling you Molly, or would you prefer we use your real name?'

This time there was no response at all.

'Very well. Molly it is. So, the thing is, even if we're not sure who you are, we believe we know why you were up on that roof. We also have intelligence telling us where you were earlier this morning, what you did, and what was done to you. It explains the way you were dressed, and why there was blood on the knife you were holding.' She paused, watching the girl for a reaction. There was none. 'Given what I've just said, Molly, would you like to change your mind and talk to us about it? It would be better for you to tell us, rather than forcing us to coax it out of you, or keeping schtum and saying nothing.'

'I don't want to talk to either of you,' Molly said, though she kept her head turned away from them. 'What don't you get about that?'

'You were so much more approachable earlier,' Bliss said, unable to help himself. 'I thought you had something about you, I sensed something in you. A difference between you and the usual kids we encounter. Maybe I was wrong.'

This drew her full attention. Bliss saw the same spark flicker in her eyes. Whatever he had noticed before was still there, though she was trying hard to close the door on it. 'You *were* wrong,' she said. 'Wrong to lie to me. I'll never trust you again.'

'If that's the price of you being alive, I'll have to cope with it. I couldn't run the risk of you going off that roof, Molly.'

'And what's to stop me doing it again the moment I get out of this room?'

'You think you'll just be released when the doctors here sign you out?' Bliss shook his head. 'Molly, from everything we've heard about what happened earlier today, you have a lot to answer for. You're probably also in a great deal of danger. Once you're discharged from here, you'll be taken directly to our station, where at the very least you'll be questioned under caution.'

The kid's face hardened as she clamped her teeth together, but then relaxed again when she realised the full extent of her plight. 'Then I'll want a brief,' she said. There was a slight quiver in her voice.

'A duty solicitor will be provided if necessary. But I was hoping to clear a few things up before we reach that point, Molly.'

'I'm not saying another word.'

'Then let me tell you what we know,' Chandler said, taking a step forward to stand over her. 'You're a drugs courier. Probably some so-called county lines mule. We suspect you are under age, so nothing will go the way you expected from this point on. Our intelligence suggests that, early this morning, you and Ryan Endicott, whose house you were staying in overnight, had a disagreement which became a physical and sexual assault. At some stage you managed to reach a knife, and along with your own defence wounds you also cut him. You then fled the scene, eventually making your way into the hotel and up onto the roof. Do you have anything to say about that account?'

The girl had snapped her head to the side once more, but colour was rising to her throat and cheeks and Bliss noticed she was shaking.

'None of what my colleague has just said will have come as a surprise to you, Molly,' Bliss said, taking up the story. 'We're as certain as we can be at this stage about the incident as described. However, what you probably aren't aware of is that Endicott followed you out of the house. Obviously he didn't find you, or I don't think you would've made it up onto that roof. But that doesn't mean he's stopped looking for you. In fact, we have firearms officers on their way here, because we believe your life is in danger. You not only stabbed Endicott – quite how badly, we don't know – but you also now pose a genuine threat to him and his business because of who and what he is, and who and what you are.

'He's a dealer. You're the mule. You courier drugs from suppliers to dealers, Molly, and that means Endicott won't be the only one interested in your whereabouts right now. Because there's someone further up the food chain than him, and let's not forget whoever's at the supplier end, either. That makes you dangerous, Molly. It also makes you a target.'

Bliss let that sit with her, motioning for Chandler to remain silent. The kid was furious with him, and undoubtedly feeling trapped and vulnerable. But her fear of others involved in the drugs business would ultimately filter through and take charge of her emotions.

Terror was a great motivator.

Her attitude both now and up on that roof told Bliss that Molly's experience ran far deeper than her tender years would suggest. She undoubtedly knew as well as he did that the vicious monsters who controlled drug gangs would threaten members with acid attacks if there was even a suspicion of collusion with the police, and that any courier who tried to walk away from a supplier or dealer ran the risk of having their anus torn apart by a blade so they would be unable to carry drugs that way for someone else. It would not take long for the girl to realise she would now be considered a threat either way.

When eventually she turned, Molly's focus fell upon Bliss.

'How bad is it?' she asked, the redoubtable glimmer in her eyes now replaced by the dark despair of a fearful child.

Bliss softened his demeanour, bringing tenderness back into his eyes. 'Tell us what happened. You don't need to mention any names other than his at this stage if you prefer not to. Yours is not the only name in the frame, Molly. Five males were arrested when our drugs team went inside Endicott's home. That's five other chances of prising someone's mouth open. On that score, both ends of the deal have bigger problems than you right at this moment. But you are one of them, so they'll be coming for you no matter what, and Endicott will prioritise you if you stabbed him. So let's start there. Did you stab him?'

Molly nodded. At first Bliss thought that was all they were going to get out of her, but eventually she opened up. 'I carried the gear up from London. I don't have anywhere to sleep, so I doss down wherever I end up each day. Night before last, I stayed in Homerton in London, and last night at Ryan's. They... they all pass me around. Carrying their gear and letting them fuck me keeps me off the streets, puts food in my belly, and from time to time I get to share a bit of product.'

'So what was different about last night?' Chandler asked gently. 'Why did you fight him off this time?'

Molly glanced at Bliss as if ashamed before responding. 'Ryan fucked me last night. But early this morning, him and one of his mates tried to… to team up on me. I said I wasn't interested, but Ryan just laughed and said I didn't have a choice. He told me to suck him off while his mate fucked me from behind. When I started to complain, he slapped me, and punched me in the stomach. Then he laughed again and bragged about how he was going to film it all on his phone and send it out so's everyone would see what a pathetic slag I was.'

'And you lost it at that point,' Chandler said.

Molly nodded, the awful moment written in her eyes.

'How did you manage to get hold of the knife?' Bliss asked, not wanting to hear any more about this young girl's sordid debasement.

'I usually sneak one out of the kitchen and stuff it under a cushion of the sofa I use as a bed before I go to sleep. There's always blokes around, and I get sick of them all thinking they can have me whenever they feel like it. Either Ryan didn't know about the blade or he never thought about it. Maybe he didn't care because he never thought I'd use it. Anyway, after the beating and the threats he ripped my knickers off and that was when I decided I'd had enough.'

'You stabbed him?'

'More like slashed him across his arm. Quite badly, I think. We fought over the knife, which was when I ended up getting cut a few times. The other bloke scarpered, but me and Ryan went at it hard. I managed to send him backwards, and he tripped over something and smacked his head on a cabinet or a table or something. He didn't move at first, but then he started to stir. I didn't hang about to see what he did next.'

'That was when you ran.'

'Yeah. It wasn't even dawn, but I saw it was coming. So I made my way through the streets and around by the back of the Travelodge. I used the door by the car park to get inside.'

'But it would have only taken you ten or fifteen minutes to get from where you were to the hotel, Molly,' Chandler said, clearly puzzled by the girl's account. 'That being the case, what did you do before going up to the roof?'

'I hid out on the stairs. I used to live in a tower block and knew my way around it from top to bottom, so I thought there would probably be an empty space somewhere above the top floor. There was no way further up on the main staircase, but off one of the corridors I found another set of stairs that led up to the room where all the lift mechanics and stuff are. I hid out there for a while.'

'How did you get inside? I'm sure the door wasn't unlocked.'

'I used the knife to slip the lock. It was an easy one.'

'What made you eventually decide to go out onto the roof, especially when it was pouring down?'

The girl frowned at Chandler, looking even more dejected. 'In the end I didn't know what else to do. I was in a state, imagining people's reactions if they saw me like that. I know someone who works on the market, so I thought if I made it to her she'd be able to help me out with some clothes and sort out my cuts. Only on my way down, I got seen by the security guard, so I ran back up to the top. I figured he'd call for you lot, so it was a case of either getting caught or going out there and just ending it. That started to look like a good idea. I mean, what the fuck did I even have to live for, right?'

'And yet you couldn't jump in the end,' Bliss muttered to himself. Molly's harrowing story had reached inside him and pulled the cork on his anger. He wanted Ryan Endicott in front of him right now;

he was desperate to vent all of his rage and fury on the man who had treated this young kid in such a brutal and inhumane manner.

'I was going to. I really was. I didn't want to go on. But I suppose I was scared of the actual fall. Sounds lame, I know.'

'It isn't lame at all,' Bliss said. 'But I'm still glad I stopped you.'

Molly blinked away a tear. Her eyes were dead and haunted. 'Yeah, well, I'm not,' she replied. 'Because it took all the courage I have, and I'll never forgive you for it.'

FIVE

By the time the detectives from the drugs unit arrived to speak to Molly, two firearms officers secured her room, standing either side of the door. Bliss had sent Chandler back to Thorpe Wood, but he continued to pace the hospital corridor waiting for his opposite number from the other squad to arrive. DI Bentley registered his surprise at finding Bliss still there, but agreed to a quick chat before questioning the girl.

'What's your interest?' Bentley asked. 'Beyond having been up on the roof with her earlier, I mean.'

'A couple of things. I hung around because I wanted to find out more about her. Wondered if she'd been on your radar and if so, what her background was.'

Bentley sniffed, eyeing Bliss with more than a hint of suspicion. 'You looking to take over this part of the investigation?'

'Not at all. I'm just after more background on the girl. She's little more than a confused child, but her awful way of life seems normal to her somehow. I wondered how it had turned out like that for her.'

This time his colleague grinned. 'Oh, yeah? So it's a personal interest, then? You looking to get your leg over, Bliss?'

Reeling his temper in, Bliss regarded his fellow DI with all the contempt he could muster. 'She's a kid, for fuck's sake. Don't even joke about it.'

Bentley laughed this time. 'You'd be wise not to let that cherubic face fool you. Yeah, we've clocked her before. A known mule, working mainly out of London. Nothing else on her, though. Not even a name.'

'She calls herself Molly.'

'Yeah, I got that. But we both know it has to be false. We don't have any intelligence about her, beyond knowing she's a street girl much of the time, who lays her head down in the homes of deadbeat druggies and scummers. She's certainly no innocent wallflower.'

Bliss took another moment to calm himself before saying, 'Just because she sees herself as worthless and gets treated like shit, doesn't mean we have to think of her the same way. Let's be better than that, eh? Let's be better than them.'

'You trying to suggest I wade around in the same cesspool as these junkies and their runners?' Bentley's stance became wider, the glimmer in his eyes meaner. 'Look, she carries drugs and cash around the country for these pricks, she snorts it up or smokes it with them and opens her legs for them. She's no different to any of them, and she's certainly no better. I deal with these people every single working day, Bliss. I think that gives me a greater insight, don't you?'

Bliss did not allow his gaze to fall away, though he acknowledged the truth in what Bentley had said. The drugs squad knew the people they dealt with – had to know them inside out, because it was a precarious business and many of the scrotes Bentley and his team came into contact with were dangerous. He didn't fully understand why he had taken a shine to this kid in particular, especially given the way they'd met and the details he had subsequently discovered about her. But the fact he couldn't explain his interest didn't mean it was pointless following it up.

'Look,' he said, deciding to extend an olive branch. 'I didn't mean any offence. I know what it takes to get through the day when you're dealing with the scum of the earth. I also know how much easier it is for us to deal with if we package them up as all being the same. Truth is, I've never dealt with a potential suicide on my own before, and I guess in trying to figure out how to make a connection with her, I got a bit carried away once I saw she was out of danger.'

Bentley nodded, accepting the apology for what it was. 'You did the right thing getting firearms on site. It's not just Ryan Endicott who'll be looking for this one.' He indicated the door to Molly's room. 'Endicott's employers will not be pleased. Not with him, and certainly not with her.'

'So what'll happen to her when she's released from here?'

'We'll arrest her and interview her back at Thorpe Wood.'

'On what charges?'

Bentley smirked. 'Don't worry, I'll think of plenty. Drugs-related, obviously, and hopefully something based around the blade she was carrying. We have potential witnesses to the fight and the stabbing.'

'Who will all blow away in the first stiff breeze,' Bliss scoffed. 'Even if a couple of them spoke about it prior to being cautioned, I'm sure in retrospect they'll realise it's best to keep schtum.'

'We may find Endicott's blood or tissue on the knife. Either way, we've reason enough to stick a charge on, see what we can squeeze out of her.'

'It would be good to identify her properly first,' Bliss said. 'Surely she must have left something behind at Endicott's place?'

'Not that I'm aware of. But if they found something it'll be sitting in an evidence bag waiting for us. It's fine, though. The clock will be running, and she'll probably want to clam up. So we'll make a big thing of her armed guard disappearing like smoke if she stalls us for twenty-four hours, hoping to walk out on bail. If she's a minor, then we'll have to get Social Care involved. It's a bloody mess whichever way it goes down.'

'But there's no immediate chance of her going back out onto the street?'

Bentley shrugged. 'You know how it goes, Bliss. A lot depends on who she gets to defend her. By the time we get the clock running on her at the nick it'll mean her being with us in a cell overnight, but beyond that is anyone's guess. It'll be a bloody minefield.'

'What are your chances of getting something to stick in terms of the drugs?'

'That's a good question. We know what she's up to, but proving anything against her is a different matter. We can't prove she was carrying a stash with her when she came up to the city. We didn't even catch her inside the flat, so our best hope is either to get her to cough or get one of the others to dish the dirt. We have a catalogue of photos and video footage showing her coming and going, but entering and leaving a drug dealer's house is not a crime, sadly, so I'm not seeing much of a case to present to the CPS.'

Bliss saw how it was likely to play out. There was what you knew and what you were able to provide evidence for, and often there was a gaping hole between the two. Molly's presence inside Endicott's home could be explained away by any number of different circumstances, none of which related to drugs or any other form of criminal enterprise. He nodded. 'Okay. Do me a favour and let me know where you're at with a few hours to go on the clock.'

Smiling, Bentley said, 'She's really got to you, hasn't she?'

'To a certain degree. I don't know her, but when she was at what must have been her lowest ebb, I thought I noticed a spark behind her eyes. It was like she couldn't help but show what was hiding beneath that front she puts up. I'm convinced I got a glimpse of her real personality, and I suppose it bothered me that she was caught up in such misery. That's all.'

'It's unlike you to make it personal, from what I hear.'

Bliss was aware of the other DI appraising him closely. Shaking his head, he said, 'Then you heard it from someone who doesn't know me at all well. They're all personal to me.'

Rain continued to beat down; the hospital car park was awash, the downpour too severe for its inadequate drainage system. Sitting in his Vauxhall Insignia while the windscreen demisted, Bliss gave some thought to what Bentley had said at the end. One of the pieces of wisdom his father, who at the time was a desk sergeant in Bethnal Green, had shared with him was that to do the job right, you had to ignore the first piece of advice they taught you at the Hendon police college. When your instructors warned you against taking people and cases personally, you nodded along and then dismissed it the moment you became a real copper. Just like the old complex – long demolished now, with the new building where the Met swimming pool once stood – those instructors were no longer around, but the ethos survived them.

'You can play at being a copper and collect your pay packet and move on,' Bliss's father said to him the day before he began his training. 'But if you want to do the job right, you've got to have heart. If you have heart, then you'll let people in and they'll stay with you. You'll often encounter members of the public at a time when an incident has become very personal to them. You ever allow them to see that you don't care as much as they do, and they'll never forget it. Don't make what might be their single experience of dealing with the police something they'll only ever complain about. But, fair warning, it'll cause you a lot of grief along the way, Jimmy. And if it doesn't, then you're not doing it right.'

Bliss seldom thought of his father these days, almost three years since his death. But the man loomed large in his mind whenever

Bliss needed him to. For instance, when he sought a reminder that taking cases and people personally was no bad thing, up popped his old man with his words of wisdom. They were always welcome, because he invariably visualised his father speaking and doing so brought a smile to his face. An imperfect man in an imperfect world doing an imperfect job, he'd nonetheless climbed out of bed every single day determined to do his best; Dennis Bliss did the right thing whenever possible. It was hard not to be inspired by that – albeit intimidated by knowing you had to at least attempt to live up to those standards.

Giving a damn about Molly and her situation was not the wrong way to go. It would be easy to dismiss her as a waste of space, taking up the oxygen of better men and women, leading her life of debauchery and wanton wickedness. The girl shifted death and misery from one place to another, across county lines, caring only about her next fix and her next warm sofa. That was how many in society regarded her kind, and a number of his colleagues felt the same way. But Bliss had been caught unawares by Molly. Disarmed by her personality, he was convinced there was more to her than what she presented every day to the world she inhabited. A girl who had not so much fallen through the cracks, as been discarded by life and left to rot alongside those whose drugs she carried.

The sharp pitch of the call tone from his phone yanked Bliss from his thoughts. It was Chandler, wanting to know if he was going back to Thorpe Wood station. His original intention after being let go for the day by the CPS, had been to complete a day's work in his office. But his conversations with Molly and Bentley had left him considering a different approach.

'Meet me outside in ten minutes,' he told her. You could get just about anywhere in the city inside ten minutes. 'I've got somewhere in mind to visit before the day manages to crush my spirits entirely.'

SIX

Gaining access to Ryan Endicott's ground-floor flat in Eastfield required an unpleasant jaunt via a dark entranceway, opposite a rise of concrete steps that smelled of stale urine. In the parking bays on the other side of a thin band of grass stood a solitary Scientific Support Unit vehicle, whose presence cheered Bliss. He and Chandler entered the property warily, using the aluminium footplates set out by the crime scene manager as pathways. They found him and an equally protective-suited tech in the living room.

'Hey up, it's the bloody Lone Ranger,' Neil Abbott said, lowering the mask that had been covering his nose and mouth. He let it dangle beneath his chin. Turning to his colleague, who was busy taking photographs, he went on, 'Peter, ignore that for a minute. I want you to take a good look at this man. You ever walk into a crime scene for the first time and see him coming the other way, you know your job just got a great deal harder.'

The younger man, who barely filled his white scene suit, looked up, frowning. 'Lone Ranger?'

Abbott nodded enthusiastically. 'I call him that because he's a bloody cowboy. Other detectives, like the estimable DS Chandler standing by his side, understand and appreciate the demands of our job. They realise we're here to scrub this place forensically before the suited and booted traipse all over our evidence. They acknowledge our skill and professionalism, and wait for *us* to give *them* the nod to proceed. DI Bliss, however, is of the opinion that he can blunder onto the scene and disrupt it any old time – often before we arrive, as he's so bloody impatient.'

Bliss waited him out. Neil Abbott was a decent bloke and a damned fine crime scene investigator, who reserved a special brand of ire for him when he decided not to delay his investigation for the sometimes several hours before the CSI unit arrived on scene. His barbs were mostly aimed in jest, and Bliss knew he was showing off in front of a new hire.

'You want to get your fat, lazy arse out of the office and on site quicker, then,' he shot back, maintaining a rigid expression. 'You bloody SOCO sperm suits are all the same.'

'And now he's going to ask for a favour,' Abbott continued. 'Treats us with disdain, makes life hard for us, even tosses in the odd insult, and then it's all want, want, want. Even a crusty old git like him knows we're no longer scenes of crime officers, but he refuses to call us CSI. At least to our faces.'

'Are you done, Neil?' Chandler asked with a heavy sigh, hands on hips, foot tapping impatiently. She turned to Peter and said, 'Ignore them. Your boss is not exactly wrong about my boss, but mine does at least make every attempt to maintain a clean site, even if he is keen to check them out. Personally, I think they're both compensating for something.'

Abbott jumped back into the conversation. 'So what can I do for you today, DS Chandler?' He was always more keen to oblige her rather than Bliss.

'We're interested in two things,' she told him, offering up her brightest smile. 'First, the amount of blood shed by Ryan Endicott. Also, there were five men arrested in the raid this morning, plus there's Endicott himself and the young girl who fled the scene, but we'd like to know if you've found any evidence of an eighth person being here at the time of the fight. Possibly even more than that.'

Fingering the hood of his suit, the crime scene manager gave it some thought before responding. 'We'll have Endicott's blood and DNA on file, so that won't be a problem. Preliminary inspection suggests he was stabbed in this room, bled as he ran into the kitchen, where he probably compressed the wound with a cloth. No suggestion of an artery being sliced open, that's for sure. Given the scene and the outcome of the raid, we're only suited up for collecting samples, but there's plenty of them. As for the suspects dragged out of here, we'll run DNA comparisons and see if we have more samples than people.'

'Thanks. Whatever you can give us, Neil.'

'And you're connected to this case how?' Abbott scratched his chin as if considering a rare puzzle.

'We've been speaking to one of the people whose blood you're likely to find in this room. The young girl who managed to escape – after the fight, but prior to the raid.'

Bliss mentally thanked Chandler for being deliberately vague. Neil Abbott's character assassination of him was more jocular than adversarial, but he'd balk at feeding them information if he knew they weren't part of the investigation team.

'Ah, the young lady who we're told stabbed Endicott. If you're thinking he might be lying dead somewhere in a ditch, then all I can say is I'd be astonished if it were anything to do with what happened here. To be honest, I've seen worse nosebleeds.'

Abbott knew his stuff and was as good as they came. Bliss valued his opinion. The news was both good and bad for Molly. Though it now looked as if she was not a freshly minted killer, she remained a marked person, and probably a high value target for Endicott and his remaining crew. That did not bode well for the kid. Any escalation relating to drugs was a worry for everyone involved, including those whose job it was to investigate.

'Thanks, Neil,' he said sourly. 'I'll pass it on to DI Bentley. Oh, there is something else. Have you come across a handbag, purse, or any kind of ID related to the girl? A mobile would be good, too.'

'All the mobiles are accounted for, I believe. Anything we bagged up matched one of the thugs who got hoicked off to the nick as far as I'm aware. We found no personal items belonging to your girl other than clothing.'

'Damn,' Bliss said. 'She had bugger all on her, and I was hoping you'd at least come across a purse or something.'

Abbott shrugged. 'Sorry. If she did have anything like that, it's not here now.'

'It's not a surprise really, is it?' Chandler said. 'In her line of work you'd not want to be carrying around too much in the way of ID or personal belongings.'

'You're probably right,' Bliss said. He'd suspected as much himself, but had hoped for more. He turned to Abbott once more. 'Nothing significant about her clothes, I suppose?' he asked.

'A short-sleeved blouse, blue denim jeans, socks, ankle boots. No bra, and the knickers we found were torn. There's also a cheap puffa jacket I think must be hers. But they're all common generic brands.'

'Fair enough.' Bliss realised they were going to find no answers here. He turned to leave. 'Enjoy the rest of your day.'

'Yeah, you too. Oh, and Bliss… be careful. Both of you, in fact. Endicott on a good day is a real piece of shit – I've had to clean up after him on several occasions. A wounded and angry Endicott is definitely someone to be avoided.'

Bliss winked. 'I hear you. Cheers. By the way, when you cleaned up in his wake, you ever find any evidence to prove it was his mess?'

'He's far too slippery for that, Bliss. And this time he's actually the victim.' He shook his head as if to question the sanity of the situation, before pulling the mask back over his face.

'We'll see,' Bliss muttered under his breath as he and Chandler exited the property. By now the rain had relented and the air was fresh and cool as the pair made their way back to his car.

'You're still worried about her,' Chandler said as they settled into their seats and buckled up. 'Molly, I mean.'

'Where can she go?' he replied. 'What are her options? If we have no evidence and no proof of her age, can her brief compel us to let her just walk free? If so, you can bet your life on Endicott sweeping her up within minutes. If it goes the other way and we manage to keep hold of her on remand, he has kids on the inside who can reach her. Middle ground is she goes into some form of emergency fostering, and how long before he finds out where she's staying? That girl has nowhere to turn and nobody to turn to.'

'She could always own up to who she is and tell us where we can find her family.'

'I don't see that happening. Molly would rather live on the streets or degrade herself with the likes of Endicott than go home – if she even has one to go to. That surely tells us all we need to know about how awful that option is for her.'

'And your suggestion is?'

'I don't have one,' he admitted. 'This kid has fallen by the wayside, Pen. One of the forgotten. My betting is she's no older than sixteen, and she's already been let down so badly by life she may never recover. Those fractures are only going to get bigger and more dangerous. Whichever way she turns, she has no chance.'

Chandler shook her head. 'I don't have any answers, either. You've always told me we have to play the cards we're dealt, right? That things are as they are, and not how we'd like them to be. Whatever Molly did, whatever she's been through, whatever she's about to face, none of it is our business. DI Bentley and his team have a few hours left with her, and then I'm guessing social services take over.'

'Will they, though? What if she never gives up her real name or age?'

'Neither can she prove she's over sixteen, Jimmy. I'm sure the Child Protection Unit will err on the side of caution and recommend she's placed into the care system.'

'Even if that's possible in these circumstances, it'll take days. What happens to her in the meantime?'

'That, I don't know.' Chandler took a breath, then gave a reflective smile. 'Jimmy, I understand why you're het up over this. You're right to be. It looks bleak for her. But we are not directly involved with her case – and to be honest, even if we were, neither of us have any answers. There are systems in place and we have to trust in them.'

Bliss shook his head and said, 'I just keep flashing back to the moment I first saw her face, Pen. I can't shift that image.'

He saw it again now. He did not own much in the way of art, but one item he had unpacked and hung on a wall at home was a framed print of *The Scream*. Edvard Munch's evocation of an endless, silent scream – of fear or paranoia – had been perfectly matched by Molly as she stood teetering on the edge of the Travelodge roof.

About to say more, Bliss was distracted by a call. The name on the screen told him it was from DSI Fletcher. He considered ducking it, but decided to get whatever it was over with.

'I need to speak to you, Inspector,' was how she began. No time for pleasantries, apparently.

'Urgently?' he asked.

'Would I be calling you otherwise?'

She had a point. It was rare for him to receive a call directly from the Super. He immediately wondered who was in trouble: him or someone else.

SEVEN

Though Marion Fletcher greeted him warmly into her office, Bliss saw concern in the look she gave him. There was no anger in her eyes; in fact, quite the opposite. He tried desperately to think of what he had done to engender her sympathy, but it was beyond him. After pulling out a chair and taking a seat, he waited for her to open up. He did not have to wait long.

'Inspector Bliss, are you aware of the human remains discovered on a building site close to Cat's Water drain in Fengate?'

The name sounded familiar to him – but not the uncovering of a corpse. At least he now knew why Fletcher was approaching this so sensitively; his last such case in the city had brought about devastation and further death. He shook his head but said nothing.

'Initially, given the location, the suspicion was that all of the remains were best left in the hands of archaeologists and anthropologists,' Fletcher continued.

'Until one wasn't, I'm guessing,' Bliss said.

'Indeed. The third skeletal form revealed was immediately spotted as being a good deal fresher than the others. Perhaps ten to fifteen years in the ground, according to preliminary findings, but we're told it'll be a while before that's confirmed.'

Bliss's shoulders sagged. Investigations involving the recently deceased were tough, but cold cases so old they were often referred to as 'freezer cases' were harder still. Evidence was generally scarce. Many potential witnesses had either passed away, or could not be traced. And the memories of those who were interviewed were often deemed untrustworthy after a decade or more of additional knowledge and experiences.

'I'm sorry,' Fletcher said with a light shrug, sensing his disappointment. 'I realise this will probably dredge up many unwelcome memories for you. However, although it's your operation as DI, it's one you ought to consider delegating to DS Bishop in respect of the daily tasks. That would free you up to take a more overall perspective, perhaps. DCI Warburton can come on as SIO as of Monday morning.'

Bliss grinned. 'You mean I should act like a normal DI in this situation and remain behind my desk?'

The Superintendent's thinning lips matched his own. 'It couldn't hurt.'

'I'll think about it, ma'am.'

They both knew he wouldn't.

Fletcher told him how to access the site, and Bliss hurried down to the second floor to gather his squad together. There was no obvious urgency in him attending the Fengate scene, so he and the team's other lead detectives discussed the three open cases they were currently working. A lorry loaded with high-end TVs had been stolen from a nearby truck stop, a lunchtime carjacking on a densely populated city centre street was taking up a lot of time, and the suspicious death of a well-known street person was the most recent case to fall into their laps.

In the opinion of DCs John Hunt and Phil Gratton, the lorry driver was in on the robbery. CID had passed the case along because he'd claimed to have had a gun pulled on him when being ordered to hand over the keys, but having looked into his background, Hunt and Gratton believed the man's form spoke for itself. He had both fraud and theft to his name, and he was a well-known purveyor of stolen goods. Their task now was to work closely with the hauliers and their insurers to apply pressure on him to confess and name his accomplices.

Bishop and DC Gul Ansari had claimed the latest case; both were keen to rid the city streets of the kind of vermin who attacked the vulnerable and needy. An ex-serviceman by the name of Adrian Summerby had been found dead in his sleeping bag on the steps of the Town Hall early on Sunday morning. Cause of death had yet to be determined, due to a backlog at the hospital mortuary, but the homeless man appeared to have been heavily beaten no more than twelve hours before being discovered.

'It's a bloody disgrace,' Bishop growled, having remained seated while Ansari delivered the update from the front of the briefing room. 'Man serves his country on three tours and that's how he ends up going out? Even in death, Ade's case is being shunted back just because he lived on the streets.'

'Do you have anything else to offer, other than political grievance?' Bliss asked. When his DS dropped his gaze and shrugged, Bliss continued. 'I understand your frustrations, Bish. And I both sympathise and agree with you when you bemoan our treatment of those who served us in battle. I realise you were familiar with Ade, so this is more than just another case to you, but if it doesn't push the investigation forward, save it for the pub, eh?'

'Yes, boss. Sorry.'

'Witnesses?' Bliss asked. 'CCTV?'

'No to the former,' Ansari replied. 'Yes to the latter. We don't have footage of the beating, but we do see Mr Summerby making his way from the alley at St Peter's Arcade towards the Town Hall.

He appears not to be walking too well. Certainly not straight, and possibly even staggering.'

Bishop coughed into his balled-up hand before interjecting. 'Normally with Ade, we'd put that down to one too many extra-strong ciders, but in this case I think he's struggling due to having taken a hiding earlier in the evening. Thing is, he appears to have sheltered in that strip between St Peter's Road and Bridge Street, and it's a good bet he received the beating there, out of sight of any cameras.'

Bliss nodded. 'Okay, keep on with it. If necessary, take a look at the shops in and around the arcade – they may have their own security cameras pointing in the right direction. Now, if you were pissed off before, Bish, you're hardly going to like this. Pen and I have a new case, so you and Gul will have to cover our current one.'

'What's come in?' Bishop asked without rancour, his outrage already pushed to the back of his mind as he sought to focus on the new information.

'My favourite sort. Unearthed skeletal remains, not that old.' He held out a warning hand. 'And before you bite my head off about why it takes precedence over the possible murder of our homeless ex-serviceman, DS Bishop – it doesn't. Pen and I will take this one, and you'll shift across to ours.' Bliss glanced over at DC Hunt. 'John, either put a delay on your stolen lorry case or pass it back to CID for the time being to babysit.'

'Yes, boss.'

'You and Phil will work Bish and Gul's inquiry for the time being. Any questions?'

'None, boss.' Hunt shook his head.

Bishop appeared to be satisfied with the new arrangement. Bliss nodded and continued. 'As for our carjacking, Pen and I have a theory. From their descriptions, the two figures who materialised out of nowhere to force Mrs McKenzie from her vehicle on Mayor's

Walk were familiar to both of us. We had a trawl through the system and we reckon one of them was our old friend Ejaz Baqri. For those of you not aware, he and his brother are notorious cut-and-shut merchants, but we don't believe Rashid ever actually jacks the motors. He's the mechanic. If this is Ejaz, then his partner this time is likely to be either Neil Smith or Raza Duranni.'

'Sounds like a good lead,' Bishop said, nodding his approval.

'Problem is,' Bliss shot back, 'the Baqri brothers never operate long in one place. The older brother, Rashid, is the brains of the outfit, and he likes to keep things fluid. We've put word out to local informants that we'd like to know the current whereabouts of their work premises.'

'Do you not have addresses?' Ansari asked.

'Yes – for both of them,' Chandler said. 'But experience tells us they'll decline to be interviewed, and we have bugger all to arrest them on. I'm sure we can still catch at least one of them in the same place as the Range Rover they jacked, because I doubt they've had time to turn it around. But I also suspect we have less than forty-eight hours before it's moved on. So, heavy emphasis on discovering the whereabouts of their new cut-and-shut operation.'

'You think you can handle that?' Bliss asked, looking directly at Bishop and Ansari. 'I realise I'm dropping you both straight in at the deep end, and shifting you all around is less than ideal, but I've been ordered to treat this new case as a priority, which means we all need to be flexible, at least until we've identified the body.'

Bishop took a few seconds to consider before responding. 'We'll give it our best, boss. If we get too stretched, I'll let you know, and we're also here for John and Phil if they run into any stumbling blocks. It's a busy time, so we'll make do.'

'Okay – thanks, everybody. I have one more thing to say before you go about your tasks,' Bliss said, walking to the front of the room to look back at his team. 'I know we were all expecting yet more upheaval with a second DCI arriving and taking over direct command of our unit. Like you, I was none too happy about it, given everything that's happened over the past few months. However, I think we've landed on our feet with Diane Warburton. You all got to know her in September, and I partnered up with her for a couple of days. She's one of us, and in my opinion that makes life a bit easier as we approach the end of what's been a tough old year. Thoughts?'

'I make you right about her, boss,' Bishop offered. 'She's bound to be a bit different now she's in charge, but we could have done a lot worse.'

'But…? I'm sensing there's more, Bish.'

'Only that her appointment still leaves us light here in the trenches. We're down one DS, and it's obvious to me at least that it's now going to stay that way.'

Nodding, Bliss said, 'We are, but in fact as I've pointed out before, we were previously top-heavy. There's always the possibility that we'll gain another DC at some point, but the whole change of structure here points to a more fluid movement of people through the units. That said, if you feel the need to blame somebody, aim your ire at me. This is not about cuts, and it's not about changes to retirement age so that old gits like me can carry on taking up space in the team. I was asked for my opinion in respect of replacing Mia, and I told Superintendent Fletcher that it was too soon. None of us are quite used to walking in here and looking at Mia's desk and seeing it empty, but I, for one, am not yet ready to walk in here and see some new face sitting there instead.'

He held his hands in the air to forestall any comebacks. 'Look, it's been a strange few months. We're all making our own way through this. I had to have my say on behalf of us all, and that was the way I decided to go. The Super went with it. If you disagree, come and find me in my office and we'll have it out. But for the time being, this is our team and we're just going to get on with our jobs.'

EIGHT

It wasn't until Bliss arrived at the building site at the end of Titan Drive in the Fengate district of Peterborough, past the single-storey industrial buildings and patches of wasteland, that he realised why the location had sounded familiar when Superintendent Fletcher mentioned it.

As he stepped out of the car and unlaced his shoes in preparation to swap them for a grubby pair of sturdy walking boots, his mind filled with a wider image of the area. Staring over the roof of the vehicle, he said, 'Now I understand why unearthing remains apparently came as no real surprise.' He pointed out across the dense scrubland to the long line of trees standing some fifty yards away. 'Just beyond there is the Cat's Water drain. You follow it left and it feeds around in a tight right-hand arc and wanders through Flag Fen.'

Flag Fen was a renowned Bronze Age historical site, which had become a beacon for national heritage tourists since it had been designated an 'Archaeology Park'.

'I had no idea we were so close to it,' Chandler said, peering through the distant trees as if hoping to catch a glimpse. She was also changing her footwear ahead of trudging over the uneven terrain and wet soil.

Bliss nodded. 'You're looking at a much longer drive to get around to it on four wheels, but yeah, it's closer to the city than people think.' He paused for a moment, gave a rueful grin and turned to point to his right. 'And I just remembered something else: if you follow the drain in that direction instead, it takes you very close to Lewis Drake's scrapyard.'

Chandler grimaced. 'Ugh, that bastard,' she said.

'Yeah. I should have been in court helping to put him away today. Yet more ugly memories. Speaking of which, are you ready for another bundle of bones?'

'As I'll ever be. Is it okay if I crack the same joke about them being lively enough for you to jump?'

He laughed. 'I'm surprised you remember that. In retrospect, I let you get away with far too much far too soon. It's why you have so little respect for me now.'

'Oh, I respect you, boss. Of course I do. I just don't like you very much.'

Bliss shook his head and made his way over to the area abutting the overgrown and neglected scrubland. A digger and a dump truck stood idle, men wearing hard hats gathered in a group in animated conversation, and a white-suited forensics team milled around several white tents erected to protect the finds from the elements. The rain had let up, but the low grey clouds looked laden with moisture, ready to unleash it upon the unwilling victims below.

A significant area had been taped off; at its entrance a forensic technician waited, armed with a clipboard to register the names of those who entered and exited the site. 'Do we need to suit up?' Bliss asked, signing his name. 'If so, we'll have to cadge them off you.'

The tech shook his head. 'Not necessary at this stage, Inspector. Both we and Dr Grant have released the remains in question for inspection prior to removal.'

'Dr Grant?' The name took Bliss by surprise.

'Yes, sir. Forensic anthropologist. She was on site anyway to process the ancient remains, but stayed to do the same when the more recent skeletonised body was uncovered.'

'It's got to be her, right?' Chandler said as they walked across to the tent the tech had indicated. 'The Bone Woman. I mean, who else could it be?'

Bliss stopped in his tracks and grinned. Heading their way was a familiar figure garbed in one of the unflattering forensic suits, its hood now pulled down around her neck. Her hair was tied up into two small pigtails. She looked pale and tired, but was nonetheless instantly recognisable.

'Dr Grant, I presume?' Bliss said, extending his right hand.

The woman slapped it away and instead stepped closer to embrace him. The hug was brief, but it felt warm and genuinely affectionate. 'Don't give me all that "Doctor" bullshit,' she said, offering both detectives a radiant smile. 'You know I don't go in for all that nonsense.'

'And yet apparently you're now a forensic anthropologist,' Chandler said, accepting her own short hug. 'What's that, your third doctorate?'

'Still just the two, I'm afraid. But I seldom use the title if I can help it.'

It was one of the things Bliss had always liked about the Bone Woman. He and Chandler had first met Emily Grant at a training event, after which the doctor had helped them out on their last unearthed remains investigation back in 2005. While the case was ongoing, she and Bliss had dated and became quite close, though their brief relationship died a rapid death when he was posted down to London. The reason for his puzzlement over her name had much closer origins, however.

'You're back to using your maiden name again,' he said.

Her smile faltered, and she let out a heavy sigh as she nodded. 'I decided Curtis didn't suit me. Neither had I earned it legitimately.'

Bliss winced, sensing her pain. In the spring, she had come to him after her husband was found to have committed suicide; Emily believed there was more to his death and he had looked into the case. Her husband having supposedly jumped from a motorway bridge, Bliss found no solid evidence to the contrary, although there were a few details that didn't quite add up. Eventually he discovered that the man Emily had married, Simon Curtis, was an undercover security services operative, murdered for getting too close to an international smuggling ring who were exploiting the armed forces transportation system. It had fallen upon Bliss to inform Emily that the man she knew and loved was not at all the man she believed him to be.

'How've you been doing?' Chandler asked. She was experienced enough to know that most women hated to be pitied, so hers was a casual question with no obvious undertones.

'Better, thank you.' Emily Grant's nod was enthusiastic. 'Good, in fact. I seem to have found my niche at last, and working takes my mind off other things. My post at Cambridge never entirely suited me, so I lecture part-time only these days, and I also loan myself out across the county on a forensic basis. I'm enjoying the different mindset required, plus it doesn't allow me to become deskilled.'

'And what do you think you have for us here?' Bliss asked, his gaze drifting over to the tent.

'Take a look for yourself if you wish,' Grant said, pulling off her gloves. 'Not that it will do you much good. I can tell you that we have a female, just like last time. Fortunately, this one was not pregnant. I'd estimate her age to be between thirty and forty, and I'll be able to narrow that down once I have her on my table. Cause of death is not immediately obvious, though we've not disturbed the remains too much as yet. Perhaps something will be more apparent when we move her.'

Bliss had to intervene. 'Sorry, Emily, but she needs to go to our own mortuary, back at the city hospital. I can arrange transportation, but given that this is also an ancient burial site, I'm happy for you to call the shots on that if you prefer.'

Grant rolled her eyes and put a hand to her chest. 'Silly me. I got carried away. Of course, this poor woman should be evaluated by your own people. Your CSI staff are here somewhere, champing at the bit for us to release the find to them. You should liaise with them as to who does what next.'

Bliss nodded. 'I will – thanks. How long do you think she's been down there?'

'The bones are neither dry nor flaky or crumbly. The discolouration is certainly not something I'd describe as archaeological. We found a number of unperishable items which I'm certain will provide a more accurate estimate.'

'Have our forensic people bagged and tagged them?'

'Not yet, no. Each piece is quite enmeshed with the general detritus of remains and soil, so they decided it would be better if the mortuary tech removed them on the table, at which point CSI will package them up and pass the bags directly to the exhibits officer. However, I think we're talking about anywhere between ten and twenty years in the ground.'

'So, similar condition to our 2005 case?'

'I'd say so. Approximately.'

'How deep was she buried?' Chandler asked.

Grant fidgeted with the hood at the back of her neck. 'No more than three feet,' she answered. 'But it's a good question. Our older remains were much deeper. In fact, if we hadn't broadened the dig in search of further bodies we'd probably have missed yours altogether.'

Bliss glanced around, taking in the industrial estate behind them, the wasteland all around, the dense line of trees away in the distance. 'If you chose the early hours of the morning, I'm guessing you'd have a fair bit of time to dispose of a body out here. But three foot isn't deep. Perhaps they encountered hard ground.'

'Frozen or baked,' Chandler muttered, appraising the soil beneath her feet.

'This is loamy soil with naturally high groundwater,' Grant informed them, nudging the earth with her foot as if to prove a point. 'The ditches and drains do such an effective job, however, that it can actually be pretty dry at times. Plenty of stones and quite flinty. If the depth is related to the toughness of the task rather than laziness, then I think you'd be able to pinpoint the most likely time of year where those conditions were met. It won't be a wide window, that's for sure.'

'You know how we like to operate,' Bliss said with a cheery grin. 'When it comes to detailed information, the more the merrier. So I'm very happy to have you working it as well, Emily.'

'Glad I can be of help.' Grant inclined her head slightly. 'Penny here was kind enough to enquire after my welfare, but I neglected to ask about yours. How are things with you, Jimmy? Still tilting at windmills?'

'To a certain degree, only my enemies are not in the least bit imaginary. And, of course, I don't take a single step without my trusty Sancho Panza by my side.'

Chandler looked at him as if he were mad. 'Sancho who?'

Bliss turned to Grant. 'You'll have to forgive her, Emily. She's both a philistine and a rube, so there's no hope at all for her.' He shook his head at his colleague in admonishment. 'It's Don Quixote, Pen. If you took your eyes out of those tawdry magazines you read, you might actually enjoy a bit of literature once in a while.'

'Donkey who? What on earth are you on about, man?'

Grant giggled. 'Oh, I have missed this. I've worked with so many wonderful, gifted people down the years, but they mostly tend towards being a little... dry. Even stuffy on occasion. Your nonsense always did brighten up my days.'

'His nonsense,' Chandler insisted, jabbing a finger at Bliss.

'Rubbish,' he said. 'You're the nut job. Anyway, Emily, in answer to your question – I'm doing great, thanks. And Pen has had some wonderful news since we all last spoke.'

'That's right.' Chandler nodded and beamed at Grant. 'I finally got to meet my daughter again.'

'Oh, my goodness!' Emily's hands shot to a position just beneath her chin, as if praying. 'How splendid for you both.'

'You have no idea. Jimmy and I went out to Turkey, and with a local police escort monitoring, Hannah and I were allowed to spend an hour together. She's called Anna now, which is fine. Until recently she thought I was dead, because that's what Mehmet always told her – he's Anna's father. Jimmy lit a fire under the security services, who in turn put a rocket up the backside of both the Home and Foreign offices, and between them and the Turkish authorities they tracked down Mehmet and got the job done.'

'Anna is absolutely stunning,' Bliss said. 'She's almost twenty now, of course. A stylish, elegant, slender, and well-spoken young woman. Everything her mother is not.'

Chandler whacked him with the back of her hand and screwed up her face in mock fury. The two glared at each other before breaking out into childish grins.

'You don't change,' Grant told them. 'And please, stay that way as long as you can. By the way, Jimmy, your avoidance of my question did not escape my attention. I suspect your life is just as chaotic as ever, but is there any prospect of us catching up some time soon?'

'That'd be nice. I expect we're both very busy, but I'm sure we can find room for a quiet drink somewhere.'

'I'll look forward to it. Meanwhile, give me what's left of today to tease this young woman from the soil. I'll arrange for transport personally if your CSI people don't care one way or another how she's moved. Is it still Nancy Drinkwater running the show at the hospital?'

'It is,' Chandler responded. 'Just tell her Ray needs it done urgently.'

Grant frowned. 'Ray?'

'It's what Nancy calls our DI here. Reckons he looks a bit like Ray Winstone.'

'I know him,' Grant said, nodding and running an appreciative eye over Bliss. 'Yes, there is a resemblance, I suppose. Is Nancy an old flame, by any chance?'

'No, nothing of the sort,' Bliss was quick to confirm. 'She's a lovely woman and we get on great, but there's nothing like that going on.'

'In fact, the boss is enduring a bit of a dry spell in that regard,' Chandler said, unable to keep the smirk from her lips. 'Thorpe Wood nick is positively swimming in oestrogen at the moment, but rather than riding the wave, Jimmy's in danger of getting swept away by it.'

'Do you mind?' Bliss said, wincing at the mental image. 'There's such a thing as too much information, as I've told you many times before.'

'Yes, boss. Sorry, boss.' Chandler snapped off a mock salute.

'And Emily,' he said, turning to Grant, 'please don't encourage her. As for our remains over there, I know I'm not about to discover anything you missed, but I'll have a quick shufti anyway. Just to tick a box if required at a later date. I guess the main thing is, there's no chance this one is going to cause the same upheaval as the last.'

NINE

On their way back to HQ, they stopped for a late lunch at Frankie & Benny's on Boongate. Over barbecued steak wraps, Chandler did her level best to provoke a response about Emily Grant and the proposed drinks meeting, but Bliss was immune to both her sardonic wit and her apparent desperation for him to be in a relationship.

'This is a clear case of serendipity,' Chandler insisted, and he knew she was not joking around this time. She had barbecue sauce above her top lip, but he declined to point it out, hoping it would remain there for the rest of the day. 'Thirteen years ago you walked out of each other's lives, seemingly for good, yet this year you've been drawn together again on two separate occasions. I call that fate. Also, you can't tell me today didn't have echoes of that evening over in Bretton Woods when she examined that skeletal young woman with us. I'm telling you, Jimmy, there's something in the air.'

'The pungent aroma of bullshit, if I'm not very much mistaken.'

Chandler waved a careless hand. 'Dismiss it all you like, but there is something going on that neither you nor I can explain.'

Bliss thought about it for a few seconds, before raising a single eyebrow. 'Perhaps more than you realise,' he said, glancing away.

'And just what do you mean by that?'

When he turned to face her, his partner had shot up in her seat like a meerkat. Bliss shrugged and said, 'I bought *The Mourinho* back on Monday.'

'Your boat?'

'Yep. I hadn't seen her in quite a while, but at the weekend I walked down by Osier Lake, and ventured out to the locks on the river for a change. I spotted a familiar blue hull peeking out from its mooring, wandered down, saw it was my old boat. The owner wasn't around, so I dropped by again on Monday evening and caught him shutting her up for the night. We had a chat, shook hands on a deal. I popped round his house later that night and signed the paperwork. It took us ten minutes to clinch the sale, and five of those we spent drinking a toast with some bloody fine Redbreast Irish whiskey. And that was that. She's mine again.'

Chandler's face was a picture of pure wonder. 'Now that *is* spooky. *The Mourinho*, some unearthed remains, and Emily Grant all back on your radar within a few days. What does *that* tell you?'

Bliss wasn't about to let her have things entirely her own way. 'Only that the cosmic tumblers turned and this is what they came up with. It's not fate, it's not karma – it's pure chance. They're three separate incidents, and when you put them all together, they still mean absolutely nothing beyond themselves.'

Chandler persisted throughout the drive back to HQ, and Bliss was more than happy to be grabbed by DI Bentley as they entered the squad room. 'Sorry to break up the party,' Bentley said. 'Any chance of me borrowing you for a short while, Inspector?'

Bliss frowned suspiciously. 'For what?'

'We have that girl in for interview. Molly. To my surprise she hasn't asked for a brief as yet, but neither was she able to nominate an appropriate adult. Says she doesn't need one anyway as she claims to be eighteen. That's clearly not the case, but it did throw up a few interesting legal issues. I had a word with a solicitor who was in on another case, and he gave me some good pointers. We managed to get hold of one of our on-site YMCA volunteers to attend as an AA. Despite that, all Molly will say is that she will only talk to you.'

'I take it you've told her it's not my case.'

Bentley flashed a sour smile. 'Naturally. Until I'm blue in the face. But apparently it's either talk to you or not talk at all. The clock is running, so against my better judgement I'm doing as she asked.'

Bristling, Bliss snapped, 'Against your better judgement? What the fuck does that mean?'

'It means I'd rather not have you in the room screwing things up for my case. But beggars can't be choosers, it seems.'

'You're such a warm-hearted tool, Bentley. Is it any wonder your witnesses won't talk to you?'

His fellow DI flashed a sharkish grin. 'Each to their own, Bliss. I get more than my fair share of wins, don't you worry about that. And anyway, she's not a witness. She's a suspect. I'm surprised you need reminding of that.'

Bliss dug his nails into his palm, trying to contain his anger. If he had been running the case, he would have initially interviewed Molly as a witness. People tended to open up more in less volatile situations, perhaps letting slip a few key pieces of information amongst the dross. Bentley's methods had set the girl against him from the off, and it would be an uphill battle now.

He sighed. 'Tell me what procedures are already under way and in place,' he said, reluctant to dance to Bentley's tune, but sensing he was Molly's best chance of getting a result.

'Okay. She's been printed, but we don't have her on record. We sent a general description, together with the name she gave us, to missing persons. I've referred her to METhub and also requested a mental health assessment. Finally, LADS were also advised so they can open up a file on her.'

Bliss nodded as Bentley spoke. He didn't care for the man's personality, but the DI was on the ball in terms of protocol. The Missing, Exploitation and Trafficking hub would immediately look into their own records, and even if Molly was not already in the system they would hopefully decide to work with the girl as soon as the police allowed them to. Likewise, the Liaison and Diversion Service – funded by the NHS but with a small team based at Thorpe Wood – would assess Molly's situation and give her advice, as well as liaising with Social Care and the Youth Offender Team if she was charged. Bentley looked to have everything in hand. There was just one thing missing: getting Molly's cooperation.

'I'll do it on one condition,' Bliss said. 'Actually, several conditions, now that I think about it.'

'And they are?' Bentley stood rocking on his heels, his hands buried deep inside his trouser pockets. He was furious at being sidelined from his own case, but it wasn't Bliss's job to become the DI's cheerleader at this juncture.

'First, I want her out of the suspect interview room and into one of the rooms we use for witnesses. Make a point of grumbling about how I'd insisted she and I talk without caution.'

'But unless I de-arrest her, she remains under caution anyway.'

'I know that, Bentley, but she probably doesn't. Your YMCA appropriate adult may object, but I'm sure you can bury the lie if you have to. Second, I want DS Chandler in with me in place of whoever you wanted in there from your team. Third, I don't want you anywhere near us.'

The DI considered the requests, using his tongue to probe various areas of his mouth while he pondered. Finally, he nodded. 'But whatever you get from her is for me and my team to act on,' he said. 'You stay out of it. This is not a Major Crimes investigation. Understood?'

'Perfectly. I wouldn't want you on one of my cases, either. But that's purely because I like to win mine.'

Bentley snorted derisively and stomped away. Bliss watched him go before turning to Chandler, who had stayed out of the entire conversation. 'Do me a favour, Pen. While we're in the room with her, watch this girl closely. I'm not quite sure how I'm going to approach things, but there's more to her than just being a mule for some lowlife drug empire. This girl is suffering inside, but she presents a front you simply have to admire.'

'Speak for yourself. I like to think I'm less of a pushover.'

'It's not like that, as you well know. She's just a kid.'

'So you'd be feeling the same way about a fifteen-year-old lad?'

Bliss had to stop and think about that. 'I can't honestly say,' he admitted. 'But I'm hoping you'll see it for yourself. She's impressively strong and direct for her age, but it's masking something. A genuine vulnerability. She doesn't want it seen or acknowledged, that's for sure.'

'But you claim to have caught a glimpse?'

'I did.'

'Up on that roof.'

Bliss nodded.

Chandler shrugged. 'I'll see whatever there is *to* see, boss. I can't honestly say I've been impressed by her so far. At the end of the day, if I think she's just another scrote, then that's what I'll tell you.'

'Fair enough. An honest opinion is all I'm after.'

'But to what end?'

He shook his head. 'I haven't got a scooby – perhaps none. She may even prove to be exactly what she appears to be, but I don't want her under my skin or inside my head if she doesn't deserve to be there.'

Ten minutes later they found Molly in the second room they tried. Whoever had used the room last had pushed the desk into one corner; the centre of the floor was now taken up by mismatched soft chairs in an L shape. The girl was not cuffed, but a female uniform stood close by. Releasing the constable from her post, Bliss took a seat at an angle to Molly; it would allow him to look directly at her without turning. Chandler sat by the girl's side. A young woman who didn't look a great deal older than Molly occupied a chair by the desk. She introduced herself as Kim Parker, acting as Molly's appropriate adult.

Bliss smiled tentatively at Molly. 'How are you feeling now?' Having checked both her hospital discharge and custody records, he already knew her wounds were mostly superficial; she had needed stitches in just two of the slashes on her upper arm and half a dozen more in an abdominal wound. With painkillers wearing off, she would feel the effects, but there was no medical reason for her not to be questioned.

'Okay, I suppose.' Molly first shrugged, then stiffened and sat up straight. 'None the better for seeing you, though.'

Bliss pursed his lips, deciding to play it hard. 'I can walk away just as easily as I came. Unlike you, I have a home to go to. I'm here because you told my colleagues that you would speak only to me. If that's no longer the case, I can go and leave you with DS Chandler.'

'Why's she here anyway? I said you, and only you.'

'You're a female minor in a room with me and no camera or observation window, just a tiny square piece of glass in the door. Ms Parker is sitting in to safeguard your interests, and my sergeant is here to safeguard mine. I haven't got time to waste, so can we please get started?'

The girl shrugged again. She wore a navy-blue sweatshirt and grey sweatpants, thick woollen socks on her feet, canvas shoes discarded beside her chair. She looked anything but the demented waif from the rooftop.

The YMCA volunteer coughed, drew their attention, then said, 'I'd just like to remind Molly that, since she was not de-arrested, she remains under caution. Therefore her right not to incriminate herself still applies.'

Molly turned away as if to register her lack of interest. Bliss conceded Parker's point with a nod before continuing. 'So, Molly, the first thing I'm hoping to clarify here is your real name. Or, if Molly is your given name, then your full name. Surname.'

The girl looked better than she had when he'd first laid eyes on her, but was still pale and obviously undernourished. The dark circles around her eyes suggested she needed to sleep for a straight week. As she shook her head in response to his request, Bliss recalled something about her. Something missing from the overall picture. He put it to one side, deciding to revisit it later.

'Molly, we're going to need that name from you at some point. And it's in your best interests to tell us. In our opinion, you are a minor – a juvenile, a child – and on that basis there's every chance of you going into the system when our twenty-four hours with you are up. We have the option to request a further twelve hours, but I doubt we'll bother. And if you aren't charged and put into detention, you'll go into emergency care. It would be easier all round if we were able to notify somebody on your behalf. An appropriate adult who is actually a close friend or family member.'

Unmoved, the girl stared at him and said, 'Easier? Not for me, it wouldn't be. You think my life was easy? What kind of cop are you, anyway? A dumb one, if you reckon I do what I do now, live the way I live now, when all the time I've got some wonderful family life waiting for me at home.'

Bliss remained equally impassive, though he detected a wry smile appearing on Kim Parker's face. 'All right. Then tell me this: do you have any family at all? Parents? Siblings? Aunts, uncles? Grandparents?'

For the first time, Molly looked confused. 'What the fuck's a sibling?'

'It means brother or sister.'

'Why didn't you just say that, then?'

He shrugged and smiled. 'It's shorter. Or at least it should be, if you don't then get drawn into a whole conversation about what it means. It usually saves wasting breath – and when you get to my age you start counting each one.'

Molly rolled her eyes, the movement exaggerated. 'I'm not talking to you about any of that. I won't. And you can't make me.'

'That's true, Molly,' Chandler said. 'But it limits our options. Your options, too. Inspector Bliss outlined what will most likely happen to you. A detention centre if you're charged and held on remand. An emergency hostel or care home if you aren't. We'd prefer to give you more choices, that's all.'

'People like me don't have choices. I do what I do. And when I don't do that any more, I'll do something else.' She glared pointedly at Bliss. 'Like throw myself off a roof.'

The kid was putting up a front, but she was hurting. He saw that in her: a thin sliver of fear running between the fresh bloom of her youth and the hard calluses she had built up to suppress it. Beneath the bluster, she was just a scared child.

'How about you tell us more about your life in London?' Bliss said. 'We know all we need to know about where you go here, and why, but you mentioned Homerton earlier. I know it well – I lived not far from there. Clapton, Hackney, Tower Hamlets all around you. Whereabouts did you live, Molly?'

'What, so's you can show photos of me around there, show my face to the local cops? I'm not stupid. I'm not a kid, and I'm not stupid.'

Bliss let it go. Her photograph, taken when she was first brought to the station, had already been sent to the nicks in and around the areas he had mentioned, just in case she was familiar to their drugs units. But in truth they had no need of identifying her at this point. Prior to the raids, relevant properties in both London and Peterborough had been under surveillance. Molly would turn up on video footage or in a photo.

He sighed and leaned forward in his seat. Molly crossed one leg over the other and began to jiggle her foot. Bliss took that as a sign of anxiety.

'You're not giving us much to work with,' he said.

A wide grin spread across her face. 'You think? Why would I?'

'Well, for starters, if you don't communicate with me then you'll be going back into the interview room with DI Bentley.'

'He's a dick.'

'You'll get no argument from me there.'

'But then you stopped me topping myself, so you're a dick as well.'

Bliss smiled and said, 'I certainly can be, and that would come as no surprise to my DS here.'

'So why don't you just ask me about Ryan? That's all you really want to know. You don't give a fuck about me, not any of you. You just want to nail him, and if you get me at the same time then that'll be a bonus.'

'Endicott is of enormous interest to us, Molly, yes. I won't deny that. And I guess you've probably seen more than your fair share of the rougher end of policing, which is why you're not so keen on us. But we're not monsters. And contrary to what you believe, we do care about your welfare.'

Molly snorted her derision. 'Yeah, sure.'

'Then explain to me why I pulled you away from that ledge. I didn't know who you were or what you had done at that point. Why would I do that if I didn't care?'

'Because you saw the knife and the blood and knew I had to be in trouble of some kind. And anyway, even if you gave a shit about me then, you don't now – because all you give a stuff about now is Ryan.'

Bliss gave Chandler the eyes, indicating for her to take over.

'Molly,' she said, shifting sideways to face the girl. 'I'm not going to lie to you and say we have no interest in Ryan Endicott and the activities he and his associates are involved in. But we don't need you for that. His flat wasn't raided on a whim today. And it's not as if we believe you have any idea where Endicott is, either. You go to the house, you see him at the house, so the house is where you know him from. There's no way you'd have a clue where he would run to.'

'He talks,' Molly said indignantly. 'He brags all the time about his contacts.'

'And we know them all. At least, our drugs squad do. Believe me, we have a number of so-called safe houses under observation as we speak.'

'Then why are you even questioning me at all?'

'Because it's our job. Prior to coming here to the station, you were spoken to unofficially and not under caution. Now we need to formalise those conversations. We want to know who gave you the drugs down in London and where you were staying. Or, to be more precise, what we need is clarification, because we already know the answers. Likewise, we'd like a statement from you naming names here, in our city. Finally, we're looking for you to tell us about the fight you had with Endicott and how you both sustained your injuries.'

Molly shot Bliss a hard look and said, 'Is she supposed to be the good cop or the bad cop?'

The stern exterior was fake, and Bliss knew it. He also believed he would pierce it, given time. 'Neither of us are bad cops. In your eyes, I guess we're not entirely good, either. You've made that pretty clear. But there's no trickery going on here, Molly. We're not trying to get you to admit to anything you didn't do, or to anything we don't already know a whole lot about.'

The girl planted both feet on the floor and leaned forward at the waist, sneering. 'I don't believe you!'

'And that's your prerogative. But before we wrap things up here, Molly, I do just want to ask you about something I remembered from this morning, up on the roof.'

'Yeah? What's that, then?'

Running drugs across county lines was nothing new. Neither was moving into smaller territories with the intention of making them your own. Not even the addition of dedicated mobile phone lines was unheard of, nor the use of children as both couriers and corner sellers. The kids were getting younger all the time, however, and the exploitation of vulnerable people was abhorrent to Bliss. One consistent theme over the years was how some chose to be paid, and it was this area that he wanted to explore with Molly.

'Your… job is to run drugs. Payment comes in the form of putting a roof over your head, some food in your belly, even a little money from time to time. What about product? Do you get a taste of that, too?'

'You don't have to answer that, Molly,' Parker said, leaning towards her. 'You don't have to answer any of it.'

Bliss glared at the woman. 'I know you have a job to do,' he said, 'but if you can't tell the difference between someone trying to help and someone trying it on, then you need to let a colleague with a bit more experience take your place in the room.'

Parker's neck and cheeks flushed. 'I'm here to safeguard this minor, and in my opinion it was time to remind her of her rights.'

'In which case, you couldn't be more wrong. I stand by what I said. I mean no disrespect, but if you're truly here to help Molly and not just to take us through your YMCA appropriate adult playbook of tick boxes, then learn to *hear* what's being said rather than merely listening.'

'For fuck's sake, stop arguing!' Molly had cupped her hands over her ears and was shaking her head in dismay. 'You're both doing my nut in. Now, what was your question again?' she asked, looking pointedly at Bliss.

'I asked if you ever got a taste of the product as part of the job.'

'Of course. It's how they control us.'

Bliss shook his head. 'It's not how they control you, Molly. I dare say the other mules stick around because they need their fix. But the thing I noticed up on that roof is your lack of track marks. Neither do you have burn scabs on your hands or lips, common with cocaine use. You're not scratching, you have no sores and your teeth are not too shabby, so I'd also rule out meth. I don't see any classic signs of heroin abuse; nor are you climbing the walls because your next fix is overdue. From a couple of things you've already mentioned, I'd hazard a guess that you've probably tried the harder stuff, but I also think the worst you do now is a bit of weed, right?'

'So? I don't like needles, I don't smoke and I don't like shoving shit up my hooter. So what?'

'Cannabis is not as addictive as class A gear. It doesn't make you as reliant on other people as those other drugs do. Plus it's cheap and you can buy it in so many places that you don't need to be under anyone's control. You'd already admitted that you don't care for the sex that your fellow mules and dealers seem to expect from you. That leads me to believe that the thing you most need from the deal is a place to stay. To be off the streets.'

'And? What's so terrible about wanting that?'

'Nothing,' he said gently, with a warm smile and a nod of encouragement. 'Nothing at all. But it tells me that if you're willing to put yourself through that stuff on a daily basis just to have a roof over your head, you've lived on the streets before and you've had the very worst kind of childhood.'

Molly made no reply.

Bliss smiled and said, 'That's something we can work towards improving. But first, you have to learn how to trust me.'

Still she remained mute – but this time, something stirred in her eyes. Bliss thought it might just have been hope.

TEN

Hunt twice turned a full 360 degrees before allowing his shoulders to surrender to despair. He stood in the middle of Bridge Street, only feet from a cart selling fresh doughnuts, hot coffee and cold drinks. Behind him was St Peter's Arcade, bookended by the Argo Lounge café bar and Middleton's Steakhouse & Grill. The walkway provided the homeless with refuge from the elements, and was known by local police officers as a beggar's trap for any pedestrians who walked through. Ahead of him, directly opposite the arcade and thereby providing the best view into it, was a store devoted to electronic cigarettes and vaping liquids.

'No sodding security cameras,' Hunt grumbled, running his eye over the three-storey building. He glanced to his right, but the HSBC bank displayed no obvious means of surveillance, and neither were there any cash machines on that side of the corner entrance. The betting shop to the left of the e-cig store gave him no hope, either.

'It was always going to be a long shot,' Gratton said, in between bites of a hot doughnut.

Hunt didn't know where his colleague put it all. His fellow DC carried no extra weight on his narrow frame, yet he seemed to be on a constant drip-feed of cakes, pies, crisps and biscuits. It sickened Hunt; if he so much as looked at any of those treats, his stomach would expand an inch. Life was so unfair.

The pair moved further along the street, before Hunt stopped in front of a bedraggled young man sitting on the pavement, his back supported by a rolled-up sleeping bag, his dog looking healthier than its owner. 'Want to earn yourself a hot drink and something to eat?' Hunt asked.

'I'd rather have the money,' the man said. He looked twitchy, so Hunt shook his head. 'Food and drink only. Spend the cash you earn today on whatever else you want, if you like. Tell me something. Did you know the man who was found dead on the Town Hall steps on Sunday night?'

'A bit. Ex-forces. Kept to himself, mostly.'

'Anyone in particular giving him a hard time lately?'

'Not so's I noticed. He put his head down somewhere close by, but I only come here during the day. This place is full of animals after dark.'

And one or more of them showed their teeth, Hunt thought. 'Was anybody else around here closer to him?' he asked. 'Somebody who might know more than you?'

'Like I told you, he mostly kept to himself. I never saw him speak to anyone longer than a few minutes.'

Hunt nodded and thanked the man for the information. He relented and handed the man a five-pound note. 'Your choice, I suppose,' he said. Just as it had been Ade Summerby's.

He turned to appraise the distance between the arcade and the building still thought of by most residents as the Town Hall, despite most of its staff having moved out into newer premises on the Fletton Quays. It seemed Ade Summerby had walked less than the length of a football pitch before stumbling and scrabbling beneath the grand portico outside the entrance.

'Let's take a look at the other side of the arcade,' Hunt suggested, nodding towards the alleyway. Gratton scoffed the remains of his snack and pulled a tissue from his pocket to wipe his lips before scurrying after him.

It was early afternoon and the street people were taking up their favourite positions outside the shops, bars and restaurants along Bridge Street, Long Causeway and Church Street, leaving the arcade empty. Its entrance from the St Peter's Road side offered a non-tourist view of the palace and the Bishop's Lodging – the formal residence of the city's most senior cleric. Beyond it, the cathedral rose up into the sky with majestic Gothic authority and confidence.

Not expecting to find anything as vulgar as a CCTV device affixed to the Palace Gardens wall that ran the length of St Peter's Road, Hunt eventually spied what he'd been hoping for on a pole outside the Car Haven car park.

'Make a note, Phil,' he said, pointing at the camera. There would be others out on Bourges Boulevard, Bishop's Road and Rivergate, but this one was critical. He walked across to stand beneath it. 'The feed we get from this should give us something.'

Gratton nodded instantly, recognising the possibilities. 'We've seen Ade entering and exiting the arcade, but once it quietens down we can focus on who comes and goes along here towards his position, because they didn't do so via Bridge Street.'

'Exactly. Given the mindset of the louts we're dealing with, if they wore hoods they probably yanked them up nice and tight on their way back after laying into Ade, but would they have done so going in?'

'I suppose that depends on why they went that way in the first place. That time of night, they were either cutting through on their way home or they went there specifically to find themselves an easy target for their fists and boots.'

Hunt sighed. It was a sobering thought, but it happened. All of his hopes now were tied into this CCTV camera, because if they were unable to identify any suspects from this location, then the chances of discovering who murdered Ade Summerby were miserable enough to be virtually discounted. Bishop would not be a happy man, and the prospect of upsetting his colleague even further twisted Hunt's gut.

'Shall I take a few photos?' Gratton said, reaching for his phone. 'Something for the files to provide context.'

'Good idea. Make sure you get one aiming all the way up the road.'

'Will do.'

'We have to nail these scrotes, Phil,' Hunt said, his voice hushed almost to the point of reverence. 'I want them so badly it's like having acid burning a hole through my stomach.'

'I know what you mean.' Gratton gave a single nod, his eyes hooded as he realised the awful truth that achieving justice for the dead man was not a foregone conclusion. 'I just hope they try to resist when we do track them down.'

***

Bliss and Chandler were not the only detectives in Fengate that afternoon. Bishop nosed his VW Passat pool car off the main road and into a wide alleyway that ran deep into a complex containing a number of businesses, most of them attached to the auto trade. At the far end they came upon the faded sign for Fox Motors, with its cartoon depiction of a smiling red-coated creature, bushy tail flaring. By the time Bishop killed the engine, the owner was already standing at the rolled-up entrance to his cavernous garage.

'Mr Fox, I presume,' Bishop said, recognising the man from a photo he had checked out earlier on the police database. He extended his arm – not for a handshake, but to display his warrant card. The man needed to know this was all business.

Grubby overalls aside, Fox did not look as if he had been working on any vehicles lately. His fingernails were too clean, hair carefully parted and held in place with product. The brown leather of the steel-capped boots he wore was barely scuffed. From inside the garage came the tell-tale clank of tools and the whining drone of pneumatic implements. A radio played in the background, the classic rock almost drowned out by the sound of manual labour.

'I'm perfectly legit these days, guys,' Fox said. The deep Scottish burr had softened, but his accent had not completely worn away during the twenty-eight years since Fox had moved south from Aberdeen. But that was not all Bishop knew about the man.

'That's not what we hear,' he said. 'Word has it you've just got better at hiding your more criminal enterprises.'

'Not true, officer. Not true at all.'

'It's detective, Mr Fox, as well you know. And don't worry, I have no real interest in you today. That doesn't mean I won't wake up tomorrow morning and decide to invest all my time and effort into making your life miserable, of course. But here's the thing: you can influence my thinking.'

'Oh, aye? And how do I do that? *Detective*.' With a world-weary sigh, Fox yanked a wallet out of his hip pocket, opened it up, and began thumbing through a wad of banknotes. 'You'll be looking for contributions to your... Christmas club, or whatever, right?'

'Are you trying to bribe us, sir?' Bishop's face became an ugly scowl.

Fox winked. 'Not at all. Like I said, I'm making a contribution to a charity of your choosing. That is what you were after, yes? Or am I mistaken?'

'Put your money away, Mr Fox – before I take it and shove it down your throat.'

The wallet disappeared like it was part of a magic trick. 'If you're sure. No offence intended. So, you said there was a way for me to influence the outcome of this conversation?'

Bishop turned to Ansari. She nodded. He nodded back. A mute agreement passed between them.

'Let's just say that if we leave here knowing where we can find the latest Baqri setup,' Ansari said, 'then we may well be far too busy over the coming days to even think about you, let alone have any genuine interest in your dealings.'

'Baqri?' Fox looked skywards, stroking his chin. 'Haven't heard that name for a while now. I don't know who you're buying your information from these days, but you didn't get your money's worth this time.'

'Is that so?' Ansari put on her best puzzled expression. 'That's strange. Because it's precisely the same source who gave us the address of your other business out in Whittlesey, Mr Fox. If you're saying our information is wrong, then I suppose we have some time on our hands after all, which we can use to take a trip over there to see for ourselves.'

Fox puffed out his cheeks. He was a tall man with a large girth; weighing in at well over two hundred pounds, was Bishop's guess. There was a lot of cheek to blow out. When his head fell to the point where his chin would have touched his chest were it not for the folds of flesh trapped between them, the DS knew they had him.

'They've got a new unit off Saville Road. Near the prison, and the self-storage place.'

'That's better, Mr Fox,' Bishop said encouragingly. 'Does Rashid use the same security protocols?'

'What d'you mean?' The man's attempt to feign bemusement was embarrassing.

'We're not stupid. We know these places are not open for business to idle browsers who just pop by.'

'Oh, aye. That. Of course. I'm not sure, but Baqri's style isn't unique or anything. You'll find the gates closed, camera staring straight down at you. If he wants you inside then the gates will open. If not, they won't.'

'What will get those gates to open for us?' Bishop asked.

'A decent set of wheels.'

'So they're not only interested in cut-and-shuts?'

'Not these days. They now have a market for top of the line motors, either in one piece or broken up for spare parts.'

'You better not be setting us up for a fall, Mr Fox.'

The big man looked genuinely bewildered this time. 'I don't know what you mean. Honest I don't.'

'Some people work to a local list and send their crews out to steal or jack to order. If they see a motor that's not on their sheet outside the gate, they'll press the panic button rather than the one that opens wide.'

Fox shook his head. 'No, that's not their way. Not that I'm aware of. Kids in the city know if they grab up something tasty, they can get a good price from Baqri. They show up, he gives the vehicle the once-over on the CCTV and if he likes what he sees, they're in. You go with the right set of wheels, you'll get past the gates. What you do then is up to you.'

In Bishop's estimation, Fox was telling them the truth. Whether it was the threat to his own business or the thought of sweeping up some of whatever Baqri would lose if he was arrested was impossible to tell, but Bishop did not care one way or the other. They had their location – and if that Range Rover was still being worked on, then they also had the Baqris. All they had to do was present the brothers with an offer they could not refuse, and he had exactly the right vehicle in mind.

The drugs unit within CID had been bragging about a burnt orange Nissan GTR with all the optional extras, snatched off a dealer working out of Bourne in Lincolnshire. They were itching to use it themselves in order to pose as potential clients, but Bishop knew that if he put the right word in the boss's ear, he would see to it that the keys were handed over to the Major Crimes team. Personally, he thought he'd look like a complete dick behind the wheel of a garish sports car, and it would be a bloody tight fit – but DC Ansari was capable of pulling it off, with him beside her as her muscle.

ELEVEN

Bliss emerged from his office having taken a call from Sandra Bannister, a reporter for the *Peterborough Telegraph*. After dashing up a flight of stairs and finding DCI Edwards away from her desk, he continued on along the corridor and talked his way in to speak with Detective Superintendent Fletcher. Aware of the arrangement Bliss had with Bannister in respect of information exchange, she noted his urgency and was keen to learn what all the fuss was about.

Bliss, whose thoughts were in turmoil, subconsciously rubbed at the small scar on his forehead as he pulled out a chair and sat down on the edge of its cushioned seat.

'During our conversation, ma'am,' he said, breathless, 'Bannister asked me if I knew the name Lisa Pepperdine. I didn't, but evidently Pepperdine was a freelance journalist who usually sold her stories to one of the Sunday tabloids. She came up to the city during the Burnout operation in early 2005. According to the journos who worked at the *Telegraph*, this freelancer tried to obtain local information from them, and then without a word just stopped calling or turning up at the offices. This was around the same time as the case folded, so they all assumed she'd gone back down to London; that, or she'd moved on to a different story in another part of the country. Likewise, Pepperdine's friends and family thought she was busy working on her own investigation.'

'I think I can see where this is headed,' Fletcher said, the look on her face now one of grave concern.

'As did I when Bannister told me. As it transpired, the woman was neither seen nor heard from again. Anyhow, Bannister tells me that after she was finally reported missing, nobody knew what to do about it. There was no evidence to suggest either way whether she had returned to London or remained up here in Peterborough. Investigations were launched by both the Met and us, but they were low-key, and you know how missing persons cases are treated when they're adults: with no suspicious circumstances, the book gets closed. She was medium risk at best, more likely placed in the lowest category. Although by that stage I was no longer on duty, I was still here in the city and I don't recall hearing about it at all.'

Fletcher pursed her lips for a moment before speaking. Bliss had always thought she looked like a bird when she did that. 'I remember a study coming out that year,' she said softly. 'The UK Missing Person Behaviour Study. Their analysis put the two highest group categories as either despondent or vulnerable. What surprised me was learning that three-quarters of missing people ended up no more than five miles from where they were last seen.'

'How many of those were dead when they were eventually located?'

'Less than a quarter. And before you ask, I have no idea if murders were recorded separately. Precisely a quarter of the men who were reported missing for the benefit of the study became fatalities, women coming in at a surprisingly high eighteen percent.'

'How do you know all this?' Bliss asked, dazed by the figures.

'I read, Inspector. Things pertinent to my job. Anyhow, from what you're saying, I'm guessing Sandra Bannister is wondering if these Cat's Water remains are those of Lisa Pepperdine.'

'Not just wondering, ma'am. Along with the remains, the dig team discovered a watch, a ring, and a necklace. We're waiting for the remains to be released so that Nancy Drinkwater can get them on the table over at the mortuary, at which time the jewellery will be freed up, bagged and tagged. As described to Bannister by her inside contact, all three items are recognised as belonging to Lisa Pepperdine – although we've yet to confirm it, of course.'

'Somebody at the newspaper must have an outstanding memory for detail.'

Bliss nodded. 'That was my initial thinking, too. But apparently, the jewellery was remarked upon by a fellow journalist because they were expensive items. The watch is a Rolex; eighteen-carat gold Datejust. The ring's a diamond cluster over platinum – the diamonds were not tiny, and they were most definitely genuine. As for the necklace, that was also platinum with a heart-shaped pendant. From Cartier, no less.'

'So if she was still wearing her jewellery when she was buried, we can rule out robbery as a motive.'

'Actually, that may not be the case.' Bliss wrinkled his nose. 'Pepperdine enjoyed wearing them in the right context, but was known to remove it all and tuck it away somewhere when meeting with individuals she didn't know or when travelling into unfamiliar neighbourhoods. All of which she freely admitted to the newspaper staff.'

Fletcher paused to consider the information he had provided. 'All right. So the jewellery items point to these fresh remains being the freelancer, and we'll be able to confirm that to a certain extent once they're examined properly. I'm still not seeing why you're in such a flap.'

Bliss nodded. 'I'm getting to that now, ma'am. When I asked Bannister if she had anything noteworthy, especially in respect of Pepperdine's visit to the city, she told me the most jarring thing worth mentioning was that Pepperdine had let a *Telegraph* reporter know about a meeting she had wangled for herself with someone she referred to as an officer high up on the Burnout investigation. And that was the last time any of them spoke to her or saw her.'

'Ah,' Fletcher said, exhaling slowly. 'Now I'm seeing your concern.'

'Justifiable concern, ma'am. Because aside from me, Superintendent Sykes and Chief Superintendent Flynn were the only two people I can think of who'd be described the way Pepperdine did at the time.'

'I see the way your mind is working, Bliss. Mine is asking similar questions, I'm sure. All the same, it's a bit of a long shot, don't you think?'

'Admittedly. I confess, any intrigue I have is mixed with anxiety. That bloody case was the beginning of the end for me here in many ways. Rightly or wrongly, it earned me an awful reputation.'

Fletcher said nothing for a few seconds, and Bliss saw she was turning something over in her mind. When she did speak again, her voice was calm and assured. 'I take it that whatever you decide to do with this information – however far you take your enquiries – you intend doing so completely off the books for the time being?'

'That is my preference, ma'am. It may be something, but it's probably nothing. With your permission, I'd like to speak off the record with both Flynn and Sykes. That was a spectacularly appalling year for so many people, and the one thing I don't intend to do is rock the boat all over again if I can possibly help it. So yes, entirely off the books, and deliberately so.'

Moistening her lips with the tip of her tongue, Fletcher leaned forward. 'Inspector, from what you've said so far you're probably right to suggest there is no cause to create a formal investigation at this stage. Certainly not one which includes the senior officers stationed here at the time. Clearly you are taking this matter seriously, and on that basis I'm granting you permission to approach your ex-colleagues prior to full identification of the remains. I'll have their contact details sent through to you. The moment you have any information, you report back to me. Is that clear?'

'Yes, ma'am.'

'As for Ms Bannister, what are her intentions?'

'She'd been preparing a column, but she's nowhere close to releasing it yet. She wants to wait for verification before splashing a fellow journalist's name all over the place.'

Fletcher drummed her fingers on the desk and shook her head slowly. 'What is it about this city? It just doesn't seem to be able to shrug off its past.'

'I think you'll find most early townships are the same, ma'am.'

'I wasn't talking about ancient history, Bliss. I was referring to that sodding year. I sometimes wonder if policing in Peterborough will ever fully recover from the events of 2005. I wasn't even stationed here at the time, but the stink seems to attach itself to everybody who crosses the threshold of this bloody building.'

He raised a crooked grin. 'I realise that, ma'am. I was deflecting. As someone who worked the two cases in question, I can safely say we've come a long way to restoring our reputation. I've only been a part of it again for a year, and while all the foundations for recovery were laid long before I returned to the city, I can still feel it.'

'And what if this new case unravels all the good we've done? What if it uncovers yet more corruption… or even worse?'

'First of all, ma'am, how likely do you think that is? I know I wasn't involved in anything unsavoury, and even if Lisa Pepperdine did meet either Superintendent Sykes or Chief Superintendent Flynn, you've seen their records, you know what kind of men they were. Joe Flynn was as decent a person as I've ever worked with in this job, and although I despised Stuart with a passion, the one thing you could always rely on him for was ruling by the book.

You never knew them – and given what we uncovered later that year, you have every right to query those who were running the station at the time. Perhaps you'll even wonder about me, since I was working the Burnout case while Pepperdine was supposedly snooping around. I'm hoping you'll regard the notion as ridiculous, as I do when it comes to Sykes and Flynn.'

'Of course. It goes without saying,' she said. 'So, speak to them, and keep it off the record until doing so starts to impinge on the new case. Brief me only.'

'Am I allowed to bring DS Chandler in on it? She was involved with that case, too. She knew both men as well as I did. Her insight will be invaluable.'

Fletcher smiled at him, and a genuine warmth lit up her eyes. 'Are you ever going to make an honest woman out of her, Jimmy?' It was a casual, throwaway remark, but it took Bliss by surprise. The Superintendent was not the kind of boss who got too closely involved with the lives of her charges. He responded with candour.

'Pen is my work wife. A friend and colleague, ma'am. Nothing more, nothing less.'

Her smile asked a question before she did. 'Does DS Chandler know that?'

'She does.' Bliss was adamant. 'And, to be frank with you, ma'am, we wouldn't have it any other way.'

'If you say so.' Fletcher's gaze gently mocked him. In a second it was gone and she was all business once more. 'Inspector, I share your concern and your anxiety in respect of this supposed meeting Lisa Pepperdine had arranged with one of our officers. It's a tricky situation, for sure. Tread carefully. I'm not entirely confident that either of us will survive any further surprises.'

TWELVE

It had been an extraordinarily long day. It never failed to astonish Bliss how much work people got through when they existed on adrenaline rushes supplemented by hot drinks, and had no real life outside the job. So far he had lurched from one issue to another in rapid succession, when all he'd been expecting was a session with his shrink and a day in court waiting for the CPS to get their house in order.

When he and Fletcher were finished, Bliss briefly considered going home. The thought lasted only a second or two, because he soon realised he had other business to attend to. He contacted the CPS in Chelmsford, only to learn that the person assigned to his case was in a meeting. He declined to leave a message, instead rattling off a quick e-mail requesting an immediate update regarding the court proceedings. Evidentiary appearances were the worst part of the job as far as Bliss was concerned. Too much time spent hanging around when he could be working. The courts did not react to lateness or absence favourably; when he was due to be in the chair, they demanded his attendance from the first until the last minute of the working day if necessary. It was not unknown for a witness to kick their heels all day without being called to the stand, and police officers were not exempt from this farcical way of dispensing justice.

Next up on his to-do list was Chandler, whom he updated on the conversation with Fletcher. She thought it was an interesting diversion and admitted that she had only a vague recollection of Lisa Pepperdine's disappearance.

'It's stretching coincidence a bit too far, isn't it, her vanishing in the middle of her investigation into Burnout?' she said. They stood in the corridor outside the Major Crimes area. It was a good place for private conversations, as you could see people coming either way along the passage and through the glass section of the door that led into the squad room, so there was no chance of being overheard.

Bliss agreed. The thought had nagged away at him since he'd started looking into it. 'I ran an eye over the records before coming to find you, and from what I can see the trail went cold very quickly. Pepperdine stayed at a B&B on a day-to-day basis, for eight nights in all. When the proprietors cleaned her room on the ninth day, they saw it was empty of any belongings and assumed she had either gone back home or moved on elsewhere. They went about their business and thought nothing more of it until we spoke to them about her.'

'How about her financials?'

'That was when everybody started taking it more seriously. Early thoughts were that she must have found another story, but when they checked, they found no charges on her credit cards, no cash taken from her bank.'

'How did she travel up here?' Chandler asked.

'In her own car. And it's never been seen since. Not taxed, not insured, no MOT, no tickets, nothing. It's as if it vanished along with her.'

Bliss told Chandler he'd requested contact details for their old bosses, explaining that Lisa Pepperdine had spoken about having a meeting with someone high up in the investigation. If she had somehow found a way in through a back door, one of them was bound to remember.

Chandler seemed to see the sense in that. 'Have you spoken to either of them yet?' she asked.

'No. I've only tried Joe Flynn so far. I got no answer so I left him a voicemail.'

'You want me to call Sykes for you?' she offered. 'I know how much you two hated each other.'

He was grateful, but decided to take the task on himself. 'No. If it was him who Pepperdine called then I'm going to have to deal with the man at some point. Best get it over with sooner rather than later.'

'If he's even still around. He's probably poisoned himself from the inside out by now.'

He laughed, but Chandler was not far wrong. Stuart Sykes had held the post of Detective Superintendent when Bliss first came to the city, and the two of them had mixed like oil and water right from the off. Bliss regarded the man as petty and vindictive, a piss-poor copper and an even worse leader. In those days, Bliss was incapable of keeping his thoughts to himself, so the pair clashed on a regular basis; at times their disagreements were heated, and on several occasions Sykes had attempted to push Bliss out of the job.

It was the Chief Super at the time, Joseph Flynn, whose strength and support had kept Bliss in the squad. He'd fought off Sykes's demands, and every time he was held to account he pulled through in Bliss's favour. It still stuck in Bliss's craw that Flynn had ultimately lost his job because of the corruption the investigation uncovered, and the two had parted as professional friends when they each left Peterborough on the same day.

Returning to his desk, Bliss pulled up the mail Fletcher had forwarded to him. His call to Flynn's mobile was met with the voicemail service once more, but when he dialled Sykes's number – a local landline – a woman answered.

'Good afternoon,' he said. 'I'm looking to speak with Stuart Sykes.'

'Who's speaking, please?'

For reasons Bliss could not immediately fathom, he was reluctant to provide his name. 'I'm an ex-colleague of his. We worked together in Peterborough.'

Mentioning the location had a strange feel about it. Sykes had been shipped sideways as a result of the autumn 2005 investigation, putting an end to a personal career ladder which the man believed still offered several more rungs to climb. Sykes's bitterness towards Bliss had spilled over in a vicious torrent of abuse and recrimination during a speech delivered at his final briefing. Still awaiting his own punishment, Bliss had sat through it wishing the ground would open up to swallow them all whole.

'I notice you avoided saying you and he were friends,' the woman said. 'I can't say I'm surprised. My father had few of them, and those he did have know where to find him these days. So what's your interest, Mr...?'

'It's Bliss. DI Jimmy Bliss.' He didn't know if the name would mean anything to her, but the pause that followed told him it did.

'So, definitely not a friend, then. May I ask why you're calling?'

Bliss wondered what she knew about him and his relationship with Sykes. Or what she thought she knew. 'If you don't mind, it's something I need to speak to him about.'

'I don't mind, but you won't reach him here anymore. My father's in Thorpe Hall. Do you know it?'

Bliss took a sharp intake of breath. He knew the place well: Thorpe Hall was a hospice, providing palliative care for people with life-limiting conditions. In spite of his antipathy towards the man, a wave of sympathy for Sykes's family coursed through him.

'I'm very sorry to hear that,' he said. 'Do you mind my asking what the… what condition has him staying there?'

'Sadly, we're talking conditions. Plural. Dad has both cancer and Alzheimer's, and he's in the late stages of both.'

'That must be very hard on you.'

'It's worse for my mother. She hates it that he requires more care than she can provide.'

Bliss paused for a moment, not quite knowing what to say. He was about to pull back from the call, but something he wasn't quite able to define made him pursue it. 'You knew my name when I mentioned it,' he said.

'Hard to forget. Not exactly a common one.'

'I doubt it was just the name, either. Your father was not my number one fan.'

'Nor you his, from what I understand. Which brings me back to the reason for your call…'

'I'm not sure it matters now. Certainly it's unimportant, given the circumstances.'

'You've taken the time to call, Inspector Bliss. Please finish what you had to say.'

Bliss gave a wry smile. He liked her style, and she appeared entirely untroubled by his intrusion. 'In that case, I will,' he said, deciding to opt for the basics only. 'I'm looking back at an old case – a missing person. There are two reasons why I thought of contacting Stuart. First of all, the missing woman was a journalist looking into a case we were working, who told colleagues she was meeting with a senior member of the investigation team, so I wondered if your father might have been the one who met with her and whether he remembered anything about it. Secondly, even if he hadn't or couldn't remember, if this lead takes us where I suspect it will, then it's likely that a more official approach will eventually be made. I wanted to prepare him for that.'

'You were concerned for him?' She sounded doubtful.

'I was. Surprised myself, actually. It's true to say we were far from close, but that was all a long time ago now and I didn't want to see him come under any undue pressure. Especially over something that happened so long ago.'

This time it was Sykes's daughter who sounded as if she did not know what to say.

While he waited for a response, Bliss considered his mixed emotions. Sykes had made his life a misery virtually from the very start of his posting. Word had it that he felt threatened by having someone from the Met on his team – especially one who arrived with a glowing reputation for his ability to solve cases. But Jimmy had also been under a cloud of rumour and speculation concerning his wife's murder and the way he had dealt with it. The torrid time he endured under the man's leadership, and his reacting to that torment the only way he knew how, had soured Bliss's mind and left the two constantly at each other's throat. Yet he would not wish either cancer or Alzheimer's on anybody, and the news left him feeling confused and more tentative than usual.

The phone crackled and Sykes's daughter came back on the line.

'Inspector, I've decided to allow you to take your chances. My father has good days, but far more bad ones. He may be in too much pain to talk; there's also every possibility of him having been sedated, or there's a good chance he'll be unresponsive and not even know where he is, let alone remember something that happened more than a decade ago.'

'That's very kind of you. May I have your name, please?' he asked, buying himself a few more seconds.

'Of course. It's Briony.'

'And this is a Stamford number, Briony?'

'It is, yes.'

'Okay. The thing is, I'm currently fitting this in around several ongoing investigations, so what I'll do is give you a bell a bit later and we'll try to arrange the most convenient time for you and your father, if that's all right by you.'

They spoke for a few minutes longer. Bliss reassured her that he would take it easy on Stuart with the questioning, and that he understood she could not guarantee a fruitful outcome. As soon as he ended the call, he redialled the number he had for Joe Flynn; it went straight to voicemail for a third time. Bliss left another message, asking his old Chief Superintendent to call him back as soon as possible, and this time telling him that it related to the Burnout operation.

When he stepped out into the Major Crimes squad room, he found DCI Warburton chatting with Chandler and Bishop. On opposite sides of their own desk, DCs Hunt and Ansari were both on the phone, and DC Gratton was feeding paper into the multi-function photocopier. The team still had two other investigations running, and they were clearly busy trying to mould at least one of them into a viable operation with some worthwhile leads to follow.

Warburton looked up and caught his eye. 'I thought I'd hang around to see if you emerged,' she said. 'Do you have time for a quick chat?'

Bliss shook his head. 'Sorry, Di… Boss. Something's cropped up.'

'Your sergeants were just apprising me of your current workload. Anything I need to be aware of?'

'This is something new. Just developing. Better if I brief you once you're behind your desk, I think.'

He chose not to elaborate. There was no way of knowing whether the missing freelancer would turn out to be connected to the Burnout operation and the remains found in Fengate, or would be just one of the many whose disappearances went unexplained. But at the back of his mind, something insisted Pepperdine had not vanished from the face of the earth willingly. He did not want to get into a discussion with his new line manager until he had further details to relate.

Bliss saw the surprise in Warburton's reaction, but he gave her full points for merely accepting what he said and not pursuing the matter. He was not at all certain that DCI Edwards would have given him the same leeway. Chandler had overheard the conversation; when she raised her eyebrows at him, he indicated that he needed five minutes, then set off for his office.

Behind his desk, entering the address for Stuart Sykes into his phone, Bliss looked up in response to a sharp rap on the doorframe. It was DCI Warburton, who peered down at his laborious single-finger method of key entry.

'I'm the same,' she confessed. 'I'm always amazed when I see my kids tapping away furiously at their phones with both thumbs.'

'It's the next stage of evolution. Hunched over and with an extra opposable digit on each hand.' He paused then and frowned. 'Kids, did you say?'

Warburton nodded. 'I still think of them that way, even though they're both in their twenties now.'

'I had no idea,' Bliss said. 'I mean, when we worked together before, I clocked the rings, so I assumed you were married, but I'm sure I would've remembered if you'd mentioned having children.'

'It was a bit of a grim and gruesome few days, Jimmy. Not much time for chit-chat or happy snaps, as I recall.'

'I suppose not.'

'Plus, you never asked.'

Bliss gave a rueful grin. 'I suppose not.'

Warburton looked beyond him and smiled. 'What's that on the wall?'

He did not need to turn. 'That is my Bliss Pissed-ometer. During my first stint here somebody got it into their heads that pinning a cardboard arrow onto another piece of cardboard, and having a range of emotions written on it to act as a guide to my mood, was somehow amusing.'

The DCI chuckled. 'It sort of is. I notice they're all dark moods.'

'Indeed. Evidently I was regarded as a bit of a grump back in those days.'

'Really? I'm astonished.'

Bliss smiled and nodded. 'Yeah, I know. Hard to imagine, right?'

As he pushed himself up from the desk, Warburton said, 'Jimmy, I do hope you won't find it too awkward having me as your DCI. We worked together well before when you took the lead, and I'm hoping we will do so again now that things have swung the other way.'

He walked around the desk, heading for the door. 'Different set of circumstances entirely,' he said. 'You had the rank, but I was in charge. It was awkward at times. But it's not going to be a problem – not for me, at least. I just need to know one thing.'

Warburton straightened. 'Shoot.'

'Do you prefer being called "Oh, Captain, my Captain," ma'am, or boss?'

Her eyebrows arched. 'A Walt Whitman quote. I'm impressed.'

'I'm even more so. Most people would have said it was a line from the film.'

'What film?'

'*Dead Poets Society*.'

She shook her head. 'Never heard of it.'

Bliss uttered a low whistle. 'Now I'm actually awestruck.'

'And gullible, it seems. Of course I've seen it. How else would I know whose quote it was?'

Bliss laughed. It was going to be all right between them. Before she could respond to his actual question, his phone rang. He held up a finger and answered; it was Briony Sykes. Following a rapid exchange, he ended the call and grimaced.

'Problem?' Warburton asked.

'Could be,' he said. 'Somebody I needed a word with has just taken a turn for the worse. I need to get cracking.'

'Then don't let me stop you. See you Monday morning.'

Bliss snatched up his jacket and gave Chandler a shout as he marched through Major Crimes, telling her he was off out on his own. According to Sykes's daughter, his one-time nemesis had reacted negatively to a new medication and his family had been warned to expect the worst. In Bliss's view, his ex-boss was enduring the worst now, and the end would be a merciful release.

THIRTEEN

The lines on Stuart Sykes's forehead and around his eye sockets were so deep they looked like bloodless lacerations. White stubble covered both cheeks, which were pinched and sunken; the look of a man whose teeth no longer resided in his mouth. Frail wisps of hair trailed across the dying man's scalp and meshed against the pillow beneath his head. Moist, jaundice-ridden eyes stared vacantly at the ceiling.

Bliss wondered what manner of drug-induced nightmare his old boss was seeing up there on the mottled tiles, as the man let out a pitiful moan and fear slithered across his ravaged, gaunt face like a storm cloud passing over its own reflection on a lake.

'He's going to be all right,' Briony whispered. Having exchanged an awkward greeting as Bliss entered the room, the pair now stood at the foot of the bed, looking down at the withering form barely rumpling the sheets upon which he lay. 'His liver is failing, and he sometimes hallucinates due to dehydration, but they've upped his drip and changed his meds so he's coming back to us.'

Fuck that, Bliss thought. He's not going to be all right at all, not in any meaningful sense. He'll never be all right again. The man was suffering; if he had been an animal, the staff would have had some compassion and put him out of his misery by now.

He understood the decision was not theirs to make, and bore them no ill-will – and in fact he found the hospice facility impressive. The majesty and feel of the original Thorpe Hall building, now more than three hundred and sixty years old, had been carefully preserved during a costly update and expansion that had taken place over a number of years. The Sue Ryder charity had pushed hard for the sympathetic redevelopment of what had been a tired, unwelcoming pile, but at the back of Bliss's mind he nonetheless regarded it as a waiting room for death.

'Dad,' Briony said, taking a seat to her father's left and reaching for his hands. At her touch, Sykes let out a stifled cry of alarm. He had not seen it coming, and the feel of her skin upon his must have hit him like a terrified scream in the still of night. His daughter persisted, and he settled. She looked up at Bliss and gave a weak smile. 'He doesn't like that initial contact. It frightens him. But I just hold on and rub the back of each hand with my thumb and it seems to soothe him.'

Bliss nodded. He understood. His own uncle had spent his final few months in a home, dementia stripping him of his very essence and dignity before eventually allowing him to slip away once every visitor's memory of the man had been tainted and scarred by what he had become.

'Dad, you have a visitor. An old colleague of yours.' Briony spoke softly, smiling at her father, seemingly unaffected by his suffering.

'Hello, sir,' Bliss said, hoping to catch the man's attention. 'It's good to see you again. I'm very happy to hear that you're recovering from your turn for the worse earlier.'

Before he'd entered the room, two members of staff had prepared Bliss, offering advice as to what to say and how to say it. He recollected what he had been told prior to visiting his uncle, but he nodded anyway as they warned him not to take offence if Sykes made the odd outlandish statement or swore at him.

At this, Bliss had come close to laughing out loud. *If only they knew.*

'I think I get it,' he told them. 'I play along with any comfortable delusions he has, especially the kind of thing that makes him feel safe or happy. I'm only to disagree if he becomes distressed, and to keep my voice even but firm during those moments. I should use his name often, nod and smile, stick to one topic at a time.'

Sykes was not currently lucid, however, and remained unresponsive. Bliss glanced at Briony, who nodded encouragingly for him to continue.

'Stuart, I just popped by to have a chat about the old days with you. Actually, I wanted to pick your brain. You always had a much better memory for people and incidents and detail than I did, so I thought you were the ideal man to help me out.'

Something lit up in the man's expression, as if a switch had been flicked on in his brain. His eyes lowered slowly and came to rest upon Bliss. 'We worked together,' he said. His voice was cracked and weak, but he was firm in his belief. 'You and me.'

Bliss smiled and nodded. 'We did, Stuart. My name is… Jimmy. It's been many years since you and I worked together, but I remember it well.'

'Yes, yes… a long time, Jimmy. You look good. Holding up well to the passing of days. Unlike me. I don't think I'll beat it this time, old man. Shan't be going home again, I don't suppose.'

Briony's grip on her father's hand tightened. Bliss closed his eyes for a moment, wishing he hadn't come. He felt like a voyeur at a stranger's long last goodbye.

'Go on,' she whispered. 'He's with us right now. He may not be for long.'

'Stuart, I'm here to ask you about a case we worked together. We didn't have operation names back then – we just called it Burnout. Do you remember it at all?'

Sykes frowned, adding greater depth to the ridges corrugating his brow. Then he nodded a couple of times. 'Terrible thing,' he said, no more than a harsh, dry croak, so low that Bliss had to move closer and lean in as Sykes repeated the same two words. The man's breath was sour and came out in ragged, uneven gasps.

'I agree, Stuart. Burnout was an awful, tragic case. Do you recall talking to a reporter? Not a local one, but a freelancer called Lisa Pepperdine? It's an unusual name, so perhaps it stuck in your mind.'

The old man was silent for a moment, still frowning, his eyes perhaps searching the past as they flicked from side to side.

'Was that too much?' Bliss asked Sykes's daughter in a hushed voice. 'Have I confused him?'

'I'm not sure. Try getting him on track again by focussing on just the name.'

Bliss nodded. He thought about the information he was seeking here, unsure how to proceed, wondering if he ought to continue at all.

'Should I carry on?' he asked. 'Now that I'm here, I don't know how much help your father can actually be.'

'I can't answer that for you.'

The room was silent for several seconds. Then, out of nowhere, Sykes blurted a name. 'Bliss!' he cried, his face creasing and eyes narrowing. 'That bloody dreadful man.'

'Try not thinking about him, Stuart,' Bliss said, knowing he had to steer the conversation away from any recollections Sykes had of their many disagreements. 'It's someone else I'm here to talk to you about. Somebody who may have been connected to the Burnout case. A woman called Pepperdine. Lisa Pepperdine. I'm sure you'd remember an odd name like that, Stuart.'

This time, Sykes shook his head vigorously. 'No, no, no! That damned man Bliss turned my head. Got me so angry. Bloody man would never do as instructed. Fuck him! Fuck him!'

'Hey, Dad,' Briony interjected, taking his hand between both of hers and clasping it tighter. 'You'll upset the other residents if you swear like that.' She smiled fondly at him. 'You know what a bunch of old fuddy-duddies they are here, and if you shout they'll hear you all the way out in the courtyard.'

'They have no bloody idea what we had to face every bloody day.'

'No, you're right, Dad. They don't. But it's not their fault. You had a difficult job to do. As did Jimmy here. You both went through difficult times.'

Unabashed by either her father's outburst or his obvious antagonism towards the man who sought his help, she gave Bliss the nod to carry on.

'This reporter, Pepperdine, said she was due to meet with a senior officer working the Burnout case,' he said, mentally scrambling around for the right path to tread. He was aware of the likelihood of families and staff wandering the corridor outside the room. 'I was wondering whether that officer was you, Stuart.'

'Oh, he didn't get away with it.' For the first time, a smile stretched the man's thin, dry, flaking lips. Bliss recalled how they had once reminded him of pink worms; now they looked to have acquired scales. 'The boy's father saw to that.'

Surprised at how Sykes appeared to recall that aspect of the case, Bliss now sought to use the momentum. 'He did indeed, Stuart. But that's not why I'm here today. I wanted to ask you about Lisa Pepperdine. The reporter. Does that name sound at all familiar to you?'

Bliss knew he was reaching. All he needed was for one thing to spark inside Sykes's mind. A light remained in those disturbingly watery eyes. His old boss was going through the motions of thinking about the question. Bliss looked at Briony and shrugged. She smiled back and hitched her own shoulders. Her guess was as good as his.

Sykes spoke again. 'If you see that bastard… please tell him I'm sorry.' His gaze was on the ceiling once more, but he still sounded lucid.

'See who, Stuart?' Bliss asked. 'You're sorry about what?'

He mentally cursed himself. Two questions. Not the right thing to do at all.

To his horror, he saw tears leaking from the man's eyes. Sykes blinked them back and started shaking his head slowly. 'I fucking hated him. Fucking Bliss. He ignored every bloody rule. He was so… so fucking insolent. Gave me no respect. None whatsoever. But you know what hurt most of all?'

'No, I don't, Stuart.' Bliss spoke gently. 'Tell me. Please.'

'The bloody man was always right. He wasn't my sort of policeman. Not by a long chalk. No discipline. No order. But he had his support from the top because he got results. Just didn't care about how he achieved them.'

'And the Burnout case,' Bliss prompted, trying to steer the awkward conversation away from himself. 'The reporter who wanted to meet with you.'

More tears squeezed out. 'I should have told him how sorry I was before he died.'

'Before who died, Stuart?'

'Bliss, of course. Aren't you listening to me, man?'

'Yes, yes. I'm sorry. I didn't realise he was dead.'

'Oh, yes. Brave young man, I'll give him that. Trained hard for six months, stepped out onto Gold Beach at Normandy and took a hit straight away. Died before his feet even made French soil.'

Bliss was deflated. These ramblings were not what he had come here for.

'What did you need to apologise for, Dad?' Briony said.

Sykes's head jerked around, his eyes widening and his mouth falling open. He stared at his own daughter without recognition for fully ten seconds before seeming to come back to the present. He nodded. Swallowed. Nodded again. Briony offered up his beaker of water, and he sipped twice through the straw.

'I let him take the blame,' he gasped. 'The one time I bent the rules. Bliss got blamed for it and I let it happen.'

'The blame for what, Dad?'

'Ball. Jason Ball. It was me who told Anthony Cox where to find him. Told him to hurry because we were about to arrest Ball.'

Bliss was barely able to breathe. Blood rocketed through his veins. This was surely pure fantasy; Stuart Sykes was a copper who lived by the book. It was his bible. Pretty much every disagreement he and Sykes had ever had revolved around the rules and Bliss's disinclination to follow them. He could not find it in himself to believe this fresh announcement was anything other than another mental lapse.

'I… I never imagined Cox would do anything more than beat the man. I would never have told him had I so much as suspected he would kill him.'

Licking his lips, Bliss took a step closer. 'Stuart. Are you sure about this? Only, it doesn't sound at all like something you would do.'

'And it wasn't.' Sykes turned his focus back to Bliss. 'I don't know what came over me that day. I knew it was wrong. Of course I did. But what Jason Ball did – not only to little Nicky Cox, but to all those immigrant families he murdered in their homes – I just couldn't let it go. Couldn't risk the possibility that he would walk free. The evidence we had against him was so flimsy…'

That was true. Bliss and the team had known how weak their case against Jason Ball was, but had feared the man would skip the country if they did not arrest him beforehand. All manner of emotions ripped through him. As difficult as it was to believe, what Sykes was saying sounded like an honest confession.

'But then I… I went on to do so much worse,' Sykes continued, sobbing in between gasps of pain. 'The inquiry turned its sights on Bliss. I wanted him gone, out of my station. This was… the ideal way. Good riddance to bad rubbish. But when it happened and he was suspended, I should have… I wanted to… but I was a coward. Never said a word. Bliss was right to hate me. By the end, I came to hate myself.'

Briony shot to her feet, her legs shoving back the hospital chair with a clatter. 'I think you should leave now, Inspector,' she said, her face a mask of anguish. 'My father is getting very tired.'

An ache ripped through Bliss's stomach, rising slowly into his chest where it remained to swell against his ribcage. He had always wondered who had tipped off Anthony Cox that day. In all these years, however, the name of Stuart Sykes would have been the very last on any list he compiled. He resented the man for having allowed him to take the blame, yet respected him for tipping off Cox in the first place. It was a curious combination of emotions.

He nodded. 'I understand. Thank you for letting me do this,' he said.

'You're welcome. I'm sure you realise that my father's mind wanders all over the place. Nothing he said here today can possibly be relied upon.'

Her eyes implored him to go along with the lie, if only to save her the humiliation of having to admit to what her father had done all those years ago. Bliss didn't even have to think about his response.

'Of course. All part of the same landscape as the Normandy landings, I expect. And Briony… you may not believe this, knowing what you do about me, but I am sorry to see your father like this. Truly I am.'

She nodded once and choked back some tears of her own.

'I'll leave you both now. By the way, where's your mother?'

Briony cleared her throat. 'She came with me. But we saw that Dad had settled again, and the nurse told us his condition had improved. My mother then decided she didn't want to be here when you arrived.'

Bliss smiled his understanding. 'Probably for the best,' he said. 'And if you're willing to take some advice from me, I'd suggest you say nothing to her about what was said here this afternoon.'

'I think you're right about that. No good would come of it.'

Turning to leave, Bliss caught himself. He looked back down at the frail, wizened man lying in the bed, ravaged by illness and no longer the presence he had once been. 'I'm away now, Stuart,' he said. 'It was very nice to see you again. Thanks for the chat. You take care of yourself.'

There was no reply – just a vacant return gaze.

He started walking towards the door. As his hand reached for the handle, Sykes said, 'Bliss.'

When he turned again, his old boss had raised his head from the pillow. The tendons stood out like cords of thin rope in his shrivelled neck.

'I'm sorry, Bliss. I hope you can forgive me someday.'

A moment passed while Bliss gathered himself. There was no doubt in his mind that the man staring back at him now did so in full recognition. He touched a hand to the scar on his forehead before nodding and saying, 'Of course, Stuart. I already do. And for what it's worth – I'm sorry, too.'

FOURTEEN

After checking out the CCTV footage from the car park cameras, DCs Hunt and Gratton finally discovered a couple of single frames in which at least two potential suspects partially revealed their faces. Printing off a number of hard copies, they returned to the city centre with the intention of showing the images to shop owners and handing them out to keep as reminders. But barely ten minutes in, Gratton hit upon an idea, and after a brief discussion they decided to pursue it.

On the steps leading up to the old Town Hall, the two detectives gathered together with half a dozen police community support officers. The PCSOs had no powers of arrest, were unable to interview suspects or process prisoners, and were not allowed to carry out criminal investigations. But despite their limited responsibilities, they were a visible deterrent, could detain people while summoning assistance from police colleagues, and were often highly motivated and keen. Today Hunt and Gratton were calling upon their vigilance.

They passed around the photos of their two main suspects, hoping for some recognition of at least one of the men. To Hunt's complete amazement, all six PCSOs not only identified both men, but also named three others who were likely to have been part of their little crew.

'Oh, yes, we know that bunch of tossers all too well,' the most senior officer remarked. 'They prowl this area after dark as if they own the place. Wherever they go we always get reports of shoplifting, intimidation… they've been known to accost people who have just used an ATM, and they're not opposed to stealing cash from the homeless, either.'

That last statement caught Gratton's attention. It wasn't beyond the realms of possibility that the crew had previously elected to rob Ade Summerby and had been fought off by the ex-serviceman. It was easy enough to imagine them making a trip into town on Sunday night with one specific purpose: to seek revenge on the man and steal what they may by then have regarded as rightfully theirs.

'I don't suppose you've detained them at any point, have you?' he asked, eager now to pursue this and get a result for the murdered man.

'Several times. And each of the little bastards has been arrested and charged on at least one occasion, I can tell you that for certain.'

Back at Thorpe Wood, Hunt and Gratton ran the records, having taken names and approximate detainment dates from the PCSOs. It took less than thirty minutes to obtain five records, together with five current addresses. When they were done, the two colleagues looked at each other, grins splitting their faces.

Hunt set his chin and pumped a fist. 'Got the little fuckers.'

Gratton offered a high-five. He stared at the monitor which showed an array of faces, each with dull, flat eyes revealing a lack of humanity. 'You lot are toast,' he said, adding an edge to the final word.

'Let's take it to Bish,' Hunt suggested. 'We can scoop them up first thing in the morning, but the Sarge will want to be in on it, I'm sure.'

Gratton nodded with real enthusiasm. 'He's going to love us for this. Absolutely love us.'

**

Meanwhile, DS Bishop and DC Ansari were in conversation with DS Ferguson in CID, to whom they had been assigned for the joint operation. They'd had no need to add the weight of Bliss's name to the discussion; CID were only too happy to exploit the Nissan GTR if it took the Baqri brothers off the map.

'We're wrapping up Gul in a hoodie so they won't clock her being a woman,' Bishop told the DS. 'They'll regard me as the muscle. I think we can pass muster.'

'You sure you're not too much muscle for them?' Ferguson asked. 'I mean, you're a big bloke, Olly. I think they'd take one look at you and sense potential trouble.'

Bishop shook his head. 'They've been in the game long enough. They'll have dealt with bigger and uglier than me.'

'All the same, is it worth the risk?' Ferguson looked at his DC. 'One of us can pair up with your DC instead, and you join in with the raid once the Range Rover's presence has been confirmed.'

'No!' Bishop snapped, jerking his head up. 'DC Ansari never leaves my side. Understood?'

He regretted his tone the moment the words left his mouth, recognising its origin. At no time since the tragic shooting of his partner had anybody suggested Mia's death was his fault. Sound reasoning and logic had long since led him to the same conclusion. They both usually held the same rank, but on that occasion it had been Mia who was the acting Detective Inspector, and it had been her decision not to wait for the expected Armed Response Vehicle before entering the disused quarry in which an armed suspect was thought to be hiding.

Bishop's shame stemmed from his having allowed the gunman, Pavle Savic, to get the drop on them both outside his caravan on the first level of the quarry basin. Logic notwithstanding, Bishop also often asked himself what would have happened had he pushed Mia harder to wait on the perimeter for the ARV unit. On each occasion, he took responsibility for not speaking up, whilst at the same time recognising his respect for her authority in agreeing to her suggestion.

There were no good responses; none that salved the wounds grief had dealt him. His friend was dead, and no amount of self-doubt or remoulding of history would bring her back.

'Sorry,' he said, biting into his bottom lip. 'It's a decent suggestion, but Gul and I know each other's moves. That will give us the edge if it gets tense inside that garage.'

'But only if you're allowed entry,' Ferguson reminded him. He was clearly unwilling to let it go.

'I realise I'm only a lowly DC,' Ansari said, raising her hand like a child, 'but if my opinion is of interest to either of you, it's this: either I do this with DS Bishop or I don't do it at all. We have no clue what we'll find behind those shutter doors, and if I'm going to take risks then I'm going to take them with the man I put my trust in every working day.'

Bishop shot her an appreciative smile. He guessed she had phrased her objection in such a way as to send him an unspoken message: she did not blame him for Mia's death. She trusted him. She had faith in his ability to overcome any odds, however misplaced her convictions were.

'We're a team,' he confirmed, meeting Ferguson's sharp look. 'We came to you with this. Let us run with it.'

The CID detective huffed through his nose and shrugged. 'Your funeral,' he said. 'Just don't make it ours as well.'

Bishop had sprung to his feet before the DS finished speaking. With no conscious awareness, he found himself with both hands wrapped around Ferguson's throat. Only vaguely aware of other hands scrabbling at his arms and the cries – both deep and shrill – raging in his ears, Bishop's sole focus remained on his colleague's rapidly exsanguinating face and terrified eyes.

'I don't know if you chose those words on purpose,' Bishop hissed through his teeth, 'but if you ever speak them again, I won't give you the benefit of doubt a second time.'

He watched as the man's face first regained its colour and then darkened further, from bright red to a bluish purple hue. He knew he was responsible, and that Ferguson was incapable of making any form of coherent reply while the life was being choked out of him. But Bishop had lost the ability to either empathise or care. Finally, heedless of the hands beating at his arms and the hysterical clamour of voices raging inside his head, he eased off the pressure his fingers were exerting and released the sweating flesh beneath.

In the silence that followed, a piercing signal ignited inside Bishop's right ear. It echoed within his cranium and sent jagged shards of glass hurtling through his brain. The room around him shifted, and he caught himself as he swayed. His eyelids flickered and both eyes rolled in their sockets. Then the floor rose up to strike him in the face, and the world turned black.

FIFTEEN

THE MUSIC WAS MERELY background noise. Floyd's *The Wall*. First album. Side one. Shorter days meant fewer opportunities to sit in the garden basking in sunshine, allowing himself to escape the troubles of the day while still wrapped in its full glory. Even so, carefully placed lighting provided an enchanting and relaxing view beyond the sliding glass doors after nightfall while he listened to the soundtrack of his younger self.

Not so different from his older self, as it turned out.

The way of Zen had come to Bliss relatively late in life, as had his slow and methodical set of exercises. Though the two were mutually exclusive – the tai chi-like physical routine keeping him both loose and centred, while Zen relied more on silent contemplation – both were intended more to lower his blood pressure and damp down his anger triggers than achieve any genuine inner peace. At his core he remained a deeply troubled human being. Bliss knew that much about himself, and it was as close to enlightenment as he was ever likely to stray.

Early in the summer he had made some progress. Following her first visit to his house, Chandler had convinced him to unpack a few boxes which had been left untouched since he'd moved back to the city. She'd insisted on him peppering the walls with paintings and photographs, encouraging him to think of his dwelling more as a home than a way station. Once he finally submitted to the power of her will, the place had instantly become more cheerful, and the displayed photos themselves brought a kind of comfort he had not envisaged. Putting his past on display was not something he had chosen to do lightly, but ultimately he appreciated Chandler's nagging approach. Anything was better than her bending his ear all the time.

And then, just as Bliss had started to think more positively about the future, a contract killer walked into their lives and shredded them. A hired gun who, along with the targets he was paid to hit, murdered four police colleagues, including Mia Short. Losing her from the team for any reason would have been enough to throw a grenade into the Major Crimes family; losing her the way they did – to a shotgun at close range, in the frantic circumstances of that awful night – would haunt Bliss for the rest of his life. Beyond his survivor's guilt, he no longer burdened himself with the weight of her loss, and he bore no responsibility for her murder. That was the work of one man's greed and lack of humanity. Nonetheless, every day spent anywhere near the office served as a reminder that Mia was not absent with illness, not on holiday, but dead, and never coming back.

Bliss took every defeat, every turn in fortune, every close call that did not go the way of the investigation, personally. It was his nature. Little more than a year ago he had come close to losing Penny Chandler, and it had just about broken him. With Mia's loss, he felt like a reed blowing this way and that, caught in the vortex of a storm whose strength never dissipated. Clarity – the kind of precision he required in order to do his job properly – evaded him.

On the turntable, the needle had skipped along to the second track. Bliss was vaguely aware of Roger Waters singing about skating on thin ice. Intense lyrics for a sombre tune, but Bliss understood the author's frame of mind. It wasn't that he had no interest in being happy – more that every time he allowed himself to start enjoying life, cracks appeared at his feet, faces from the past swarmed around him, and when he took the inevitable plunge below the surface, hands pulled him deeper into the icy water while his own scrabbled for purchase and that one final gasping breath.

'You're depressed,' Jennifer Howey had insisted during their initial meeting. She had repeated it in their last, too.

On the first occasion, he'd shrugged. The next time, he shrugged again but said, 'Then you've not done a very good job, have you?'

'That's because you refuse to let me all the way in.'

'I don't have time for this. I don't have time to be depressed, either.'

'It's not a choice, Jimmy. And it's not a weakness.'

'Neither is it a strength. I'm with Gary Cooper on this one.'

'Gary Cooper?'

Bliss dismissed her lack of movie knowledge with a flap of the hand. 'Look,' he insisted. 'Depressed or not, I have a life to live and a job to do. I'm not about to top myself, so please just let me be.'

The memory brought back his conversation with Molly. If there was one thing he was certain of, it was that she was not quite ready to take that last step into nothingness. Otherwise, by the time he'd arrived on that rooftop he would already have been too late. But, if he was reading her right, Molly was closer to taking her own life than she had ever been. If circumstances did not soon turn in her favour, she would do it. Whether she stepped in front of a bus, took an overdose of an unfamiliar drug, or found herself another tall building to leap from, that was her destination, the final stop on her own personal ride to hell.

He was damned if he knew how or why the girl had found a way beneath his skin, but she was there now and Bliss knew better than any shrink just how much he was driven to protect. He didn't know what to think of Howey's saviour complex theory, but was inclined to believe it was mere psychobabble. Even so, something inside compelled him to take notice of this young girl. Molly was not his responsibility, nor his suspect or witness. But he thought of her lying in her overnight cell back at Thorpe Wood and accepted the reality that he would get little, if any, sleep in the coming hours.

After leaving the hospice, his old boss's words still rattling around inside his head, Bliss had driven back to Thorpe Wood, intending to update himself on the team's ongoing cases before heading home for a relatively early night. The moment he saw DCI Edwards prowling the corridor he knew something was amiss. Trapped inside her office for the next twenty minutes, he sat and listened as she told him about DS Bishop's outburst.

'I think we all understand what set him off,' Bliss said, defending his sergeant without equivocation. 'But none of us are Bish, and therefore none of us can know what kind of stress he's been working under since Mia's death.'

'Which is why I have calmed the waters,' Edwards said. 'While DS Bishop was being treated by the on-call FME, I obtained an account of what took place from DC Ansari, after which I spoke to DS Ferguson.'

Bliss's immediate concern was for Bishop's welfare. If the forensic medical examiner had been summoned, then Bish must have been in a dreadful state of mind. 'Have you spoken to the FME since?' he asked.

'Briefly. In layman's terms, DS Bishop saw red. Provoked by a thoughtless comment, whatever stress he had been keeping a lid on exploded out of him. From what I understand, at one point somebody pulled a baton with the intention of using it on him before he went too far. As if he hadn't gone far enough by that stage.'

'But understandably so, boss. The main thing, surely, is that he drew himself back from the brink.'

Edwards looked up sharply. 'No. The key issue here, Bliss, is that DS Bishop attacked a colleague and caused the man both pain and distress.'

'Ferguson's not pressing charges, is he? If so, let me have a word with him.'

'There's no need. He'd intended no offence. He merely used a common saying; it was thoughtless, not intentionally cruel, so he is the injured party here. However, he doesn't want to get a colleague into trouble over a flare-up, especially considering everything Bishop has been through. He's happy to let it go. As am I, provided of course that DS Bishop agrees to more counselling.'

Bliss exhaled a sigh of relief. He empathised with Bishop; had been there himself, swallowed up by that red mist enveloping the senses and incapacitating all reason. 'You're not putting him on leave, are you?' he asked. 'We've got too much on, boss. I need him out there.'

'I should tell him to go home and take a week at least. That would also allow things to settle, especially with CID still disgruntled about the reason behind their initial disagreement. However, I'm confident that provided you have a word with DS Bishop first thing tomorrow before he does anything else, we can all carry on as we were. But – and I cannot stress this enough, Inspector – you and your team must keep a close watch on your colleague. The moment any of you see him heading towards a similar breakdown, you step in. Understood?'

He had. In the circumstances, DCI Edwards had acted reasonably. The uncharitable notion that she did so because the unit would be DCI Warburton's problem from Monday flickered across Bliss's thought process. But he quashed it. Edwards was a changed woman in so many ways, and he accepted that she was doing the right thing.

After a brief chat with his team, he put a call into his uniformed colleague, Inspector Kaplan, hoping to find a curry partner for the evening, but Lennie had a prior engagement. Instead, Bliss had come home alone as usual, in the mood to ruminate and indulge himself with some music.

With The Eagles now playing in the background, Bliss went online. Usually he avoided running a Google search on victims, suspects or witnesses, as the internet had a habit of turning up at least as many incorrect hits as factual ones. In this case, though, it was worth a shot; Lisa Pepperdine was likely to feature on a number of sites whose sources were impeccable, and he was sure he'd also find one or two of her own contributions.

In the fifteen minutes he spent searching, he found very little. A brief biography attached to a website asking for information about her disappearance mentioned her growing reputation, but in what looked to be a relatively short career she had shifted across to the more sensational area of journalism rather quickly. The site contained a link to a *News of the World* article, but it was dead. He checked to see if the now defunct tabloid had maintained a web presence since 2011 when it closed its doors for the last time following the phone hacking scandal, but found only a single page saying goodbye to its readers. Bliss managed to find some references to a few older items, but they were also dead links.

The search did produce a number of articles in which the reporter's disappearance was mentioned. Some pointed the finger of blame at police inactivity and even outright lack of interest. The same articles contained a line or two of balance, citing a police spokesperson explaining that in the case of a low-to-medium risk missing person, there was only so much they could do, all of which had been done. Other columns referred to a couple of exposés written by Pepperdine, and it was one of these that held Bliss's attention.

The first decade of the new millennium saw the emphatic rise of the extreme right-wing British National Party, following first 9/11, and then after UK-born Muslim terrorists struck in London in July 2005. In some ways, an upsurge in nationalistic fervour was to be expected, but it was not a star that burned too brightly nor for too long. However, it appeared that in 2004, Lisa Pepperdine had focussed heavily on the BNP and its chief players, so it was no leap of faith to imagine her doing the same with regard to the New Crusader Movement in Peterborough.

The week of what became known as the 7/7 bombings, in 2005, was etched into Bliss's memory. For him it began five days earlier with the Live 8 concert at Hyde Park. He'd watched most of it on TV; The Who were terrific, but he was far from alone in his eager anticipation of the Pink Floyd reunion that night, and the band put on a legendary final performance. Then, just the day before terrorists struck in the heart of London, the city was chosen to stage the 2012 Olympics. It had seemed to be one of those weeks when nothing could possibly go wrong…

Researching Lisa Pepperdine, he found a woman who looked to be hell-bent on reaching deep into the far-right movement and staking a journalistic claim. The Burnout case had been and gone before the summer, and Bliss thought he had a good idea of what Pepperdine would have made of the tragic events on that Thursday in early July, and the aftermath that saw a marked change in the attitude of many people in the UK towards both the Muslim population and those who swore to fight them. She would undoubtedly have regarded it as an opportunity to exploit. But it was looking very much as if, by then, Pepperdine had already been murdered.

The last site Bliss checked out was the one devoted to finding Pepperdine. It was a website run and sponsored by her sister, who firmly believed that Lisa had not gone underground to infiltrate a movement, had not merely tired of everything and taken herself off-grid, but had disappeared in circumstances in which the police should have taken more interest.

Afterwards, Bliss used his work laptop to access the criminal records database, and found the entry relating to Pepperdine's reported disappearance. Along with the electronic data entered directly into the system, he also discovered scanned notes written up by officers who had been involved with interviewing relevant people. Typically for a missing adult deemed not to be vulnerable, there was little for Bliss to wade through. The owner of the B&B at which Lisa had stayed was listed, as were individuals working at the city's newspaper. Despite what Sandra Bannister had told him – that the internal grapevine believed Pepperdine had arranged a meeting with a police officer – there was no record of this in the crime log.

Bliss thought back to the comment by Pepperdine's sister regarding the police taking more interest in her disappearance, and he couldn't help but wonder if she was right.

SIXTEEN

Checking his watch as the night gloom gathered around him, Bliss drew in a sharp breath and decided to stir himself. He killed the turntable and made the first of three planned calls.

'Hi, Mum,' he said when the ringing stopped. 'It's your favourite son.'

'And what makes you say that?'

'Mainly because I'm your only son.'

'That you know of, Jimmy. That you know of.'

Bliss laughed. 'You been up to no good with one of those Blarney-kissing widowers you hang around with?'

Shortly after his father's death in Spain – where his parents had lived for a number of years – Jimmy's mother had returned to Ireland, the land of her birth. In coastal County Clare, she had found herself a group of elderly people living alone after lengthy marriages, and had formed a bond with many of them.

'You mean my Moonies?' She chuckled at the name he often called them, but the laughter gave way to coughing, her throat sounding wet and slack.

'You all right, Mum?' he asked, eyes narrowing in concern. This cough had lasted longer than usual, and her breathing rattled in her chest. 'You been back to the quack's about that virus you had?'

'Oh, what do doctors know?'

'Of course. Them with all their degrees and years of experience treating medical conditions. No better than Google, right?'

'Don't be bloody cheeky, Jimmy Bliss. You're not too old to put over my knee and feel the palm of my hand on your backside.'

'I think you're wrong about that, Mum. Also, you'd have to have bloody long hands to slap me from there.'

'Language!'

'You said it first. Exact same word.'

'Well, I'm your mother. Have respect for your elders.'

'You're sounding more Irish every time I speak to you. You last another year, and there'll be no telling the difference.'

More laughter. More rattling.

They chatted for ten minutes. He didn't see his mother as often as he would have liked, but occasionally took a long weekend to fly over; Stansted to Shannon was a short hop. When he was done, he scrolled through the contacts on his mobile and jabbed an entry marked 'Hedgehog'.

'Hi, Jimmy.'

Bliss smiled. Hanna Jez, an ex-colleague who had found herself in trouble back in the spring, lost her job with the National Crime Agency but had found employment with a private security firm while she awaited the outcome of her IOPC investigation. The wheels and cogs within the Independent Office for Police Conduct turned slowly, despite being freshly engineered. He knew all about them, his own inquiry having been closed only a few months ago.

'How's everything with you, Hedgehog?'

'Good, actually. My solicitor thinks I'll get a deal. No jail time. They've accepted my claim that I was put under obscene pressure to give up details on the case I was investigating, and that nothing I did played any part in the subsequent events other than losing out on that single shipment.'

Bliss remembered it well. A task force in Essex, surveillance and a planned hit on a hardened villain – only Hanna's tip-off, after threats made against her family, had left the task force empty handed. His friend had paid with her career, and it was right that she suffered no further consequences. His letter of support had been submitted long ago.

'I'm glad about that. And the new job?'

'It's not the NCA, but it's a living. It still gets the juices flowing from time to time.'

'You do close protection work, too?'

'Oh, yes. Always a buzz.'

'And your love life?'

'What love life?'

He grunted. An all too familiar story. People who weren't in the job had little comprehension of the strain it put on a relationship when one of the couple was seldom not on call, and where the quality hours spent together often amounted to less than a dozen each week. They never realised it required a complete lack of communication about the daily grind slowly wearing away at every nerve ending. Outsiders often thought of the lone copper as a cliché, but as with all old chestnuts, there was an inner core of truth.

Bliss felt better having spoken with his old pal. She was a sweet woman with a lively personality and a heart of pure gold, and he missed working alongside her. More than that, he still enjoyed the connection to her, in the way he did with so many people he had worked with down the years; even Stuart Sykes had left his mark, as ugly as their relationship had been.

He made his final call – to Sandra Bannister, the *Peterborough Telegraph* reporter. There were a couple of things he wanted to run by her, and their association was such that they shared information as it suited, without crossing any hard lines. The journalist greeted him warmly.

'To what do I owe this dubious pleasure?' she said. Bliss pictured her readily. Tall, easy on the eye, with a smile that suggested intimate knowledge. It was the latter he was interested in now.

'I have a couple of favours to ask,' he said, pouring himself two fingers of whiskey from a new bottle of Jameson. More of a beer man, Bliss nonetheless enjoyed the occasional spirit, but only ever in moderation. He remained on his feet, preferring to pace the carpet as he spoke.

'I'm all ears,' she said smoothly. 'Sounds as if you'll owe me afterwards.'

'A little. First up, are you working the raid on Ryan Endicott's home this morning?'

'As it happens, I'm not. And before we go any further, I need to offer my congratulations. Rooftop hero rescues potential suicide victim. Were you wearing your cape, Jimmy?'

'Not this time, no.' Bliss knew she was only being friendly, but he was tired and wanted to get on with it. 'Look, I'm hoping you'll share with me any background information you have on Endicott – known associates, stash drops, flop houses, whatever dirt you can dig up.'

'Looking for that one thing your own intelligence may not have?'

'Exactly so. Oh, and just so's you know, when Nancy Drinkwater's mortuary tech removed Lisa Pepperdine's jewellery, it was all precisely as you described. I got a call from our forensics people just after leaving work tonight. It's not enough for a formal ID, of course, but I'm happy for us to start looking at Lisa Pepperdine's life very closely. For our purposes, that begins with the Burnout op that she came up here to look into.'

'And what do you want from me on that score, Jimmy?' Bannister asked.

'We're going back to 2005, which is way before your time here in the city, so I don't know how much you actually know about the investigation. You touched on it when you mentioned the jewellery and her supposed meeting with someone high up in the operation, but only as information you'd picked up from people who worked at the newspaper back then.'

Bannister paused for a moment, before speaking again. 'That's true enough. I admit, much of my previous focus was on what happened later in the year, although I did a bit of digging into Burnout as well prior to writing my book.'

'So you know that our op was concentrated on Jason Ball, a white supremacist.'

'Yes. I recognise the name, and I have a vague understanding of who and what he was.'

Bliss was happy not to have to go through the man's history. 'Were you aware that when he wasn't co-opting young children into committing arson for him and burning out immigrant families, he was murdering a boy by the name of–'

'Nicky Cox. Whose father went on to murder Ball.'

'Okay, so you know enough. Currently I'm unofficially following up on the meeting Pepperdine said she had – but while that's cooking, I also want to look beyond that point as part of the wider investigation we'll now be running. The case we were working at the time was all about Ball, and if she went digging in his direction then I doubt she would've liked what she unearthed.'

'I see what you mean. I suppose you'd like me to delve into our archives to see what we have in relation to that period?'

Bliss sensed her smiling around the words. 'You suppose right. I'm interested mainly in Jason Ball, but also the group he ran with. Usual background stuff. Supporters, affiliations. You know the drill.'

'Any specific time period?'

Bliss thought back to that year – one of his worst in the job. Some aspects he recalled too vividly; the bodies and the lingering echoes of burning children. He had no desire to dwell on those memories, so reached instead for another, infinitely happier one.

'It began in earnest for me on the first of May,' he told her. 'The reason I remember it so well is because the day before, a mate of mine drove up from London and took us both on to Bolton, where we watched Chelsea win the Premier League title for the first time in our lifetimes. Having planned to drink ourselves into a stupor in celebration, we stayed overnight. The next day, shortly after he dropped me off at home, Penny called and informed me that a boy called Nicky Cox had gone missing. Didn't seem like much at the time, but when I think back, that was a pretty significant moment in my career.'

'It certainly signalled the start of a bad run for you.'

Bliss nodded absently to himself. He wasn't sure why he had unloaded all of that detail on Bannister, but the point she made was a good one. 'Agreed. So I'm interested in that period, but obviously Jason Ball and his far-right shit in particular. Oh, and I'll need a chat at some point with anyone at the paper who worked with or spoke to Pepperdine. You think you can sort all that out for me?'

'I don't see why not. It's going to cost me by way of time, though. What would be my recompense?'

'Dinner?' he asked before he had time to filter the thought out.

What was he thinking? She was too young, their careers clashed, and she was out of his league. During her initial silence, Bliss broke out into a cold sweat.

'Now there's a first,' Bannister said eventually. 'I'm usually prepared for you, Jimmy. But this time you've taken me by surprise.'

'Yeah, me too, if I'm honest. I'm not at all sure where that came from. I'm happy to settle for something else if you prefer. I'll owe you.'

'No, no. I wasn't about to reject your offer. But I do have one condition.'

Pulling himself together, he said, 'I was certain you would have. Fire away.'

'When we're out, I'm going to call you Jimmy as usual. And at long last, you *are* going to call me Sandra.'

After they had made arrangements and Bliss was left alone with his thoughts, he tried to imagine where the dinner invitation had come from. Not that Bannister wasn't attractive; granted, she was taller than he preferred, but on the few times they had met he had found himself appreciating her more. Her being a reporter meant he had to be on his guard, except during the interviews he gave by way of payment for another favour. She was writing a book about the travails of the city police in the autumn of 2005, and his prominence in the case that tore the force apart at the seams put him front and centre of her work.

The interview sessions had gone well – better than he had expected. Bannister had been far less aggressive in her questioning than he'd anticipated. Even so, moving from a rather uneasy alliance to a dinner date was a direction he had not foreseen. By the time he had finished his drink and climbed the stairs to bed, it wasn't only the alcohol that conjured a warm sensation in his stomach.

SEVENTEEN

The following day, Bliss was at the station by 8.30am. Intending to have a word with Molly ahead of her next round of interviews, he was both surprised and irritated to learn that she was already in the room with DI Bentley. After checking with the custody sergeant and noting that the interview had been going for thirty minutes, he lingered in the area until they emerged for a comfort break.

With an encouraging smile and a nod of greeting to the girl and her appropriate adult – the same young woman from the YMCA – Bliss brushed by them and put himself in front of the drugs team DI.

'What's your bloody game here, Bentley?' he demanded. 'I realise the *Interview Techniques for Dummies* book is like a bible to you, but can't you see that dragging this specific kid in at stupid o'clock in the morning is only going to alienate her further?'

The taller man looked down at Bliss, giving a sly grin as he shook his head. 'What's it to you? Did I get it right yesterday? You got a semi on for this girl?'

Bliss took a beat to reel in his anger, his mind slipping to Bishop's altercation with Ferguson the previous evening. He wet his lips and cleared his throat before responding in a low voice so as not to be overheard.

'That's the second time you've made that crack. If you know anything about me at all, Bentley, you'll think long and hard about doing so again. Your tactics are shit, is all I'm saying.'

'All? You don't reckon that's disparaging and condescending enough?'

'I suppose.' Bliss met the other man's gaze head-on. 'But you're the one fucking things up right now. You treat her like that, she's going to blank you all the way until it's time for you to shit or get off the pot, and she'll walk out of here with you none the wiser. She'll outlast you, Bentley – because believe me, this kid has been there, seen it all, and has the T-shirt.'

'What the hell do you know about her that I don't?'

'Nothing. Except that I was the one on that rooftop with her. Not you. She'll yawn away the last few remaining hours you have with her, leaving you with nothing more than you started with.'

'Is that so?' Bentley squared his stance, making himself larger, a peacock putting its feathers on full display.

Bliss shrugged, opening his hands. 'Put me right, then. Regale me with everything she told you over the past hour. Go on, Bentley. I have all the time in the world.'

The DI huffed out his own anger before angling himself sideways, pushing past Bliss to continue along the corridor. Muttering to himself and shaking his head, he strode away quickly, hands balled into fists.

Because you know I'm right, Bliss thought.

As he headed across to Major Crimes, a uniform called out to him from the top of the stairway. 'Inspector, somebody here to see you – down in reception.'

Bliss checked his watch. He had time before the team briefing – ish. He'd be late, but they wouldn't start without him, and he had already left word for Bishop to hang around until they'd had a chance to catch up. He raised a thumb at the constable and took the stairs down two flights. Using the badge on his lanyard, he let himself through the electronic security door and walked out into the well-lit entry hall. There were no chairs – visitors were not invited to linger. But standing by the entrance, hands buried deep into his pockets, stood a familiar figure.

'Very good to see you again, sir,' Bliss said, advancing with his arm out. Smiling, the two men shook hands firmly.

'Not "Sir" these days, Inspector,' the man said. 'Just plain Joe Flynn in my dotage.'

'Old habits,' Bliss explained. 'This the first time you've been back here since you left us?'

'It is. I was thinking on my way over that it's thirteen years since I walked away. I have to say, I was astonished to learn that you're back in the fold.'

'The proverbial bad penny, that's me.'

'Still tilting at windmills?'

Bliss laughed. 'Funnily enough, I ran into someone else just yesterday who asked me the exact same thing. Let's just say it's not been the easiest of years. You want to go into the canteen, or shall I find an empty room somewhere?'

Flynn nodded towards the door Bliss had entered by. 'I have no intention of walking back through there, Jimmy. Not today, nor any other day if I can possibly help it. I'm in the city until late this evening, so any chance of finding time to meet up for a drink? Lunchtime or after work is fine by me.'

Bliss nodded. 'Either – or both, if nothing big breaks in the meantime.'

'Let's settle on lunch just in case. How about the Draper's Arms on Cowgate?'

'I know it. Sounds good.'

'Half-twelve suit you?'

'Perfect. I take it this is about the message I left for you?'

A shadow passed across Flynn's long, narrow face. 'What else? When I got your voicemail I realised it must be something I couldn't afford to ignore.'

Without going into any detail, Bliss relayed the basic facts relating to the progress of the operation, then told Flynn about his visit with Sykes.

'Poor bugger.' Flynn sounded genuinely sympathetic.

'Yeah.' Bliss made no mention of his old boss's confession; he still didn't know what to make of it himself.

The two men shook hands again before going their separate ways.

Chandler caught up with him the moment he was back on the second floor, a long, square parcel in her hand. 'It's for you,' she said. 'Don't worry, we've had the bomb squad and the HazMat team give it the once-over. We all know how over-zealous your fan club can be.'

'Very funny,' he said, noticing how ridiculously pleased she was with her joke. 'Mind you don't cut yourself on that rapier-like wit.'

He unwrapped the package and his eyebrows rose; seventeen-year-old Balvenie DoubleWood single malt did not come cheap. Chandler had already removed the card that had been taped to the wrapping paper, and was reading it unbidden.

'What does *my* card say?' he asked her, a wry smile on his lips. 'Who's *my* gift from?'

She handed it across. 'Aw, how sweet,' she said. 'It's from Joe Lakeham. To thank you for remembering him on the anniversary of his wife's murder.'

Bliss was pleasantly surprised. Annie Lakeham's vicious murder had been his first case upon returning to the city, and her husband's devastation had gnawed at Bliss for a long time. Concerned by the man's state of mind, Bliss had kept in contact. He'd visited Joe on the anniversary, knowing how the old man would feel that day, having experienced those awful series of firsts himself: first birthday, first wedding anniversary, first Christmas. Bliss had made a point of reaching out on each of those important days, saving the personal visit for the one ugly memory.

'How did he know you liked a tipple?' Chandler asked.

Bliss shrugged. 'Must have come up in conversation.'

'How's he doing?'

'As well as can be expected.'

'You still worried about him? I remember you telling me he was a possible suicide risk.'

'Yep, I'm still worried.' Bliss sighed. 'A year is nothing. No time at all.'

'It's nice that you keep in touch.'

Bliss did not want to discuss it further; he regarded the conversation as an intrusion into Joe Lakeham's misery and loss. 'Come on,' he said. 'I'll pop this on my desk and then we'll get cracking.'

Taking up his usual position at the head of the room, Bliss delivered the morning briefing in a tone that brooked no remarks. 'The three items of jewellery found with the human remains tell us only part of the story,' he said, 'as does the approximate year of death. Both point towards this body being that of Lisa Pepperdine. We know why she was in the city at the time, and we know she subsequently went missing. We don't know for certain that our most recent set of remains are hers, but until we have a firm answer either way my decision is that we look hard at those dark days back in 2005.'

He omitted Pepperdine's alleged meeting with a high-ranking officer. He did not like taking the case forward with his team out of the loop about a specific and viable angle worth investigating, but he remained acutely aware of how sensitive the situation was. If police corruption – perhaps even involvement in a murder – erupted again in the city, this time they would all be caught in the blast. It was for their own good, and Chandler had agreed to conceal the lead until he decided otherwise.

'Finally,' he continued. 'By now, you will have all heard about Bish's… squabble with DS Ferguson in CID yesterday.' He paused while all eyes flashed across to Olly Bishop, who was wedged into his favourite chair, looking straight ahead and chewing on his lip. 'I need you all to understand that whilst what took place cannot be condoned, I think I speak for the entire team when I say we recognise the provocation all too well. Furthermore, it would be hypocritical of me personally to lambast DS Bishop for his response to that incitement; none of us are immune to anger. My view is this: it happened, let's accept it for what it was and move on. If anybody here is unhappy with that, you know where my office is.'

Twenty minutes later, Bliss was at his desk checking the case record when Chandler knocked on his doorframe. He looked up from the keyboard he was wrestling with. 'Do you come in peace, or have you been nominated to speak for the others?'

'There's nothing to say,' she told him. 'I don't think you'll find any disagreement out there, boss. No – I came to ask you about Joe Flynn. I heard he was here earlier.'

Bliss relaxed, pushed back in his chair. 'He was. I'm seeing him later on for a pint and a chat.'

'The missing reporter?'

'Yep. He looked anxious.'

'That's because he's sane. Only someone like you would fail to be concerned.'

'I was concerned enough to reach out to him and Sykes.'

Chandler shrugged. 'I suppose so. You want some company? I'd love to see the old Chief Super again.'

He shook his head. 'No, I think this is best left to those of us who were running the Burnout case. He may not feel comfortable discussing some of the issues in front of you. He did say he'll be in the city for the day, so I'll try to arrange a meal for later on if you're up for that?'

'Please do. It'll be great to catch up. What do you think his apprehension is all about?'

Bliss grinned, remembering the man's attitude and approach back in the day. 'If he's anything like the man we worked under, Pen, he won't be reacting to this by halves. My money is on him wanting to go for some plain speaking.'

Chandler snorted. 'Well, that should be right up your alley.'

His mobile rang; seeing Bannister's name, he answered right away. 'I do hope you're calling with good news,' he said.

'And good morning to you, too, Inspector.'

'Same to you. Now, what do you have for me?'

'Such a charmer. You could sweep a woman off her feet with that seductive manner.'

'Sorry. I'm busy, is all.'

'I'll put you out of your misery, then. I'm still looking into Jason Ball and his acolytes – there's a lot on file and I don't just want to skim it. As for Ryan Endicott, we have surprisingly little. Seems to me that he's not the biggest fish in the pond.'

'He isn't. It's the way these people work now. Little cells, all interlinked but all individually run. He's a main player, but he's not at the top of the food chain. He's answerable to someone who's answerable to somebody else.'

'But he's nonetheless a very dangerous young man. Endicott served time: three stints which were drugs-related, and two for using a knife.'

'That much will be in our own records,' Bliss said. 'Where's my juicy bone?'

'Okay. I'll assume you have a list of properties connected to both him and his associates. But I have two things of note for you. First of all, during one of his spells behind bars, Endicott was introduced to a man by the name of Thomas Holt. Now, Holt was inside on drugs distribution charges, yet he's apparently been clean since his release. I have notes here to suggest he started working differently, perhaps even in the way you just described. Oh, and Holt has connections to a person of interest called Eric McManus.'

Bliss nodded thoughtfully. 'I'll speak to our drugs unit, see if either are on their radar. Thank you for that. And the second thing?'

'Ryan Endicott has been spotted on several occasions with Courtney Jacobs.'

The name was familiar, but for a moment Bliss could not place it. 'Remind me,' he said.

'One of the new wave of celebrities. You know the kind; you're not quite sure what it is they do, or where they came from, but suddenly they're all over the TV and splashed across the news. Usually for all the wrong reasons.'

Bliss chuckled. 'You sound cynical.'

'And you'd know, right? Sorry, but there was a time when people had to earn their fame and fortune, actually achieve something in their lives.'

'And people say we've progressed. Yeah, I remember Courtney Jacobs now. That's something we're unlikely to have in our records. Thanks for that – I appreciate it.'

'Was it worth a second dinner?'

'I don't know if I'd go that far. Dessert after the first, maybe. Anyway, I have to go. I appreciate the information. I'll call you about… the other thing.'

When he disconnected and looked up, Chandler was staring at him with a curious expression on her face. He'd forgotten she was in the office, and now realised he'd made a couple of verbal slips during his conversation.

'What was that all about?' she asked, unable to keep the smile from thinning her lips.

'What was what?'

'That? Have I stepped into a parallel universe and been transported into the wrong office? I was expecting to find Inspector James Bliss, he of the granite exterior wrapped around a steel interior. Instead, I got the Bliss with a soft gooey centre. That was a woman you were speaking to. Tell me I'm wrong.'

'It was my mother.'

'Your mum just called to talk to you about our drugs unit and a big-boobed celeb.'

'Yes. She wants to be more involved in my life.'

Chandler stared hard at him and then her face creased into a broader smile, her eyes becoming round and wide. 'Oh em gee! You have a woman. Jimmy Bliss is dating.'

Bliss winced and took a pace back as if retreating in disgust. 'First of all, it's every bit as quick and easy to say "Oh my God" as it is to say "OMG", so please use proper sentences. Secondly...' He turned his own easy grin on her. 'The rest is none of your damned business.'

'None of my...? Are you crazy? Is this why you were so casual about the Bone Woman, because you already have a floozy?'

Bliss made no reply, but her words snagged against something inside him. Last night when he'd invited Bannister to dinner, the impetus had come out of nowhere – except he knew that was impossible, because all actions were taken either consciously or subconsciously, even if the reason wasn't immediately apparent. Now he wondered if he had made the date with Sandra in order to eradicate Emily from his mind. If so, it had not been effective.

EIGHTEEN

'What's this I hear about you summoning armed officers to protect a suspect yesterday, Bliss?'

Edwards started speaking before looking up, but by the time she was finished her eyes had found his. The DCI had collared him moments after he'd finished discussing his love life with Chandler; her beckoning finger was all it took to uproot him from behind his own desk. Now he sat on the other side of hers, knowing he was in the shit again.

'I've no idea what you're talking about, boss,' he said.

'You're telling me you did not order an armed guard for this Molly Doe or whatever her name is? The young girl you… encountered on the rooftop.'

'Oh, her. Well, at the time I was under the impression she was a witness. That's where I got a bit confused. Apologies.'

Edwards folded her arms across her chest, tapping the fingers of one hand on her ribcage. 'Seriously, Bliss? That's the story you're going with?'

'With respect, boss, isn't it irrelevant whether she was a suspect or a witness? Either way, she was both vulnerable and exposed.'

'Was there not already a uniformed officer outside her door?'

'PC Lamb seems like a good copper, ma'am, but I'm not sure she'd be any match for Ryan Endicott and his crew if they steamed in there all tooled up. From what I've heard about him, he's crazy enough even when he's not wounded.'

'You make a decent point, but since when have we been in the business of providing armed guards to suspected drugs mules who happen to have had a run-in with their fellow traffickers?'

'Since this one came ready and willing to tell us everything she knows about Endicott, his rabble of a crew, and the London end. That's when.'

His boss studied him for a few moments, uncertainty flickering in her eyes. 'Ready and willing to cough and spill her guts on what amounts to dozens of very dangerous men. Is that what you're telling me, Inspector? Because that is not what I am hearing from DI Bentley – who, by the way, is not at all happy with you accosting him outside the interview room first thing this morning.'

Bliss scoffed and rolled his head back. 'He told you? What a dickwad.'

Fletcher leaned forward and took a grip of her own hands as if keeping them away from his neck. 'Actually, it wasn't Bentley who came to me. A colleague did so on his behalf.'

Cutting short a derisory laugh, Bliss said, 'All due respect, boss, but you know as well as I do that he instructed her to do that. Sent her to do his dirty work. Doesn't want to be seen as a baby telling tales out of school, so gets a loyal subordinate to come running, probably horrified by the way her guvnor got treated by that spiteful Bliss bloke.'

'Her?'

'I'm assuming it was his DS. Warren, I think her name is.'

Edwards hissed through her teeth as she settled back in her chair. It was a good sigh, Bliss thought. His boss was spent. He waited while she chewed on her lip, her head rocking slowly from side to side. Now she was running it all through her mind, moving towards a decision. When she looked up at him, he saw that he would come out of it okay.

'You're putting me in an awkward position, Bliss,' she said, speaking as if each word caused her physical pain. 'Especially in light of DS Bishop's mad moment yesterday evening. You do realise that come Monday morning, DI Bentley will be reporting to me. My heading up CID is a temporary measure, but I still have to work with the man and his team.'

'So on Monday tell him what a turd you consider me to be. Believe me, boss, I'm steering clear as much as I can, but I call it as I see it – and he ruined any chance he ever had of getting Molly to open up the second he made it confrontational.'

'It is perhaps your good fortune that this Molly girl seems to have things to tell you that she refuses to share with anyone else,' the DCI said. 'I'm guessing it got pretty fraught up there on that roof. You did a fine job, from what I hear.'

'Thank you, boss.'

Bliss heard the slight pause and knew there was more to come.

'So why do you then undo all that good work by breaking the rules and ordering an armed detail for a suspect?'

'I think you'll find I bent them, boss. The rules. I bent them as far as their inner tension allowed without snapping, but I didn't break them. Look, I know I walked a fine line. Hands up on that one. But Molly is not only vulnerable to a revenge attack, I also genuinely consider her to be more of a witness than a suspect if we play it right – well, if the drugs team do.'

'From what I hear, they have very little evidence to process her further. And you did at least get her to engage.'

Bliss nodded. 'We only have her until late afternoon. Any danger of you wangling me another crack at her?'

DCI Edwards tilted her head to one side and rolled her eyes to the ceiling. 'Let me see if I have this right, Inspector. You would like me to have a word with DI Bentley – the man you accosted and insulted and swore at – and persuade him to allow you back into the room?'

'That's about the size of it, boss. Seems reasonable enough to me.' He shrugged as if he meant it.

The DCI let out a long and weary exhalation. 'I'll say this for you, Bliss. You've got some bloody nerve.'

'Does that mean you'll do it?'

'It means I'll think about it.'

'Good. And then you'll do it, yes?'

Running both hands through her stylish short dark hair, Edwards said, 'Just go, will you? In a few days you'll be someone else's problem. I'll do what I can if you promise not to darken my doorstep again this week. Deal?'

Bliss shook his head. 'I figured this was what you wanted to talk about, given you were out of the office yesterday, and allowing for the fact that I dealt with the Super regarding the remains in Fengate. So I took the liberty of telling DI Bentley that he was wanted here in your office' – Bliss checked his wristwatch – 'right about now.'

***

According to Bentley, Molly had maintained her defiant attitude throughout all her interviews with him, refusing to budge on her family or her age. Kim Parker from the YMCA had also spoken privately with the girl, but even their conversations had yielded nothing further.

'I don't think she'll give it up for me, either,' Bliss said, feeling two pairs of eyes turning to him.

The DCI had made room for the meeting, though Bliss had endured the bollocking he richly deserved for putting her in such an awkward situation. She had grudgingly accepted because, in her assessment, time was running out and decisions needed to be made. Her gaze switched to him as she spoke.

'You two have a rapport, from what I understand. And earlier you were extremely keen to get back in the room with her.'

'She doesn't trust me because I grabbed her away from that ledge. Before that, though, I'd got her talking. She also spoke to me when Pen and I met with her in hospital. And you're right, I do want to have another crack. All I'm saying is that we shouldn't expect to hear her real name or true age, because she probably realises we'll struggle to reach any decisions until we know for sure how old she is.'

'The girl insists she's eighteen,' Bentley said with a brusque shake of his head. 'And there's no way that's true. I'm betting she's at least three or four years younger.'

Bliss was inclined to agree. 'But unless we can identify her, whether she's a minor becomes a debatable issue. To my mind, we need to decide right now if she's going to be charged. Because if she isn't, I'd be interested in contacting Social Care to see if we're able to put Molly under some kind of order that ensures she goes nowhere.'

'Who needs to decide about charging?' Bentley said, raising his eyebrows. 'Not you, for sure.'

Bliss held up a hand. 'Yeah, okay. Somebody actually working the case needs to make that decision. All I'm saying is it shouldn't be some last-second throwaway when the twenty-four hours are up. I want to... sorry – I think you ought to consider having a procedure in place whereby she is moved immediately from custody to whatever secure provision we can come up with.'

'What about that?' Edwards said, looking at Bentley. 'Where are you on charging this girl?'

The Inspector's cheek protruded as his tongue raked the inside. His shrug betrayed his frustrations. 'We're not there yet. And I have to admit that I don't see that changing before our time with her is up. I can extend it by twelve hours, but it's probably pointless.'

'What exactly do you have?'

'Nothing from any of the men we swept up from Endicott's place. They won't even acknowledge she was there, and all of them are now out on bail. All we have are snapshots of her leaving the place in London and arriving at the flat in Eastfield. It's enough to associate her with them and Endicott, but not to nail her as a county lines drug mule. We don't have her prints on file, either.'

Edwards took a beat to consider his words before responding. 'Presumably you allowed her to make the delivery so the product would be sitting there when you raided the flat yesterday morning?'

Bentley nodded. 'Precisely, boss. We were able to arrest, detain and charge the others, because they were found inside the flat together with the drugs. With Molly, we don't have that advantage. We have no way of proving she was the courier, nor that she ever has been. As for the knife she was carrying, most of the blood on it was her own; we suspect she slashed her own midriff up on that roof. There is another blood type on the blade, and it matches Endicott's, but DNA results won't be with us until tomorrow at the earliest. The whole thing is a sorry mess. We planned to wrap them all up with a nice neat bow on top, but the fight between her and Endicott yesterday morning screwed us.'

'Why didn't you raid the place shortly after she arrived?' Bliss asked.

'We wanted to see if anybody turned up to collect the product. The flat was under observation at all times. If somebody had showed, we would have gone in. We decided to give it the night and take them early doors while they were still foggy with sleep. It would have turned out the way we hoped if Endicott and Molly hadn't fallen out.'

'What did you get from the men you detained?' Edwards asked.

'Bugger all once they were in the room with representation. With regard to Molly, all we have is an early informal statement from one of them who laughed at the fact we'd missed out on Endicott. During his arrest he mentioned a girl, a fight, the knife. Got a real kick out of it. Said he wouldn't want to be the girl for all the money in the world.'

'Which has been my point all along,' Bliss said. 'Assuming Endicott's wounds are not severe, he's already after Molly. He's either paying for information as we speak, or he already has it. He and his crew will be trying to work out what happens to her next. If she was provably eighteen, she'd be bailed to appear – or even released without bail and left to her own devices.'

'Is that our way in, then?' Bentley interrupted. 'We tell her we believe her story and she's being released. We also wish her the best of British, knowing Endicott and his pals are lying in wait for her somewhere.'

'Nice,' Bliss shot back, sneering at his fellow DI. 'You're a real prince.'

'Don't tell me you wouldn't be thinking the exact same thing if you weren't so sweet on her.'

Bliss shot to his feet, glowering. 'I warned you before about that crap, Bentley. I've had enough of your bullshit.'

Bentley feigned bewilderment as his smiling gaze turned to Edwards. 'What did I say?' he asked. 'What the hell is his problem?'

'When you two children are quite finished, can we get back to the matter in hand?' Edwards said. Poker-faced, she gave it a moment and allowed the silence hanging between them to do its work. Eventually she nodded and went on. 'Thank you. DI Bentley, this is hardly the impression you want to be giving me only days before I officially become your line manager. And DI Bliss, don't be baited so easily. I thought you were beyond that now. Both of you, let's think about Molly and what's best for her.'

It wasn't easy for him to admit, but Bliss relented. 'DI Bentley is not wrong. In his shoes, I'd be doing precisely as he suggests. Whatever Molly is or is not, the one thing I know she has in her armoury is intelligence. She comes across as a whippersnapper, but she'll have weighed up the consequences, and like us she won't have the first clue as to the best option available to her. It won't hurt to remind her of the threat that's waiting for her out there. It may not buy us her name, but she might well admit her true age.'

'Good,' Edwards said. 'I agree. Which is why I want you to be the one who whispers that thought in her ear.'

'Me?' Bliss said.

'Bliss?' Bentley blurted out at the exact same time.

Edwards smiled. 'Of course. DI Bentley, Molly clearly has no faith in you. What you say will rock her. But will it challenge her emotionally? I doubt it. Whereas if Bliss tells her and is seemingly indifferent to the consequences, it will hurt just that bit more, which may well cause the reaction we're looking for.'

'With respect, boss,' Bentley said, 'it might also make her clam up entirely.'

Bliss loathed himself for nodding. 'I hate to say it, boss, but he's right. Molly needs to believe she has someone in her corner – someone who cares about her. We need to give her someone to turn to for support once she accepts the predicament she's in. DI Bentley has to be the one to tell her. After which, we give her me.'

A lengthy pause followed, but finally Edwards gave in. 'Very well. Sort it out between you. Bad cop and good cop.'

'Yes, boss,' they said, in unison.

'Good,' Edwards said, rising to her feet, a broad grin on her face. 'Isn't it nice when we all agree and get along together?'

Which was the moment Bliss realised he and his DI colleague had been played.

NINETEEN

Although the pub was a Wetherspoon's, Bliss considered the Draper's Arms to be anything but a chain-run establishment. The former nineteenth-century draper's shop frontage benefitted from floor-to-ceiling windows which opened the place up to both light and closer examination of the atmosphere within. Its relatively narrow interior shone with lights that reflected off mirrors behind the highly polished wooden bar, and its imposing charm offered the prospect of a good time.

Bliss found Joe Flynn already seated in a high-backed booth of wood and stained glass. The pub did a better trade in the evenings, especially at the weekend, but there was still a decent lunchtime crowd in. The menus were basic but cheap, and the beer was excellent. Bliss bought two pints of the guest ale and took them over to the table, sliding himself onto the smooth bench seat with the ease of a man experienced in such manoeuvres.

Flynn proved to be every bit the same person he was when Bliss had worked under his command. He was older, of course, and had a decent amount more timber on him; less hair, too, and what remained was sparse and more white than grey. The lines on his face were deeper, eyes perhaps receding into their sockets. But still the same kind and straightforward man Bliss had always known.

'Hell of a shame about Stuart,' Flynn said, slowly easing his head from side to side. 'I had my issues with the man – who didn't? – but nobody deserves to fade away like that.'

'I held a grudge against him for the longest time,' Bliss acknowledged, painful memories lingering on his conscience. 'Sometimes it was as if I had acid in my veins. But when I saw him lying there in the hospice, nothing but skin and bone and grasping for his memory, all I felt was sympathy.'

Bliss recalled thinking how Sykes struggling to remember things had reminded him of a cat pawing at a pinpoint of light; an abundance of futile effort for no ultimate reward.

Flynn nodded absently. 'It's a harsh world that allows people to leave it barely more compos mentis than when they entered. Genuinely tragic.'

For the first time since he had decided to contact Flynn, Bliss realised how little he knew about his old boss. The man's softly spoken words were not tossed carelessly away; there was a depth to him that Bliss had not previously been aware of. When they worked together, Flynn's integrity had always been the quality he admired most of all, but now he was going to have to rethink the former Chief Super all over again.

The two spent the whole of their first drink catching up on the last thirteen years. Neither mentioned the job, concentrating instead on their lives outside the boundaries of law, order and justice. Not that Bliss believed he had often achieved the latter – at least, not fully. He thought of justice as an almost amorphous concept these days – perhaps even something that no longer truly existed. If, indeed, it ever had.

Upon his retirement from the job half a decade earlier, Flynn and his wife had bought and still ran a tasteful B&B establishment in Norfolk. Other than the odd difficult customer, Flynn explained, it was a completely different world. The large Victorian property was both a home and a source of income, and the couple were enjoying life to the full. Joe's enthusiasm was unforced, and it was clear to Bliss that his old boss had found peace away from the police service. He wondered if the future held such promise for himself.

With two more pints on the table, frothy white heads as yet unbroken like a fresh dusting of snow, it was Bliss who brought them on point.

'So what do you make of this Lisa Pepperdine woman, and her claim that she had a meeting arranged with someone high up in the investigation?' he asked, searching Flynn's eyes for any signs of discomfort. Something passed across them, but it was slow-moving and vague, as if a veil had been drawn over.

'Until I heard your voicemail I'd pretty much forgotten all about her,' he answered; it seemed to Bliss that he was slowly releasing each word after careful vetting. 'I came here to speak with you because I can't help but think I let her down.'

Intrigued, Bliss pushed him for more.

'There was no pre-arranged meeting,' Flynn insisted. 'At least, not with me. Pepperdine did doorstep me, though – outside Thorpe Wood nick, of all places. It was obvious to me that she had an angle. She was pushing the notion that we were moving slowly and showing a lack of interest because the arson victims were foreigners. Even in those days, TV programmes showed crimes being solved so easily, in a single episode, and daft people like her began to believe that's how it was in real life. I made it clear that we were doing everything in our power, but she didn't want to listen. Started shouting and screaming over me. In the end I just pushed past and thought nothing more about her until sometime later when I heard she had gone missing.'

'I don't understand,' Bliss said. 'Your reaction seems perfectly understandable to me. In what way did you let her down?'

'Ah. That came when we were asked to look into her disappearance. It was a torrid time, and I can't even recall who brought it to my attention. Either way, I gave it little thought or energy, and it did not feature high on our list of priorities. I would imagine we did the least anyone would expect of us, and no more. If memory serves, my immediate impression was that she had probably moved on to other matters when her biases found no traction here. I would assume both we and the Met thought the other force would do the hard graft. That said, low-risk missing adults have never been a priority for our meagre resources.'

'Surely somebody must have kicked up a fuss afterwards. After all, she had family, friends. Are you telling me they just shrugged and moved on?' Bliss found that idea difficult to comprehend.

Flynn bit into his lip and ran a hand over his face. 'I'm ashamed to say I don't have the foggiest idea, Jimmy. It came across my desk and it slipped off the other side. If I ever thought about it again, I'd be astonished. I dismissed it from my thoughts and carried on as if it had never happened. Had it been our only case, then of course I would have given it the utmost concentration. But you know yourself how certain cases can get lost in the mix.'

'So you're not aware of anything in relation to her since then?'

'I wasn't. Not until your message. I've become quite a dab hand at the old laptop, so I set to work running searches and linking from page to page until I built up a bit of a picture. It brought back some memories about those days and some of the people we encountered. You'll remember the New Crusader Movement, I take it?'

Bliss did. A rapid shudder passed along his spine. 'Jason Ball's neo-Nazi group.'

'Yes, and a nastier bunch of shits you'd be hard pressed to find. It pretty much died a death when he did… Except that when I ran a trawl through modern-day equivalents, I turned up something surprising. There's a group who call themselves Britain For The British. You heard of them?'

'Not that I recall, although I had to interview someone of the same ilk earlier this year. Bloke by the name of Ritchie – but his mob were Britain Unites.'

'My antennae started twitching when I had a look at their website, because a couple of the names were also associated with the group I remember from the Burnout case. So I dug a bit deeper. Buried away on one of the pages was a name that caught me entirely by surprise: Craig Ball.' Bliss raised his eyebrows and Flynn nodded. 'Yes, I had exactly the same reaction. I delved deeper still, and found out that Craig is Jason's son.'

'Well, now that is interesting.'

'Isn't it just? But it gets more so, Jimmy. It listed Craig as an ex-member, so I switched my attention to him. Turns out he still gets his kicks out of being an activist, only now he does so with a bunch calling themselves Antifa-UK.'

Bliss frowned. 'Are you sure about that?'

'Yes. Why the scepticism?'

'It's not that I'm sceptical,' Bliss said. 'Not entirely, anyway. In theory, Antifa are the polar opposite of groups like Britain for the British. They're anti-fascists.'

Flynn looked perplexed. 'That makes no sense whatsoever.'

Bliss sipped his pint then leaned closer, lowering his voice. 'Except that it does. It depends on what lies behind these groups. See, whilst Antifa claim to have an anti-fascist agenda, in some ways they're as fascist in their approach as any far-right organisation – more so, in some circumstances. They go masked, they stamp down on free speech if the voices are not saying what they want to hear, they rule by fear and strength of numbers, intimidate those who oppose them, and often resort to violence to get their message across. The thing is, they're regarded as being on the right side of the debate, so their nastier aspects are pretty much ignored by our politicians and the media. But many of them are wrong 'uns, and I can see why a thug who enjoys a demo and a scrap would relish being part of that group. This mob are accepted by the establishment, supported by many of them. They fly beneath the radar that way.'

Flynn blew out his lips. 'You learn something new every day. Like father, like son, it would seem. I realise we're straying off the point, but it occurred to me that if Lisa Pepperdine was pursuing this, she more than likely encountered Jason Ball and his bunch of thugs.'

Bliss sat back and gave that some thought, having had the exact same notion. Flynn had all but lost the sibilants of his Liverpool accent, but the scouse in him reared up when he got excited. The man's eyes were gleaming, and his breath came in short, sharp puffs. Once an investigator, always an investigator, apparently. Bliss was impressed.

'The same thoughts strayed across my mind, too,' he said, taking a pull on his pint and savouring the bitterness on his tongue before swallowing. 'In fact, I'm already looking into it.'

Grinning, Flynn said, 'I thought you might say that. I'm not sure how much it helps, what with Jason Ball no longer being around, but I suppose it may be worth seeking out others from the NCM to see if they remember her.'

'If we can locate any who are willing to talk to us. Most of them probably still blame us for Jason's death.'

'I'm not sure what else you can do, Jimmy. It sounds very much as if Stuart is a dead end – excuse the choice of words. Pepperdine probably did seek him out after getting short shrift from me, but even if you got him to recognise the name, you couldn't be sure that anything he told you about her was factual.'

Bliss nodded his acceptance, but then had an idea. He took out his mobile and scrolled through the contacts list. Moments later he was connected to Briony Sykes. 'I hope you don't mind my calling,' he said, 'but do you think your father would be up to another visit?'

He listened, nodding occasionally, before thanking her and laying his phone down on the table. 'She reckons if we give it a day or two he's likely to be in a different frame of mind altogether – which could be either good or bad.'

Flynn nodded. 'What's she like?'

'Pleasant. Even to me, and evidently mine was not a name much cherished in the Sykes household in the mid-noughties.'

'I don't imagine it was. You two clashed so often I thought I was going to have to separate you, one way or another.'

'I never got the chance to thank you fully for the way you treated me.' Bliss stared off into the distance, where the past lay in wait to either captivate or horrify, depending on its mood. 'You were scrupulously fair, when it would have been far easier to have favoured the Super.'

Flynn paused, pint glass raised to his lips. 'I very much disagreed with the decision that came down from Cambridgeshire HQ to have you answerable directly to Stuart following the Burnout debacle. I saw no reason why you were singled out to bypass the usual lines of responsibility. And I was disgruntled about the gardening leave you were persuaded to take. I probably gave you the benefit of the doubt because of that.'

Bliss snorted in disgust. 'And to repay you for your kindness, I cost you your job.'

'No. I did that to myself,' Flynn argued. 'Where you acted, I hesitated. Where you put yourself in the firing line, I held back to wait out the storm. I knew something was rotten in the state of Denmark, Jimmy. Those bones that bunch of kids discovered in Bretton Woods were telling us a story, and you were the only one with the balls to not only listen to what they were saying, but act upon it. I let you smash through the barriers ahead of me, and that was a mistake. It was right that I paid the ultimate price for it.'

Bliss reached a decision he had been toying with since walking into the pub. 'I have to tell you something, Joe. Something Stuart said to me yesterday. The man was spouting nonsense at times – talking about me as if I wasn't there, going off on some Normandy beach fantasy – but right at the end I think he came back. I think I was listening to the real Stuart Sykes. He told me he was sorry, because it was him who tipped off Anthony Cox shortly before we were set to move in on Jason Ball. He said he never imagined it going as far as it did, but that he should never have let me take the blame.'

For a moment, Flynn failed to respond. When he did, it was with evident uncertainty. 'And you think at that point he recognised you? That he was lucid? That it was his intention to confess this to you?'

'In the moment, I do,' Bliss replied without hesitation. 'He came and went, but when he spoke directly to me, I believe he was telling me something that had been weighing on him all these years.'

Flynn breathed out heavily. 'Well, I'll be buggered. Isn't that something?'

Bliss nodded. 'Not that it matters now, I suppose. I'm not even sure it mattered that much back then, either.'

'It does to me, Jimmy,' Flynn said, setting his glass down hard on the table.

'Why should it? It was me who took the grief for something I didn't do.'

'And that's precisely why it does matter. It means I got it wrong. Again. I sat back and let it happen. Again. You think I was a friendly and supportive presence in your first stint at Thorpe Wood, Jimmy, but in fact I seem to have been the architect of your downfall.'

'No. Not the architect, Joe. Sure, your inaction gave others the confidence to pin it on me and give me a hard time in the process, but you weren't to know.'

'What if I didn't want to know? Did you ever think of that?'

Bliss fixed his gaze on the man, mulling it over before he spoke. 'I never did, and I never will. We all know about hindsight, Joe, and we can all be brave in retrospect. Which of us can hold our heads up high about those two cases that year? You lost your job over it, I had to leave Peterborough, and Stuart was shuffled sideways. Looking at the three of us now, do you still believe he got the best end of the deal?'

After a few moments of silence, Flynn raised his glass, swirling the dregs around at the bottom. 'To those we were unable to save,' he said. 'And to the things we got right in the end.'

Bliss tipped his own drink towards his old boss. 'That's a toast worth making,' he said, the past slipping into his pores and filling him to the brim with melancholy.

TWENTY

Molly sat still, absorbing the news that she would probably be released at any moment, and that Ryan Endicott was bound to be waiting for her with open arms when she stepped outside the safety of Thorpe Wood. As far as Bliss could tell, the news hadn't fazed her at all. He didn't know whether to be impressed or angered by her lack of reaction.

'You were thinking of killing yourself,' he said, deciding to say what was on his mind and leave her to adjust. 'But even if dying doesn't bother you, I'm sure how it happens is more of a concern. If Endicott snatches you up before you have the chance to top yourself, then your eventual death is going to be both a lingering and painful one.'

'And who do I have to thank for that?' Molly shot back at him, still unruffled.

'I did what I thought was right at the time – and if I had it to do all over again, I would. You may think you would have been better off if I'd stayed in the coffee shop rather than traipsing up onto that roof, but once I got there I was always going to do my job. Believe me, I was perfectly happy, poised over a mocha and a lemon muffin. I'd just cut into the bugger and seen all that delicious curd ooze out when my breakfast was ruined by that bloody shout.'

Molly hugged herself. 'And what a great choice *I* have now. Thanks for that.'

'Because you were doing so well beforehand. Do I have to remind you why you were on that roof in the first place? Or what kind of state I found you in? Like a drowned rat, half naked and with blood smeared all over you. Yours and Endicott's.'

The girl showed the first flicker of interest. 'So I really didn't kill Ryan, then? I thought you and that other cop were hiding something from me, using the threat of Ryan to make me talk. But I can see by the look on your face that you think he's alive – and if that's the case, then he's bloody well after me with a vengeance.'

'What look, Molly?' Bliss asked, taking a chance. 'What look do I have on my face?'

She studied him for a few seconds longer, searching for something more behind the mask he was presenting. Eventually she frowned and whispered, 'If I didn't know better, I'd say it was concern.'

'It is. Concern for you. See, Molly, I'm not interested in what you do on a day-to-day basis right now. The matter of you humping drugs around the country can come later. Neither do I give a toss if you deliberately harmed Ryan Endicott with a carving knife, because I'm pretty sure you were provoked into defending yourself. Plus he's a dealer, so fuck him. But I do care about you walking out of here and falling into that bastard's clutches. Either that, or finding another rooftop and this time taking your final step.'

'Why?'

'Why what?'

'Why do you care?'

The answer came easily. Bliss sat back, feeling spent, releasing a long sigh. 'Because you're a young girl, presumably under age, who should have been protected from the life you've endured. Protected by your parents, family, social services… somebody. Instead, your childhood has been tossed away, and in its place you've surrendered to what you consider to be the inevitable. You courier drugs from one shithole to another, giving yourself up to the depravities of others in order to move from one meal to the next, one bed to the next, one roof over your head to the next. It makes me sad, to tell you the truth. And it makes me bloody angry, too.'

Molly's voice crumpled in disbelief. 'With me?'

Bliss shook his head, hoping his eyes revealed the compassion he felt for her plight. 'No. Of course not. I'm angry with everyone who let you down, with every single person whose negligence allowed you to end up in this room. On that rooftop. In Ryan Endicott's flat.'

The girl nodded; her lustreless hair barely moved. 'Yet here we are. And there's fuck all you can do about it.'

'If that's the case, then I'm pissed off about that as well. But Molly, if you believe we can't avoid the inevitable outcome, do you at least accept that we can delay it? That we could and should try to prevent it happening for as long as we can?'

'I don't know what you mean,' she said, head tilted.

But you're interested, aren't you? Bliss thought. *I've got your attention now.*

He edged forward in his seat, maintaining eye contact. 'Molly, the moment our twenty-four hours are up, DI Bentley will process you out. He's not applying for additional time. Because we have no evidence to the contrary, he will reluctantly accept your assertion that you are of age, and you will be free to make your own arrangements to leave. You'll walk out of our doors and we'll turn our attention to the next person who needs us. The only thing that can stop that happening now is for you to tell us the truth about your age – or, at the very least, to tell us you are not eighteen and that you thereby request support and protection as a child.'

Bliss was fully aware this was not the case, but the YMCA woman had agreed to remain quiet as he told his carefully constructed lie. By rights, if social services agreed, the police could hold on to Molly, provided they were all convinced she was a minor. Kim Parker had elevated herself in his estimation by seeing sense in his plan to try compelling Molly to agree, rather than forcing her into a decision. Compliance was always better than confrontation.

'And what happens then?' Molly asked after a long delay. Bliss saw her gaze disappear inwards as she turned possible scenarios over in her head.

'As you're not being charged with anything, but are effectively homeless – with no family ties that we can ascertain, unless you want to tell us otherwise – Social Care will deploy their child protection team to replace the YMCA. They'll talk to the Liaison and Diversion team and meet with myself and DS Chandler here, plus my boss and possibly DI Bentley. We'll report to them and they will make a decision in your best interests, based on what we have to say.'

Rolling her eyes, Molly said, 'I still don't understand what any of that means.'

'In my opinion, it's likely they will either find a place for you in a children's home of some sort, or apply for emergency foster care.'

Molly hugged herself again, lines thickening across her forehead. 'A home? That means sticking me in with a load of other kids just like me?'

'It does,' Chandler said, speaking up for the first time. 'Whereas emergency foster care would place you with a family. DI Bliss and I have already discussed this, and given your unique situation, our recommendation will be to find you a couple with the right level of experience who currently have no other children in their home. Or at most one other, ideally a much younger kid.'

'That's to ensure you're not placed in a family where Ryan Endicott might have a contact living in the same property,' Bliss added.

'He'll find out where I am eventually.'

Bliss decided to be honest with the girl. 'We can't guarantee he won't. We have no idea who within social services or even our own ranks is susceptible to a bribe or blackmail of some sort. But let me tell you this: it will take a while for that information to trickle down, and longer still for Endicott to react to it. Meanwhile, we will endeavour to erect barriers. That means myself and DS Chandler will do our level best to have you removed from the city and transported to another county, whose child protection team will do exactly the same. And we'll repeat as many times as necessary to filter out the possibility of any details moving with you. You'll find yourself in a place where even we have no clue where you are.'

'On my own?'

'Well, in foster care – but yes. Are you not alone now?'

Molly ignored his question. 'Can't you do it?'

Bliss sensed Chandler stiffen by his side. Whether in surprise or to stop herself from laughing he did not know, but his partner was holding her breath in expectation of his response.

'You mean foster you?' Bliss asked Molly, uncertain which part of the process she was referring to.

'This emergency foster care, or whatever you said.' She looked at him as if she were asking for nothing more complicated than a drink of water.

Stifling a self-deprecating laugh, Bliss said, 'Even if I wanted to, it wouldn't be allowed, Molly. It's impractical for so many reasons.'

'What reasons? Why can't you?'

The urgency in Molly's voice unnerved Bliss. 'For starters, my job is too unpredictable. Being a Detective Inspector in charge of a busy team with a full workload is incompatible with providing the care you require. My hours are long and varied, so I'm never sure when I'll be home. My age hardly works in my favour, either. Then there's the fact that I'm a single man living alone and you're a female child, which I suspect would be another major negative in the minds of people who make such decisions.'

'But you don't know for sure, do you?' Molly argued. 'You only think those things – you haven't actually asked anybody if you can do it.'

'About the last two issues, no, I'm not a hundred percent certain. About my lifestyle not matching your needs – yes, I'm positive about that. Any request I made would be rejected out of hand.'

Dejected, the girl fixed him with a tight stare. 'And you don't want me anyway, right?'

Bliss considered his response. He did not want her. Not the responsibility, nor a complete stranger living in his house. A child, no less. And a girl, at that. What did he know about raising a kid her age? Why she had even mentioned it was beyond him, and he was struggling to form a reply. Fortunately, Chandler was in the room and she knew exactly what to say and when to say it.

'Molly, that's not what DI Bliss meant. There are genuine practical reasons why such a thing is impossible, so it's not worth wasting time even speculating. But I understand why you would ask. DI Bliss is the man who somehow managed to get you chatting up on that roof when all you wanted to do was throw yourself off. He's also the detective you chose to speak to when others made you feel like clamming up even more. Equally, you've recognised his concern for your circumstances – you've realised he wants to protect you. It's only natural that you would wonder why he isn't either prepared or able to see things through by taking care of you when you leave here. And knowing my boss like I do, Molly, I'm betting he wishes he could do exactly that. He doesn't want any harm to come to you, and normally the best way to ensure that is if DI Bliss is involved.'

'I'm not sure how much of that is true,' Bliss admitted with an appreciative smile in his partner's direction. 'But what I can be certain of is that if you do it my way, then you have a chance of a better, brighter future. To make something of your life, far away from the mess it's in right now. Not in this city where you are known, and not in London for equally obvious reasons. We'll rule out any other places you've been sent carrying drugs.'

Molly's features became pensive as she reflected on all that she had been told. 'I don't know. I've heard some seriously fucked-up shit about foster homes.'

'Much of which is probably far-fetched bullshit. Molly, I'm not denying there are some immoral people who end up fostering for all the wrong reasons. You may have to kiss a few frogs along the way. But it gets you away from here, keeps you off the streets, and if you get lucky with the couple who take you in it will make a huge difference to how the rest of your life pans out. It gives you the opportunity you need to become more than the sum of your parts. It could be the only chance you'll ever have.'

The girl huffed and put her head down. Bliss was aware of the reputation social services had, of the sexual deviants who passed themselves off as loving foster carers, and of the misery some children endured while being raised by the state. Those were the issues heavily dissected in the media, because tragic stories make for better copy than the happy ones. Yet there were plenty of heart-warming tales out there waiting to be told, accounts of abused kids removed from their parents or swept up off the streets and going on to achieve great things – which, for some, merely meant living a normal, healthy life free from ill-treatment.

'We came in here to explain your options,' Bliss finally said. 'But it has to be your decision, Molly. I intervened yesterday morning both because it was my job and because I wanted to; I saw someone worth saving up on that rooftop. I won't even try to pretend it will be easy for you, and nor do I know exactly how things will go for you in the future. Even if you get the best foster carers on the planet, you will have to make radical adjustments to the way you think, the way you approach each day, your overall outlook. I think you have it in you to do that and come out the other side. But I can't make that decision for you.'

'So what would you do?' Molly asked, looking at both of them. 'If you were me, right here and now, what would you do?'

'I'd confess to being younger than eighteen and ask for protection,' Chandler replied instantly. 'No question.'

'Same answer,' Bliss said. 'In a heartbeat.'

Molly nodded. 'Then let's do that,' she said. 'I'm Molly, I'm fifteen years old, and I want to be protected.'

TWENTY-ONE

THE STRIKE TEAM HAD spread themselves out in three separate vans parked close to the site where, until recently, a used-car business had plied its shady trade. On an industrial estate in which every third vehicle or so was a van, their mode of transport did not look out of place. One of them had taken up a position directly opposite the Baqri location, its driver having nipped into the premises to make hasty arrangements with the owners of the steel manufacturing business for them to park up. None of the undercover vehicles were visible from the garage.

Fresh from a hastily arranged session with Jennifer Howey, Detective Sergeant Bishop had earlier returned to Thorpe Wood and immediately drawn Ansari, Hunt and Gratton into a huddle.

'What I did yesterday evening was unforgivable,' he told them. 'I reacted to a throwaway comment as if it had somehow personally insulted Mia. Knowing her as I did, she would have been ashamed of my behaviour. And believe me, she would have let me know all about it, too. But as the boss said this morning, what's done is done. We move on. Anyone have a problem with that?'

No one did.

Bishop had obtained permission from Bliss to rope in both Hunt and Gratton for the sting operation. The boss believed the entire team would soon be called in on the skeletal remains op, now named Survival, which he regarded as particularly unsuitable. The feeling within CID was also one of trepidation – that if they did not hit the Baqris now, the Range Rover would be long gone by the time they got around to it. Bishop agreed; he wanted it over as much as they did, if not more so.

He was buoyed by one result, however. The thugs most likely to be responsible for murdering Ade Summerby – for little more than being a homeless man in a vulnerable situation – had been picked up early that morning and brought in to Thorpe Wood. Aged between sixteen and nineteen, the lads were known to be all bravado and spite when together in a gang, but liable to fold like lawn chairs when separated. During questioning, the interviewing officers had not mentioned Summerby's death, and three of the five young men had coughed to beating and kicking him when he refused to hand over his cash that night. Emboldened, the CPS had declared open warfare on the entire crew and all of them had been charged with murder.

Bishop was delighted. Voluntary manslaughter was the safer charge to go with because, as expected, all five solicitors had raised the spectre of the boys having no intent and suffering loss of control during the robbery. Hunt and Gratton had pushed for murder, because of the obvious resolve to cause grievous bodily harm. The agreement from CPS came as a shock, but with attacks on the homeless becoming commonplace events, a clear message needed to be sent out.

There was a sense of relief for the team as a whole, but Bishop had taken it more personally. His brother, an Iraq veteran, had experienced a period on the streets shortly after leaving the army to become a civilian again. Olly had seen, all too easily, his own flesh and blood in the badly beaten and helpless form left to die alone on the steps of a building where decisions about providing shelter for such people had been made for so long.

He had therefore entered the meeting with CID in an excellent mood. After a brief but sincere handshake with DS Ferguson, Bishop went over the simple plan for everyone involved in the sting and strike operation. Assuming they made it past the checkpoint at the gates, he and Ansari would announce themselves as detectives the moment they were inside the garage. DC Hunt had volunteered to conceal himself in the tight space behind the front seats, so Bishop and Ansari would draw those seats forward as they got out to allow greater manoeuvrability for when Hunt exited the vehicle. It was Bishop's job to find the location of the security camera monitor and gate release, at which point he would open it up again, together with the shuttered door.

Neither Bishop nor Ferguson was concerned about the possibility of firearms being on the scene. Whether Baqri and whoever else worked in the garage would give themselves up without a fight remained to be seen, so tools were the main items to worry about. If something went wrong, the units standing by outside the property would utilise multiple entry points over fences or walls to gain access. The steel shutter doors of the garage itself were another matter, but the feeling was that Bishop alone was capable of fending off a few frightened men in order to open things up. The trio of Bishop, Hunt and Ansari certainly could.

If he was being overly protective, so be it. Bishop never again wanted to see a colleague die, nor be wounded or even slightly injured, for that matter. If his back was up against the wall in defence of one of his team, Bishop had always considered himself to be the kind of man to come out with all guns blazing – metaphorically, at least – and that grim determination had only increased following Mia's death.

Ansari appeared to be having a whale of a time behind the wheel of the Nissan. Claiming a need to familiarise herself with the garish speed machine, she had nudged it up to just over the limit on the parkway roads, shrieking with unfettered joy at one point as she blew by a pearl-white Tesla. Bishop became instantly more aware of the grumbling engine sound as they nosed into the industrial estate, close to HMP Peterborough. Outside the Baqri site there was a rutted gravel drive some thirty feet in length that led up to the solid-looking gates.

'Security camera is on your side,' Bishop said to her. 'Perched on top of the brick pillar that supports the gate. Remember: don't smile, don't wave. Don't check it out, not even once. Stare straight ahead and wait.' They had covered this twice during the planning stage, but to Bishop's way of thinking, it never hurt to throw out a reminder.

If the gates didn't open, the agreement was for them to drive away and try again in an hour. Bishop swallowed thickly as Ansari drew the rumbling machine up to the stopping point, her foot on the brake. She sat with both gloved hands on the wheel; black leather gloves were a no-brainer for any respectable carjacker, and she made sure they were on full display.

Thirty minutes earlier, the local radio station had agreed to a police request to put out a fake news item about the car being taken in Westwood Park Road, a wealthy area of prime real estate. The hope was that the Baqris would hear the feature and pretty much be expecting the vehicle to pull up outside their premises.

Bishop had just started to consider driving away when a metallic groan came from the mechanism on the gate and it slowly began to swing open. The gravel drive curled away to the right, in front of the large, flat-roofed garage whose shutters remained down. He assumed there were more cameras following their progress as the gate closed behind them. Ansari had barely touched the brake before the rolled-steel shutters ground upwards, shrieking as if the movement caused them pain.

'Ready?' Bishop whispered.

'Ready,' Ansari said.

Hunt echoed the single word a moment later.

Bishop stared straight ahead. He could feel his heart thumping in his chest, and his mouth was dry. He told himself to relax, but as soon as the shutters had risen high enough to allow them entry, he realised they were screwed.

TWENTY-TWO

Sand Martin House was situated in Fletton Quays, a redeveloped complex sandwiched between the river Nene and the railway lines, on land adjoining the new buildings where both the old Whitworths' flour mill and the original gin distillery had once stood. In excess of £120 million had been poured into the quays on the site of the long-forgotten Peterborough East railway station, closed since the mid-sixties, and the modern premises were proving popular. This was the place of work to which staff from the Town Hall on Bridge Street had relocated, and it was here that Bliss and Chandler found the Social Care offices.

After being asked to wait for ten minutes, the two detectives were eventually led into a vast, airy meeting room, in which three people were already seated. Marie Collins, a squat and sturdy woman of mature years, had a pale face with stern features, and Bliss wondered if he was about to get into it with a petty bureaucrat. As the assistant service director for children's services and safeguarding, Collins was probably the most powerful person in the room.

The representative from the Liaison and Diversion Service was a man by the name of Hugh Ellis. He was young and earnest and both looked and dressed like a hipster, right down to the straggly little beard. Bliss wondered whether the tinted Quicksilver spectacles were an affectation, as he saw no obvious distortion in the lenses. Ellis's remit was to act in support of Molly, and to prepare a report for what was known as the Integrated Front Door, which encompassed the work of various child care departments including the emergency duty teams, METhub, and the Multi Agency Safeguarding Hub.

The third person on their side of the table was Kim Parker.

Collins elected to begin the conversation by saying, 'I take it you're aware of the July 2018 changes to Code C of PACE?'

'We are,' Bliss answered for them both. In truth, his knowledge was vague, but he had an idea that their situation related to the first few lines in the summary of amendments. In effect, it enforced the provision of the Police And Criminal Evidence Act guidelines that anyone who appeared to be under eighteen – and in the absence of any evidence to the contrary – should be treated as a juvenile. In such circumstances, social services would represent any individual who fell between the cracks.

Collins sniffed dismissively. 'And yet you opted to lie to Molly. In effect, you painted a rather ugly picture for her in terms of what she would face if she left your care.'

Bliss flashed an angry look at the young woman from the YMCA, but she was busy writing notes with her head down. When he confronted Collins, his tone betrayed no animosity.

'What I told Molly was the reality of the situation if she walked out. Yes, I knew there were ways of preventing that from happening – although not indefinitely, it has to be said. But in my opinion, her remaining under our influence had to be the girl's choice. If that meant lying to her, so be it. If she wants protection, it helps us to provide it.'

'Very well. We can agree to disagree on your methods, but fortunately we've arrived at a healthy place. So, the first thing to establish, logically, is whether there is also general agreement on the basic assumption that Molly is, indeed, under eighteen.' She had brought a thin folder into the meeting room, from which she now withdrew a sheet of paper. Her eyes dropped to the document for a few seconds, before moving to hold on Bliss's own gaze. 'Molly's appropriate adult, Kim Parker, believes the girl to be a minor. I gather you consider Kim to be inexperienced, Inspector Bliss, but would you like to accept her recommendation or wait for me to visit with the girl myself?'

Bliss shook his head. 'I think it'd be obvious to anybody who spent even a few minutes with her that Molly is a juvenile. If Kim is of the same mind, then of course we're happy to proceed to the next stage. Plus, I managed to get Molly to agree and state her age as fifteen.'

'Hmm. I'm not sure how that holds up legally, Inspector Bliss. From her point of view she may now accept what we offer by way of protection, but if she really is a minor then her agreement is void. However, the next stage you mention is, I gather, Molly's impending release from Thorpe Wood.'

Bliss swallowed. Now they were down to the meat of it, and he knew he had to play this part right. 'That is the situation we're facing, yes. If we took her at face value, she'd walk away without a backward glance and we'd wash our hands of her. But in addition to being a juvenile – as we've now all agreed – she's also vulnerable. Not only did she attempt to kill herself yesterday, she's also being hunted by a dangerous drug dealer. Frankly, if we were to let her go, I doubt she'd survive the night.'

Collins nodded, though her expression barely flickered. 'Our role is to protect Molly, and clearly in her current situation it's of paramount importance that we work closely with the police. We would be able to squeeze her into one of our residential children's homes, but I understand you object to that because you feel she'd be vulnerable should any of our other residents have a connection with this Endicott character.'

'That's our chief concern, yes. Endicott has a wide reach in the city, and it's no stretch to imagine Molly running into another minor who has previously worked for him – or even one who still does. I'm confident that Endicott has kids working for him who live in these homes, and by now they will be looking out for the girl.'

Collins shifted gear all the way up to haughty. 'I hope I don't need to remind you, Inspector, that the police have no say in this matter. While you are entitled to express your preferences, the final solution is ours to devise, and ours alone.'

Resisting the temptation to respond in kind, Bliss replied carefully. 'No, there's no need to remind me of that. It is our stated preference, and it seems to me the most logical and secure way to proceed. I'm convinced Molly will be exposed, and therefore extremely vulnerable if placed in a large home.'

Having made her point, Collins took a step back. 'Which leaves us with foster care. And at this late stage, we'd be talking about an emergency placement for up to seventy-two hours.'

'Ideally with carers who currently have either no other children, or a much younger child. Three days would allow us to make progress with our investigation… it removes Molly from the immediate firing line, whilst also giving us time to plan for a more enduring placement.'

'What do you mean by enduring?'

Bliss was prepared for the question, and had already planned his response. It was vital that he state his lines with care. 'I think it's critical for Molly's welfare that any long-term placement is located far away from either Peterborough or London. Before she leaves Thorpe Wood, I'd like to have one final conversation with her to identify any other places in which she has drug connections so that we can rule them out, too. In my view it's imperative that she's removed to a place where she is completely unknown. And – not to point fingers at either of our organisations – I would go as far as to suggest that any relevant communication is limited to a very small number of us, to a point where we can be relatively sure that Endicott won't be able to put a bounty on her head and have it snapped up by an adult whose job it is to protect her.'

'We realise no arrangement is foolproof,' Chandler said quickly. 'If Molly is in the system, then she resides on a database somewhere, but obtaining information that way requires specialist skills. In these early stages, it's more about reducing word of mouth.'

Bliss nodded, thankful that his DS had remembered the lines they had both practiced in the car on the way over. This meeting had to be about more than deciding upon a temporary solution for Molly. Before they headed back to HQ, he wanted a firm commitment from social care to fully engage in securing a long-term placement somewhere far away from the life she was accustomed to.

Collins glanced at Hugh Ellis, who arched his eyebrows but said nothing. A typical fence-sitter, Bliss thought. If the hipster had an opinion, he wasn't about to share it. Collins tapped a finger against her lips before finally nodding. 'This girl is vulnerable in several obvious ways – that much is clear, and I have to make allowances for that. Inspector, please arrange with Hugh here a time for us to come and collect her. In the meantime, I'll upgrade the file that the YMCA opened when they attended the girl's first interview, and get cracking on finding an emergency placement.'

'Thank you,' Bliss said, relieved to have achieved more than a semblance of security for Molly.

'It may not be easy,' Collins warned. 'In such cases, we have to advise the carers about *all* potential risks, and Molly's connection to a prominent drug dealer – especially one currently wishing her harm – is obviously a substantial threat.'

'You can't put her in a home with other kids,' Bliss reminded her, hearing the clipped urgency in his tone. 'It's far too risky.'

'You made your case, so I understand the problem, Inspector. But you also need to understand ours. We can't force carers to open their doors to such a very real danger.'

Bliss did understand. It was a tough ask. But anything less would put Molly back in the firing line. He was surprised, to say the least, by the next thing that came out of his mouth. 'How about me?' he asked. 'Is there any way she can be placed in my care for the next three days?'

'Are you a registered foster carer, Inspector Bliss?'

'No. But I'll do the appropriate paperwork right here and now if necessary.'

Collins was shaking her head. 'I'm sorry, but that's not going to happen. The procedures include initial enquiries, a home visit, and the completion of a training programme prior to approval.' The woman smiled for the first time. 'There are no shortcuts for serving police officers, Inspector. But don't fret. I said it would not be easy for us to find a couple for the girl; I didn't say it would be impossible.'

'Okay, but what happens to Molly in the meantime? She's going to be released shortly, and she needs to be moved somewhere.'

'On the advice of Miss Parker, we already have an emergency protection order in place. Believe me, one way or another, Molly will be safeguarded until the foster placement can be made.'

Realising he was behaving unreasonably, Bliss sat back in his chair. An EPO was easier than a care order to receive at short notice, so the young woman from the YMCA had done well. This was Collins's bailiwick, and he had to allow the woman to get on with her role in protecting Molly. After all, his was close to being over.

Chandler's phone emitted a tone. She took it out of her bag and read the screen, then turned to Bliss, huffing out a long sigh. 'That was a text from a friend in CID. DI Bentley has not done us any favours. He's called a halt to enquiries: Molly is no longer under arrest and is free to leave.'

'Give us an hour at least,' Bliss said, looking over at Collins. 'We'll head back to HQ now and walk Molly through our plan while she's being processed out. Assuming you won't have a home for her by then, I can easily detain her further by consent. She'll play along. Just call me when you're ready for her.'

If he'd been annoyed with Bentley before, he was now furious. It was as if the DI was toying with him, either not realising or not caring that in doing so he was also messing with Molly's life. He was glad for the ten minutes or so it would take to drive back to Thorpe Wood; perhaps by then he would have calmed down enough to only beat Bentley to a pulp instead of killing him.

TWENTY-THREE

Having already washed his hands of Molly Doe, DI Bentley had been called out to another investigation, sparing Bliss any immediate interaction with his opposite number. Instead, he spoke at length with the girl and eventually convinced her to remain at the station while Social Care made arrangements for her foster placement. After pacifying Molly, he went up to Major Crimes, arriving at the same time as the raiding party.

Bishop told the team it hadn't been anything he'd noticed that disturbed him as he, Ansari and Hunt had prepared to enter the garage. It was more a case of what wasn't there: the Range Rover. In that instant he'd had to make an instinctive decision, but in his opinion a tactical withdrawal would not have been the right move. The location was blown anyway, and his only thought had been to salvage something from the op if at all possible. At that stage, the odds remained in their favour due to the element of surprise.

He had given the 'Go' command three times as Ansari nosed them into the garage – each flat, hard cry more urgent. He'd extricated himself from the sports car with a great deal of effort, remembering to flip his seat forward as he exited. His shouts mingled with those of both his colleagues as they informed the garage workers who they were and that the premises were being raided. The shutter was still rolled up, which was one less job for him to think about. He spotted an office away to the right and headed for it. On the periphery of his vision he became aware of two figures running for the wide open entrance, but was confident they would be scooped up by the rest of the raiding party. His primary concerns had remained inside the garage.

'I managed to reach the office, located the gate button and sorted that without any aggravation. As for the Baqri brothers, neither of the buggers were there. I'm also reliably informed it's not looking good for any of the three motors that were being worked on at the time. All of them appear to be legit.'

'And no Range Rover,' Bliss said sympathetically.

Bishop shook his meaty head. 'It can't have been gone long. Our one hope is that forensics pulls a rabbit out of the hat for us. If they left behind a single VIN tag or plate, we'll be able to take a run at them. Otherwise, it was a complete bloody failure of an op.'

'It happens,' Bliss said, patting his disappointed colleague on the arm. 'If there's an old oil drum close by – one that looks as if it's been used for barbecues – my money is on anything Range Rover-related being inside it. Could be they didn't have time to fully destroy what they burned.'

Bishop raised a thumb and turned his attention to DC Gratton. 'Phil, give the crime scene manager a bell. Ask him to have someone search for that drum, please.'

'Things have moved on a bit elsewhere,' Bliss said, eyeing each of his colleagues in turn. 'We're formally regarding the human remains discovered over at Fengate as those of Lisa Pepperdine. I'm awaiting final confirmation of that from Nancy Drinkwater, but all signs point to it being her. My initial suspicion is that she came up here to find a different perspective on the Burnout case, and whatever she stumbled upon got her killed. Pen and I will be having a word with whoever at the newspaper is still around, see if we can dig up more than we currently know. We also know that, although Pepperdine's main focus was to give us a pasting, she also had it in for the far-right groups at the time. My money is on her getting too close to one of those – perhaps even a local group here in the city.'

He hated keeping information from them, but he could not afford to have the names of either Joe Flynn or Stuart Sykes dragged through the mud. Nor his own, for that matter. Stories like that spread like wildfire; the smoke and flames scattered far and wide, often unchecked. Bliss would not allow rumour and suspicion to fall upon anyone from that old investigation if it were possible to prevent it. By the time questions were asked – as they inevitably would be – he wanted to know all the answers.

'Pen and I are also still involved with the girl who stabbed and fled Ryan Endicott's clutches. It's not our op, but if it's a choice between keeping a young kid safe now and a case that's well over a decade old, I know which will be my priority. So, with the team concentrating on Pepperdine, we'll want a full background on her, plus as much as we can gather relating to the days she spent up here in 2005. The *Telegraph* is ours, so you lot need to start talking to relatives, friends, and her editors. If she had a solid story going on, then it's possible she mentioned it to someone. Bish, get some actions started. Oh, and with DCI Warburton about to take over, make sure you have your TIE forms completed for her inspection just in case.'

The Trace, Interview and Eliminate procedure was long established and widely used, even if not always to the same structure. Bliss preferred to refer to it as Trace, Interview and Evaluate, while other areas replaced Interview with Implicate. It was essentially the same set of protocols, though some recorded them better than others.

'What if she'd already sold her story, boss?' Ansari asked. 'Or the idea of it, at least.'

'It's worth looking into, Gul. I doubt it, because no editor came forward to shout it from the rooftops when she went missing, but spare it an hour if you need to.'

'How about the jewellery?' DC Hunt said. 'Any joy there?'

'No, but you can certainly make sure that gets moved on for trace and latents in a timely manner. I'm told it was all bunched up, probably in a pocket. From what I understand, that usually meant she was either meeting someone she didn't know or trust, or was heading into a dodgy area. If she died where she was found, that's the second part of that equation covered, because it's not somewhere I'd like to linger, especially after nightfall.'

'What about a purse, or a bag?' Chandler prompted. 'She may have carried a notepad in her coat pocket, but I'd still expect to find a bag nearby, with a purse inside it. If they aren't found, does that open it up to a potential robbery? A chancer grabs what he can, not realising the real swag is tucked away elsewhere.'

Bliss smiled and nodded with satisfaction. He enjoyed this stage of a case: the saturated hypotheses, questions and often answers bouncing from team member to team member. There were no airs or graces, certainly no egos; if you thought it, you said it. He liked Chandler's idea, as he'd not considered the bag. Nor a coat, for that matter. Modern clothing always left behind remnants, be they plastic or metal hooks or buttons.

'Check and see if one was found,' he said. 'Now that you've mentioned it, I'm surprised the jewellery wasn't inside a bag.'

'I'm not. In a robbery, what are they most likely to snatch? No, if I were to remove my jewellery for safety I'd have somewhere more secretive to keep it. Perhaps a small pocket inside my skirt or trousers.'

'There were remnants of clothing found on her. Anything natural would be gone, but synthetics and leather must still be in place. I'm expecting a full report later on.'

Bliss was happy enough with the progress being made on operation Survival, though he remained anxious about exactly how and where it would start to impinge on the Burnout case and the senior officers involved. Thirteen years was a long time, and memories were going to be shaky, so there was every chance that Pepperdine had not been about to meet a senior member of the team at all. Still, she had been killed for a reason, and it remained his job to find out why.

TWENTY-FOUR

When Bliss's mobile rang, the caller's identity surprised him. After the briefing, he had returned to his office, hoping to type up a report on Molly and the meeting over at the Social Care offices. But he wasn't great with words, and everything he wrote came across as stilted and overly formal. So, when he heard his phone going off, he was glad for the break from the computer. Until he saw who was calling. For a couple of seconds he panicked, caught between gathering his wits to talk and letting it go to voicemail. He felt like a teenager again, instead of the drooling old fool he was.

'Hi, Emily,' he said after eventually thumbing the answer symbol. 'Do you have some information for me?'

Yeah, that's it, Jimmy. No 'Hi, how are you?' No 'Hi, I'm so glad you called.' Assume she's calling about business and that way you won't be disappointed.

'Oh, sorry – no. Were you expecting anything from me?' Emily sounded hesitant, as if she was already regretting calling him.

'Not that I know of. I was… I wasn't expecting to get a call from you, is all.'

'Well, if I'm being perfectly honest, I called on the spur of the moment. It's just that since yesterday I've found myself thinking about you. To be blunt, despite the awful circumstances, I was very pleased to see you.'

A warm glow lit up the inside of his stomach. His smile was immediate, and he took a beat before responding. 'I have to say the feeling is mutual. After everything that happened earlier in the year, I wasn't quite sure if I'd left things with you in the right way. I should have done more in the weeks and months after you lost your husband.'

'Oh, Jimmy, you mustn't think like that. If it hadn't been for you, I might never have found out what happened to Simon.'

'If it weren't for me you might never have found out Simon wasn't Simon at all.' His words spilled out much faster than his mind could filter them, and he bit down on his lip too late.

'But that was also something I needed to know,' Emily said, seemingly unfazed. 'Jimmy, everything you did for me at the time – everything you put yourself through, including the favours you asked for on my behalf, and even welcoming me into your home – you should know that I very much appreciated it all. Genuinely I did.'

'That's nice to hear, but it's not only the case and its consequences I'm referring to. You were in shock, still grieving, and I pretty much let you get on with it without knowing who else was there for you.'

'I think the fact that I ended up staying with you for a while tells you nobody else was there for me, Jimmy. But you surely had to realise that was my choice. Whether you remember it or not, you did make yourself available to me. You offered a shoulder to cry on, and I shunned it. Not because I wasn't appreciative, nor because I didn't want anything to do with you, but because I wasn't sure I deserved it.'

Bliss frowned. 'Why would you even think that, Emily?'

'Because I was the one who gave up on us all those years ago. You had no choice but to go back down to London, and in spite of everything we discussed and the arrangements we put in place for a long-distance relationship, I was the one who bailed on us. I know I hurt you, and so even though I came to you for help when Simon died, I didn't think I deserved your compassion.'

'Emily, all of that is in the past. We're both very different people now. We had our separate lives, time moved on and it took us with it. Of course I wanted to support you after your loss. You were – you are – absolutely worthy of any compassion I possess.'

After a momentary pause, she said tentatively, 'Seeing you again out there in that field yesterday brought back so many vivid memories of the one and only case we worked together.'

Bliss smiled to himself. 'Given our respective jobs, I guess it's hardly surprising that we would meet again under similar circumstances. Which reminds me: was it a good find for you and your team?'

'It was amazing. Five bodies in all. A family, we believe.'

'Any clue as to why they were so far outside the perimeter of the Flag Fen site?'

'We won't know for sure until we've completed all our tests on the bones, but one theory is that they may have all suffered from the same disease, perhaps a virus of some kind. It's even possible that the actual cause of their illness – if that is why they went off to die – was misdiagnosed. A common cause of severe illness was kidney disease caused by parasites – giant kidney worms up to a metre long. We found that most prevalent out at the Must Farm settlement due to the proximity of freshwater marshes, but it wouldn't have been uncommon at Flag Fen, either.'

Bliss raised an eyebrow. 'Must Farm? I don't think I know that one.'

'It's on the way out to Whittlesey. Close to the McCain's factory. You would have gone past it many times, I'm sure. That actually became our best-preserved Bronze Age site so far.'

Bliss loved hearing that familiar enthusiasm. When they first worked together, he recalled questioning the depth of her immersion into the investigation, her fervour spilling over into the terrible case of a young woman who had been used and abused by those sworn to protect her. But it was a relationship that led first to familiarity, and then affection. Emily brought something out in him he had not felt since the death of his wife, and he had suffered following their breakup more than he had ever cared to admit. He couldn't help wondering if she had called hoping to rekindle those feelings.

Then he remembered that he had arranged to take Sandra Bannister out for a meal. He thought they both understood it was about more than repaying a favour, but there was nothing more than that between them yet; certainly nothing that could not be undone. On the other hand, he was not sure about taking what would be a major step back with Emily. He had long ago accepted their time together had come and gone, yet her voice had reawakened emotions still living beneath his surface.

Realising he had not spoken for an uncomfortable amount of time, Bliss quickly said, 'I'm so glad I arrived on site in time to see you again. Bumping into you was so much more natural than if I had phoned you.'

'Would you have, though?'

'What, phoned? As it happens, I have given it some thought recently. It occurred to me that an appropriate amount of time had passed, and maybe I could call and ask how you were doing, how you were managing, that sort of thing. Just chat without any awkwardness.'

'Merely to find out how I was, or in the hope of something more?'

Bliss swallowed. There was the question, starkly put. He responded in the only way he could. 'I'll be honest with you, Emily – I don't know the answer to that. I'd like to say I've not given us much thought over the years, but that'd be a lie. On each occasion, however, I've come to the conclusion that what's done is done. Never go back, right?'

'Yet still you wanted to call.'

'Yes. If only to put an end to the wondering once and for all.'

'And so here we are. I'm the one who called you. What do you think we ought to do about that, Jimmy?'

His chest rose and fell. Both palms felt sweaty. That awkward teen was back again. 'I reckon the very least we owe ourselves is a conversation. Somewhere neutral, somewhere quiet, somewhere we can just… talk.'

Emily was quick to respond. 'I know you no longer have Bonnie and Clyde, but do you ever still stroll around the lakes at Ferry Meadows?'

'When I can. I even find the December cold and rain bracing sometimes. How about you?'

'I like it just fine. And after all, what harm can it do? No expectations, no recriminations. We walk, we talk, and at the end we decide if we have something worth pursuing – or not.'

Bliss's smile broadened. It was obvious to him now that she had experienced similar emotions. Whatever fears he had about not going back, or the possibility of shadows from the past forming a barrier between them, he also owed this to himself.

'You know what I do for a living,' he said. 'And you know what I'm like when I'm doing it. I'm in the middle of a couple of things right now, and of course there will be something following on behind. But how about, in between, I give you a call and we'll make arrangements?'

'Sounds great.'

'I'm happy you think so.' Bliss licked his lips and heaved a long sigh. His mind drifted back to the walks they had taken, the time they had spent together, and the life they had begun to form. In relation to the years and months he had been circling the drain on this planet, their star had thrust itself skyward and exploded in the blink of an eye. Yet it had left its mark upon him, and he knew better than most that not all scars are visible. 'And Emily?' he said. 'I'm very much looking forward to it.'

TWENTY-FIVE

BLISS HAD BEEN OBSERVING the quaint ivy-festooned cottage for nigh on forty minutes before the first set of car headlights caught his attention. He had found a nice spot in a pub car park, from which he had an unobstructed view of the curving road in both directions. The cottage stood no more than a hundred yards away, and there was no easy access to the rear of the property in which Molly was hopefully tucked up in bed and sleeping off the past two days of stress and strain.

He and Chandler had accompanied Social Care earlier in the evening when they transported the girl to the home of her temporary carers, Lance and Abigail Paxton. Bliss had immediately taken to the childless couple, both of whom were at pains to put everyone at their ease. Even Molly – sullen throughout the drive over – had perked up after spending a few minutes in their company. When he and his partner had left, she gave them a smile and a nod; the look of gratitude in her eyes spoke more eloquently than any words.

Four hours later he was back – this time tucked out of sight – watching, waiting, and fretting about how Molly and the Paxtons were getting along, and concerned about Endicott discovering the whereabouts of this hastily arranged accommodation. Such were

Bliss's anxiety levels that he became tense when the headlights first flared in the distance, his muscles remaining taut as the bluish-white wash of colour grew bigger in the sprawling darkness.

Alert to all possibilities, he watched in silence as a light-coloured Kia SUV rolled by and kept on going, around the bend and then up and over the hill, until its taillights were nothing more than a red smudge on the distant horizon. Before they had completely disappeared from view, he caught a second flicker of headlights heading his way; this time, they turned off the main road and into a side street.

Surrounded only by the night once more, Bliss settled back in his seat. It groaned beneath his shifting weight, the sound leaving him less than impressed. In June he'd had to replace his two-year-old Insignia with a new model after it had ended up in a lake during a chase. Six months in, and already the new car seat mechanism was complaining. Bliss was still thinking about that when he became aware of a presence moving swiftly and silently through the darkness towards him. A face appeared at his nearside window, and he cursed himself for not reacting sooner.

'I could have been anybody,' Penny Chandler said as she clambered in alongside him, closing the passenger door with a soft click. 'A tooled-up Endicott instead of me and you'd be in trouble, old man.'

'How the bloody hell did you know I'd be here? And where I'd be parked up?'

'I saw you eyeball the pub earlier when we drove by. I knew you wouldn't be able to resist coming back out here tonight and sitting on the place.'

'I was feeling restless. I took a drive and ended up here.'

Chandler fixed him with one of her speciality doubting smiles. 'Of course you did. Just keep telling yourself that.'

'You were in the motor that turned off down that side street a couple of minutes ago, I take it?'

'Yep. Just shows you how easy you are to predict sometimes. I was so confident I'd find you here, I didn't even have to check the place out first.'

Bliss blew out his lips. 'Well, what else was I supposed to do? Mr and Mrs Paxton are a lovely couple, but in some ways that only makes matters worse. That's three of them in danger now, not just Molly.'

'So… what, you're going to guard them for the next three days?'

'Just the nights.'

'And work during the day, leaving you to sleep when exactly?'

'It's Thursday now, so… Sunday.'

Chandler shook her head in despair. They were silent for a few minutes before she spoke up. 'So, tell me, Jimmy, would you have taken her in if you'd had to?'

'You mean if they'd let me.' Bliss gave himself some time to ponder. 'I wouldn't have wanted to, insofar as I don't exactly relish the prospect of having a fifteen-year-old kid under my feet. Plus there's the language barrier to consider.'

'What language barrier?'

'I don't speak teen. On the other hand, having played a part in preventing her from taking a dive off a rooftop, I'd do pretty much anything to keep her safe.'

'Your answer is yes, then.'

He grinned. 'I suppose it is.'

'There's no shame in admitting it. You feel for her, you want to protect her.'

'My saviour complex,' he said softly. He told her Jennifer Howey's thoughts concerning his protective nature.

'That's the problem with shrinks,' Chandler said. 'They boil everything down to a condition of one sort or another so's they can understand it. Label it. To them, things can never just be what they appear to be.'

'Which is exactly what I told her.'

'Great minds think alike.'

'Fools seldom differ,' they said in unison.

Following a brief lull in conversation, during which they watched another vehicle breeze by them and away out of sight, Chandler nodded towards the cottage. 'Do you actually believe Endicott would be stupid enough to turn up here?' she asked.

'He's desperate enough, certainly. Angry enough, too, I shouldn't wonder.' Bliss thought about Molly wounding the dealer, wondering how much more painful it had been to his pride. 'That kid has a price on her head now, make no mistake.'

'The Paxtons are incredibly brave taking on that kind of responsibility. Not only do they have a real tearaway on their hands, but one of the city's most notorious villains is after her blood. I'm not sure I'd be too keen.'

Bliss nodded. 'People like them think only of the child's welfare; they wouldn't be on the emergency register otherwise. It's not about the money, of that we can be sure.'

A moment later, Chandler shifted sideways in her seat and said, 'What is it about you and this particular kid, Jimmy? Seriously, why are you going out on a limb for her?'

Bliss gave himself time to prepare a response. 'I'm not sure. Maybe it's because she's the first person I've saved in such circumstances, and I want to keep her alive long enough to start making different choices. She's like one of those bedraggled mutts you see on the RSPCA adverts on TV.'

She smiled at him, her eyes wide and perceptive. 'You'd have made a great dad to some lucky kid.'

He licked his lips. 'I'm not so sure about that. To be a great parent you need to be present in the child's life.'

'Your work ethic would have changed if you and Hazel had had children. You would have adapted. Plenty of people do.'

'True. But all the ifs and buts and maybes count for nothing in the end, Pen. Speaking of parenthood, though, how are things between you and Anna?' He knew that Chandler now maintained regular contact with her daughter via social media and spoke to her regularly by phone.

'Great,' Chandler said now. As ever, when she thought about Anna her face lit up. 'Couldn't be better, in fact. We've arranged for her to travel over at Christmas.'

'That's terrific news,' he said. He was delighted for his partner, who had endured her loss for so many years with enormous dignity, never once giving up her search or her annual pilgrimage to Turkey to hunt for the girl.

'She's looking forward to getting to know you better. Or will you be going over to see your mum?'

'I'm not sure. Depends on the shift rotas. Either way, I'll make sure I'm around for at least a day to catch up with Anna. Just keep her on a tight lead… I don't think the young men of Peterborough are quite ready for someone so exotically beautiful as your daughter.'

Chandler's smile broadened. 'Oi, hands off, old man. If I'm too young for you, my offspring certainly is.'

'Can't a man pay an innocent compliment these days?' He laughed.

Her eyes narrowed. 'I'm not convinced anything about you is entirely innocent, but I reckon even an old perv like you respects certain boundaries.'

'Thanks. I think.'

'And to bring us back to the here and now, tell me honestly: this chemistry you seem to have with Molly – is there not even the tiniest bit of it that feels paternal?'

Bliss thought about that, and as he did so something solid and uncomfortable pressed down on his chest. His two dogs, Bonnie and Clyde, had been like children to him, even more so following the death of his wife. As for himself and Hazel having their own kids, it had always struck him as a surefire way of inviting pain and misery into their lives. Great joy, too, of course; pride as well, and an overwhelming love. But his mind had also taken him to darker regions of the human experience. Hazel had once told him his reluctance was because of all the things he had seen, the harsh reality fate had in store for some. His father had agreed, having endured it himself.

'I genuinely don't see it as paternal,' he eventually replied. 'I think of it – if I think of it at all – as simply human. This is why I disagree with Dr Howey – one of the reasons, anyway. I don't believe I have a saviour complex, because I don't want to save Molly. I want to protect her so that I never have to save her. To me, they're not the same thing at all.' He shrugged. 'If that makes any sense.'

Chandler nodded thoughtfully and then changed the subject. 'Flynn was in good form earlier, don't you think?'

The pair of them had joined their old boss for a drink and a meal at the Paper Mills in Wansford, on the western edge of Peterborough. Without the barricades of rank standing between them, the trio spoke with abandon; none of them had anything to hide, and no subject was considered taboo. The old days were discussed at length, provoking both laughter and melancholy.

'He was,' Bliss agreed. 'Did you find anything odd about that?'

'In what way?'

'Something dragged Flynn back into the city today. My call yesterday sparked his decision, but there's no way that alone would compel him to drive over here to discuss it in the way he did. Anything he had to say could just as easily have been said over the phone. Plus, I got the impression he was more keen to listen than speak.'

'Don't tell me you think he has anything to do with Lisa Pepperdine going missing.'

'I won't – because I don't. But he may have his own suspicions.'

'You mean about Sykes?'

Bliss shrugged. 'Possibly. Or even me. If he knows it wasn't him, who would you put money on to have met with a freelance journalist back then – me or Stuart?'

'Neither,' Chandler said, shaking her head emphatically.

'But if you had to choose one of us? Suspect one of us?'

'I don't, and I won't play that game.'

He smiled. 'Good. Because I know it wasn't me, and I don't believe it was Sykes, either.'

His partner frowned. 'But that leaves nobody.'

'I'm not so sure about that, Pen. I realise language isn't everything, but when Sandra Bannister first told me the story, she said Pepperdine had apparently mentioned meeting with a high-ranking officer. Not detective. Officer. So what if she meant a uniform?'

'Were there any working the Burnout case?'

'Actually, yes. Because of the arsons and the connection to immigrants and asylum seekers, the man I'm thinking of liaised on a daily basis with Stuart Sykes.'

'Who?'

'Robert Marsh. Chief Inspector Marsh.'

Wagging a finger in his direction, Chandler said, 'Yes, I remember him now. He moved on about a year or so later, didn't he? Got a posting down on the south coast somewhere. I suppose if we're ruling out the Major Crimes unit, then he's not a bad shout.'

Bliss was of the same opinion, and not only because he didn't want it to be someone closer to the team. He had no desire for Pepperdine's meeting to have been with anyone based at Thorpe

Wood, nor anywhere else in the city for that matter. But neither was there any denying Marsh's reputation at the time as a man looking to establish a name for himself. One who enjoyed seeing his name splashed across the pages of the daily newspapers.

TWENTY-SIX

Like most regional newspapers, the *Peterborough Telegraph* survived because of its online presence. Having moved to its current location at Unex House opposite the Rivergate car park, in the same road as DS Chandler's own apartment block, the paper had streamlined and modernised, Suite B being one of several units in the two-building complex. Bliss had known London's thriving Fleet Street newspaper empires well, but those halcyon days of limitless budgets were now the smouldering embers of a funeral pyre forged by the impact of technology and a rampant twenty-four-hour news cycle.

Sandra Bannister met them in the reception area. Bliss noticed how frosty Chandler's greeting was as she and the journalist shook hands, and he wondered how much of that was due to his own uncommon enthusiasm towards the woman. Without further comment, the reporter led them into a large glass-walled conference room, in which three people were already waiting.

One of the two men looked to be roughly Bliss's own age, though he was a great deal heavier and seemed to be clinging desperately to the few remaining wisps of grey hair swept across his scalp. His suit was showing signs of neglect, and had likely been inexpensive when it was first purchased. Bannister introduced him as Andrew Regis, one of the newspaper's senior editors. The second man, Mark Southern, was considerably younger, probably closer to Chandler's age. He wore a thin leather jacket over a crew-neck sweater, neatly pressed Chinos and snazzy socks. *To prove he's a character*, Bliss thought, *which means he isn't*. Janis Ward, the third member of staff, was clearly the powerhouse among them, seated at the head of the rectangular table and peering disapprovingly over the frame of her spectacles.

Sandra Bannister had prepared the trio for the two detectives' agreed line of questioning, but remained in the room as Bliss opened up the meeting.

'Thank you all for agreeing to speak to us off the record like this,' he said, making sure to remind them that nothing they said at the meeting could be revealed to the public. 'I'm hoping we won't have to keep you too long. Just to put you in the picture, at this time we have no formal identification of the remains uncovered yesterday at Fengate. Post mortem results and associated reports were due in last night, but they are running late. Even so, we firmly believe the remains to be those of Lisa Pepperdine; both the approximate burial date and the items of jewellery discovered with the body point to it being her, though we may yet be proven wrong. Assuming there are no surprises, then, what we are looking for from the three of you is some insight into the woman you met and came to know back in the spring of 2005.'

Ward, who until that moment had looked like she had a nasty smell under her nose and regarded the two police detectives as the source, leaned forward across the table and narrowed her gaze.

'You do realise how long ago that was, don't you?' she said, a sneer puckering her mouth.

'I do,' Bliss snapped back. 'I got my maths A-level, so it was relatively easy to calculate.' He hadn't, but she didn't need to know that.

'And you expect us to recall specific conversations we had with an individual whom we barely knew in the middle of the last decade?'

'We don't *expect* anything,' Chandler jumped in, her lips curled and her eyes blazing. 'We're here asking questions and hoping for answers. I hear what you're saying, Mrs Ward, but Lisa was a visiting journalist, one who wrote features for the nationals, here during a time of great scandal, fear and tension within this city. Frankly, I'd be more surprised if you *didn't* remember her well.'

That put the supercilious woman in her place, Bliss thought, nodding his agreement.

'Look,' he said, 'we're not after state secrets here. What we'd like from you are your impressions, recollections… any scraps of conversation you can recall. I know already that one of those memories points to the possibility of Lisa meeting with one of our own, but we would very much like to know who that was. The where and when, plus anything at all which will allow us to gain a perspective on her last movements.'

Regis nodded eagerly. 'And we'll do everything in our power to help, Inspector Bliss. None of us are without compassion. However, you have to realise that Lisa was little more than a fleeting presence in our lives, so our recollections may be hazy.'

'I fully appreciate that. Let's just see what we can pull out, okay? Now, which of you liaised most with Lisa?'

'That would probably have been me,' Mark Southern said. The fingers of one hand massaged the knuckles of the other. 'I was the most junior of the three of us. And while you're right to point out that Lisa was writing pieces for the nationals, we hardly welcomed her with open arms as a rising star from the capital, here to show us all how it was done. That said, she was one of us…'

'Which means you two swapped information,' Chandler said, getting to the meat of it in a way Bliss admired.

'To a certain degree.'

Bliss had a sense the response was guarded. 'What does that mean?' he asked.

'Only that we journalists are extremely protective of our sources and the information we get from them. Lisa mostly wanted an insight into local people, and I was perfectly happy to provide it as long as none of it conflicted or crossed paths with my own leads. I think it's safe to say we both had the same level of reluctance to reveal all.'

'What exactly was the thrust of her own story?'

'She didn't believe enough was being done to find the arsonists. In her opinion, this was because the victims were immigrants or asylum seekers.'

'To which your response was…?'

The man looked up sharply. 'I was blunt, Inspector. I told her I disagreed. What's more, I also let her know that this newspaper did not officially agree, either. None of which appeared to dissuade her. She insisted on continuing down that same path while we focussed on the events themselves.'

'We regarded what she was doing as sensationalism,' Janis Ward said, sniffing and turning her head slightly to one side. 'The woman veered between raging at the right-wing groups for promoting discrimination, and your lot for letting them get away with it. She ignored the actual tragedies – the people killed, injured and made homeless – instead indulging in wild speculation and passing it off as news.'

'Clearly you didn't approve,' Chandler said.

'We report the news. We did then and we do now. We will seek it out where we believe it exists, but we do not do so with the intention of creating sordid headlines. I got the impression Ms Pepperdine was mostly interested in getting a centre-page spread in the *News of the World*, even if her story had little basis in reality. I regarded her as someone who did not want to earn her reputation by following traditional avenues. I don't like to speak ill of the dead, you understand, but to my mind Lisa Pepperdine was a typical example of the gutter press I so despise.'

'Lisa did seem to think she was on the fast track to fame and fortune,' Southern confirmed. 'I remember her telling me that the story behind the story was often more interesting.'

'And on that occasion, the backstory was how the authorities didn't care about foreigners being murdered,' Bliss said. The thought angered him. He understood it was an impression some members of the public had – especially when it came to the police – but they were wrong. He turned his attention back to the three journalists around the table. 'Which brings me to what we understand was perhaps her final conversation with any of you. She said she had arranged a meeting with a senior officer working the case. Which of you did she say that to?'

Andrew Regis cleared his throat and said, 'That was me. Lisa popped in to ask for any current updates, and while we were chatting she told me about her meeting. She was extremely upbeat and excited about it.'

'She mention a name?'

The man was furiously chewing gum. Bliss had noticed him feeding stick after stick into his mouth while the others were talking. The sweet, sickly smell of Juicy Fruit wafted over from his side of the table. Perhaps he was trying to stop smoking, or had simply formed a habit. Either way, Bliss disapproved of all the lip smacking going on.

'No. That was where she drew the line when it came to exchanging information.'

'But she definitely said it was with a high-ranking officer?'

'Yes. I remember that specific exchange particularly well.'

'Not detective? She didn't say a high-ranking detective?'

Regis sighed. 'It was a long time ago, but like I said, that conversation stuck in my mind, mainly because I had never seen her that ebullient before. I can't swear to it, but yes – I'm as sure as I can be that she said officer and not detective.'

'For what it's worth,' Ward said, tossing back her wavy brown hair with a flick of her head, 'that's precisely how Andrew related it to me, as far as I am able to recall.'

Bliss paused and glanced at Chandler. He had already admitted that language was not all-important, but he wondered if someone like Lisa Pepperdine would have failed to be precise when describing her forthcoming meeting. He frowned. That was unlikely – unless she had been deliberately vague or misleading in an attempt to throw the *Evening Telegraph* reporters off the scent. In which case, both Flynn and Sykes were firmly back in the frame.

'Are you suggesting it wasn't anybody from CID or Major Crimes?' Ward pressed him. 'That in fact Lisa was scheduled to meet with a uniformed police officer?'

'You were talking about an officer but thinking detective at the time?' Bliss suggested, ignoring her question.

The three journalists exchanged glances. Each of them nodded. 'That's what we assumed, yes,' Southern admitted. 'Only one uniformed officer ever attended media briefings. Other than him, it was detectives all the way.'

'And he was?' Chandler asked.

'Chief Inspector Marsh.'

That name again. Bliss took a breath, composing himself. He had a decision to make, but it came easily to him. 'We're convinced Lisa was attempting to lead you astray,' he lied. 'There were only three detectives she could possibly have been referring to, and none of us arranged to speak with her. There would have been no logical reason to have done so.'

Southern leaned back and stretched an arm out across the back of his chair. 'I have to confess, we all eventually reached the same conclusion. I don't think any of us were convinced she had a lead at all.'

Bliss chose to mention something that had been bothering him. 'Despite her approach being one you clearly all disagreed with, Lisa was one of your own. You still reacted that way around her, I take it – that she was, at the end of the day, a colleague of sorts?'

'Of course,' Ward said dismissively.

'Then why the lack of interest when you learned she had disappeared rather than moved on?'

'I don't know what you mean.' Her birdlike mouth twitched then pursed after speaking.

'What I mean is: one of your own was last heard of here in your own city, in your own offices, and yet you covered the story as if she were like any other missing person.'

It was Regis who filled the resulting awkward silence, his jowls quivering as he shifted uncomfortably in his chair. 'Inspector Bliss, the simple truth is that Lisa Pepperdine came and went like a ship in the night, and her absence left us unaffected. I recall a staff meeting at which the issue of her disappearance was discussed, and the general take on it was that she would eventually turn up, basking in the spotlight.'

Bliss sensed the man couldn't care less, either, even now that Pepperdine's fate had been revealed.

'And afterwards?' Chandler prompted. 'When she failed to materialise and was later legally regarded as dead?'

'The nationals ran with it for a while. We settled on an appeal for information.'

'But there was no journalistic investigation into her disappearance?'

'No. You have to bear in mind that we are a city-based newspaper and we largely focus on local news. Lisa Pepperdine was one of us in respect of being a reporter, but not a Peterborian, Inspector Bliss.'

'So, no theories?' he asked. 'I'd imagine in a job like yours, as in my own line of work, there's a fair amount of speculation.'

'A little,' Ward confessed. 'But it was idle. If we referred to her at all, I think it was still in anticipation of her eventual return.'

'Well, you were wrong about that,' Bliss pointed out. 'It's looking increasingly likely that she never even left.'

That was pretty much it. Nobody was able to offer anything further of note.

A few minutes later, as she and Bliss walked across the road towards the car park, Chandler was quick to question him about his earlier lie.

'I take it you were attempting to divert them,' she said. 'That you didn't want them sniffing anything out, especially regarding Chief Inspector Marsh.'

'Precisely. They've disregarded it all these years, and we don't need them poking their noses anywhere close to where we're going to be looking next.'

'So you like Marsh for this?'

'The meeting with Pepperdine?' Bliss nodded. 'I think it's a distinct possibility. As for anything above and beyond that, I'd like to think not. It's a shitstorm I don't want any part of.'

'I reckon those three bought it. I'm not quite so confident when it comes to your girlfriend, though.'

'My girlfriend?'

'Oh, come on. I clocked the looks you were giving each other. Especially when she said goodbye a moment ago.'

'There were no looks.'

'Yes there were. All dewy-eyed and yet at the same time furtive.'

'You're wrong. Mutual respect is what you saw between me and Sandra, and any other inference is a result of your warped mind overheating. By the way, good job confronting them head-on back there. I was proud of you. Reminded me of me in some ways.'

'Cheers. But don't change the subject.'

Bliss's phone rang and he cut Chandler off by answering it.

'Bish,' he said. 'What have you got for me?'

'She's gone, boss!' DS Bishop shouted. 'Molly's been taken.'

TWENTY-SEVEN

The night before, Bliss and Chandler had each taken turns to grab some sleep while the other kept watch over the Paxtons' cottage. Other than Bliss's snoring and his partner's somnolent chatter and cute little chipmunk noises, the hours passed without incident. They left at dawn believing Molly was secure until nightfall. But Ryan Endicott had been busy. He was also proving to be unpredictable, striking during the day rather than waiting for the cover of darkness.

Mr and Mrs Paxton were both unharmed, but still in shock and visibly unnerved by the time Bliss and his DS arrived at the scene. As they sat at their breakfast bar, Lance Paxton described in a rush of words what had happened an hour ago.

It had all been over in less than a minute. A middle-aged woman dressed smartly in a navy-blue pin-striped business suit and carrying a clipboard had presented herself at their front door, which he had opened only after scrutinising her through the door's central glass panel. She flashed a warm smile and said she'd like a word about plans for a proposed supermarket development. As he slipped off the security chain, the woman stepped aside and four masked men burst in. Each of them carried a large machete.

One of the figures rested a sharp steel edge against Paxton's throat and asked where the girl was, his request echoed by the large man who stood on the threshold, barring any bid to escape. When Lance tried telling them he had no idea who they were talking about, the blade had bitten into his neck and drawn a thin line across it. He admitted now that the warm trickle of blood had caused him to freeze.

By this time, one of the intruders had forced Abigail Paxton out of the kitchen, where she had been baking cupcakes, and dragged the terrified woman into the hallway to join her husband. One of the masked men spoke up, telling them that if either of them lied again the other would be badly wounded and permanently marked. The voice was raised this time; seconds later, Molly appeared at the top of the stairs.

'Get your fucking evil hands off them!' she roared, making her way down the staircase without taking her eyes off the figure holding Lance. 'It's me you're after, you twisted fuck. They've done nothing wrong.'

'All we want is you,' the man said to her.

'I'll come with you. If you leave these people alone, I won't even make a fuss.'

Lance Paxton related all this to Bliss, Chandler, DS Bishop and DC Ansari. He shook his head in wonder. 'That girl hardly knew us,' he said, his voice low and unsteady. His hands were still trembling. 'And yet she gave herself up so that those men wouldn't hurt us. Can you imagine…?'

'I can. That kid has spirit,' Bliss said. His heart went out to the girl, whose fate now lay beyond his control. The thought brought tension to every muscle. He felt hot blood rip through his head, causing an ache at the base of his skull.

'As they led Molly out of the door, I told her how sorry I was. That we'd let her down, you know? She had this curious look on her face, as if she didn't quite understand. Then she shook her head and said we had nothing to apologise for, but that she did because she'd involved us in her fight.'

'She slipped away with them as if she'd known it was going to happen,' Abigail said, twisting a small gold pendant at her throat. 'Like it was inevitable somehow.'

'She probably thought exactly that,' Chandler suggested. 'Girls like Molly have seen and done it all. They've learned to expect nothing from life other than torment and misery.'

'Did you happen to see the vehicle they drove away in?' Bishop asked, moving anxiously from foot to foot. The sharp creases in his face revealed his anger.

'Yes. It was a maroon Ford minivan. The numberplate started with LS10. I'm sorry, I couldn't get the rest.'

Bishop thanked him. 'That means it was registered in Stanmore, eight years ago. It won't give us the owner, but it's still helpful. Anything at all on the four masked men?'

Mr Paxton took his time to reflect before nodding. 'I'd say three of them were of average height, slim build – but the other was a beast of a man. Tall and wide, though he did nothing more aggressive than stand there holding his machete. The first to speak, the one who had hold of me, was the smallest.'

'Accent?'

'Oh, locals. Fenlanders, I'd bet money on it.'

'You didn't happen to catch a glimpse of skin colour, did you? Hands? Neck?'

The Paxtons both shook their heads. They appeared confident, despite still suffering the after-effects of the traumatic incident.

'But you can provide a description of the woman who knocked,' Bliss said, nodding reassuringly. 'That will be a great help to us.'

Guilt pressed against him, sharp corners feeling as if they might pierce his flesh. He had not suggested that the Paxtons care for

Molly, but he had approved the decision. His presence in the pub car park overnight was evidence of his misgivings, and his presence here now told him he should have listened to himself more closely. Leaving Molly with this couple had put them both in the firing line, and Bliss wished he had done more to protect them.

'I know you're trying to cheer us up, Inspector,' Lance said, offering a tentative smile. 'But I will never forgive myself for being duped like that. We were on high alert, warned by both yourselves and social services, but seeing that woman at the door completely threw me. She looked so ordinary. Had she been younger, or dressed differently, I would never have opened the door, but she was so… believable.'

'That's understandable,' Bliss told him. 'It's what they were counting on. Look, I'm going to leave you with one of my detectives here, and I'd like you to provide a more detailed description to them, but is there anything about her that you can remember as being immediately obvious? Besides her age and style of clothing, I mean.'

'I'm pretty sure she was eastern European,' Abigail said. She thought about it some more and then gave a grim nod. 'I didn't see her, but I heard her voice from the kitchen. She was trying her best to hide it, I think, but she sounded Polish, Lithuanian, something like that.'

'Yes,' her husband said, nodding emphatically. 'Now that Abby mentions it, I can hear her voice again in my head and I'd agree she was Polish. She had pale skin, short blonde hair. She was quite tall and slender, though she did have quite wide shoulders. A swimmer's build, you might say.'

Bliss nodded. 'Okay. That's great stuff. It gives us plenty to work with. Thank you. Thank you both.'

Other than the gratitude, which was heartfelt, he didn't mean any of it. A vehicle that was probably ablaze in a field somewhere as they spoke, four unidentified masked figures, and an eastern

European woman in an area that had seen the highest increase of immigration from that region in the entire country. No – none of it was great, nor plenty. It was nigh on useless.

On the other hand, Bliss mused, none of it mattered. Ryan Endicott was responsible, even if he himself had not taken part in the abduction. Bliss's heart skipped a couple of beats as he thought about the girl in that evil bastard's clutches. If she was still alive then she was most likely suffering. His guess was that the crew would pump her for information: how had she got picked up? Who interviewed her? What questions did they ask? What did they offer her in return? And what did she give up?

Twenty-four hours, he thought miserably. That's all she had. Maximum. A day at the very most for his team to find Molly and prevent her life from ending in the way she had long imagined.

'Have either of you been up into Molly's room since she was taken?' he asked the Paxtons.

'No,' Abigail replied, shaking her head. 'It never even occurred to me.'

'Is it okay if we pop up there to check it out? I'm sure we'll find nothing, because she had nothing, but I'd hate for a note or something to be sitting up there, only for us to neglect to look.'

There were no objections. Though the room was tiny, as cottage bedrooms tend to be, the Paxtons had decorated it tastefully. Its furniture was made from good-quality oak, with solid wood flooring and a single bed centred in front of a wide window overlooking the back garden. Molly's only property had been the thin, baggy nightdress she had been wearing when Bliss first encountered her, which was now sitting inside a plastic bag in an evidence storage locker. The clothes she had been given to wear were clearly still on her, as neither the top nor the tracksuit bottoms were lying anywhere in the room. The Paxtons had provided her with some toiletries, which were kept on her own shelf in the bathroom. They had planned to go shopping for clothes over the weekend. Bliss had expected to find nothing. He found even less, and the very thought choked him up.

The bed was made, everything tucked in. Not a wrinkle on the sheets or a crease in the duvet – almost as if she had never been there to make an impression. Back downstairs, Bliss asked Mr and Mrs Paxton if they had stuck to their instructions in not allowing Molly to use the internet or either of their mobile phones.

'Absolutely,' Lance said, nodding firmly. 'Molly is not the first child we've provided emergency care for, Inspector Bliss. We stick rigidly to the guidelines. All she had access to was an Xbox to play games on.'

'An Xbox?' Chandler piped up, her eyes widening. 'Please tell me it wasn't connected to the Wi-Fi.'

'It can be, in order to download updates, that sort of thing. But it's only for games.'

'And some games have a messaging facility. If you saved your access credentials last time you connected to the wireless router, it would have been possible for Molly to reactivate them quite easily.'

The woman's hands flew instantly to her mouth. 'Oh, my God. Did we do this? Please tell me we're not responsible for what happened here.'

'You *did* not and you *are* not,' Bliss said, adding some heft to each emphatic inflection of his voice. 'If Molly chose to reach out to somebody against all advice and that person gave her up, then that's on them.'

'But we may have given her the mechanism to do so.'

'You couldn't have known.'

'Of course we could have,' Mrs Paxton shot back. She looked up into her husband's moist, blinking eyes. 'And we should have. She's just a child.'

'There may be nothing to worry about,' Bliss said. 'If you can provide my detectives with access to the router, we'll have it checked out. If Molly used the Xbox to access the internet, the router's system logs should tell us. In which case, we'll take a look at the box itself.'

Less than twenty minutes later, DC Ansari spoke to Bliss while Chandler kept the Paxtons busy in the kitchen. The constable confirmed Molly's use of the Xbox to gain access to the internet. She was also able to ascertain which game the girl had played. 'It was Ghostbusters. And there's no part of that game that allows for instant messaging.'

Bliss blew out a sigh of relief. Before he had a chance to respond, Ansari held up a warning hand and said, 'But she wouldn't have needed to, boss. Xbox Live has a central messaging facility, allowing you to chat with other Xbox Live users. There's only one Xbox tag created for the Paxtons, but its credentials are saved on the device, so Molly could easily have used it. I found no messages in the message centre, but she could have used it and deleted the thread. We have no way of knowing. Sorry, boss.'

He shook his head. 'No, thanks, Gul. You did well. Molly's bright enough to have cleaned up behind her. It would be a comfort to know that nobody back at HQ or at social services had given up this address – that Molly had done so herself to someone she assumed was a friend. But of course, we always live with the possibility that information is being bought.'

'I can't think of any checks that would allow us to know one way or the other, but if we bring the device and router back with us, then we can have our tech people look them over.'

'Good idea. I'm sure you're right about not being able to trace messages if they've been deleted, but anything is worth a go if it leads us to whoever ratted her out.'

And if I ever get my hands on that person, they'll bloody well tell me what I want to know, too.

Bliss allowed himself a few seconds to gather his thoughts. He attached no blame to the Paxtons; this stealthy approach was something nobody had anticipated. He had Endicott down as the kind of punk who would screech to a halt in a flash car and take the front door off its hinges with shotguns, screaming and shouting and not caring who knew about it. Why would anybody doubt the smiling face of a charming female visitor? Molly's life had switched from security to maximum danger in an instant, and the only thing he had on his mind now was finding the girl and getting her back.

Shortly afterwards, with arrangements having been made for the equipment to be removed and transported back to Thorpe Wood, Bliss thanked Mr and Mrs Paxton, turned to Chandler and said, 'Come on, Pen. Let's go get our girl back.'

TWENTY-EIGHT

Long before it became known as Crowland, the small town in the South Holland district of Lincolnshire had been attainable only by boat; it had effectively been an island, surrounded by North Sea water. Trinity Bridge, a unique three-way stone arch construction, had spanned the confluence of the Welland river and one of its tributaries, but after considerable rerouting of the waterways it now had pride of place as an historical marvel on the roadside. Bliss had no time either to admire the fourteenth-century design or to contemplate its history as he and the convoy behind him blew past with lights flashing.

Blues, but no twos. They did not wish to be heard as they approached their target.

On the northern tip of the town, just off a tight two-lane road named Cloot Drove, lay a detached property which had once been a barn housing farming equipment and to dry out hay. Bliss believed there was a good chance it was currently being used for the interrogation of Molly, having spotted the remote location on a list provided by Sandra Bannister.

His first port of call after leaving the Paxtons' had been Thorpe Wood police station. There, he and DI Bentley pored over duplicate hard copies listing the various properties known to be used by Ryan

Endicott and his crew. After a couple of minutes, Bliss shoved his sheet of paper aside and shook his head. 'This isn't going to work. There's no way Endicott will be holding Molly somewhere he knows we're bound to have on our radar. The man is not that dumb.'

Bentley agreed, but wondered where that left them.

'Screwed,' Bliss muttered beneath his breath. 'But let me make a call and see what else I can come up with.'

When Bannister answered the phone, her natural instinct was to assume Bliss was calling about Lisa Pepperdine. Instead, without preamble or explanation, he asked her for a list of known haunts frequented by Endicott and his associates. The urgency in his tone had done the trick. When a list came through in a mail barely five minutes later, he and Bentley compared it to their own records. The property in Crowland was the only one not on the police intelligence database, and Bliss reckoned that gave it the edge in being the single stalk of straw they were searching for.

It was the Major Crime team's good fortune that a fully loaded Armed Response Vehicle happened to be in Peterborough when Bliss placed his request for a firearms unit to join their raid. A second unit had been arranged to provide additional backup in the event of a siege or significant escalation, but Bliss was more than happy to crash the converted barn with just the four heavily armed crew members at his disposal. He certainly did not have time to waste waiting for reinforcements to arrive from Huntingdon.

As the lead officer on the ground, it was Bliss's decision as to how they approached the incident, though the ARV team leader had to agree on tactical deployment of firearms. In Bliss's opinion, this was not an appropriate situation for hostage negotiation; Ryan Endicott had not hunted Molly down for any reason other than to silence her. He would do so either by using threats backed up by examples of how much pain he was capable of inflicting, or by ensuring she could never speak to anyone again. Bliss was undecided as to which of the two would be worse for Molly, but he was convinced that if he gave the dealer any time for rational thought, Endicott would not hesitate to end the girl's life. Fortunately, the most senior armed officer available agreed with his assessment of the situation.

Bliss took a drive-by in order to get a look at and a feel for the place prior to engagement. The barn conversion was simple and effective. The two-storey, red brick building looked sleek and modern and was approached by a short gravel driveway, with a two-car garage and room for a further two vehicles on a block-paved parking area. A Mini Cooper stood close to the front door, which was positioned a third of the way along from the left-hand end of the structure.

After returning to the spot in which the fleet of police vehicles had gathered, out of sight of the barn, Bliss asked Bishop to run an eye over the place from his own car. When the burly sergeant returned, the two compared notes. Neither had seen any sign of activity. Both wondered why the Mini had not been tucked away in the garage, and they agreed on the most likely scenario: it had been moved out to accommodate more recognisable vehicles which were identifiable as belonging to Endicott and his crew.

Bliss requested a PNC check, and the police national computer came back with the name of Shannon Fitzgerald as the Mini's owner, a young woman with no record who was not a known acquaintance of Ryan Endicott. This bothered Bliss, and he placed another call to his contact at the local newspaper.

'How certain are you of your intelligence relating to this address?' he asked Bannister.

'It's in our Endicott file. The source is, unfortunately, no longer with us; he emigrated to Canada earlier this year. However, knowing the way he worked and the pride he took in his job, if he entered those details then he did so with good reason.'

'Would you stake your reputation on it being accurate?' Bliss asked.

'No. Why do you ask?'

'Because I may be about to do just that.'

The journalist laughed and said, 'You? What reputation?'

That brought a smile to his lips. She was right; he had none to protect. But neither did he want to steam into an innocent's home, stormtroopers powering their way through every room, perhaps terrifying children and animals as they spread like a virus. Then his thoughts drifted back to Molly and whatever torture Endicott might be inflicting on her at that very moment. In the end, it was an easy decision to reach.

Ten minutes later, they went in hard and heavy. The big red key – the force's affectionate term for their hand-held battering ram – took the barn's heavy front door down on the third blow. Standing behind the firearms officers, Bliss watched the door, counting the blows, and was concerned by the apparent lack of a metal bar – often used to protect against a forced entry, or at the very least delay it enough to allow dealers to flush away their product. It was what he would have expected to find on a property used by drug dealers, and he began to feel the dull weight of anxiety lodge in his chest.

It took less than three minutes for his qualms to become reality.

Molly was nowhere to be found, and there was no evidence of her ever having been inside the home. Nor was there any sign of Endicott, and no drug paraphernalia of any description. Further searches were unlikely to result in anything substantive. A trained canine would sniff something out if it was there, but Bliss already knew they had made a mistake. That *he* had made a mistake, driven by a perfectly rational desire to free Molly from the clutches of a monster. Sandra Bannister's source had not been wrong to add the property to the dealer's file; it was just the context they were missing.

Shannon Fitzgerald told her story, standing guard over a bewildered child who was no more than five or six years old. She had never married Endicott, and they had dated only half a dozen times before splitting up acrimoniously when she discovered what he did for a living. Still, it was enough time for him to impregnate her; their son, Tyler, was the result. Endicott had wanted nothing to do with either her or his kid, but rather than have to deal with a protracted court case to settle his financial commitments to the boy, he had bought Shannon the converted barn and left them to it. Bliss believed her when she said she had not even laid eyes on Ryan Endicott in close to eighteen months.

Though frightened, and furious with Bliss at having been subjected to the raid, the young woman listened to his explanation and accepted his sincere apology. She would make no official complaint provided the police paid up for the door to be replaced.

As each unit in sequence stood down and drifted away from the scene, Bliss walked back outside on his own to get some fresh air. The sky was low and grey, threatening more rain. The wind that whipped across the flatlands carried a chill. He stood on the front path in a daze, and a creeping sense of unreality settled over him. It had been too easy, of course. Too rapid a conclusion. On the drive over to Crowland, he had been fully expecting to rescue the kid – again – but on reflection he ought to have known better. Nothing ever quite worked out as planned.

All of which left him nowhere. And as far away from rescuing Molly as he had been at the beginning. The knowledge gnawed at him, like a parasite digesting his intestines. He was sickened, frustrated, and angry. He wanted somebody to take his rage out on.

His phone rang, pulling him back into the moment; it was DC Hunt. Bliss sighed, and with a leaden heart he answered.

'Boss,' his colleague said urgently. 'We have Ryan Endicott on the line. He wants to speak with you.'

TWENTY-NINE

'Tell me what you want,' Bliss said when Endicott answered.

He had immediately called the number Hunt provided; he knew it was a burner phone and had no intention of even attempting to trace it. He could also guess why the man was calling him, and the thought sent a chill scuttling between his shoulder blades.

'I want you and Bentley's mob to walk away and forget you ever heard my name. I've tret the girl fair until now, but that can change as soon as I want it to.'

The Fenland accent can be difficult to pin down. It is a curious mixture of the Norfolk and Lincolnshire accents, depending which county border is closest – and the closer to those borders people live, the more similar it becomes. Yet it is also associated with the northern reaches of Cambridgeshire. The use of specific words provided clues, and the moment he heard Ryan Endicott speak for the first time, Bliss knew for sure. When the dealer referred to himself it came across more as "Oi" and his use of "tret" rather than treated was a dead giveaway.

Fists balling, Bliss had to unclench his jaw before responding through the tightest of lips. 'I think you must know that's a guarantee I can't give,' he said. 'The taxpayers expect us to find, arrest and punish drug dealers, not strike bargains with them. Besides, what can you possibly offer me in return for us turning a blind eye to your operation? You're not about to give her back to us, are you?'

'Course not. I ent stupid. But I can promise not to hurt her.'

'I strongly suspect you already have, Ryan.'

'Fuck her up more, then. Fucking bitch disrespected me and cut me. I couldn't let that go. You know what I mean?'

'I do, unfortunately. But let me tell you something, Ryan. However badly you've hurt her makes all the difference in how much I hurt you. So for your sake I do hope you've been careful. Think of what you've done to her and multiply that by ten. That's how much pain I'm going to inflict on you by the time I'm done.'

'Who the fuck are you to threaten me? You're nothing. Nothing. I'm the one in control here, yeah?'

Bliss swallowed back bile as anger rose up inside him, a thick, black poisonous coating that threatened to devour him whole. 'For now,' he admitted reluctantly. He paused, rested the cool glass of his mobile screen against his forehead for a moment, then continued, 'But think about what you're threatening, Ryan. You go too far, then what's stopping me from tearing you apart limb from limb?'

'What the fuck…? You're the filth, you can't say shit like that.' Endicott sounded demented as his voice rose and flexed.

'I am today, Ryan. But tomorrow, who knows what I'll be? If you damage that girl – or worse – then I resign, hand in my warrant card, and I make it my life's work to hunt you down. When I find you, I won't be able to arrest you. Instead, I'll take you to a nice quiet place where we can chat without being disturbed. It'll be quite some conversation. Tell you what: stab yourself in the eye, then think about how that's the very best you're ever likely to feel again if you hurt her.'

Silence.

Bliss liked to think he was bluffing, but when he looked deep inside himself he was not entirely certain. He had it in him to hurt the man on the other end of the connection. As for how far he would take matters, he did not want to find out what his limits were. Especially not where Molly was concerned.

'I'm fucking reporting you,' Endicott blustered eventually. His incredulity made its way through the mobile phone network. The sheer idiocy of what he'd said did not seem to register.

'You know where that ranks among the fucks I don't give, Ryan? Right there at the top, old son. You harm that girl and find out the hard way if you want. But listen, I realise that puts us at an impasse. That's a stalemate to the likes of you. I can't tell you we won't hunt you down, and if you have a single brain cell bouncing around inside that thick skull of yours, then you probably won't want to be hurting the girl again. Neither do I expect you to give her up to me, because I'm not stupid. So where does that leave us, Ryan?'

'You tell me. You're the fucking crazy guy making all the threats.'

'We're both in a bind, that's where we are.' Bliss gave it some thought, decided to delve deeper. 'Now you, Ryan, you have to be wondering how others perceive you at this moment in time. Your supplier can't be too happy that a shipment is sitting in our evidence locker as we speak, nor that some of your crew got grabbed up in our raid. They're all out on bail now, but who knows what they coughed to while we had them? Then there's whoever stands above you on the ladder. They must be looking down asking themselves if you're still worth the risk. Not only are they missing out on their cut, but they'll be aware that one of your couriers was in custody for twenty-four hours. That's liable to make them a bit itchy, Ryan.'

'Fuck that. I got that under control. I got the bitch back, yeah?'

'You did. But what they'll be asking themselves is what she told us in the meantime. Now, between you and me, despite her hating your guts for taking advantage of her and letting others do the same, she never gave you up. That kid is many things, but a rat is not one of them. So you're safe on that score. But will those at the far ends of your operation see it that way, Ryan?'

'Man, what the fuck are you on about? You're doing my head in.'

Bliss heard the panic setting in. The voice, initially calm and collected, was now discordant and shrill. Bliss had wrested control away from the dealer; now he had to hold his nerve and push harder still.

'Think about it, Ryan. You can tell them everything is okay. I dare say you already have – probably within minutes of getting the girl back. Thing is, will they believe you? Do they trust you anymore? You let them down. You got raided and you had one of your own turn on you. My guess is they're looking for someone to take your place even as we speak. As for what they do with you, Ryan… I'm sure your fertile imagination can work that one out.'

'No. No fucking way. I'm their man, they're mine. They know I'm a stand-up guy, and I already showed them how I take care of things here in my city. You're trying to get inside my head, and it ent working. So fuck you. You hear me? Fuck you.'

'All right, all right. Take it easy.' Bliss gave a grim smile of satisfaction. He was under Endicott's skin and burrowing deeper all the time. 'Let's say you're right. Let's say they're angry, but willing to give you another chance. Then you go and top the girl and that brings down all kinds of madness from me and my team.' He snorted loudly. 'You know, when I think about it that way, I won't even need to handle you myself, Ryan. As much as I would love to rip you apart with my bare hands, I'd just as easily opt to ruin your business and have others do the job for me when they realise you screwed them a second time.'

He heard heavy, undulating breathing at the other end of the line. Bliss wondered if Ryan Endicott had ever had a conversation like this before. From what he knew of the man, he had been a part of the drugs trade for around two decades of the twenty-nine years he'd been alive; had run his own crew at the age of fourteen, and had enjoyed a lofty position in the city since before his sixteenth birthday. Bliss was willing to bet that nobody had spoken to Endicott this way for a very long time – if ever – and he would not be enjoying it one little bit. Moreover, he probably had no idea how to react.

Now was the right time to show the man a way out.

'I think I have a solution,' Bliss said. 'It's less than ideal for either of us, but it's a compromise that provides us both with options. As I said before, there's no way I can guarantee me and my team will leave you alone, and I certainly can't speak for the drugs squad or CID. And I accept you're not likely to give up your trump card now that you have her back. So how about we settle for that? You keep her, but keep her safe. No forced sex, no violence, no nothing other than you feed her, water her, keep a warm roof over her head. Make sure she comes to no harm. As for us, we'll do what we do and see where it leads us. If that ends up with us standing on your doorstep, well, we can always react to that change in circumstances at the time. I see little point in continuing to exchange threats or make demands. You with me on that, Ryan?'

It took a couple of minutes, but eventually Endicott muttered his agreement before killing the contact.

Around him in the car, Chandler, Bishop and Ansari released their breaths as one; Bliss's phone had been switched to speaker, so they had listened to both sides of the exchange. Bliss remained still behind the wheel, his mind turning as many somersaults as his stomach.

'That was intense,' DC Ansari said after a few seconds. She laughed as if expelling any lingering apprehension over what she had just heard.

'I don't mind admitting you gave me chills there for a moment, boss,' Bishop said. His eyes suggested he remained unsure whether he'd heard a genuine threat from his superior or a simple gambit from someone entirely familiar with how the game was played. 'I reckon he believed every word you said. He'll be off changing his underwear right now.'

Chandler – the one who knew him best – was pensive. 'You think he'll do as you suggested?' she asked.

Bliss shrugged. 'I can't say for sure, but I think at the very least it bought us some time. My aim was to rattle him, but also to make him realise he had less to fear by keeping Molly alive and well than he did by making good on his own threat.'

'Then I reckon you succeeded. As you say, it buys us time to locate her.'

'I noticed you never once referred to her by name,' Ansari said. 'Was that deliberate?'

'It was,' Bliss answered. 'I don't know for sure how much he knows about her, and if Molly happens to be her real name I didn't want to feed it to him.'

Chandler rubbed her arms and shuddered. 'Gul is right. That was incredibly intense. I felt the air grow colder in here. If I'm Ryan Endicott, I'm convinced that the copper I just spoke to is willing to give up his job and come gunning for me. I'd believe he's that bloody crazy.'

'Maybe I am,' Bliss said, following it up with a sly grin. 'Let's just hope he never has to find out for sure.'

THIRTY

It was hard to focus on anything other than Molly, but avoiding operation Survival was not an option. In Bliss's absence, Nancy Drinkwater's pathology report had come in. DNA samples taken from the remains matched those held on record for Lisa Pepperdine. Now that it was official, Bliss realised that media relations would have little choice but to release the name of the victim. Given the reason Pepperdine had driven up to Peterborough, the newspaper and TV people were going to have a field day. Speculation would become conspiracy theory before the first cycle of news was completed. Social media would pick it up from there and spin its own web of misinformation.

Leaving Chandler to work up a fresh contact list with DI Bentley – hoping to rattle something loose in the search for Endicott's bolthole – Bliss went looking for Patrick Grealish. The uniformed sergeant was the longest-serving copper working at Thorpe Wood. For a long time the two men had harboured only ill-will for each other, yet during the past year they had reached an understanding, even a mutual respect. Bliss figured if anybody was both willing and able to dish the dirt on Chief Inspector Robert Marsh, it would be Grealish.

Bliss found his target chatting with several colleagues outside the cell corridor ironically known as the Green Mile, due to the colour of its vinyl flooring. He asked for a word in private; with arched eyebrows, Grealish agreed, and the two stepped into a side office barely large enough to contain them both.

The first thing Bliss noticed was how much weight the sergeant had lost. His protruding belly had all but disappeared; Grealish had gone from looking bullish and robust to hollowed-out and gaunt. There had been no talk about any ill-health that Bliss was aware of, but his former enemy did not look at all well.

'How're things?' Bliss asked, searching for any sign of evasion in the response.

'Not so bad. Yourself?' Grealish was clearly wary. The two had not exchanged words since Bliss's road accident back in June.

'So-so. Look, I'll get straight to the point. You knew and worked under Chief Inspector Marsh, yes?'

'Robert? Yeah, for the better part of ten years. Why, what's up? Something happened to him?'

Bliss's head jerked up. 'Why would something have happened to him?'

Grealish shrugged. 'I don't know. You're here, which is unusual, and you've come up with a name I've not heard in a bloody long time. I assumed the worst.'

Bliss nodded, not quite buying it. 'He's fine, as far as I know. But I would like to learn more about him.'

'Such as?'

'For instance, who did he pal around with here? What was the sense you had working under him – was he widely respected? Was there any… talk about him?'

Grealish shifted his stance. His physique no longer carried any threat, but Bliss recognised when the man was suspicious. 'Why do you ask? What's this all about?'

'It's not what you think – not entirely. I'm not looking to rake up dirt on the man, and especially not in connection with all the shit that went down before. I just want to find out what kind of copper he was, and who he was most likely to confide in back in the day.'

'Sounds to me as if dirt is precisely what you're after. Tell me what it's about, then I'll see if I can help you out.'

It went against the grain to share information on a case which was still partially informal, especially where ex-police officers were involved. But Bliss got the impression that Grealish knew something and would not be averse to discussing it in the right circumstances. Reluctantly, he laid out the background concerning the human remains uncovered at Fengate, the subsequent identification of Lisa Pepperdine, her mention of a meeting, and the logical paths Bliss and Chandler had followed which had led them to Robert Marsh.

'Does that sound like Marsh?' Bliss asked. 'I mean, the part about him agreeing to talk to a freelance journalist who was looking to make a name for herself?'

After a long moment, Grealish finally huffed air through his nose. He ran a hand across his face and looked around to make sure they were not being observed. 'Robert was a good man and a bloody fine leader of men. But yeah, he did have his weaknesses… He was partial to getting his name and face in the paper, and on the local news. Where most avoided the media like the plague, he loved the attention – a bit like your old boss, Sykes, in that regard. I'm telling you now there's no way it went any further, but sure, I can see him taking that meeting.'

'You never heard any rumours about it at the time, though?' Bliss pushed.

'No. He'd drone on about plenty of different things, but he was also bloody secretive when he wanted to be. He came across as gregarious, just one of the boys, only of superior rank. We all knew it was mostly bullshit, but we liked him. As I say, he was damned good at his job. Still, we also knew to stay tight-lipped around him. Our team's boat leaked information a bit too often for our liking, and not one of us took a bet against him being the sieve.'

Unsurprised, Bliss sought further clarification. 'So from what you're saying, whilst there's every possibility he's the top man who set up a meet with our journo, you don't believe he shared that information with anyone. Certainly not a fellow copper.'

Heaving a long sigh, Grealish nodded and said, 'That's about the strength of it. You mentioned pals before, and nobody immediately sprang to mind. As decent as he was, Marsh was still a boss, so we kept our distance outside the job. But, now I think about it, there was a strong rumour that went around for about six months...'

'About Marsh?' Bliss leaned in, feeling the blood pulsing in his neck.

'Yeah. Him and a female admin worker. Don't get me wrong – Robert had mates, I suppose, but nobody in the job, that I can recall. You have to remember what it was like back then in terms of ranks. He couldn't have been good friends with anyone below Chief Inspector, so his choices were limited. But yeah, we all knew he had a bit of a fling with Fern Wilder.'

As soon as he heard the name, Bliss had a flashback to the woman's face. Early twenties, pretty – so red-cheeked and fluttery her colleagues joked about her being a Disney princess. But even if Robert Marsh was seeing her, did that necessarily mean their relationship had been close enough for the man to reveal more about himself than he otherwise would?

'Thanks for that,' he said. His mind was working hard, but he was grateful to Grealish. 'Believe me, I'm not looking to stitch him up for anything.'

'But if he's a wrong'un then you'll go after him.'

Bliss knew precisely what was going through the sergeant's mind. He saw the memories in the gleam of Grealish's eyes, and took a breath. 'For stepping out on his wife? No. For betraying operational confidences to a journalist? No. But anything more than that, and he's fair game, don't you think?'

The sergeant didn't have to think about his response. 'I do. We've all moved on, Bliss.'

'Good. I'm glad to hear it.' As he spoke, Bliss was struck again by his colleague's appearance. He leaned in and said, 'You sure you're okay, Patrick? You're looking a bit under the weather, if you don't mind my saying so.'

Grealish regarded him closely before responding. 'I have Crohn's disease. The consultant tells me it's not going to kill me, provided I avoid complications. I'd be lying if I said it wasn't a pain in the arse – literally at times – and you can see the effect it's had. It's a terrific diet plan, but that's about the only thing it's got going for it.'

'I'm sorry to hear that,' Bliss said. 'I mean it.'

'Cheers. Bugger all I can do about it now – but I have put in my papers. My police pension is waiting for me, and my state one starts paying out in five years' time. I leave at the end of the month.'

'I hadn't heard.'

Smiling briefly, Grealish said, 'Yeah, well, we don't exactly move in the same circles.'

Bliss stuck out a hand. 'All the same, I wish you luck. With both retirement and your illness.'

Grealish accepted the handshake. 'Cheers, Bliss. Before long there won't be any of us real coppers stalking these corridors anymore.'

Bliss thought about his own team, and decided the sergeant was wrong about that. 'You take care,' he said.

'You too. Especially if you end up looking more closely at Marsh.'

The words were spoken half in jest, but they reminded Bliss of something he'd forgotten to ask. 'On that subject, there is one last thing. You say Marsh courted publicity. Do you happen to know who his contact was at the newspaper offices at the time?'

It took a few seconds for Grealish to dredge the name up from his memory, but he eventually wagged a finger and said, 'I do, actually. Her name was Janis Ward.'

THIRTY-ONE

Following a late lunch of burger and fries grabbed hastily from Five Guys, the first person Bliss spotted in the Major Crimes squad room was Diane Warburton. The DCI was perched on the edge of a desk chatting with the rest of the team. She wore a black skirt that finished just above the knee; the thin material had risen somewhat as she sat back. Bliss remembered the days when he'd noticed Chandler's skirts doing the same, and realised he hadn't changed as much as he thought over the past decade or more. He was a leg man, pure and simple. He saw no harm in looking, because in his head it did not equate to objectifying. Staring would be creepy. But the odd appreciative glance… well, if that was no longer acceptable, then he was glad his time was mostly behind him.

The atmosphere inside the room seemed relaxed, yet for some reason Bliss was immediately and instinctively on his guard. His new boss looked up as he approached, offering a wide smile that was echoed in the natural warmth of her eyes.

'I'm surprised to see you here,' Bliss said. He checked out both Chandler and Bishop, but their expressions gave him no cause for concern. He started to relax, though he remained confused by the new DCI's presence.

'Not half as surprised as I am to be here,' Warburton replied, standing up and folding her arms across her chest. Her thick wavy hair was fixed in a French braid, the tail of which she shifted to hang over one shoulder. 'Superintendent Fletcher contacted me. There was some concern that you were being pulled in two different directions at the moment, so she asked if I would help out by getting an early start. She explained everything to me, Jimmy, and I've just informed your team that both Joseph Flynn and Stuart Sykes may be implicated, however ambiguously.'

Bliss was taken aback. Trying hard not to show his irritation, his eyes widened. 'You gave my team information the Super and I had previously agreed to hold back until its relevance was established?'

'Yes. She and I discussed the issue at some length, and the decision was made to release those details to the team.'

'And you don't think I should have been part of that decision-making process? Need I remind you this is my case?'

Bliss realised his mistake the moment he reacted. He had backed Warburton into a corner in front of the entire team, openly questioning her authority before she had even officially taken over the reins. If she was ever going to gain their respect, she now had no choice but to slap him down a peg or two.

'I apologise,' he said quickly. 'That was bang out of order.'

'Yes, it was.' The DCI's face had lost its glow. Instead her cheek pulsed and her jaw worked as if she were chewing on a hard toffee. 'From what I gather, Inspector, you are to be granted a certain leeway because you get results. I'm more than happy to go along with that, provided I also receive the required level of professionalism and respect from you.'

Bliss squirmed. The bollocking was muted, but it rammed its point home: she was right and he was wrong. He was annoyed that Fletcher and Warburton had come together to change course and had also acted upon their decision in his absence, but showing his disdain in such a petulant way did the new DCI a massive disservice.

'I agree,' he said. 'I was being a dick.'

'In which case, I accept your apology... and admit, in return, that you're right to be miffed. I think it was the right decision to share this information with your team, but you ought to have been involved prior to my doing so.'

Her features were less rigid. There was no longer any hint of a smile, but her anger at his response had clearly dissipated and she had moved on. Bliss was grateful to her for that. He informed the team of his conversation with Grealish, but his colleagues looked to be struggling with what any of it meant.

'I remain convinced that neither Flynn nor Sykes ever arranged to meet with Pepperdine,' he said, putting his own theory out there. 'I don't know about Marsh, either, but he does look by far the more likely candidate. Sykes was a media hound as well, no question, but his desire for publicity was about showing off his authority and intelligence. As I recall, Robert Marsh was all gleaming gnashers and perfectly coiffed barnet, but without any of the patter. He wanted the attention on a personal level. Joe Flynn courted neither.'

'Is it not possible that Flynn met with her on the quiet to set her straight?' Bishop asked. 'After all, if she was gunning for us, then he was going to get it from all sides, as well as above and below. He may have wanted to deflect her attention, and so perhaps he would have chosen to do so away from the public glare.'

'I'm not about to say you're wrong, Bish,' Chandler said, scratching at her cheek. 'What you say makes a lot of sense, actually. But the boss and I spent some time with Joe Flynn yesterday, and I can't think of any reason why he wouldn't have told us if that were the case.'

'There is one reason, surely?'

All attention switched to Gul Ansari. She blinked back at them and said, 'I wasn't around in those days and I never met the man, so

I think that puts me at an advantage in looking at this dispassionately. If you all agree that he was willing to meet with her – with every intention to steer her away, I'm sure – then is it not remotely possible that something went wrong when they did meet? Could she not have said something that so enraged him he momentarily lost control and… lashed out?'

Bliss noticed all eyes turning his way. Chandler had worked with Flynn as well, but it was Bliss who had been running the team back then. Bliss who later uncovered both murder and collusion much closer to home than anyone had ever imagined. They now looked to him for answers, and he chose to keep nothing from them.

'I admit to one thing,' he said, with measured reluctance. 'It bothered me that he chose to drive all the way over here to offer us so little. When he asked for me and I met him downstairs, my first thought was that he had come looking to provide me with something solid concerning our uncovered remains, but that was not the case. Not in my lunchtime meeting, nor at dinner when Penny was also present. I won't go as far as to suggest he was trying to tease details out of us, but neither was he giving us anything to work with.'

'So you're wondering why he was so interested that it drew him back to the city,' Bishop said, nodding gently.

'I did at the time, and I suppose I still am. That's not to say I believe he did anything wrong; I just don't see that in the man. I may be blinkered, but to me Joseph Flynn is no killer, even if he does turn out to be the person who met with Lisa Pepperdine.'

'Even in the heat of an argument, as Gul suggested? In a rage he was unable to contain?'

'That's just it, Bish. Flynn is one of the most unflappable people I've known in my entire life. I don't recall ever seeing him lose his rag, and I never heard any reports of him doing so, either.'

'I have to agree,' Chandler interjected. 'Doing the job we do, we all understand that anyone can lose it in a second and do something completely out of character.' She was careful not to look at Bishop. 'But Flynn was the most easy-going man I have ever worked with – as placid as they come. It would have taken something catastrophic to have pushed him over the edge, and there's no way Pepperdine had that kind of ammunition.'

'But nothing is impossible,' Ansari said softly.

'No. Nothing is impossible.'

'But it's still the most unlikely option,' Bliss said, getting them back on the track he wanted to be travelling along. 'I didn't know Chief Inspector Marsh very well, but he's definitely in the frame when it comes to having met with our freelancer. And given he's not Joe Flynn, I consider him to be much more likely to have lost his cool with her if they got into a heated exchange.'

DCI Warburton, who until now had stood quietly, observing and taking it all in, sighed and said, 'Then somebody has to have a chat with him, and with this Fern Wilder woman. It's unavoidable, I'm afraid. Right now we have Flynn, Sykes and – with all due respect to Major Crimes – you too, Bliss, as well as Marsh. The four most senior police officers involved in that particular investigation.'

'Burnout,' Chandler reminded her.

'Thank you, Penny. So let me tell you all how my conversation on this subject with Superintendent Fletcher went. The way she sees it, we look hard at everyone – and I mean *everyone* – before we eventually have to turn our thoughts to your own DI. None of you are going to like investigating your own boss, and frankly I won't allow that to happen. If it comes to it I'll have another area come in to carry out interviews. But there's no escaping the fact that DI Bliss is among those upon whom attention will fall if we don't put this to bed quickly. That's an added pressure we can all do without, but it's not of our choosing, so we deal with it.'

Bliss understood what Warburton was saying, but he was growing increasingly uneasy. 'You're not considering asking me to stand aside on this case, are you?' he asked.

The DCI met his gaze without flinching. 'Here and now? No. But if we TIE the others on that very short list and don't come up with answers, then there's no way you can remain in charge of an investigation in which you have become a potential suspect.'

He had seen it coming. It was inevitable, and he thought he was prepared. Only he wasn't. It was a harsh and ruthless decision, though in both his heart and mind he accepted that Warburton and Fletcher were only doing their jobs. He respected them for it, but he didn't have to like it.

'I won't create any ripples when the time comes,' he said. 'I'll continue working this with my team, and of course when we run out of options, I'll remove myself from the case.'

'Which brings me to a question I have to ask,' the DCI said. She looked around the room and put back her head as she sighed. Then she turned back to Bliss. 'Jimmy, given how involved you are in this business with the girl from the rooftop, have you considered seconding yourself to that investigation more fully and leaving operation Survival in the hands of myself and your trusted sergeants?'

The truth was, he had not. Jennifer Howey would not have been amused, given she had pushed him so hard to accept delegation as a positive step in the process. He shook his head. 'Honestly? No. I don't think the time is quite right. But I do understand what you're getting at. My seconding myself to that investigation avoids my having to step down from this one, which is better all round for everyone concerned.'

'Yourself included,' Warburton reminded him.

'Of course. All I'd ask is that you allow me to be the best judge of when it happens. I've not forgotten my doubts about Joe Flynn, but my sense is that we're about to make a breakthrough by following the Chief Inspector Marsh lead. I'd like to see that through before walking away, at least to the point where you and my team can follow one clear route without distraction.'

Warburton gave it a few moments, her eyes never leaving his. Finally she nodded and said, 'The ball is in your court, Jimmy.'

'Thank you, boss.'

'May I make one suggestion?'

'You're the boss.'

She smiled for the first time in a long while. 'I guess we'll see about that. I do also think it would be best if you excused yourself from interviewing the Chief Inspector. However ex he is, his rank will sit there between you in the room. Far better for me and DS Bishop to take him, while you and DS Chandler talk to his bit on the side. What do you say?'

'I say you're not the boss without good reason. It's the right decision, and one I'd probably not have made.'

Warburton studied his face for a few seconds, her gaze narrowing. 'You were about to suggest that arrangement yourself, weren't you?'

Bliss laughed. 'Yes, boss,' he said. 'But I thought I'd give you your moment in the spotlight.'

THIRTY-TWO

A MARRIED WOMAN WITH THREE children, Fern Wilder was now Fern Lockwood. Not wanting her past to come anywhere close to the present, she opted to meet with the two detectives in a restaurant at the Springfield Outlet Centre in Spalding, where she worked as a manager at a jewellery store.

If anything, Bliss thought, the woman had grown even more attractive in the intervening years. She had lost the youthful perkiness that had contributed to her nickname, but although she was no longer a Disney princess, neither was she exactly the wicked witch. Lockwood was understandably nervous, and her hands shook when she took the tea Chandler had bought her.

'I don't know what you think you're going to find out from me,' she said, after Bliss had made the introductions and the three of them had settled into their chairs around a wobbly table that irritated him the moment he first leaned on it. 'I barely even knew Robert.'

'And yet you were sleeping with him,' Bliss pointed out. He had no time for the delicacies of the situation.

'That doesn't mean I knew him.' Her eyes flared momentarily, but then she dropped her gaze back down to her hands. 'It's no excuse for having an affair with a married man, I know, but I was young, naïve and easily led in those days. He was all charm and attitude, so confident, and when he flirted with me he made me feel special.'

'He sounds like a bit of a hound,' Chandler remarked, shooting Bliss a smirk. 'Were you aware of any other notches on his bedpost?'

'You make it sound so unsavoury.'

'And you're suggesting it wasn't?'

'Why do I feel like I'm under attack here? Robert played his part, you know. More so, given he was the married one.'

'Neither of us has any desire to attack you for what took place,' Bliss assured her. 'But we can at least agree to call it what it was. This was no great love affair. You've already admitted to hardly knowing the man you were… sleeping with. What you had was about sex, pure and simple. Even so, there must have been some pre- or post-coital chat. Let's begin with the man himself: what was your overall impression of him, Mrs Lockwood?'

Her hands shifted around the mug of tea, steam spiralling from the rim up towards the ceiling. The woman briefly withdrew into herself before edging forward slightly in her chair. 'It's hard for me to admit that someone I slept with had so little impact on me,' she said, 'but the sad truth is that's exactly how it was. Robert and I met for sex. For me, at that age, the physical side was fulfilling enough, as was the excitement of it all – being the other woman was a bit of a rush, I suppose. When we were together, I didn't want to hear about his job, and I certainly had no interest in his home life. He enjoyed a game of golf, and he liked his fishing. Other than that, I can't tell you much more about the kind of man Robert was.'

'So he never made any promises to you,' Chandler said. 'No expressions of love to go with the passion. No talk about leaving his wife for you, or anything along those lines.'

These were not questions, but firm statements, as if Chandler were reading the woman's thoughts.

Lockwood barked a quick, humourless laugh. 'Leave his wife? I told you, what we had was all about the sex and that was it. I didn't ask for more – or expect it, for that matter – and he certainly never offered. He found it hard to stay in the same room as me after we were done. He always had some excuse to dash off as soon as he'd dumped the condom in the bin.'

'This took place where? In your home, or at a hotel?' Bliss asked.

'My flat. Always at my flat. It lasted a few months, at which point I confess I got bored by it all. The sex was pretty routine – I wasn't even enjoying it any more, so I called a halt. It really is that simple. That crass.'

Bliss decided to take a different approach. 'Mrs Lockwood, do you recall the Burnout case, as it was known? The period during which we had several fatal arson attacks in the city?'

'Of course. It was all anyone talked about. You were heavily involved in that yourself, if I remember correctly.'

'You do, and I was. But tell me, were you and Marsh seeing each other at the time?'

She had to think about that one, but then nodded with some certainty. 'I'm pretty sure we were. Why do you ask?'

'Did he ever discuss it with you?'

'I told you, we barely spoke when we were together.'

'But it can't all have been wham, bam, thank you mam. There must have been the occasional conversation. You were in lust, but you were also both human beings. Humans talk.' Bliss pushed on, determined to get answers if there were any to be had. 'For instance, did he ever mention talking to a journalist? A freelancer up from London, looking to run a hit job on us for dragging our heels?'

Lockwood shook her head. 'I don't know what else I can say to convince you, Inspector Bliss. Of course Robert and I talked sometimes, but it was everyday stuff, office gossip, or more likely how to switch things up in the bedroom. He never discussed the job in the way you're suggesting. Not once.'

'Okay, so was there a time when his behaviour changed? Did he at any point become more distant, preoccupied even? Perhaps a slight change in personality – growing more evasive, or getting angry over the little things...'

Bliss saw it in her face before she replied. Her cheeks flushed, and he could see her swallowing as if trying to force down something solid. After a while she nodded and said, 'Now you mention it, that's exactly what happened. He cancelled one of our evenings together. A quick call, just to tell me he'd been held up at work. We were due to meet again three days later, but he never confirmed. Finally, more than a week later, he came over unannounced, and there was something not right about him. Actually, to say he was preoccupied is a bit of an understatement, if I'm being brutally honest. At times it was as if he wasn't even there. Not in the same room, nor even in the same world. We went to bed, but we didn't... Robert was far too tense. We only saw each other a few more times after that.'

This was something. Bliss was certain of it. If Marsh's mental state had altered, especially in the midst of an investigation that was spiralling out of control and leaving senior people exposed in the spotlight, it was hardly indicative of any one issue. Yet Bliss suspected the Chief Inspector's behavioural change was not due solely to the pressures of work. It was possible he wanted to believe it so much that he wasn't thinking straight, but Bliss genuinely believed this might be important.

The team had agreed to wait until this interview was over and its details discussed before hauling ex-Chief Inspector Robert Marsh in for his own grilling. There was every chance of something arising from it which would be useful to prod Marsh with if he attempted to clam up. Affairs were always messy things to deal with, no matter how many years had passed. If the man was still married to the woman he'd cheated on, it opened up a chink in his armour. Whether the change in his demeanour was sufficient to force a wedge into that fissure, only time would tell.

'One last thing,' Bliss said to Lockwood, who now appeared drained and anxious to leave. 'Did it seem to you as if Marsh was unhappy in his job, that he craved something more?'

Seemingly on safer territory, Lockwood smiled. 'Oh, yes. He always wanted more than he had. Hence his fling with me, I suppose. But no, Chief Inspector was not enough for Robert. He had Chief Constable of Cambridgeshire in his sights, no matter how many ranks stood between where he was and what he was aiming for. He'd scramble over the men ahead of him if he had the chance, especially if they stumbled somehow. One of the few times he did open up to me – although he might have been a bit drunk – he said all he needed was a single opportunity to carve through his superiors, and he would leap on it.'

'And what did you take that to mean?' Chandler asked her.

'I suppose that he was hoping for their failure and his eventual success. Ironic, now that I think about it.'

'What do you mean by that?'

'Only that if he had hung around before moving on to another county, he'd have been in the city when all hell broke loose later in the year. People of rank lost their jobs left, right, and centre, as you know. If he'd stuck it out, he would have got his wish.'

Bliss ignored the fact that he was mostly responsible for lobbing that particular grenade into the job in the autumn of 2005. Instead he focussed on Fern Lockwood's observations about her lover, and began thinking about how best to use that information when DCI Warburton and Olly Bishop spoke with the man himself.

THIRTY-THREE

There was time for the team to discuss all relevant and current information before parting ways again. DCI Warburton and DS Bishop were awaiting the arrival of Robert Marsh, whose acceptance of the invitation had been curt and derisory. Fortunately he had moved back to the area after retirement, and so was able to make it in at short notice. Bliss and Chandler were also putting together a plan to locate and talk to a potential link to Ryan Endicott.

Concerned about the creeping reach of the investigation, Bliss sought to reel it back in. Clarity and a sharper focus were required at this critical stage, and it was his job to make sure that he and his team were all on the same page.

'So far we've mainly concentrated on our own people,' Bliss said, explaining his decision to expand the operation while at the same time maintaining a tight grip on the reins. 'Rightly so, because the aim is to stamp it out before it spreads and we become a media target. But I also feel the time is right to explore alternative theories, and we can't ignore Lisa Pepperdine's history with organisations like the BNP. In 2005, during the Burnout case, a right-wing extremist group calling themselves the New Crusader Movement had some momentum in this area. After the bombings in London, their numbers swelled alarmingly, but they were not an inconsiderable force even before July.'

Chandler picked up the thread from him. 'The NCM's top dog was Jason Ball, and to say the man was pond life would be doing a disservice to leeches. The boss and I discussed this connection, and with Pepperdine's significant interest in bringing down extremists, her attempting to contact or even infiltrate the group would have been a logical step to take. Our hope is that this is where we'll find her killer.'

'That was before my time,' DC Hunt said. 'But I remember it well, seeing as I lived here in Peterborough. The BNP were on the rise, and we all thought the New Crusader Movement was just grabbing hold of its coat-tails, but without any real clout. Even so, there were a lot of whispers about Ball and his family.'

'They were a right bunch, but Jason was by far the worst of them,' Bliss said. 'He used kids to do his dirty work, including a young boy by the name of Nicky Cox. Many of you will recognise the name, but Pen and I worked the case. Fearing the kid was going to blab, Jason Ball abducted Nicky and eventually murdered him.'

'Didn't the boy's father then kill Ball?' Warburton asked. 'I seem to remember that case went nationwide.'

Bliss swallowed, thinking back to the final words Stuart Sykes had spoken to him just two days ago. He wondered how life in the police force, reaching its tentacles out into the city and beyond, would have been different had Sykes not provided Anthony Cox with the name of his son's killer.

'Yeah, the father managed to reach Ball before we were able to scoop him up. Anthony Cox was convicted some eighteen months later and sent to Hull prison. He was subsequently transferred back here to Peterborough, where he'd originally been banged up on remand. He was always a class B prisoner, because the only person he ever wanted to murder was already dead. Consideration was given to his motive, and so he was allowed the move to be closer to family. Except that, a month ago, he supposedly hanged himself. The investigating team are unconvinced about the suicide, mainly because they can see no reason for it. But neither do they have any evidence to the contrary.'

'What a tragic state of affairs.'

If you only knew the half of it, Bliss thought. 'As sad a case as I've had the misfortune to lead. But therein lies the problem with this new line of investigation. If we speculate that Lisa Pepperdine may have been killed by somebody from the NCM, then our prime suspect is already dead.'

Realisation spread amongst the gathered detectives. 'Which leaves us where, boss?' Gratton asked. 'As in, where do DC Hunt and I even begin?'

'Good question,' Bliss said. 'There are a few members of that organisation still around. Some splintered off and started calling themselves Britain for the British; one or two may also have drifted across to Britain Unites. But the starting point, I think, has to be Craig Ball. He's Jason Ball's son, and evidently he's just as big a prick as his old man.'

'Oh, joy,' Hunt said, rolling his eyes in a dramatic fashion. 'Interviewing Nazi psychopaths is always the highlight of my day.'

Bliss sympathised, but then revealed what he had learned from Joe Flynn. 'That's not who Craig Ball is associated with anymore. However, in my opinion, the rabble he is involved with are no better. He and his wife are heavily linked with Antifa-UK.'

Bliss explained how Antifa's methods were more akin to fascism than those of many of the groups they protested about. It became obvious to him that many of his colleagues were unaware of how the group worked. Given their methods were counter-intuitive, he understood their confusion.

'Whatever you do, don't try fooling him by pretending you agree with his ideas,' he warned. 'With some of these idiots, if you feed their egos they'll share a few pints with you and at some point they'll let something slip, but let's not assume Craig Ball is dumb purely on the basis of his thirst for violence and anarchy. Get a feel for him – the way he lives his life, who he spends time with. If you think his inner circle can be infiltrated by one of our undercover officers, then we'll give it some thought. For now, just sound him out and report back. There are others in the groups whose names you can look up online. As you do, please feed them into the case file.'

'Should we mention Lisa Pepperdine's name when speaking with these people?' Gratton asked.

'Only if you think you have to. Use your nous on that one. Raise the issue first by mentioning the local press, that sort of thing. If he doesn't bite, then go for it. You'll do fine. Both of you.'

'Which reminds me,' DCI Warburton said. 'I took a call from pathology. We now have confirmation that Pepperdine was strangled to death.'

Unsurprised, Bliss nodded. 'Bear that in mind as you question people,' he said to Hunt and Gratton. 'But don't show your hand.'

Warburton gave a firm nod of satisfaction. 'Bish and I will tease as much out of Robert Marsh as we can before throwing Fern Wilder's name into the mix.'

Bliss agreed. 'Now with him, I'd suggest you do pander to his ego. He's a complete narcissist from what I can gather, so if you play to his old rank it'll make him warm to you.'

'Good idea. And you, Jimmy? How do you feel about this possible link to Endicott?'

In response to his new boss's question, Bliss offered a half-hearted smile. 'Desperate times and all that,' he said. 'I think I managed to worry Endicott during our phone conversation, hopefully enough to make him think twice and without causing too many problems for Molly. I'm now worried about those who pull his strings. If they decide she has to go, even if that also means he has to be taken out as well, then nothing I've said or done so far is going to prevent that.'

'I'm sure we all wish you the best of luck with it. We'll meet back here later, yes? Say around six-ish?' Warburton kept it upbeat, and he appreciated that.

What he had in mind next wasn't much of a plan, but for the time being it was all they had. Bliss had found it difficult to lend any focus to the murder of the missing journalist, his thoughts constantly turning instead to Molly and how much suffering she might be enduring. It was tying him up in knots, and he struggled to concentrate. Even so, at some point he'd remembered the name of Courtney Jacobs being mentioned by Bannister in connection with their drug dealer. Having researched further, he and Chandler had discovered that due to paparazzi intrusion, Jacobs now hid herself in a walled estate whose only approach was barred by heavy wrought-iron gates. Without a warrant to search her home or for her arrest, he wouldn't be able to speak with her in any formal setting.

Chandler, however, had chanced upon a link to a phone app which appeared to monitor the young woman's movements. 'It's basically tied into Courtney's social media pages,' she explained to Bliss, who after more than thirty minutes reading inane reports about Jacobs had pretty much lost the will to live. 'So, despite her pleas to be left alone, everywhere she goes she updates her Instagram, Twitter and Facebook feeds. Some bright spark has developed an app that picks up the updates and feeds them into a single map pinpointing her every movement. It's called *Follow CJ*.'

Bliss hadn't quite known how to respond. Jacobs had found fame by enlarging her breasts and showing them off as often as possible, and made her fortune by exploiting that fact in the eyes of the gullible. TV reality shows fought to sign her up, mainly because she was willing to say or do just about anything to debase herself in the name of money and success. He seldom felt older or more out of touch than when some celebrity game show came on the TV and he knew literally none of the participants.

The phone app Chandler had described was dubious in his opinion, a borderline stalking offence. Yet it was the ersatz celeb herself who provided the ammunition, and according to everything he had read protested too much about it for her outrage to be taken seriously. There was no doubt that behind the collagen and plastic, Courtney Jacobs was an attractive young woman, and if her personality wasn't as manufactured as her chest then she genuinely had something going for her. Bliss was not particularly looking forward to tracking her down like some sleazy fan in a mucky raincoat, but Chandler was right: it was an opportunity they ought not to ignore.

As everyone else in the team left to tackle their tasks, Bliss remained at his chosen desk in the main working area, sitting opposite Chandler. One of life's stoics, she seldom revealed her emotions. Even when it came to her own woes she pretty much took every blow on the chin and if it knocked her down she got right back up again. That was how she had managed to survive the long years without her daughter, and she brought that steadfast approach with her into the job every single day.

Chandler caught him looking at her. 'What's up?'

He hitched his shoulders. 'Nothing,' he said. 'Just thinking how I could probably have done a lot worse when it came to partners.'

She grinned. 'You certainly have that advantage over me.'

He flipped her two fingers.

'How old are you? Don't be such a child. Use your words.'

'How about my fists?'

'When you're big enough. You're already ugly enough, so you have that going for you, too.'

Bliss shook his head in mock weary despair. 'You always have to have the last word, don't you? I seem to remember I began this conversation by paying you a compliment.'

Chandler tilted her head. 'You did, didn't you? You must want something from me.'

He fluttered his eyelashes and leered at her, prompting a roar of laughter. Choking it back, she said, 'Yeah, well you're not getting any of that, I can assure you. I'm a prime cut these days, and way out of your league.'

'You're a cheeseburger at best. A McDonalds one, on a good day.'

'And yet still way too good for you.'

'That's not what your lips told me back in June. And we both know lips don't lie.'

This time he was on the receiving end of the two-fingered gesture. He grinned and winked at her. A drunken coming together when both of them feared his world was collapsing was the only intimate moment they had ever shared, though often their flirtations were mistaken by others for something more.

'So thrill me with the life and times of our voluptuous celeb,' he said. 'I'm itching to nail this little fucker, Ryan. Molly better still be breathing and in one piece or I'll rip his lungs out.'

According to Chandler, today's lunch of watercress and Berkswell cheese risotto had been enjoyed at Prevost in the city centre, where Jacobs had remained long after the assigned lunchtime opening hours; with a selfie alongside her main dish appearing across all major social media platforms, the restaurant manager was hardly going to argue the point. Having established her vegetarian credentials by passing up on the roasted hake, Jacobs and her all-female entourage had moved on to take both John Lewis and Primark by storm.

'And you found all this out by checking your phone,' Bliss said in wonder after Chandler had reeled off a series of updates from the app. 'Modern technology at its very best, I'd say. What the bloody hell is Berkswell cheese when it's at home, anyway?'

Her thumbs flashed across her smartphone. 'It's a hard cheese made from unpasteurised ewe milk and animal rennet.'

His mouth hung open. 'Sorry, I'm none the wiser. What on earth is animal rennet?'

Another search, another rapid response. 'It's derived from the stomach of a calf, lamb or goat while their diets are still limited to milk, and if I'm reading this right it's typically 90% pure chymosin.'

'Now you're just taking the piss,' Bliss said, wincing and turning his head away. 'And doesn't that blow her veggieness out of the water?'

'What can I say? Clearly her boobs aren't the only fake things about her. And before you ask, chymosin is some sort of enzyme.'

'Did you have to look that up?'

Chandler shook her head. 'No, for some reason I knew that bit.'

'Which is more than I did.'

'Maybe I should be the DI instead of you.'

'Please,' he said. 'Do take my job. You'll be doing me a favour.'

'Yeah, you and the rest of us.'

There was that last word again. He knew better than to pursue it. Now that he'd mentioned this particular quirk of hers, Chandler was never going to let him best her. Not in this exchange, at any rate. He got to his feet, groaning, and stretched out his spine, arching backwards. 'Looks like we have a shopping trip to Queensgate to look forward to,' he said. 'I hear Primark is a great place to buy knickers.'

As she slowly rose from her own chair, Chandler turned her feline eyes on him and said in a smoky voice, 'Why, Inspector Bliss, whatever makes you think I wear knickers?'

THIRTY-FOUR

Anthony Clarke had long ago decided that if – as seemed to be the case – white folk were confused by a clean, well-cut black man in a suit and tie, unburdened by bling, then he was definitely going to fuck with their heads. Today he was wearing not far off ten grand's worth of bespoke Huntsman whistle, while the Northampton-made Crockett & Jones boots on his size twelve feet had set him back a monkey. Five hundred quid was nothing to lay out for foot comfort.

Wherever Clarke went he drew looks. He knew what they were thinking: a boy from one of London's many black ghettos done good. Investment banker, entrepreneur, perhaps even someone who had made it big on TV or in the movies. The thought always brought a thin smile to his lips. If only they knew how he really made his money, their tiny little heads would explode.

In the way he presented himself to a largely narrow-minded society, Anthony had avoided being stereotyped. As for how he was able to fund that lifestyle and afford to make the decision in the first place, well... he had to accept that being a villain fell right in the middle of people's expectations of young men with his skin colour. Except that he was no ordinary face. He was no iron-pumper, had never swallowed a steroid in his life; he was a whelp who looked in need of a good steak dinner. Even so, he had the intelligence, patience, self-awareness and absolute detachment from humanity to become the enforcer he was.

If he was spoken of, it was in hushed tones. He was the bogeyman wise souls warned their children about. He was the Kraken others released. He was Keyser-fucking-Söze.

In a council maisonette just a goalkeeper's punt from Homerton railway station, Anthony sat in an under-stuffed armchair leaking its filling through the worn seams, listening to a man arguing with himself. Leroy Kelly filled his sofa like Jabba the Hutt, and smelled as pungent as Anthony had always imagined the bloated slug-like creature would have, had he been real. It was all he could do not to be violently ill, so powerful was the stench of the man's body odour and halitosis.

'Ain't no bitch gonna slide onto my dick even if she can find it,' Leroy had been known to say, shrugging as if that was all that mattered. As if that excused him from taking a shower once in a while, or brushing his big old horse teeth. Man, he was one ugly fucker.

But enduring Leroy Kelly's malodorous presence was the price one had to pay for retaining his interest and penchant for ordering enforcement opportunities across the country. Anthony reckoned he had earned enough to buy another ten suits and just as many pairs of shoes out of Leroy over the past few years, so spending a few minutes in fetid squalor was something worth putting up with every now and then.

Only this time, Leroy had already talked himself out of giving this particular job to anyone at least half a dozen times in the past thirty minutes. It was obvious to Anthony that the big man was out of sorts because of this Ryan Endicott dick, who resided some eighty miles north of the capital. One minute he only wanted the guy to be taught a lesson, the next he was demanding Anthony take him off the map completely, only to then smack his own ears and convince himself once more that a warning and a sharp word would suffice.

'What's the deal, Lee?' Anthony finally asked, using the shortened version of the man's name as he preferred. 'What's fucking with your head, man? I've never seen you like this before.'

That wasn't quite true. He'd witnessed Leroy Kelly's internal-but-vocal disputes on several previous occasions, but never with three different outcomes at stake.

Another smack of his ears.

'It ain't this Ryan motherfucker,' Leroy said, throwing both arms up, a movement which caused a wave of putrid air to bounce off Anthony. Boy, that man had some fucking bingo-wings on him, sitting there in his Adidas wife-beater and letting the fat swell out like some glutinous ooze. 'I never met him, never want to meet him. I'd have you enforce that motherfucker into a meat mincer without blinking if I had my way.'

'So what's stopping you, bro?'

'Fucking Eric the Eyeball.'

'Eric the… what's that, some cartoon character or something?'

The slug frowned, his forehead seeming to fold in on itself. 'You never heard of Eric the Eyeball? Where the fuck you been, man?'

Anthony couldn't help himself. He laughed and shook his head. 'To be honest with you, Lee, it sounds like you made the geezer up. Eric the fucking Eyeball?'

'That's just what we call him. Eric McManus. Fucker's only got one eye. He don't even cover up the socket with a patch or nothing, he just lets it sit there and dares you to stare at it.'

'All right. And he's the source of your problem how?'

'Ryan's his boy. Took him under his wing, brought him on in the business. Anything goes down with Ryan, it reflects on Eric. I'm fucking hurting after losing that supply, man. I mean, how fucking shit is this Ryan bloke anyhow, letting some bitch stick him with a blade and then losing my product in a raid? How come he didn't get warned by his own 5-0 piglet, is what I want to know.'

Anthony blew out air through his teeth, almost too embarrassed to continue. All this 5-0 and piglets shit when referring to the police was so fucking last century. He kept his cool, though it was becoming increasingly difficult to do so while trapped in this small room with this rancid excuse for a human being.

'How about instead of paying this Ryan prick a visit, I go and have a chat with your man Eric?' he suggested. It was a logical leap, and one that both gave him the chance to earn and made a potential future employer aware of his existence. He knew how to impress with more than just his style.

'And say what?' Jabba asked.

'Ask him how he feels about losing out on business the way it went down. Kind of calming the waters, but also finding out whether he'd stomach losing one of his own at your hands.'

Leroy punctured the air with a pointed finger. 'That ain't a bad idea. Not a bad idea at all, motherfucker.' He grinned, all dull yellow teeth. Then he winked and tapped the finger against his temple. 'You got some fucking brains on you, man. That's why you and me fit, you know what I mean?'

'I do, Lee. I really do. Let me take care of this for you. I'll drive up later tonight or first thing in the morning, have a word in Eric's ear – I take it he's still got both of those, right? – and then see how things stand. If there's some enforcing to be done, I'm all over it. If it's just a warning and a physical ticking-off, then consider it sorted.'

Leroy Kelly laughed and held up his hand for a high five. When Anthony left him hanging he laughed again, rubbed both hands together as if trying to start a fire, then gave mean and moody his best shot and said, 'Make it tonight, Ant. Yeah?'

Anthony nodded and winked. Fuck that. He had a date with a girl whose body sent him crazy every time he saw it naked. 'I'll do that, Lee,' he said anyway. 'I look forward to my eggs and bacon in Peterborough.'

THIRTY-FIVE

With approximately sixteen million people a year passing through the Queensgate shopping centre, security staff often use the warren of corridors hidden inside the main structure to move from one area to another more quickly, appearing from behind one of the many mirrored sections of wall separating the store units. The security officer monitoring the CCTV observed every movement Courtney Jacobs made, and two more tracked her from within the centre's walls. When Bliss arrived, he popped his head in to the security communications office to request an update.

The celeb had shopped at both John Lewis and Primark, and was now enjoying a drink at Costa, by the escalators. Bliss had another security worker, Mike Johnson, show him and Chandler the way through the internal corridors to a point close by. The three of them emerged into the centre itself without anyone noticing. Jacobs and her entourage of five sat less than twenty feet away.

'How do you want to do this?' Johnson asked, his eyes scanning the thickening crowds.

Bliss had previously explained their intention to extract Jacobs as quickly and quietly as possible, with the minimum of fuss. Tricky at the best of times, testing with so many other people passing by.

'We crack on as soon as they're on the move,' he said. He turned to his partner. 'Pen, if Johnson and I walk behind them on either side of their group with you between us, you can swoop in amongst them and have a word in her ear without even breaking stride. To anyone looking – and they will be – it'll appear as if you're one of her people. We'll try keeping the others quiet by distracting them.'

'And what if she kicks off? She's hardly known for her dignified behaviour.'

'Threaten her with arrest if she starts going off on one.'

Chandler shook her head. 'You genuinely don't understand modern culture, do you, boss? There is no such thing as negative publicity for these people. I threaten to take her in, she'll make sure it happens in the full glare of other shoppers' phone cameras. The likes of Courtney Jacobs never do anything quietly.'

'So what's your brilliant plan?' Bliss countered.

'We wait until we're close to one of those mirrored doorways, then we snatch her and drag her behind it. It'll get her out of the public gaze in a single swift movement, which will mean she has nobody around to play to. It's the only way we'll get a crack at the real person rather than the reality celeb persona.'

Bliss liked the idea, and they discussed the security officer's role. Shortly afterwards they were off in pursuit. Their escort gave them the heads-up about where the doors were before disappearing behind one. A couple of minutes later, another popped open up ahead. Bliss and Chandler converged on the six young women, infiltrating their tight group, ignoring a few loud objections. Then, as they drew level with the now wide-open mirrored doorway, the pair made a lunge for Jacobs. Each took an arm and steered her forcefully off to the side and behind the door, which slammed shut behind them. And all with barely a cry of outrage from either those who remained outside or the celeb herself.

'Who are you? What's this about?' Jacobs demanded, her voice a high-pitched squeal. The narrow passageway was gloomy, but the confined area put Bliss less than six inches away from the woman. Behind the slathered makeup she was more attractive than he had realised from her photographs, but there was no plastered smile, no perky 'can-do' personality showing through. In its place sat fear and a complete lack of comprehension.

'I apologise, Ms Jacobs,' Bliss said immediately. 'We're detectives working out of Thorpe Wood police station. Sorry for being so abrupt and physical, but we needed to spirit you away with as little fuss as possible because we'd like a word with you on a serious matter.'

Without waiting for a response, he looked over at Johnson. 'Closest room?' he asked.

The man, no more than mid-twenties himself, was barely able to drag his eyes away from the alluring celebrity. He gave a vague nod of understanding and turned to walk back the way he had come.

Courtney Jacobs said nothing until she, Bliss and Chandler were sitting around a table in the small room that was normally used for staff breaks. The young man from security offered her some water before taking his leave and standing outside the room.

'Sorry for the theatrics,' Bliss apologised again. 'We thought it would save even more drama if we did things this way.'

'What do you want with me?' Jacobs asked. 'Are you allowed to snatch me away from my friends like that?'

'Don't worry about them. Right now, another couple of security officers will be explaining everything to them.'

'Well, then, can one of you can explain it to me, too?'

Their initial move had taken her off-guard, but she was recovering quickly. Indignation had fast become unrestrained anger. Bliss did not blame her, though he was untroubled by guilt. This was important, and he needed information. All bets were off.

'We have to ask you about Ryan Endicott,' Chandler said. 'This was our best way of separating you from the public, which we had to do because we need to talk openly.'

'So why didn't you drive up to my house and ask to come in?'

'Would you have let us, without first calling your agent?' Bliss asked. 'Time is a factor, so we couldn't hang around to let all the usual niceties play out. I won't sugar-coat it, Ms Jacobs, so please listen. Ryan Endicott has abducted a young girl from foster care and is holding her against her will. If we don't find her soon, then things might spiral out of control very quickly.'

'Woah, what?' Jacobs stared at Bliss, open-mouthed. Her hands were raised, palms out, as if protecting herself from being struck. 'Why are you talking to me about any of this? I barely know Ryan.'

'We hear differently. From a reliable source.'

'And I'm telling you the truth. Yeah, me and him got together a few times. People only knew because I got papped outside a nightclub in London, and Ryan was sort of holding me up after I'd had a few too many. But I don't get involved with the stuff he's into. No bloody chance.'

'I'm not suggesting you were, or that you knew about his movements,' Bliss said softly. 'But having spent some time with him, you may know more about the man than you think you do.'

'Like what? We didn't talk about his business.'

'It would help us if we knew where to locate him. His flat got raided on Wednesday morning, so we know he hasn't gone back there. We also know that's not his only address, that he has a house out in Deeping where he prefers to live when he's not dealing. He's not there, either. We have a list of places associated with him and his crew, but again there's no sign of Ryan at any of them. A bloke like him is always going to have stash houses or boltholes dotted around. Ms Jacobs, did he ever discuss any of them with you? Did he mention anywhere that you can think of?'

'Do I need a solicitor?' Jacobs asked, trepidation touching her eyes.

She was on unfamiliar ground, Bliss realised, caught without her so-called advisors – those girls who may have been close friends, but could just as easily be parasites looking to exploit their friend's temporary dalliance with the big time. She was uncertain, and that left the doorway open enough for him to make some headway.

'You've done nothing wrong,' he assured her. 'And we're not suggesting otherwise. If what you had with Endicott is over, then you're well out of it, but that doesn't mean you don't know something we can use. Again, I'm not saying you're keeping anything from us, only that it would be easy for you to have forgotten all about it.'

'We'd like you to think back,' Chandler said, taking the young woman's hands in hers. 'You and Ryan did spend some time together. Perhaps you got high, maybe you got drunk, but either way there were probably times when you just talked. If he opened up, then it's possible you heard him say something that meant nothing to you at the time but which you now recall. Some place he took you, or bragged about, or just said he liked to spend time at.'

For a few seconds, Courtney sat in silence, shaking her head. Bliss wondered if she was engaging in some kind of internal debate or had switched off from the conversation, but just as his patience expired, she spoke up. This time her head was nodding, energised by what she had to say.

'Yes, yes, yes. Of course. He took me there once. Said it was his favourite place in the entire world. A place only his closest friends even knew about. Somewhere he sometimes went to switch off for a few days, especially when things weren't going well for him.'

'You remember where it was?' Bliss asked.

'Yeah, of course. It was a house that once belonged to his grandma. Out by Longthorpe Tower.'

'Along Thorpe Road?' Chandler said.

'Yeah. Ryan was always complaining about how much it had expanded around there, what with all the new housing estates springing up. Said it had ruined the place and so many of his memories. He told me him and his mates used to play over at Holy Wells; said if the roads then had been as busy as they are now he'd never have been allowed to go.'

'Can you show us?' Bliss asked. 'I mean, unless you remember the number or are able to describe it perfectly, can you come along with us and point out which house it is? We'll make sure you can't be seen, I promise you.'

'You're seriously telling me Ryan snatched a kid and is using her against you?' Her voice was soft now, resigned to the truth.

Bliss nodded. 'Yes. And you can help us get her back,' he said, hardly daring to believe that their long shot had paid dividends.

THIRTY-SIX

Ex-chief inspector robert marsh had proven to be both an obnoxious misogynist and a major stumbling block to the investigation, DCI Warburton revealed. The team had reconvened in the incident room as planned, and the meeting was already running hot after Bliss had related his and Chandler's news.

'I don't think I allowed his comments to get under my skin,' the DCI said, although her forlorn look suggested it was possible. 'But I couldn't read the man at all well.'

'Me, neither,' Bishop confessed. He appeared troubled by the experience. 'Clearly he considered having to talk to the boss here as beneath him. Kept saying how she wouldn't have had the job back in his day, and said it like that was a good thing. We pandered to him long enough, then started bringing him down to earth. You should have seen the look he gave me when I reminded him that our addressing him by his rank was purely a courtesy now, as he was no longer in the service.'

'The man still has his wits about him, though,' Warburton said. 'He was extremely careful about what he did or did not say. Anything he decided to tell us flowed like shit off a shovel, but when it came to something contentious, suddenly he had problems with his memory and clammed up.'

'There's a lot of that around,' Bliss said, thinking about Janis Ward's failure to mention her connection to Marsh. 'So he didn't cough to meeting with Lisa Pepperdine, I take it?'

Warburton shook her head. 'I'm afraid not. He claimed not to know anything about her at all.'

'Bugger it. That leaves us with a bloody great loose end. The Ward woman has another chat coming her way, but I wouldn't bank on her giving anything up, either. Hopefully John and Phil will have something positive on Monday.'

DCs Hunt and Gratton were still off-site, running TIE sheets on local far-right group members and those now affiliated with Antifa-UK, though Hunt had already phoned in to tell them that Craig Ball was out of the country and not expected back until Sunday evening.

'Are you not calling everyone in for at least tomorrow?' Warburton asked.

Bliss heard surprise in her tone, and he understood why. But he was prepared. 'What those two are working on can wait a couple of days. They're not due in, so why waste our budget on unnecessary overtime? John will be glad of the time off. As for Phil, I reckon his mind won't wander far from the case, in fact I wouldn't bet against him digging into it in his own time over the weekend.'

'And what about Ryan Endicott and his crew? You don't see Hunt and Gratton as being up to the task of taking them on?'

As Bliss had already explained to the team, after the intervention at Queensgate, he and Chandler had taken Courtney Jacobs for a ride. Although she had ducked down in the back seat as they travelled along Thorpe Road, she was nevertheless able to call out when they drove past the house that had once belonged to the dealer's grandmother – and now presumably to him. Bliss was having the Land Registry checked as they spoke. Having whisked Jacobs back home – ensuring she made no social media updates on the way, and cultivating her silence afterwards by suggesting she would become a target if she revealed anything to anyone – Bliss discussed the next stage of his plan with his colleagues back at HQ.

Handing out hard-copy printouts of an area he had isolated using Google Maps, Bliss had walked them through it step by step. The property was accessible via a narrow drive alongside the Post Office which led to a car park at the back, with spaces allocated for use by those enjoying either the tennis courts or bowling green. That left a six-foot-high brick wall as the only barrier to overcome.

Not that they would have to force entry blind.

During the single drive-by, Chandler had noticed that the house immediately opposite had an abandoned air and a For Sale sign out front. She made a mental note of the estate agent and gave them a call after dropping Jacobs off outside her own gates. The agency manager had readily agreed to them taking the keys and using the empty house as a base to run a stakeout. Two specialists on loan from CID were currently there, updating the Major Crimes team every time they spotted movement.

Bliss brushed off his new DCI's question concerning the dependability of his two male constables. She did not know them well, and had mistaken his decision for lack of trust. 'I've got complete confidence in both of them, boss – I just don't think they are needed. We already have myself, Pen, Bish and Gul. Firearms are on the way, and we have additional backup from both CID and uniform.'

Warburton accepted this with a shrug. 'Assuming the young girl is actually being kept inside this property,' she said.

There was no mention of Crowland, but Bliss heard it anyway. An unspoken criticism of his going in hard and heavy without any end result. 'I'm thinking of ways to find out for sure about that, boss. Or at the very least, to confirm Endicott's presence there, which for me will be enough.'

'Ideas so far?'

'We send a couple of people in acting as cold callers or political candidates. Anything that gets whoever is inside that house to open the doors.'

'And what if that person is not Endicott?'

'If someone is there, then there's every chance he is as well. It's his grandmother's place, after all. Or was. He took Courtney Jacobs there once, so we know he still goes there occasionally, and the fact we were previously unaware of it makes it as good a place as any for him to stash Molly. We've covered every other angle, so this may be our final shot at it.'

'And your stakeout duo have reported what so far?' Warburton's tone was muted, conversational rather than confrontational. Bliss understood, and was happy to fill in the blanks for his new boss.

'No sign of movement so far. But there are nets up at the windows and no need for lights on just yet. Nobody has come in or out. If we send a couple over there to knock on the door, they may be able to hear something from inside even if nobody answers – TV, perhaps even a conversation.'

Warburton nodded. 'Get it done. Let's establish as early as possible that this property is occupied.'

'It'll be sunset inside the next half-hour or so,' Bliss said. 'We see lights coming on, we'll know for sure.'

'Unless they're on a timer. I've made that mistake myself before now.'

Bliss acknowledged the point with a nod. 'I'm hoping any light that comes on will expose anybody who's in the house. Either way, shortly after sundown I'll have them run the knock, see if we can catch a glimpse of the man himself.'

'I'm guessing you don't like the risk, Inspector.'

Bliss was taken aback. He thought he had hidden his trepidation well. He shrugged. 'If whoever opens that door gets so much as a sniff of our callers' motives, then the op is blown. Without the element of surprise behind us, Molly won't come out of there alive. Unless Endicott decides to run before we even get a chance to force our way in.'

'The pair running the knock are experienced, I take it?'

'Of course. This is not a time for novices.'

'So trust them,' Warburton said.

'I do. That doesn't stop me fretting about the risk.' He smiled. 'I'm being truthful, boss. You asked, I answered.'

Warburton matched his smile with one of her own. 'Then ask yourself if the lights coming on will be enough.'

'For me, they would be. However, I was wondering whether to take our knock team from firearms. Put them in civvies, weapons covered by jackets or coats. They can give the green light and go in themselves if they spot our target. We have both front and rear deployment at the same time that way.'

'Have you spoken to Eric Price about this idea?'

'Not yet. It's just an idea at this point, not a firm strategy. I realise Eric will want a full risk assessment first, before he lets me use any of his crew.'

Warburton sighed and swept her gaze around the room. 'Anybody want to join in?' she asked with a faltering smile. 'You're all part of this, so if you have something to offer now is the right time.'

'I like the boss's idea,' Bishop said. '*My* boss, that is. DI Bliss.' He coughed and flushed red. 'You know what I mean. Two armed officers rather than plain-clothes uniforms at the front door gives us a further advantage. They can green- or red-light it as they see fit, from a far better position than any of us will have.'

'And if nobody answers their knock?' Warburton asked.

'Then they can take the door off its hinges,' Chandler said. 'I'm with both the boss and Bish on this. If Molly is inside that house, she's already on borrowed time. If we get even the slightest sniff of movement inside the place, we need to go in decisively.'

'So we wait for confirmation that lights have come on. If they do, we suit up and get this done.'

'We?' Bliss said, narrowing his gaze.

Warburton nodded. 'I did tell you once that I'm not usually as hands-on as I was when you and I worked that case together, but this is my first op here in Peterborough. I can't sit back and watch you lot having all the fun, can I?'

THIRTY-SEVEN

SITTING IN THE FADING natural light of the ground floor study in his substantial home in Wymondham, slightly west of Norwich, Joseph Flynn leaned back in his faded leather Chesterfield chair, sipping a thirty-year-old Delord Frères. He was no connoisseur, and the Armagnac had been a gift from his father-in-law, but he recognised the difference between this drink and a younger version. Neither the heat nor the earthiness were as pronounced, the spirit having been tamed over the years, softened by time to produce a far more nuanced taste. He would have settled for his usual Jack Daniels, but had found himself in the right mood for something expensive and brooding.

He was both meditative and concerned. For two days now, ever since hearing Jimmy Bliss's, voicemail, Flynn's mind had seldom strayed from Peterborough, seventy miles west. The four-hour round trip had resulted in his back muscles complaining and his head throbbing with an almost gleeful persistence. The more he tried to forget about it, the more it pounded, so he had finally relented and gone in search of peace and a drink to dull the pain.

At the core of his anxiety lay not the unearthed remains of Lisa Pepperdine, but rather the dogged and tenacious resolve of Bliss.

Over the years he had been asked on several occasions who, of all the detectives he had known, he would choose to investigate a crime against a loved one. Never had he hesitated before speaking the name of Detective Inspector James Bliss. Conversely, he was precisely the person you did not want on the trail of a case in which you would prefer some questions to remain unanswered.

This was one such case. Bliss had the smell of it in his nostrils, too, and that meant only one thing: he would not give up. No stone would be unturned, no path left unexplored, no thread not fully unravelled or unexposed.

Flynn took another sip from the lead-crystal glass, admiring the curvature of its bowl and the precision of its diamond-cut lines. Although his palate was far more conservative by nature, he had acquired a taste for some of the finer things in life when attending police functions at which senior ranking officers mingled and enjoyed fine wines, brandies and cigars. It was a rite of passage, and despite being a man with his own mind and methodology, he had immersed himself in the formalities of the service wherever and whenever possible. He respected tradition, even if he was not always comfortable with it.

A heavy sigh disturbed the silence. His study window overlooked the back garden and beyond it a vast meadow, with a hill rising up to a dense thicket of elderly chestnut trees. The sun had fallen behind the swell, casting a deep orange glow over the land, crimson fingers raking across the sky as if tearing away its very fabric. The beautiful vista was sorely at odds with his sombre mindset, and the disparity was like a physical blockage in his throat, about to choke him to death.

The uncovering of the journalist's body and Bliss's subsequent phone call had sent Flynn hurtling headlong through time and space, back to the most miserable and toxic period of his entire life. The spring of 2005 had lit a match beneath the city; arsonists targeting foreign settlers had created a ripple effect that consumed the population in a way he had never encountered before. The ill-feeling and deep mistrust felt by some of Peterborough's varied communities was already creeping like lava across the cityscape, scorching everything in its path, when a second eruption was caused by the July bombings in London. Those fractures were barely healing when the autumn discovery of a young woman's bones reignited the flame which had been flickering steadily within the local police service, setting ablaze the flimsy construct of conspiracy and murder that had lain dormant for the better part of fifteen years until Bliss and his team began their investigation.

If that third and final straw had broken him, it was the Burnout case that most directly affected him. Through a friendly contact in a senior position at the *Evening Telegraph*, he had learned of Lisa Pepperdine's interest. The woman was consumed by spite, bigotry, and animosity aimed at the entire police service, and placed her ambition ahead of everything else – including the truth. Her hatred of extreme right-wing factions was understandable, and the stance she had taken against them admirable, but her insistence that the police in Peterborough were happy to allow such venomous people to target immigrants and asylum seekers was a poison she sought to inject into the bloodstream of a city already ravaged by fear and misunderstanding. In Flynn's mind, one more jolt would push them all over the edge and he was not about to let that happen.

He remembered the point at which he'd decided Pepperdine had to be stopped.

He remembered then seeking the counsel of a colleague. A man he ultimately ordered to liaise with Lisa Pepperdine, with the sole aim of deterring her from ever writing a single word against the Peterborough police service and its attempts to root out a sadistic killer of numerous foreign men, women and children.

Ex-Superintendent Stuart Sykes also had a view of the setting sun. He was aware of what he was seeing, if not entirely what it meant. The sun came up, the day got brighter. The sun went down, things gradually became darker until another source of illumination was switched on. He knew there were terms for the sun coming up and going back down again, familiar to him once but now lost in the cloud of confusion that mostly overwhelmed him.

As for where the sun came from or went to, he was convinced that he ought to have answers… Perhaps later on, as he struggled to switch off and fall asleep, it would come to him. It didn't matter if he had to wait until tomorrow, a week from now, or even a month, provided it came back to him eventually. Was there a chance that specific chunk of knowledge would never return? He wasn't certain, but he assumed it was possible; anything was possible these days. Except for a full recovery, that was. This much he knew and retained, though for how much longer was anyone's guess.

Oddly enough, it was these lucid moments that he had come to fear most of all. Because only when the thought process was less woolly and the pieces slotted together seamlessly was he able to fully comprehend all that he had lost. His physical deterioration was a result of the mental decline, not the other way around. Until his mind had started to slip, he had been in pretty good shape and looking forward to a dotage spent in the warm bosom of his family: wife, daughter and grandchildren. On the days when his capabilities were at their peak, he remembered all that had lain before him, and understood the incredible loss of a future he would never now enjoy. The outcome was a pain so deep and so all-consuming that he mentally begged for the lights to go out inside his mind once again, leaving him stumbling around in the dark, groping blindly for everything he had earlier sought to eschew.

The cancer had begun eating away at him more recently, its appetite voracious, its momentum unstoppable. It was a toss-up as to which would pull his plug first. If he had his way, he would do it himself. Here and now. Better that than have to see the pain and pity in the eyes of both his wife and daughter ever again.

Tears ran unchecked from both eyes. Hot and salty, they trailed down his cheeks and dripped from his chin onto his clean paleblue sweater. The moisture dwelled on the cloth for a while, like an array of islands cast adrift in a vast ocean, before evaporating and leaving behind only the vaguest notion that they had ever existed.

This past day or so had provided him with more episodes of genuinely living in the moment than any he could recall since moving into the hospice. But rather than his mind focussing on his wife or daughter, it was Bliss's face that swam towards him out of the murk.

Bliss, the man who had openly defied him on numerous occasions.

Bliss, the man who had disregarded the respect owed to men of greater rank and instead argued with him, swore at him, poured scorn over his every thought and deed.

Bliss, the man he had allowed to take a fall which had not been his to take.

Bliss, the man whose life he had tampered with in ways a better man would not even have considered.

Bliss had visited him. He wasn't sure how long ago, but the man had stood right here in his room and spoken to him as if nothing untoward had ever passed between them.

What had he wanted? Apologies were made concerning the tragedy that befell the Burnout operation. Shame still scalded his cheeks in that regard, and rightly so; he had thrown a fellow police officer to the wolves.

It had been wrong of him. Bliss was not bait, nor a false trail to lay upon the ground as if he were less than human. Still, he had hidden his own wrongdoings behind the maverick figure Bliss presented to the world.

Was an apology what Bliss had come for?

Sykes heaved himself upright, eyes widening as an unbidden memory filtered through the encroaching fog. He beat away the haze yet also embraced its return, both hating and loving it at the same time. At its core, he continued to see Bliss. Older, yet still a presence not to take lightly. The Bliss of now, not of yesterday.

And yes, his visit had concerned Burnout, but not the case itself. No, this was more specific. A journalist. Not one of those from the local rag, either. Some name reporter from London, freelancing and looking to pull up weeds.

Lisa Pepperdine.

The mist rolled closer, enveloping him. He recoiled at its icy touch, a miasma caressing his bare skin and leaving goosebumps in its wake. But before it swallowed him whole, he had time for one more thought.

Lisa Pepperdine and the meeting.

***

Robert Marsh had no idea where he was. He had stopped for a drink at the first pub he saw on his way out of the city, and there he had remained. Probably have to get a cab home. Better that than disturbing Marlene while she was at her book club. They were having an author visit this evening, and his wife had been looking forward to both the reading and the Q&A. He refused to pull her away from that just because he'd chosen to have several too many in a boozer whose name escaped him.

He didn't like to admit it, even to himself, but the interview at Thorpe Wood had left him shaken. Having a woman grilling him about his past movements, his operational decisions, just about drove him crazy. She would have considered herself fortunate to spend her days typing for the police when he first came into the job, but now she sat there looking down her nose at him, at the same rank where his career had ended and with still some way to climb up the career ladder. It made him feel sick to his stomach.

But not half as much as the things she'd had to say.

As for the DS sitting alongside her, now there was a proper copper. Big, strong brute of a man. Someone you'd fear tackling in a dark alleyway. Not like the fruit fly taking the lead. Skinny little thing. Attractive, that was for sure. Long wavy hair, sharp features, great eyes, no more than a nice handful each up top and a splendid arse if those tight trousers of hers were anything to go by. But real coppers didn't wear a bra and knickers.

Give the DCI her due, though, she knew how to run the room. Softened him up by using his old rank, then when he failed to budge an inch, she turned a full 360 on him. He'd taken it all in his stride, and the lies had come easily to him.

Of course he knew who Lisa Pepperdine was.

How could he not?

THIRTY-EIGHT

At eleven minutes past four, a light came on in a downstairs room. After calling it in, the two highly trained police officers observing it set their digital video camera to record, and also began taking photographs. One of them made a note in the stakeout log book. The other never took his eyes off the house.

Less than an hour later, Bliss found himself standing with his team behind a group of suitably attired officers, both armed and unarmed, who were all set to breach when given the green light. They had driven silently down the narrow drive alongside Longthorpe Post Office, parked up and disembarked equally smoothly and efficiently. Aluminium ladders with rubber tubing wrapped around the upright struts in order to muffle sound now leaned against the wall separating the car park from the property in which somebody had earlier switched on the lights in one room.

It was a moment of high anticipation. Each officer knew that one false step, one loud noise, might disrupt the relatively simple plan. Bliss waited for every man and woman there to be primed and coiled before giving the instruction for the knock team to go ahead.

Through the brooch microphone pinned to the female officer's overcoat, Bliss, Chandler and Eric Price were able to hear everything happening on the other side of the property. The scraping of leather soles on paving... two hard raps with a heavy brass doorknocker.

A count of ten... eleven... twelve... thirt...

Two more knocks.

Another pause. A grating noise, followed by a juddering and then the sound of muted voices.

Somebody had answered the summons of that doorknocker. Bliss barely had time to revel in the thought of Ryan Endicott falling for the very same trick he himself had used on Mr and Mrs Paxton.

'Good evening, sir.' The voice of firearms officer Jessica Bright. 'I'm sorry to disturb you, but we're here this evening to talk to you about the environment and whether, as a home owner, you'd be willing to undertake substantial alterations in respect of energy consumption in order to help the fight against man-made climate change.'

Make it as dull and boring as you can, Bliss had suggested, just so long as you're topical and believable.

'I ain't interested. I'm not the owner.' The voice was clipped, urgent. Local, it sounded to Bliss. He glanced at Chandler, who shrugged.

'Perhaps we could speak with the owner then, sir,' Bright persisted. Light and breezy. Not pushy at all, but reacting to circumstances.

'He ain't here. Call back another time, yeah?'

Before either of the knockers had a chance to respond, the distinct sound of a door closing heavily filled Bliss's ears.

Footsteps again. Then: 'Have identified Endicott's number two.' The male firearms officer, this time. 'Paul Grayson. Confirm, Paul Grayson is on site.'

That was enough for Bliss. If Endicott's right hand man was holed up in the house, then Endicott would be with him. 'Green light,' he said. 'Go, go, go.'

Not in complete silence, but with great care, the teams surmounted the ladders and were over the wall in seconds, spreading out into their identified areas in the garden and making their way towards the rear of the house. Meanwhile, Bright and her partner were back, hammering on the knocker. As Bliss clambered into the garden and began jogging along a path covered in slate chippings, he heard the door being wrenched open with a clatter and the two officers identifying themselves as armed police. Bliss knew their guns would now be drawn and aimed at their target.

Bliss wondered if Endicott's number two had returned to throw open the door, or if the man himself had done so this time. Either way, the distraction was everything those approaching from the rear needed.

In went the windows and doors, followed by flashbang grenades; no smoke, but plenty of noise, aimed at confusing those inside at worst, terrifying them at best. Seemingly without pause, the various units entered the premises. There were loud cries, rapid movement, but no shots as far as Bliss could tell. He was unable to distinguish the action taking place at the front of the house from that which came from his side, but if the others had stuck to their planned roles, a team whose job it was to crash their way through suspected drug dens had joined the two armed officers who had gone in through the front door.

More voices now. One pleading not to be shot. Another howling their outrage. As Bliss entered through the dome-shaped conservatory, he saw a figure on his knees, hands clasped behind his neck, a large forearm pressing him down closer to the floor. Into a narrow passageway, ignoring a room in which there was no activity at all. Then into the living room, and Bliss came upon his prize.

Ryan Endicott was a disappointment in person. Thin, reedy, looking like a stiff breeze might break him in two. Either that or cause him to shatter into hundreds of pieces and blow away in the wind. The dealer sat on the edge of an old cloth armchair, wrists bound behind his back. He glared at everyone who passed across his vision, but when his eyes fell upon Bliss, they narrowed and hardened.

It wasn't a look Bliss found intimidating in any way; he imagined it was designed to work on Endicott's own kind. But then, he reasoned, you didn't have to be physically menacing in order to stick someone with a knife or pull a trigger on them. All you needed was the will to do so, and Endicott was more than psychotic enough for that. That much was obvious in every tic of his cheek and the lifeless eyes emitting pure hatred in Bliss's direction.

Bliss heard his name being called out, along with the rattle of a banister rail and stairs being shaken beneath the weight of a fellow officer. It was a uniform out of Thorpe Wood, his cheeks red and veins protruding on his forehead. The older copper jerked his head back the way he had come. His features were set and solemn, but Bliss found succour in the fact they were not crumpled and devastated.

'Molly,' he whispered to himself. He set off in pursuit of the uniform who was already disappearing back upstairs.

He found the girl in a small bedroom at the back of the house.

She had been bound to a wooden chair with adhesive tape, and gagged with more of the same. A heavy chain had been threaded around and through her legs and padlocked to an old cast-iron radiator. Her chin lay on her chest and her lank hair was draped like a blanket over her face. As he entered the room, Bliss spoke her name.

Molly's head moved. It came up slowly, thick clumps of hair falling to one side, revealing a tight mask of anguish beneath. She looked at him and the hollows around her eyes appeared to darken and recede further into her skull before eventually crinkling around the edges. Bliss stepped forward, peeled the tape gently from her mouth and then began to tear free that which fastened her to the chair. Over his head he called out for bolt cutters.

'I'm here,' he whispered, turning his attention back to the girl. 'You're safe now.'

'About time,' Molly said, her voice dry and brittle. 'I'd just about given up on you, Jimbo.'

THIRTY-NINE

Three hours in A&E, followed by a further couple at Thorpe Wood. Now, at 10.31pm, Molly was fast asleep in Bliss's bed, protected by not just two carers but eight – two of whom were armed. Kim Parker had just come back downstairs after checking on the girl. She nodded and said, 'Soundo. Not quite sure how. That is one tough kid.'

'She wears the armour well,' Bliss responded.

'Armour?' Parker looked puzzled.

'Yeah. The thick skin so many of these kids grow when they live the way they do. Like feral animals. We mostly see it when they're the perpetrators of violent crime – they become desensitised. But it works the other way, too, acting as a shield to protect them emotionally, if not physically.'

'Our boss is quite the philosopher,' DS Bishop said in response to some of the looks Bliss's words had garnered. 'Not just a pretty face.'

Laughter rattled the walls of the living room. In addition to Bliss, Chandler, Bishop and Ansari, there was DCI Warburton – who, despite Bliss's assurances, had been determined to join them – plus the two firearms officers who had knocked on Ryan Endicott's door. After ninety minutes of negotiation with social services, it had been agreed that Molly's immediate care and protection would be best served by this group of dedicated coppers, provided Kim Parker was allowed to accompany them as a neutral observer. Bliss struggled to think of a better team to have around him, and for the time being it meant Molly was safe.

'She must know it's not over, though,' Ansari said. 'Today we managed to fix one of her problems, but that's not the end of it for her.'

Both of Bliss's sofas were occupied. On one, the DC was perched on the footrest that swung out when the mechanism was set to recline, Chandler taking up the cushioned seat itself. Bishop and Warburton replicated their positions on the other. Bliss himself was swallowed up by a fold-out travel chair.

He regarded Ansari and nodded. 'Far from it, Gul. When she's awake she won't be thinking too far into the future. Endicott was a massive threat to her, but other more dangerous people are still out there, just waiting for their opportunity to get their hands on her.'

'What can we do about that?' Chandler asked. 'Besides what we're doing right now, I mean.'

'We keep to our original plan as best we can. Molly needs to end up in the back of beyond somewhere, after being passed around between the regions, filtering us all out to the point where none of us know where she is. If we don't know, then we're unable to pass that information on.'

'Her details and address will still be on record,' Warburton pointed out.

'They'll be buried as deep as they can be,' Parker assured them, looking around the room. 'A new background, a new home. The works. Details available only to a select few. She is under the protection of Social Care, and they will do everything they can to make sure it's effective.'

Bliss did not doubt either her words or the dedication of the people who would be involved in delivering Molly's care and supervision over the next few months. In time, assuming Ryan Endicott was the only one to take a hit, his employers might not worry if they lost the girl's scent. She was only a problem to them if she intended them harm. One of the discussions earlier at Thorpe Wood had centred around that notion. Though she had provided little information so far, Molly had plenty of names and addresses sitting inside her head. Valuable intelligence, especially for DI Bentley's unit. But Bliss had been determined to hammer out a deal for the girl that saw her testimony limited to Endicott and his immediate crew. Word of that, he'd insisted, had to go out so that the criminal underclasses became aware of the situation sooner rather than later.

'Molly is safe with us tonight and over the weekend,' he said. 'But come Monday, she has to be on the first of those moves. If Endicott cops a guilty plea in exchange for a few favours, she will never have to come back here. That's our goal.'

'She's some kid,' Warburton said, her voice hushed. 'I can't begin to imagine what must have been going through her head since she was snatched from the Paxtons, but you'd hardly know anything had happened judging by her reaction after we picked her up. And if you don't mind my saying so, Jimmy, that kind of spirit takes more than armour.'

Bliss dipped his head in acknowledgement. 'No, you're absolutely spot on. She wears it well, but beneath it she's tough, resourceful, bright and… impressive.'

'And you saw all that in her on day one,' Chandler said. 'Somehow you knew she was different. Someone worth fighting for.'

He nodded, feeling the weight of the day settle over him like a second skin. There was some lightheadedness, the first incapacitating signs of fatigue creeping into his bones. His Ménière's disease often flared up as a reaction to stress, which had been a constant companion since Wednesday morning. This was not the time to buckle, however, and there would be no sleep tonight. Tomorrow, he and the team would draw up a rota, assigning shift patterns to provide Molly with round-the-clock protection. Bliss just had to make sure he made it through the night relatively unscathed.

Chandler must have noticed something in his response. Her eyes had not left him and when he glanced up, she narrowed her gaze. He raised a feeble smile and winked. Knowing his partner, she would now be keeping an eye on him, monitoring his every movement, hanging on every word he spoke. She had become accustomed to the vagaries of his illness and recognised the signs of an imminent attack. But he was well enough to push on, provided the vertigo heading his way was mild.

Excusing himself, he went upstairs and sat alone in the darkness of his spare room for a couple of minutes. It took only a dozen deep breaths and lengthy exhalations for him to relax, after which he popped his head into the bedroom to check on Molly. As he was about to pull his head back and retreat, she lifted hers from the pillow.

'Everything all right?' he asked, stepping inside but remaining by the door.

Molly gave a drowsy nod and a weary smile. 'Bet you never imagined having a young looker like me in your bed, eh?'

Blood drained from his face in an instant. 'Don't even joke about shit like that,' Bliss said, striking hard with the rebuke. 'I know you're only screwing around, Molly, but you have to cut it out. That kind of thing is something the old Molly would say. It's not something I want to hear from the new one.'

She gave him a cool, appraising look, so much wiser than her years. 'The differences are only inside your head,' she said. 'I'm still me, whether you like what you see and hear or not.'

'So for my sake, at least pretend. Make an effort. Put up a front to disguise your baser instincts. Please, Molly. What you are now is not all you can be – you may not believe that about yourself, but I do. I have faith in you. The harder you push the person you think you are, the more the real you inside will be squeezed out.'

Molly smiled, leaning up on one elbow. 'Like juice from an orange.'

Bliss nodded. 'Without the pulp.'

'Did anyone ever tell you how weird you are, Jimmy?'

'Many times. That's *my* real me. The juice.'

Shaking her head, she said, 'No, I don't think so. I reckon you never let people see that part of you. And you should. From one unhappy and lonely person to another, if I can make such a big change in my life, then so can you.'

'Ah, but I'm much older than you.'

Molly blew a raspberry. 'That's just an excuse, and you know it. But you should listen to me. Come Monday I'll be gone, and who will remind you who you are afterwards?'

'That's why I keep Penny around,' Bliss said softly. 'It's just about her only use.'

They both laughed and spoke further. Molly told him how much she liked his garden. As usual he pretended to have put in all the hard work himself getting it into shape, whereas the truth was he had paid a team of landscapers to do the work. Molly remarked that she had never had a garden of her own, and Bliss felt an immeasurable sadness creep over him. For a moment they were silent, then Bliss ducked out, telling the girl to catch up with her sleep.

'You'll miss me when I've moved on,' Molly said, snuggling her head back into the pillow. Her voice was gentle, drifting away.

'Not a chance,' he said, firmly shaking his head.

'Yes you will. G'night, Jimbo.'

Bliss laughed to himself as he headed back downstairs. Molly was some kid. He made drinks all round and found an open packet of chocolate digestive biscuits which he tipped onto a plate. He brought the tray of steaming cups and mugs into the living room and set it down on the floor, no table being available. He told everybody to help themselves to milk and sugar.

'That was a textbook raid earlier,' he said, raising his own mug of tea. 'Owing, in no small part, to our armed officers here. But you all did extremely well, so thank you.'

The female firearms officer was out in the hallway, standing at the foot of the stairs. He hoped she had heard and was hoisting her own hot drink in celebration. The other took a satisfied sip of his coffee and continued to study the back garden through the sliding glass doors, still on high alert.

'I'm not sure I've come down yet from the rush it gave me,' Ansari confessed, holding a hand to her chest. She did still appear to be in the throes of excitement, what with the glow of her skin and her two wide eyes staring back at everyone. 'What an incredible feeling!'

'I know what you mean,' Bishop said. 'But let's be thankful it went down as well as it did. I've seen it go the other way before, and at such close quarters it can get ugly fast if you let it.'

Bliss understood exactly what his DS meant. You could do all the recces you liked, but the moment you went beyond the threshold you were in control of nothing. Anything could – and often did – happen, and it had been their good fortune that Endicott's crew had quickly recognised the futility of attempting to take on an armed unit when they themselves were equipped only with knives. No matter how big or sharp or intimidating those blades were in other circumstances, they were no match for a Glock.

Dogs and guns. They were the real equalisers. Bliss was glad to have had them on his side when dropping the hammer on Endicott and his crew.

'Right now, Molly is in the safest place in Peterborough,' DCI Warburton said, 'possibly even the whole of the UK. And given this current arrangement is not on any official record, the only way her location gets out this time is if one of us sells her out.'

'Us, or Marie Collins at Social Care,' Chandler said. 'Though I trust her implicitly.'

'Me too,' Kim Parker chipped in. 'She's a fierce champion of juveniles like Molly.'

'What if she were threatened?' Ansari asked.

'There's no way Marie would tell them anything. She'd rather die.'

'What if somebody in her family was threatened?'

The room fell quiet.

Moments later, Parker said, 'Bloody hell, who exactly do you think is after this girl?'

'Just about anybody,' Bliss answered, his voice deep and curt. He wanted them to listen, to understand. Their lives depended on it. Ansari's question had been idle, but she made a good and critical point. 'Believe me, the bastards who supply the product and those who make their living selling it will not be resting on their laurels. The moment they hear what happened to Endicott – and they will, if they haven't already – they'll put something in motion. Wouldn't surprise me if whoever they've sent is already here in the city, but at the very least we've got until tomorrow morning before anything happens. And Gul is right to question Marie Collins's ability to keep this location to herself. Same goes for each and every one of you, too. We are all vulnerable if they find a way in behind our defences.'

FORTY

Anthony Clarke had delayed his drive up to Peterborough until he'd finished with the woman, but nonetheless he was having his eggs and bacon at the Holiday Inn half a mile from Thorpe Wood at shortly before eight on Saturday morning.

Overnight he'd received a barrage of texts from Leroy, each more strident than its predecessor. What had begun as a bit of an errand when they first discussed it had rapidly become a full-blown crisis. Ryan Endicott, who had been due a slap at the very least, was now in the unslappable position of being banged up in a holding cell at the local nick. Leroy, raging, had bayed for blood in most of his messages, but reason had obviously set in before he sent the last one. In it, he merely instructed Anthony to obtain permission from Eric the Eyeball to reach out from the inside once Endicott went on remand, or to take action himself if the dealer was released on bail. As for the kid, she was nothing to do with Eric and therefore fair game. It was open season on that bitch.

As he wiped his plate with the last piece of buttered toast, Anthony gave careful thought to the girl and what her recapture by the police now meant for him and his boss. He had only ever known her as Molly. Some meaningless scrap of a kid who occasionally ended up on the sofa at Leroy's drum, but who kept to herself and always looked closed off from the rest of the world. Her life was so alien to him. She bumped across counties like the silver ball in a pinball machine, buffeted and whacked around, seemingly without caring what became of her. She was a nothing who had rapidly become a something. A major something, at that. One who needed taking care of in the most terminal of ways.

His bet was that Molly was now being held at the nick just down the road. For her own protection, of course, though the cost of that would be a full statement naming names and places. He thought long and hard about her and married his conclusions up against everything he knew about Ryan Endicott. In his estimation, Endicott was the bigger threat. Not only did he know more about the operation and those at both ends of it, but he was also far more likely to cave than the girl. A coldness lived in her eyes the likes of which Anthony had seldom seen before – perhaps matched only by what he saw in the mirror every day.

With Molly still uppermost in his thoughts, Anthony pulled his sleek royal-blue Audi R8 Spyder out of the hotel's car park and blew the early morning cobwebs away as he headed north towards Deeping St James. It was not a roof down day, so he tweaked up the bass and let his playlist run through on the car's Bang & Olufsen sound system. The journey went far too quickly. As he guided the growling vehicle along Eastgate, it drew plenty of admiring glances, and his wide, easy grin said everything about his mood.

Anthony was frisked by the muscle who'd opened the front door, and deprived of his SIG Sauer, cosh and flick-knife before being shown through the house and back outside again. Eric the Eyeball's modern detached property came with an enormous garden, and the muscle preceded Anthony along a winding gravel path which led to a raised deck overlooking the river Welland. The man himself sat at a low glass-topped table, a coffee cup to his lips. He was wrapped in a thick, heavy dressing gown, the weather being still bitterly cold in the morning's pale sunlight.

Fuck, Anthony thought. *His face sure lived up to its billing.*

Skin puckered around the vacant eye socket like a sphincter, causing the remaining eye to appear large, wide, and round. If you didn't know better, you'd swear it was made of glass. Eric was white, looked to be in his mid-fifties, tall and bulky. His hands were huge, his thick fingers barely able to cope with the handle of the coffee mug he now set down.

'So, you're Leroy's boy,' Eric said, looking him up and down. 'Come to help us out with our bit of business, is that right?'

Anthony bristled at being called anyone's boy, but he pushed it to the back of his mind. This was Eric's turf, after all. Let the guy have his moment.

'I'm here to do what I can, yes.' He sat down opposite Eric, waving away the offer of a hot drink. What he really wanted was to get inside; it was bloody freezing out here. Didn't this clown know it was mid-December?

'Much has changed overnight,' Eric told him. 'You up to speed on that, Anthony?'

'Yeah. Leroy filled me in. The way I see it, we have the same number of problems, they're just in different places now.'

Eric laughed, his wide shoulders heaving. He coughed a couple of times, a wet, chesty sound that made Anthony question the man's choice of location for this meeting. 'Leroy told me you weren't easy to rattle,' Eric said between chuckles. 'I like your style.'

'It is what it is, man. When me and Leroy spoke about the Endicott problem, we were going to ask you to have a word. Just a slap and a telling off, nothing too drastic, you understand? But now… I'm thinking you're looking for something more severe where he's concerned, yeah?'

'Even if we are, what makes you think we can't take care of it ourselves?'

Anthony kept his gaze firmly on Eric, though he remained aware of the man's two henchmen standing close by. Big blokes, suited and booted. Looked the part. 'No worries on that score, Eric,' he said. 'See, this is an offer from Leroy. A gift from him to you. He acknowledges the fact that Endicott is your man, but he feels some responsibility considering it was him who introduced the girl into the mix. Look at it as his way of paying you respect, offering to do the dirty work on your behalf. Saving you the bother, keeping your own guys' hands clean at the same time.'

'And the girl?'

'That's our mess to tidy up, man. As far as Leroy is concerned, he wants you to sit back and relax while we take care of business. He wants to get this sorted.'

'You mean he'd like to start up the production line again as soon as possible.'

'I imagine that's part of his thinking.' Anthony shrugged. 'But if so, surely that benefits everybody.'

'I take it when Leroy says "we" what he really means is you?'

'Of course. Leroy is not a hands-on sort of guy. If he was, he wouldn't need me.'

'Your reputation is well-earned, Anthony.' The man sipped some more of his drink, nodding, keeping that one bulging eye fixed on his visitor.

Uncomfortable beneath the cyclopic glare, Anthony gave a shady grin. 'Which can only ever help in my line of work.'

After a long pause, Eric said, 'Then let's see you earn it. You do well, we'll see about putting some more work your way in the future.'

'Mine is not a reputation I'm going to give up without a fight, Eric.' He flashed his wide, toothy grin once more, cocked one leg over the other and spread both arms along the back of his chair.

'See, this is who I am. It's all that I am. And if I can enforce Leroy's world in London, I see no reason why I can't do the same up here in your city.'

'You're very confident.'

'You think I'm arrogant, and you'd be right. I've got a lot to be arrogant about. But that don't mean I let my guard down. Not ever.'

'That's good to hear. So tell me how you intend to proceed if I give the nod.'

Anthony sucked down a lungful of chilled air and then slowly released it. 'Endicott is either going to be held on remand or he's coming out on bail. I can get to him either way, and I'm prepared to go as far as you want. He can be crippled enough that he'll never walk again and will only ever eat through a straw. He can be cut up so badly even his dear old mum won't recognise him anymore. Or he can go away altogether and never trouble your thoughts again.'

'I like that last option,' Eric said. He finished up his drink and waggled his fat fingers. 'Go on.'

'The girl poses more of a problem. Our sources say she's dropped off the radar.'

'Same here.'

'Which suggests to me they have her tucked away inside their main nick.'

'Same here.'

'Which means either she's talked already, or she will. But that's not an issue, because she still has to testify in court, and that will never happen. In a day or two they have to do something with the kid. They have to place her somewhere. If a guy like Endicott is capable of reaching out and finding her, then there's no way I won't be able to do the same. Yeah, they'll double up this time. They'll put a defensive ring around her. But you have my word, man. I can make sure she doesn't testify by cutting out her tongue or cutting out her heart. Makes no difference to me, either way.'

'Once again I prefer the latter option, Anthony.'

Clarke got to his feet and reached across the table. 'It's a deal, Eric. Pleasure to do business with you.'

The two men shook, their eyes locking. 'You know what this means if you fail, Anthony?'

'I do. And don't worry, if that happens you'll never see me again.'

He didn't mean it the way Eric would imagine. But if the impossible did occur and he failed in either job, he really would make sure the man did not see him again. However, his voice would be the very last thing Eric the Eyeball ever heard.

FORTY-ONE

It was just the five of them now. A delivery of four folding cot beds had arrived in the early hours of the morning, and at the moment both the female armed officer and the young woman from social services were grabbing some much needed rest. The other firearms cop took up a position by the foot of the stairs – the ideal spot from which to defend both sides of the house.

Bliss had recognised him immediately, and decided now was the right time to have a quiet word out of earshot of the others. 'You were one of the two snipers who took out the gunman at the quarry, right?' he said without inflection.

'Yes, sir.'

'I hope you know you did a good thing that night. I hope you sleep easily.'

The officer gave a shy grin. 'I'm okay with what I did,' he said. 'It took me a while to recover. Had my counselling. But it was a good shoot. I only wish the order had come down sooner.'

Bliss patted him on the arm. 'We all do. But hindsight is a wonderful thing. I'm just glad you've come through the other side.'

He hefted his firearm. 'I won't hesitate to use it again, sir. If that's what you're worried about.'

'I'm not. I don't think you'd be here now if you had any doubts. And I have none about you.'

Under normal circumstances, Bliss would not feel entirely secure. Ryan Endicott was a major player in the Peterborough drugs business, but fairly insignificant within the wider empire. That larger aspect of the operation had a great deal of reach and clout and often wielded it aggressively. If they discovered where Molly was being kept, they would have no hesitation in coming in all guns blazing so as to silence her for good.

Yet he was unperturbed; so few people were aware of her current location, and those who did know would never trade that information for anything as tawdry as money or influence. Even so, Gul had raised an interesting question last night, and it got Bliss thinking now about Marie Collins.

Collins's involvement in protecting the kid who'd twice escaped the clutches of Ryan Endicott had to be common knowledge; there was a network of informants spread out across the whole city. With no leaks coming out of Thorpe Wood or the social care department, those who both supplied Endicott and earned from him would think in more specific terms this time.

A worm of worry began niggling at him.

Bliss slipped outside into his back garden, closing the sliding doors behind him. A watery sun offered no heat but, wrapped in a fleece, he rubbed his arms and stamped his feet to keep warm. He called the mobile number Collins had provided, and she picked up on the third ring. He explained his misgivings and asked where she was most likely to be vulnerable.

'In too many areas to even think about it rationally,' Collins admitted. 'I have a husband, three children and two very young grandchildren.'

'Is there any way for you all to disappear off the map for a couple of days?' Bliss realised he was asking a lot, but this was where they were weak and he wanted to ensure he did everything possible to plug any gaps.

'At this short notice? I'm really not sure, Inspector Bliss.'

'If it's about practicality, think about the big picture instead. You can be got to, Mrs Collins. If they find this chink, they will exploit it. They may not be the Mexican cartel, but they don't like to be threatened, and us having both Endicott and Molly is a very real threat to them. Removing you all from the board is our best way of making sure nothing happens. I can have a word about protection, but the kind of numbers we're talking about will be impossible to muster. In my view, it'd be both better and easier if you all took yourselves off somewhere until this blows over.'

'Thank you for your concern, Inspector. I'm just not sure that I can uproot my entire family every time somebody makes a threat against me. In my job, it's pretty much par for the course.'

Bliss was disappointed. The woman clearly failed to grasp the peril she was in. 'With respect,' he said, 'this is in a different league altogether to anything you've encountered before.'

'And with equal respect, Inspector, you have no idea what kind of people I am forced to deal with every week of every year. I hear what you're saying, however, and I will certainly consider it.'

'I don't want to have to worry about what's going on behind the scenes.'

'And I've told you I understand,' Collins snapped. 'I will run this by my family. If we decide to take your advice, I'll let you know. Now, is there anything else? I have things to do.'

When she ended the call, Bliss remained irritated by her manner. He was trying to help, yet her clipped tone suggested annoyance at being disturbed from her weekend routine. He had no choice but to accept it, however. When he returned indoors, Bliss told the others his concerns, and heard them out when they voiced their opinions. Chandler agreed with him that Collins and her family ought to pack their bags and move out for a few days at least. Kim Parker sided with her superior, but only up to a certain point.

'If it were me, I'd probably do as you say,' she admitted. 'But I also see her point. Our jobs come with daily threats as part of our contracts. She's at the top of the pyramid, so she bears the brunt of them all. If she moved out every time someone threw a hissy fit, she'd never unpack her bags.'

'This is a little bit more than a hissy fit,' Chandler argued. 'These men are dangerous and they will stop at nothing to get their hands on Molly again. If they think of this route through – and if we can, they can – your boss and her family will be in a lot of trouble.'

'And I'm sure she'll take that into account. But she'll also do things her own way.'

'Which leaves me feeling decidedly uneasy,' Bliss said. 'Because if she allows herself to become exposed, then by association so are we.'

Moments later, Bliss took a call. This time he stepped into the kitchen before talking. It was Janis Ward responding to the voicemail message he had left on her phone prior to the raid on Endicott's place. 'Thanks for getting back to me,' he said. 'I'm hoping you can clear something up. See, try as I might, I cannot recall you mentioning your relationship with Chief Inspector Robert Marsh when we met at your offices yesterday. Only, it seems to me you would have done. I mean, there we were discussing potential links between a journalist and a senior police officer, and yet somehow you neglected to inform us of this significant detail.'

He let the resulting silence go on for a few seconds longer than necessary before giving it a stir. 'Mrs Ward, if you're honest with me now, then unless Marsh was as bent as a nine-bob note, nobody needs to know the sordid details.'

'There was nothing sordid about it,' she said, her voice carrying a hard edge. 'It was purely business.'

'You mean you paid him for information?'

'We *exchanged* information on occasion. It was a two-way street, Inspector. Such arrangements are commonplace, as I'm sure you appreciate.'

Was that a veiled threat? Was Janis Ward aware of his own relationship with Sandra Bannister?

Bliss shook the thought aside. Ward knew about the interviews he had agreed to undertake with Bannister, and he decided she had been referring to that specific arrangement and nothing else. 'Tell me, Mrs Ward,' he said. 'In the days leading up to the disappearance of Lisa Pepperdine, did you and Marsh *exchange* any information that may have been relevant to our discussion yesterday?'

'No, we did not. Had we done so, I would have mentioned it, I assure you. Look, I kept quiet because there was no relevance. Had Robert and I spoken about Lisa at all, I would have told you.'

'And afterwards? After it became clear that Lisa had left the city, and later – when she was reported as missing – did you discuss the matter with him then?'

'No.'

'You're certain about that?'

'I am. I'm not suggesting it's something I would have remembered out of context, but I'm positive it would have come to me while we were talking about it around the table.'

Bliss considered both her words and the situation, before saying, 'Do you not consider that odd? Weren't Lisa Pepperdine's interference in an ongoing investigation, and her subsequent disappearance, precisely the kind of issues you and he would have discussed?'

'I… I suppose they were, yes. I can't say I'd ever considered it before.'

Bliss knew and understood people better than most, and he wasn't getting any feeling of hidden guilt from Ward. He sensed nothing guarded behind her words. He was inclined to let it go, but he asked one more question. 'Mrs Ward, upon reflection, can you think of anything Marsh said to you that now gives you pause?'

'No,' she said eventually. 'In fact… as you say, Inspector, the oddest aspect of that period is that he asked me nothing about Lisa Pepperdine. Had it occurred to me at the time, I think I would have been troubled by the lapse.'

Bliss let her go. He had hoped to uncover something they could work with, but he believed in the woman's innocence. When he was done, he shook his head at Chandler, who had been loitering close by, then made another call of his own. DCI Warburton heard him out, but when he requested an armed unit outside the Collins' home she took a step back.

'I can't authorise that, Jimmy. That's three teams over each twenty-four-hour period, which amounts to more budget than I can allocate. I'd need to confirm with the Super.'

'I'll wait for your call, then, boss.' Bliss grinned as he spoke.

'You expect me to call Marion Fletcher on her day off?'

'Do any of us really have days off?'

'Your Superintendent does, Jimmy. Of that I can assure you.'

'Do you agree with me at least?' he asked.

'As it happens, I do.'

'Then need I say more?'

Bliss knew it was enough. He'd placed his boss in an awkward position, but the safety of everyone involved came first. Warburton promised to call him back within the hour. He slipped the phone into his pocket, and looked at Chandler and Parker.

'I suppose there is another way to tackle this,' he said. Both women regarded him with interest.

'I'm all ears,' Chandler said. 'Because now that you've raised the possibility, I have to say I'm anxious about our current position.'

'Well, if Mohammed decides not to go to the mountain, we should consider having the mountain move instead. What I'm saying is: if Collins refuses to move out to protect her family and prevent herself from revealing this location, then we leave this location. We three plus our firearms officers. And Molly, of course.'

'And where exactly would we go?'

Bliss shook his head. 'I haven't thought that far ahead.' He shrugged. 'But I'm open to suggestions.'

FORTY-TWO

THE HEAVY TRAFFIC SLOWED first to a crawl, then came to a complete standstill. At this point, Bliss started to question the wisdom of his decision.

The answer to their dilemma had come to him as he'd exchanged thoughts and ideas with Chandler and Kim Parker. They needed a place to go where nobody would think of looking for them – a safe house unattached to any of the small group. And it had to be somewhere large enough to comfortably contain the six of them until Monday at the very least.

It occurred to Bliss out of nowhere that the bed-and-breakfast establishment run by Joe Flynn and his wife was the ideal spot. It was a good way out of the city, and nobody was going to associate Bliss with Flynn, nor Flynn with accommodating them. His ex-boss had taken some persuading during a phone conversation lasting close to fifteen minutes, but with rooms available and Bliss arguing his case both articulately and with some force, the man finally relented.

Next came the practicalities. The firearms pair raised two perfectly viable objections. First, they would not take their weapons with them without first notifying their immediate superior. This closely related to the second issue: Bliss's plan would take them into a neighbouring county. Shifting an armed crew beyond the Cambridgeshire boundary required its own form of bureaucracy, but Bliss believed addressing both issues fully would mean involving too many people. He persuaded Eric Price to agree the location change without first running the matter by command or any of his own superiors. Instead he would write a note for himself and have it on his list of things to do should anybody ask for an explanation later. Bliss appreciated his armed colleague taking on the risk.

That left Kim Parker, who was vehemently opposed to any plan that would uproot Molly from yet another supposed safe house without Marie Collins's knowledge. She crossed her arms, as if to seal the deal.

'Don't you see how that negates the whole point of moving?' Bliss argued. 'The only reason I want to leave here is to protect both us and Marie Collins, and we do that by her having no idea we've even moved on, never mind where to. There's no point in my going through the motions only for you to call her up and tell her everything when I'm finished.'

Parker regarded him with scorn. 'I get what you're saying, of course I do, and please don't talk to me as if I'm a bloody fool. But I have a responsibility to that girl upstairs, and I discharge that by doing my job and doing it properly. Protocol insists I inform my boss if we change location. In this case, Mrs Collins has taken on the role as my boss, and so neither Molly nor I can go anywhere without asking her first.'

Bliss paused, sighed then said, 'How about if I call her myself? Rather than ask permission, I'll explain what we're about to do and why. Except that, instead of revealing where we're going, I'll tell her only that we are leaving here and going dark until further notice. Agreed?'

In truth, he did not much care whether the young woman from the YMCA concurred. So far she had been extremely open and communicative, flexible in her thinking and direct with her responses, and he understood why she now wanted to look higher up the totem pole for answers. But he did not have time for the debate to drag on; neither did he care if she went with them willingly or considered herself forced to in order to remain with Molly. Even so, he was glad Parker relented and allowed him to make the call on her behalf.

Collins hadn't liked the idea at all. Once again she sounded as if she were being put out, and was clearly unhappy about not knowing where Molly was being taken. 'I understand the limitations you are working under, Inspector,' she said. 'All I'm asking is that you appreciate my own responsibility in this kind of situation. Molly is officially under my care at the moment, and I must be informed at all times as to her whereabouts.'

Resisting the urge to ask how that had worked out when Molly was placed with the Paxtons, Bliss added an edge to his voice when he spoke next. 'These are exigent circumstances, you have to see that.'

'I do. Nonetheless, I must insist.'

He had hoped for greater understanding, but now it was his turn to be adamant. 'Look, you do whatever you feel is necessary by way of complaint, but we are relocating Molly. For her safety, I believe the fewer people who know where she is the better. So let me tell you what I am prepared to do. If she agrees, Miss Parker will remain part of the group. She can continue to act as Molly's guardian, and although our precise location will not be identified, I'll have her keep in regular contact with you by phone.'

Collins had attempted to argue one last time, but Bliss refused to budge an inch further. Less than thirty minutes later, their small convoy had been on its way, and now here they were, going nowhere fast.

Wondering if the Canaries were playing at home, which would certainly explain the stalled traffic, Bliss shifted his gaze to the rear-view mirror. Moving his head slightly allowed him to look at Molly in the back of the car, alongside Kim Parker. The kid continued to surprise him, and he found himself increasingly impressed with her attitude. Over a breakfast of toast and juice, she had listened to his plan for relocating her yet again, and he'd waited for an explosion that never came. Instead, when he was through explaining, Molly had shrugged; he knew best, she said, and she would go along with whatever he decided. Her reaction was further proof that he understood absolutely nothing about the workings of a fifteen-year-old mind.

Before setting off, Chandler had driven Bliss's car to the Serpentine Green shopping centre to buy Molly some clothes, plus a bunch of toiletries for them all. Staying for two nights at Joe Flynn's B&B was a strictly short-term measure, but there was no need for any of them to stink up the place. Bliss slid her a sidelong glance as he nudged the car forward a few yards before hitting the brake again. His partner had been markedly quiet all morning, and they hadn't found an opportunity to speak in confidence. She lacked her usual sparkle, and the trio of deep lines on her brow concerned him.

About to ask her what was up, Bliss was distracted by his mobile ringtone. He frowned at the screen; the call was coming from the ARV behind them. When he was done, he nodded towards the windscreen and said, 'There's been an accident up ahead, apparently. That's why we're breathing exhaust fumes.'

The car was filled with groans, but nobody voiced their annoyance. He noticed Chandler was busy thumbing her phone. A moment later, Bliss's device announced an incoming text. His own frown this time was severe.

Say nothing. Don't want Molly to get scared. But I don't like this. Feel exposed.

Bliss nodded. He wasn't good at texting, and it took him ages to shape a reply.

Is that why you have a face like a slapped arse?

From the corner of his eye he caught Chandler closing both of hers and biting down on a retort. A moment later her fingers flew once again.

I went with you on this to present a united front. But I'm not comfortable with it at all. Prefer to stand ground if cornered than be out in the open.

What did she imagine would happen? Collins had no idea where they were going, and nothing was officially logged by either DCI Warburton or Eric Price at the firearms unit in Huntingdon. The only people who knew both where they were now and their ultimate destination were in either this vehicle or the one behind it. Oh, and Joe Flynn, of course, but in Bliss's mind that was as good as keeping it to themselves. This wasn't a government organisation coming after them, a faceless mass with all the surveillance equipment of GCHQ at their disposal. It was a bunch of lowlife drug dealers. Vicious as they come, psychopathic without a trace of empathy, for sure. But they had no way of discovering where this weary band of travellers were, nor where they were bound. It just wasn't possible.

That was when Bliss heard the motorbikes.

He checked his mirrors. Way back in the queue of traffic, a gang of them wove in and out of the vehicles. He didn't blame them. After all, if they were able to make their way through the logjam, then why would anybody else complain? Bliss all but dismissed them from his thoughts, but as a number of bikes came steadily closer, he spotted something odd. The bikers were paying a lot of attention to the vehicles. Instead of focussing on the staggered path through the traffic, they were looking across both lanes of the dual carriageway, occasionally even ducking down to peer in at the occupants. As if they were...

Bliss stood on his accelerator and rammed into the Italian hatchback ahead of him, shunting it a couple of yards forward. He then reversed and, with the right angle now available to him, he swung the wheel left and aimed at a gap between the vehicles alongside him. The opening was no more than six feet wide, so Bliss's big Vauxhall slammed into the rear wing of a dark saloon, shifting it both sideways and forwards. He reversed sharply once more and repeated the manoeuvre, ignoring the screams and cries emanating from the back seat and the expressions of horror of those in the vehicles around him. Twice more he slammed into the car to his left before he'd created enough space to drive through the opening, shuddering off the tail end of a small van in a desperate bid to reach unobstructed space. His right foot hit the accelerator and he clipped the same van one more time, nudging it aside as he made it through and up onto the grass verge.

Checking his mirrors, Bliss saw the ARV had followed suit. No questions asked. No phone or radio calls. They were the security for everyone in Bliss's car, and they would stick to him no matter what. Beyond the police vehicle, Bliss observed that his wild manoeuvres and the crash and clang of metal against metal had drawn the attention of the bikers. Some of them were making their own way over to the same verge.

Straightening, and oblivious to whatever his passengers were yelling, Bliss shot alongside the caravan of vehicles, tyres straining for purchase on the ridge of damp grass and mud that separated the road from the open space beyond. Up ahead, past the next couple of fields, Bliss noticed a dense woodland away to his left, the trees' bare limbs now a pale shade of grey and appearing to be twisted and knotted together. The closer he got to the denuded forestation, the more conscious he became of the bikers gaining ground behind him. The ARV was right on his tail, and he hated to think what that heavy front end had demolished on its way through.

Bliss clenched his jaw as he saw what he had been hoping for. Two tall telegraph poles appeared to mark a turnoff, but there was no signpost telling him where it would take them. He regarded that as a good sign, because he did not want to move whatever this was into a densely populated area. He understood that the moment they were off the verge and onto anything remotely resembling stable ground, those bikes with their superior acceleration and manoeuvrability would catch up with his Insignia very quickly.

As he approached the turn, Bliss hit the brake and spun the wheel violently to the left. The car shimmied before righting itself, bucked slightly then took off as he swapped brake for accelerator. In his rear-view, the firearms unit's white SUV stuck close to his bumper in a startling feat of driving.

'What the hell, Jimmy?' Chandler's voice rose up out of the discordant sounds ringing in his ears. He flashed a quick glance her way and caught the look of terror on her face and the questions in her eyes.

'Those bikers are not on their way to some convention,' he said, eyes back on the narrow track leading deep into the woodland, grateful it was at least straight at this point. 'They were checking out vehicles as they made their way through the jam. They're searching for us. They'll be armed this time.'

His partner sat upright and turned to look back over her shoulder. Bliss angled his head to check on Molly. Her expression radiated fear; when his eyes met hers, he saw disappointment. Right from their initial encounter he had promised to keep her safe, yet everything he had done so far had put her deeper into harm's way. Beside her, Kim Parker had raised her legs and wedged herself back into her seat and was now sobbing uncontrollably.

Up ahead the road forked, curving both left and right. To the left, he saw only open fields. No cover if they had to make a break for it on foot. He hit the tight bend without braking, all four tyres squealing as they somehow retained their grip on the uneven surface which was little more than a thin layer of broken tarmac, fast becoming a shifting, unreliable crumbling crust. On the positive side, the woods now began to embrace them, providing more options if they had to flee across country.

Behind the ARV a number of motorbikes ate up the ground in pursuit, gaining all the while. It would not be long before they drew level and then pulled ahead, barring the way. The moment they did that, they would be in control; there was no way Bliss was letting that happen. His eyes scouring the landscape ahead, he ran the permutations through his mind and reached a decision.

It was time to bail out.

On the one hand, it exposed them to the bikers. On the other, it exposed the bikers to the firearms officers. Bliss viewed that as a win for his side.

Spotting a dirt patch up on the right which ran about twenty feet into the wooded area, Bliss slammed his foot down hard on the brake and steered towards it, gripping the wheel tight as the car fought against him.

'Out, out, out!' he cried as they came to a jerking halt. He flung himself out of the car and dashed around to the rear door. Yanking it open, he pulled Molly out and threw her towards the trees. Chandler soon came up behind him, the hysterical Parker gripping tightly onto her upper arm. 'In there,' he said, pointing to the woods. 'But stay close.'

Bliss had a momentary twinge of guilt about leaving the armed officers. But he was doing the right thing. It was his duty to get Molly, Parker, and his partner as far away from the bikers as possible. The firearms pair knew their job, and he would only hinder them if he stayed put. Their role now was to secure the scene from a position behind their vehicle, keeping the motorcycle riders at bay with loud warnings, followed by shots from their Heckler & Koch weapons if necessary.

He kept on running, virtually dragging Molly behind him. Her legs pumped hard, but he was taller and even at his age more athletic, so she struggled to keep up. 'Push harder,' he said, panting as he scampered across the woodland floor. 'You're doing great, but do better.'

Bliss pulled out his mobile, cursing when he saw he had zero bars of signal. Chandler threaded her way through the woodland by his side, pulling Parker along as if she were a human trailer. Sweeping away overhanging branches with his arms, Bliss kept his eyes flicking between the uneven ground and the circuitous pathway through the trees ahead, desperate that none of them should catch and twist their ankle in a root. The likelihood of a break was severe, but even a lousy sprain at this point might prove fatal for all four of them. All the while his mind was in overdrive, straining for answers, shocked and dismayed at how quickly they had been discovered.

It was impossible for anyone to have figured out their destination. Yet still someone knew enough to have sent in a team on bikes to hunt them down. Bikes and not cars. Bliss wondered now if the accident on the road ahead had been faked, a deliberate shunt designed to close down the two lanes running east.

But how?

That was the real question here.

It made no sense, unless…

Unless someone had been following all along.

If Molly's location inside Bliss's home had somehow been compromised, a lone watcher – or even a team of them – could have followed the two-vehicle convoy out of the city. It was also feasible that somebody had stuck a GPS tracker on his car overnight. All it would have needed then was a call to summon others, plus the creation of two lines of stationary traffic. Not easy to set up in such a short space of time, but not impossible either.

Behind them, Bliss heard raised voices which brought him hurtling back to their immediate predicament. Moments later a number of shots rang out. It was odd how the gunshots seemed to come from ahead of them, their explosive power dulled by the dense lines of trees and foliage, but of course that was impossible.

Just as it was impossible to know where we were, Bliss had time to think, before a group of four masked men wearing body armour and holding assault weapons across their chests appeared in front of them.

FORTY-THREE

'That was good,' Anthony Clarke had said to Marie Collins when her conversation with Bliss was over. 'Very convincing. So, anyway, before you took that call, we were discussing Molly's current whereabouts, yeah? And as I was saying before we were so rudely interrupted, all I need from you is an address. If I don't get that right now, then I'll force you to watch your family suffer until you change your mind. We found you, lady, so we can find them just as easily.'

He smiled at the memory. The woman had soiled herself at the thought of him carrying out his threat. He was no monster, though. Not if he didn't have to be. He even allowed her to shower and change her clothes before handing her off to a couple of rough-looking eastern Europeans supplied by Eric the Eyeball. Their instructions were to take care of her in some out-of-the-way location until they received a call to let her go.

Obtaining the social worker's address had been an easy enough task once they had her name and a few other details; the electoral roll provided sufficient information if you paid a premium fee. Gaining access to her home had been no less simple, Clarke flashing a fake police warrant card through the glass door panel when Collins answered his knock. After outlining the many ways he would make her family suffer if she resisted him, the woman became instantly malleable and had played her role to perfection. Quite how it would have gone down had her husband or children been at home at the time, he didn't know, but thankfully that was a bridge he hadn't needed to cross.

Deciding upon the strategy that had put him and Collins together had not taken a great deal of thought. When weighing up everything he had learned about the police snatch the previous evening, Anthony concentrated on the individuals who were now responsible for maintaining Molly's safety. Eric had multiple police contacts on his payroll, but the filth were playing this one close to their chest. As he'd suspected, the girl had been held at the main nick for a couple of hours after being rescued from Endicott's house, but had later been spirited away beneath a blanket of secrecy. No word was making it back as to where. His next concern was to figure out who else would need to be made aware of Molly's ongoing situation. A handful of phone calls later and the names of Marie Collins and Kim Parker were floating around inside his head. Parker was surely too low-level and insignificant for a job this important, and besides she could not be located. Which had left Collins.

Sometimes it was that easy. If you didn't allow panic to set in, if you used some plain old common sense, applied logic and reason to the problem, solutions always appeared out of nowhere.

Leroy's contacts in the area were at his disposal, and Eric had agreed to loan out as many bodies as were needed to get the job done. One member of the crew had bought information about the detectives involved from a traffic cop working out of Thorpe Wood, and Anthony had arranged for Leroy's best men to sit on their homes. Not so close that they'd be noticed, not so far away that they would miss anything important. Meanwhile, Anthony started to piece together a strategy based on everything Collins had told him.

Moments after making the decision to direct all manpower towards the house and its current occupants, word came in that Bliss, two women, two armed cops, and the girl, were all on the move. Anthony cursed his bad luck. Another hour and he would have had them surrounded by his own gunmen, with a plan to take the door off its hinges followed by a swift and bloody raid of their own. Reacting to the rapid change in circumstances he gave the order to follow and observe, for his men to report back direction and positional changes every five minutes. He withdrew the watchers from the other homes and pulled them into action, ordering them to catch up to the lead car and rotate position with it so as to prevent being made by any of the cops they were in pursuit of.

It didn't take as long as he'd expected to pull all the pieces together, even if some of them remained scrambled and waiting to form the single picture he'd imagined. Information based on local knowledge provided by the followers suggested a specific route was being taken, and Anthony realised that to be effective and make time for armed intervention, he would have to slow the cops down. One conversation was all it took to arrange the van and lorry collision. Two brothers living in Thetford – and therefore ahead of the cops in their two vehicles – did as they were told and got the job done. The bikers were another simple matter to organise, though arming them was not quite as straightforward. It irritated Anthony that they were not better equipped, but handguns and shotguns would have to be enough. By sheer weight of numbers if nothing else. For an ad hoc plan, it wasn't too shabby.

The unit inside which he currently waited impatiently for news stood on the Maxwell Road industrial estate in Woodston. It had originally been a tooling workshop for engineering components, but for the past two years a shell company belonging to Eric McManus had been paying the lease. Its business designation was unknown, and it had never traded. But the utility bills were paid, so both the water and electricity were still on, and a Calor gas tank provided heating as required. Eric had suggested it as an ideal place for Anthony to wait for the arrival of the girl – and hopefully even a copper or two – in the back of a large plain van.

Alone inside the vast unit, Anthony had turned the thermostat up to its maximum setting to take the chill off the air. The interior was musty and dirty and, judging by the dust settled over every surface, it hadn't been used in some time. He wondered for a minute what kind of business was done here, but a few tell-tale patches of dried blood soon told him all he needed to know. He still wasn't entirely sure what he intended to do with Molly, but if that van rolled in loaded with cops as well, then the large work area was going to have its walls and floors newly decorated in vivid red.

He waited patiently. First for the phone call confirming that the girl had been secured, then for her arrival. Whatever her ultimate fate, he would make sure she told him everything she knew. His methods for extracting information had never failed to work, though some interviewees coughed quicker than others. He was no sadist; if his victims crumpled and fell apart at the mere sight of a set of pliers or a toothed-grip vice, then he was happy enough not to get his hands dirty. But those who clung on to some noble, yet sorely misplaced ideal of being able to resist and never break, were every bit as enjoyable to ply his trade upon. It was remarkable, he thought, how many ways there were to inflict pain. Anthony was certain he had not yet explored them all. Perhaps today would be the day for fresh inspiration.

FORTY-FOUR

DETECTIVE CONSTABLE PHIL GRATTON had woken that Saturday morning feeling restless and uncertain. Having spent the previous day in the company of unrepentant right-wing extremists, he had come home in desperate need of a shower, but also with a head crammed full of confusing and contrasting information.

Many of the radicals were straight out of film and TV casting: shaved heads, ugly tattoos – some depicting Nazi insignia – and loud voices set not to stun but to intimidate. They spoke openly and with great enthusiasm about cleansing the mongrel nation their beloved country had become, and they laughed and fist-bumped one another without shame at the thought of asylum seekers dying in rough seas as they sought the sanctuary of UK borders. Their general consensus was that it served the freeloaders right. Each of them, whether man or woman, behaved as he'd expected.

It was the other kind who confused Gratton, leaving him unable to define the people he had spoken to as one specific type. He and John Hunt had discussed their interviews afterwards in the pub over a pint of Stella, and both agreed that if they had met someone of the latter category in any other setting, they would probably have enjoyed their company. These people were funny, generous with their time, and fully open and reasonable in their views. Generations of men and women who had no desire to deport settled immigrants, other than those who brought only crime and misery to the country. Entire families drawn from all classes who worried about the changing culture and the influence of foreign enclaves. People who did not believe it was right that their children were still waiting for social housing when so many newcomers already had homes. Ordinary folk who believed they were entitled to their opinions, yet were constantly ignored by what they saw as a liberal-left elite making decisions favouring the minority.

Gratton had found it hard to dislike them for their views. He heard no outright bigotry, nor racism, no intent to cause harm or incite violence. Only concern based on their everyday experiences. They were people who lived the life from within, not observing from the outside. He didn't agree with everything they had to say, but he had found himself accepting that their views were based not on colour, nor on race or religion, but solely on cause and effect as they perceived it. None of it was entirely compelling, but he certainly understood them better afterwards.

Still he was dissatisfied. When it came to the more extremist movements, he had yet to be in a room with any of the leadership. It was their minds he sought to unlock, especially those attached to the New Crusader Movement, and even BNP activists from the mid-noughties. They would have to keep for another day, perhaps even a different investigation. After all, the cycle of intolerance never stopped.

Instead of continuing to chase down the main far-right targets, Gratton found himself at a community centre in the heart of the Fletton district. The decades-old building was let out for functions, and late on Friday afternoon he and Hunt had learned that Antifa-UK were holding a meeting there today. Hunt was committed elsewhere for the entire weekend, so Gratton had gone on his own.

His arrival inside the hall caused heads to jerk up, eyes narrowing in suspicion as they zeroed in on a stranger in their midst. Several of the burlier men edged closer before swarming around him.

He was about to run through the script he had rehearsed about being interested in joining the group when another figure appeared at the shoulder of one man who now openly barred the way. They jabbed a finger in his direction and said, 'This one's Old Bill. Him and his mate were in the Anvil yesterday, asking all sorts.'

Gratton's mind rapidly sought a plan B, but the only way out of this now was to be upfront. He squinted at the man who had picked him out and said, 'How the hell do you know where I was yesterday? What's Antifa doing in a watering hole for white supremacists?'

'We have our spies in all kinds of places, pal. I'm one of them, and I saw you myself.'

'What of it? I've come to ask the same sort of questions I was asking yesterday,' Gratton said, changing tack. 'I'm not here for any other reason.'

'No? Then why the jeans, boots and hoodie underneath your jacket? Yesterday you were a shirt-and-tie man.'

'Because yesterday I was on duty. Today I'm not. Look, I'm not going to pretend I have any interest in what you're all about. Neither am I here to gain intelligence on anything you might be cooking up here today. I have specific questions for specific people. Things I want to ask of those who know a bit about extremist groups back in 2005. I need ten minutes of their time at most.'

The man who had recognised him withdrew with one of his taller, wider pals and they spoke in hushed voices. Gratton heard the low grumble of protest from all around the hall at his presence now that word of who he was had filtered through. The so-called anti-fascist groups despised the police, and the establishment in general, almost as much as they proclaimed to hate fascism. He chose to stand his ground, eyes locked on the two men who were still in discussion, both now gesticulating with their hands. Eventually, the larger man looked up and flexed his fingers in a 'follow me' motion. Gratton took a breath and went after him.

At the back of the large hall was another meeting room, this one much smaller. Gratton saw the big man rap on the door with his knuckles before entering. The bruiser held up a finger for him to wait where he was, stepped inside the room and closed the door behind him.

A couple of minutes later it opened again; the man dipped his head and stood to one side to make way. Swallowing his anxiety, Gratton walked in ahead of him and heard the door being closed firmly at his back. Spread about the room were stacks of cardboard boxes. A couple of them were open, flaps pulled back. Inside one Gratton saw T-shirts with an emblem across the chest, but the folds of the cloth prevented him making it out clearly. The other box contained what looked like newsletters bearing the Antifa-UK logo. In the centre of the room was a table, around which six people were seated.

'You asked for ten minutes – you've got five,' said the only female among them.

Her narrow gaze pierced Gratton as if searching for the slightest sign of bias or intent to cause disruption. He was very much out of his depth here, but he had thrown the dice and now he had to see the game out.

'Thanks,' he said, his voice faltering momentarily. 'I'll get straight to the point. In early 2005, a journalist by the name of Lisa Pepperdine came to the city looking for a scoop. She told fellow journalists she wanted to expose the police for doing relatively little in combatting the arsonists who were attacking foreigners during that period. However, because of her previous articles, we also believe she was here to delve deeper into the right-wing movement in Peterborough at the time.'

'And what of it?' the woman asked. 'What's that got to do with any of us?'

Gratton aimed a nod back over his shoulder towards the door. 'I've already noted the wide range of ages out there. I'm guessing some of them, one or two here included, were locking horns with the BNP and the New Crusader Movement around the time of those arsons. I also think some may even have intimate knowledge of those organisations. So I'm–'

'You better not be about to suggest that any of us carried out those racist attacks before switching sides,' she interrupted, anger pinching already tight cheeks around the bone.

Gratton put her age at mid-forties. Though not without its appeal, her face betrayed every hard knock she had taken throughout her life and, if he was any judge, there had been many.

He shook his head. 'I wasn't going to imply anything of the kind. We've known since that spring who was responsible, and he's no longer around to give us his side of it. But some of you may have known Jason Ball. Some of you probably knew other members of the NCM, too. I'm not looking to rake over cold ashes, but I am here to ask if any of you met with Lisa Pepperdine, or know of anyone who did. You may or may not be aware, but her body was discovered on Wednesday. Pathology tells us she was murdered during her visit here to the city, and it's our job to find out why – and who killed her.'

'What makes you think any of us have the foggiest idea about any of this?' the woman asked, rising to her feet. She glared at him, fury twisting her face into a tight scowl. With her hair pulled back into a tight bun atop her head, her features became hard and mean.

'Because Jason Ball's son did not follow in his father's footsteps. Craig Ball found another outlet for his rage – here, with Antifa-UK. And we don't believe he was the only one.'

The woman started walking around the table towards him, her lips puckering. 'You tell us you're not here to carry out some sort of inquisition, but then you make it clear you think one of us knows who killed this journalist.' She stood three feet away, contempt etched deep into her worn-out face. 'How typical of you people to go for the soft target.'

Gratton held onto her gaze, unwavering. 'Is that a guilty conscience I'm hearing? Because all I said was that we believe she might have met with somebody who is now one of your members. Nothing about them murdering her, just that she was murdered.'

'Yeah, and we all know what you meant, even if you didn't have the balls to say it.'

'No,' he shot back, shaking his head vigorously. 'You only think you know. And you either think it because there's some truth to it, or because you're paranoid. I'm not looking for a killer here today, only answers.'

'Then you'll be disappointed.' The woman slid both hands to her hips, swaying from side to side. 'And I reckon your five minutes is up.'

Ignoring her this time, Gratton said, 'I notice Craig Ball isn't here today. Are you expecting him later on?'

'No. He's in Portugal, not due back until tomorrow evening.'

Gratton cursed his memory. He had completely forgotten all about an informant's phone call telling them that Ball was away. 'Would I be able to speak with him when he returns?'

'No. Now do yourself a favour and fuck off out of it.'

'Look, I don't know who you are,' Gratton said, injecting some steel into his voice, 'but given you're the only one speaking up, I'll assume you're some kind of big deal around here. So I'm here to tell you not to be so bloody stupid.'

'You what?' Her hands clenched, and for one awkward moment he thought she was about to attack him. Two men stood up from the table, their chairs screeching back on the hard wooden floor. The large bruiser who had escorted Gratton into the room took a single step closer. That confirmed the woman's status in Gratton's mind, now all he had to do was push back.

'I've come here today, off duty, holding out an olive branch. A couple of simple questions to ask, looking for a couple of truthful answers. In and out, no fuss. But if I walk out of here now with nothing, how exactly do you think things are going to go from there? The woman is still dead. The investigation into her murder continues. Now, I can either stand up at our briefing on Monday morning and report that I've interviewed your group and eliminated you from our enquiries, or I can tell them you weren't willing to cooperate and have them rolling out to inconvenience you in your homes and your places of work.'

'You think you bunch of fascist mugs intimidate us?' the woman scoffed. 'We already know the police are either bent or psychopaths using a uniform to cover up their own violent urges.'

Gratton gave a harsh chuckle. 'Believe me, you know nothing about intimidation. But you've never been on the wrong side of my boss before. See, if he thinks you're hiding something from us – and he will, if you kick me out on my arse now – he'll rain down on you a kind of intrusive power you cannot even imagine. He will dig into your lives, your homes, your jobs, your families, your history. He'll turn your worlds upside down until you no longer know which way is up. And the thing about my boss is, he's not only relentless, he's the one man I've ever met who genuinely does not give a fuck. Your lives will be made a misery if he decides to go that way. And all for the sake of a couple of questions asked and answered right here, right now.'

Nobody said a word for what seemed like an eternity. Gratton didn't know if he had made a breakthrough or was about to get his throat slit and his body dumped in a ditch out in the Fens somewhere.

When she eventually responded, the woman's features remained set hard, her body taut, and her eyes brimming with distrust. 'My name is Debbie Ball,' she told him. 'I'm Craig Ball's wife. Because he's not able to attend this meeting today, I have his voice at this table.'

Gratton breathed out slowly, trying not to show that he had been holding it in for so long he had become giddy. 'So, you're willing to cooperate?'

'Just ask your questions,' she told him. 'You said you had a couple. I suggest you make them work for you.'

FORTY-FIVE

BLISS'S IMMEDIATE REACTION TO seeing the four armed men was to pull Chandler, Molly and Parker behind him. He spread his arms wide, making himself a bigger target. Then he took a better look at the group and lowered his hands, moving a couple of steps forward.

'What the bloody hell are you lot supposed to be?' he asked, appraising their attire and recognising the weapons now for what they were. The four of them stared back at him in complete silence. They appeared to be in as much shock as he was.

Bliss knew some people enjoyed the thrill of paintballing, dressing up in combat clothing and playing with guns. But these were unreal. All four wore black military-style warfare body suits, complete with head protection and masks… When his eyes fell back to the weapons they carried, he saw he'd been wrong. The guns did not carry paintballs.

He pulled his warrant card from his jacket pocket and held it up for them to read. 'What are those weapons?'

'They're just airsoft rifles,' one of the men said, having removed his mask.

'Airsoft?'

'Yeah. They fire 6mm plastic BB pellets.'

Bliss nodded. He remembered reading about them in a briefing newsletter. The weapons were capable of shooting their projectiles at around four or five hundred feet per second, depending on upgrades and modifications. He realised he had led the others into an area where men and women looking for a quick thrill took part in combat-style social events. Airsoft was a bit more hardcore than paintball, and judging by the way this group were dressed, they obviously took it far more seriously than the majority of weekend war-gamers.

'Where's this all based? Where can I find the organisers?' Bliss's strident voice snagged their attention. He was breathing heavily and casting anxious glances over his shoulder.

'Back through the woods,' one of the others said, hooking his thumb in the direction they had come. 'About three-quarters of a mile.'

Bliss thought quickly. Shots were popping off all around them, but he had no idea if any were coming from either the firearms officers or the bikers. He had to think worst case: men armed with deadly weapons were tracking them down right now, moving swiftly in their direction. He promptly reached a decision, and hoped it was the right one.

'Give me your rifles and your BB ammo,' he said to the group. 'Don't argue, just hand them over. Then you get your arses back to wherever you came from. Tell whoever is in charge to dial triple nine and report four police officers and two civilians in trouble, facing down armed men wearing motorcycle gear. Have them prevent anybody else coming out here and get them to call as many people in as they can. There's a very real possibility that we'll have live ammunition flying around these woods any minute now, and I don't want anyone believing these dangerous men are armed only with BBs. You got that?'

Two of the four nodded, while the others stood mute and blinking back their bewilderment. It was all too much for them, and nothing like what they had signed up for.

'I'm going with them and taking Molly with me,' Kim Parker said in a flat, decisive tone. She took hold of the girl's arm but the kid wrestled from her grasp, slapping the hand away before squinting sharply at Bliss.

He shook his head and moved to stand in the way. 'No. I considered that. It sounds good in theory, Kim, but remember this: those men back there are not after me or Penny. It's Molly. She is their target, and if you take her anywhere near other people then you put their lives in danger, too.'

'Well, we're hardly safe out here,' Parker pointed out. Her eyes looked as if they had been pushed back into her skull, all colour leached from her face.

'No, you're not,' he admitted. 'But neither are you any safer elsewhere, so all you'll do is make others less so.'

'I'm not going anywhere with her no matter what she says,' Molly piped up. She scowled at Parker and tensed as if about to flee.

'Don't worry,' Bliss told her. 'We're all staying put.'

'Jimmy, these rifles are no match for whatever those bikers are carrying,' Chandler said hurriedly, casting fearful glances over her shoulder.

He swivelled his head, eyes scanning the woodland behind her. 'I know that, Pen. But if we find a decent spot to tuck ourselves out of sight, we can pick them off at distance. Those BB pellets are harmless, but the sound of gunfire will at the very least make whoever's out there think and take cover. Slowing them down may buy us some time.'

'Fair enough. But still...'

She let it hang out there, leaving Bliss less certain about his decision. To his mind, they had three options: accompany the four men back to the organiser's premises and risk putting more innocents in harm's way; continue on alone and hope the armed men in their wake would somehow fail to catch up with them; or stand their ground now and take the fight to the bikers. None of these was ideal, but that did not stop their current situation being dangerous for everyone concerned.

As he turned it over, Bliss heard a loud snap, back along the jagged path they had taken. He squatted, peering through the gaps between trees and undergrowth, searching for the slightest sign of movement. His body became taut, forming a rigid shell. He saw nothing, but he felt something shift. The hushed whisper of encroachment, carried on a current of air that drew the attention of the subconscious. And whoever was out there, they were coming his way.

'Down,' he hissed behind him, emphasising his instruction with a hand gesture. Everyone obeyed, including the four men looking for combat thrills. He turned his head and motioned for one of them to pass him a rifle. The man did so as if the weapon had suddenly become red hot. Bliss looked it over, recognising the automatic mechanism. He'd be able to get off a few rounds without having to reload. Even as the thought rumbled through his mind, he wondered what return fire he would draw. Had he made a mistake in deciding to take a stand?

Something shifted ahead, across to his right. It was hard to make out anything in the thick woodland, but a figure was slowly picking its way towards them. Bliss's finger rested on the trigger of the airsoft rifle, and as he applied a small amount of pressure he recognised the absurdity of what he was about to do. Instead, he kept the weapon pointing outwards but then gave a cry of warning.

'Hold it right there!' he cried out. 'Armed police! If you continue with your approach I will fire upon you!'

Silence for several long seconds… and then a lone distant voice. 'Inspector? Inspector Bliss? It's Constable Jackson.'

Bliss closed his eyes and gave an easy sigh of relief. A genuine firearms officer had joined them, armed with a lethal weapon and not a powerful toy. He stood upright and waved the man towards them. Jackson stepped out from behind a tree and quickly reached them.

'Where's your sergeant?' Bliss asked, peering beyond the officer but seeing no sign of further movement.

'She's holding most of them back, sir. We had the bikers pinned down, but a small group broke away and entered the woods. Sergeant Bright ordered me to get in here and make sure you were covered.'

'Which left her alone to fend off the rest.' Bliss understood why Bright had instructed Jackson to track down and protect, but he worried about her exposure and vulnerability.

'Yes, sir.' Jackson smiled and shrugged. 'But you don't argue with Sergeant Bright. We managed to get a comms message out the moment we went off-road, so reinforcements are on the way. Some of the bikers weren't up to the task and rode off again, but there are two or three of them in the woods with us somewhere, and perhaps twice that number back out by the ARV.'

'You in touch with Bright?' Bliss asked.

Jackson gave an affirmative nod.

'Good. Let her know you found us. Tell her we're staying put, taking our own stand right here.' He'd noticed the officer's eyes all over the four combat-dressed men. 'Don't worry about them. They have their own job to do right now.'

Bliss turned and spoke to the group while Jackson raised his sergeant. 'Okay, help is on the way and coming fast. You lot get yourselves back to where you came from and warn others to move as far away from here as possible. These woods are dangerous now;

make sure they understand that. I don't want any weekend warriors out here looking for an extra rush of adrenaline.'

He did not have to ask twice now that things appeared to have settled down. The four disappeared through the trees and merged into the woods. Bliss watched them go, then turned his attention to his own group.

'You two okay?' he asked, nodding at Molly and Parker. The pair were clearly distraught, but they nodded and stared at him, waiting for him to speak. Bliss slipped a sidelong glance Chandler's way. Her soft features now came with hard edges, but her composure and strength of character shone though. He sucked down some frigid air before continuing.

'I realise staying put feels illogical, that it goes against the fight-or-flight instincts that are telling you to run. But for all we know there are a dozen more people like those four spread across these woods. I don't want anybody to get hurt who doesn't deserve it. There are bikers close by looking for us, and movement attracts more attention than standing still. So we get low and wait it out until backup arrives. If they happen to come in this direction, then we warn them off. And if necessary, Constable Jackson here is trained to handle this situation. Those coming our way are not. Remember that.'

Having finished advising Bright of their position, Jackson nodded and shifted his semi-automatic carbine. 'Inspector Bliss is right. This is not a great position to be in, but the more we move, the more we expose ourselves. Stay behind me, keep down, and we'll be okay. Don't worry, more crews are on the way and the moment my sergeant has everything wrapped up out there, she and the others will make their way to us.'

'What if the bikers find us first?' Parker asked, her voice laboured and tremulous.

'You let me worry about them.'

He sounded more confident than Bliss felt, and he nodded his thanks at the young man. No older than mid-twenties, Jackson carried an air of authority way beyond his years. Training and experience will do that.

The woods echoed to fewer sharp reports now, but the sounds had not ceased entirely. 'You two get off any rounds?' Bliss asked the ARV crew member.

'Yes, sir. We returned fire. Once we did, they got their heads down and they stayed down. It's one thing to fire a weapon, something quite different to have one spitting real bullets your way.'

Having undergone firearms training while with the National Crime Agency, Bliss understood what Jackson was telling him. You never did know how you would react under fire, but you had a much better chance of doing the right thing if you had years of training behind you.

A sound snared his attention. He wasn't sure what it was, only the direction from which it had originated. Jackson had heard it, too, and reacted instinctively by taking a knee and peering down his rifle sight as it moved patiently from side to side. Another disturbance, louder this time. Hushed voices flaring angrily.

'Armed police!' Jackson called out. 'Stand still and lay down your weapons! Then approach me slowly with your hands raised in the air! If you do not do as I say, I will open fire if I feel you pose a threat!'

Twigs snapped and branches whipped in the air as whoever was out there reacted. Composted leaves stirred underfoot. Bliss guessed whoever it was had responded by crouching low and taking cover behind a tree. When there was no reply, Jackson stepped it up a gear.

'Lay down your weapons! Interlace the fingers of both hands together and place them over your head! Then slowly – and I do mean slowly – approach the sound of my voice! I warn you again, I *will* fire on you if I sense any imminent threat!'

Two figures emerged into view. They walked slowly as commanded, hands on their heads. Neither appeared to be carrying a weapon. At least, not a firearm. The pair approached silently and with caution. Jackson kept the business end of his weapon trained on them.

Bliss did not trust the situation. He knew that hired muscle like these men were fine when it came to handing out a beating, or holding and even using a gun on others, provided they were always in control. Such men invariably unravelled when faced with the prospect of a highly skilled firearms officer facing them down, but these two had conceded their positions too readily for his liking. He wondered whether a third biker had escaped into the woods, and where that man might be hiding right now.

Shuffling forward, Bliss leaned down and whispered in Jackson's ear. 'Only two of them. That feel right to you? What if someone else is circling around, looking to get the drop on us?'

Jackson nodded. 'Keep an eye out,' he replied. 'Let me do the talking.'

Bliss switched his gaze. Sweeping it left to right, he peered deep into the woodland and kept his focus out there.

As the two figures reached a small clearing a dozen yards away, Jackson called out to them once more. 'On your knees! Keep your hands where I can see them! You move, I fire! No questions asked! And to your other mate out there, wherever you are, you'd better join your friends! Because otherwise, once I have them secured I'm coming for you and next time I fire first!'

Bliss heard the third figure before he saw him. 'Okay, okay!' came the panicked cry. The biker shambled into view. He'd forgotten to place his hands on his head, and Jackson's response was immediate, reminding the man to do as instructed or he would fire. The woods echoed to his stern demand, and this time the man complied fully.

Seconds later, the bikers were grouped together. As Bliss and Jackson stepped towards them, the firearms officer handed Bliss a batch of plastic flexicuffs, never once shifting either his gaze or his aim. The men remained subservient while Bliss first searched them for additional weapons, then secured their wrists behind their backs and pressed their faces lower into the ground. Meanwhile, Jackson messaged his partner as the sound of approaching sirens filled the cold winter air.

Bliss's shoulders lost their tension for the first time in several long minutes. Pulling moisture into his dry throat, his mind latched onto the many ways in which everything could have gone wrong. Outnumbered and taken by surprise, Bliss had made a series of choices, all of which would be examined in minute detail by more senior investigators. He mentally reviewed each step… and declared himself satisfied. Others would undoubtedly have made different decisions, but he had done nothing incorrect. As with all actions viewed in retrospect, his choices were open to debate – yet as far as he was concerned, not one of them was also open to challenge.

'You okay with these pricks?' he asked Jackson. The constable nodded, his composure admirable.

Bliss turned and walked back over to his partner, smiling, then switched his attention to Parker and Molly, who were still huddled together. He winked at them. 'It's all over,' he said. 'We're done here. You can both breathe easily again.'

FORTY-SIX

HE WAS BETWEEN VISITING hours, but had been persuasive with the nursing staff. A veiled reference to his own ill-health – though he was feeling as fit as the proverbial butcher's dog – and a more overt description of a horrendous journey had done the trick.

Sykes was napping, so Flynn quietly eased himself into the bedside chair and waited patiently. The cacophony of wet wheezing sounds emanating from his old colleague's chest was disturbing, but better than no breaths at all. Bliss's observations had prepared him for the worst, but seeing Sykes for himself caused goosebumps to rise beneath his shirt sleeves, and a shudder worked its way down the full length of his spine. This was how mortality appeared in its most unsettling guise, but Flynn vowed this would never be his future.

It was many years ago, during a holiday in Italy, that Flynn had looked out over Lake Como and reached a decision from which he had never wavered. That night, as he walked with his wife along the Viale Benedetto Castelli, he had told her of his wishes. For him there would be no care home, no hospice; no indignity, nor strangers bathing him, changing him. Neither did he intend imposing upon his wife to shoulder that burden while his body, mind, or even both shut down and turned him into an infant once more.

'Either I'll kill myself or you can help me if I need it,' he'd told her. 'But whatever happens, don't leave me to fade away into insignificance.'

The man lying in the bed before him now was doing precisely that. The palliative care would, Flynn was certain, be comprehensive and carried out in a humane and professional manner. But how was this a fitting way to go out? Relying on others for your every single need. A slow, lingering death that caused more pain and misery than anyone should have to endure? If Stuart Sykes were a dog and this place run by veterinarians, he would have been put down. A painless, compassionate end. Instead, here he lay, slowly fading into the shadows.

'Who's there?' A low, rasping voice.

Flynn snapped out of wherever his head had been. Sykes was awake, eyes open. Guarded, perhaps even fearful.

'It's Joe Flynn, Stuart.' He smiled at the man in the bed. 'Do you remember me? We worked together at Thorpe Wood.'

Moist eyes blinked back at him. The frail, undernourished, supine figure was merely the husk of the upright, shoulders-back-chest-out man Sykes had once been. Flynn thought of his own bowed gait as he walked, the aches and pains he carried, the extra effort almost everything required these days compared to when he was in his prime. And he was still relatively healthy and vital, someone who exercised and ate well. Miserably, he wondered how much of his ex-colleague was even left.

'Remember me, Stuart?' he prompted again. 'Chief Superintendent Flynn. You were my Super, running the show for me.'

Was that a glint of recognition?

Flynn went on. 'Those were the days, eh, Stuart? An entire city police force operating like a well-oiled machine. The uniforms were the ringleaders, of course, but it was us suits who were the stars. They just held the ground for us, parted the way to allow us entry. We didn't secure a crime scene, we got our hands dirty. We solved cases. Hundreds of them. The glory years, Stuart. Perhaps even the last of their kind.' He laughed at his own words. 'Just like you and me, Stuart. We were the last of a kind, too… other than Bliss, of course. But then, to be perfectly honest with you, I was never absolutely convinced he wasn't a species all of his own.'

Sykes winced. 'Bliss,' he croaked, swallowing thickly. Flynn picked up a plastic cup with a straw poking over its rim. 'Here, Stuart, have some water, mate.'

Sykes sucked hard and managed to wet his lips, pulled some more into his throat. The effort appeared to drain him and he let out a soft groan.

Flynn wondered if he ought to leave. Even if he got Sykes talking, he'd never be able to trust the ramblings of a dying man, much less a dying man who was also losing his grip on reality.

Sykes resolved the conundrum for him by reaching out and grabbing his wrist. 'You knew what I did,' he said. 'To Bliss. You knew what I did to Bliss.'

Flynn nodded and patted the man's hand. 'I did, yes.'

'Why… why did you never tell him?'

'Perhaps I did. In my own way.' By treating Bliss better than he deserved at times, although Flynn had always secretly admired the Inspector's iron will and fierce determination.

'Bad… egg…'

'He could be, Stuart. But his heart was invariably in the right place.'

Sykes nodded. Understanding, or agreement? Flynn couldn't be sure, but he took the opportunity to press on with what he had come here for. The moment Bliss had contacted him to explain that he and his entourage were no longer coming, that they had been rumbled and had decided to shelter elsewhere following an incident in some woods, Flynn had an overwhelming urge to cleanse his own guilt. For that he needed Sykes. A Sykes who, even if only for a second or two, had to be present in the room and fully aware. This was that opportunity.

'Funnily enough, Stuart, I was only recently talking to Bliss. He hasn't changed that much, I can tell you. He's working on something involving a journalist. She wasn't from here in the city. Up from London, piecing together a scoop. Woman by the name of Lisa Pepperdine. It reminded me that you and I spoke about her once. Remember?'

'We did?' Sykes's eyes closed tight as he concentrated, lines deepening across his forehead.

'Sure. She came to me demanding a meeting. There was no way I was going to allow that to happen, so you and I discussed her. We agreed she was a major pain in the arse. You must remember that, surely? Especially her name: Pepperdine?'

This time Sykes nodded, and his eyes cleared as if a cataract had been removed. 'Yes. Of course. Pepperdine.' His mouth puckered into a jagged grin. 'Bloody stupid name.'

'Yes, yes. We had a good laugh about that, Stuart. Remember I asked you to fix it for me? How I refused to meet with her, and told you I wanted her gone from the city because she was only here to exploit what was already an explosive situation? I was wondering how you accomplished that? Because I never did hear from her again, did you? Did you hear from her, Stuart? After you... met with her. Persuaded her to leave somehow.'

'You think *I* killed her?'

Flynn reeled back in his chair. It was partly the unexpected forcefulness of the words, but also that when he looked into the man's eyes he knew that Sykes was genuinely in the room with him. Living the moment. Remembering the past. Flynn laughed it off and said, 'No, of course not. Why would you say such a thing? When I asked you to solve our problem, we both knew I did not have that solution in mind.'

'I'm not quite sure what you were thinking, Joe. I'm not even certain you cared much one way or the other, just so long as she was gone.'

'That's not true, Stuart. The aim was to have her move on. Perhaps to make things uncomfortable for her, apply some unusual pressure, but never anything more than that.'

Sykes huffed and waved a hand in the air. 'What does it matter now? It's unimportant what you had in mind – only what happened, yes?'

'Yes.'

'Then I'll tell you. You made your problem mine. I made it someone else's.'

Flynn's heart lurched and then began to thump behind his ribcage. 'Not… not Bliss, surely?'

'Bliss?' Sykes regarded him as if he were insane. 'You think I would ever have asked *him* to take care of a difficult situation on my behalf? The man would have laughed me out of the office. No, no. Robert Marsh was the right man for that job. I knew he would get it done for us.'

'Get what done?' Flynn's mouth was bone dry; as much as he needed to know the answer, he also wanted to stand up, leave the room and never return so that he would never have to hear it. He took a sip of Sykes's water. 'What was it you got done, Stuart?'

Sykes smiled. A smile of great cunning. A smile from the past. The kind of smile he reserved for those times when he wanted to hurt or demean, or both. Then in a low, wheezing voice he said, 'We did what I thought you wanted from the very beginning, Joe. We arranged to get rid of our problem.'

FORTY-SEVEN

THE SLAUGHTERHOUSE ON THE outskirts of Maxey was a useful backdrop to a spot of intimidation, and Anthony was suitably apprehensive. The only reason Eric had chosen to meet him here was that Anthony would be forced to sit and reflect on his failure while surrounded by blood-spattered walls and floors, with the sounds of machinery grinding bones and taking apart huge chunks of meat in the background. The setting required no psychoanalysis.

For the past thirty minutes he'd been doing his best impersonation of a brass monkey, sitting in a cold room whose hooks dangled from the ceiling like foul windchimes. Every so often a chilled breeze caused them to twitch and stir. He'd been ordered to wait alone, while the two blokes who had accompanied him from the unit in Westwood remained outside. The psychological impact of his immediate predicament rather than the stark surroundings themselves was intended as a punishment. Anthony wondered if there was more to follow. Which, he realised, acted as a further emotional scouring in itself.

He had perhaps underestimated Eric. There was more to him than pure greed or bloodlust. Therefore, it came as a relief when the man himself walked into the room. Anthony knew that his own reaction was also part of the plan. To be both fearful of, and grateful to, another human being granted them power over you and mastery of the situation. *Kudos to you, pal*, he thought. *But I'm not as mentally weak as you imagine.*

'Tell me what went wrong,' Eric said. There was no edge to his voice, and his manner remained reserved. He stood with his hands behind his back, opening himself up, his body language suggesting he considered the man before him to be no threat.

'Pure misfortune, from what I can gather.' Anthony kept both his tone and his manner neutral. Concerned, but unfazed. 'The people we tasked with doing the necessary had the girl in their sights. The plan was for four of them to draw alongside the copper's Vauxhall and, before the ARV crew had a chance to respond, spray the interior with as many rounds as a Browning Hi-Power pistol holds.'

'Which is how many?'

'Thirteen each.'

Eric pursed his lips. 'After which they ride away into the sunset, yeah?'

'Not quite. But we had two brothers who live in the area cause an accident which blocked the A11 eastbound. And by brothers I don't mean *bruthas* – I mean actual brothers.' He paused for a second to chuckle at his own joke. 'I realised the ARV crew might get a few shots off themselves before all of our guys managed to get away, so another part of the plan was for a couple of bikes to draw up alongside their motor as well, stopping the doors opening. It wasn't foolproof, man, I admit it, but I didn't have much time once I knew Molly was on the move.'

Eric acknowledged this with a tilt of his head and no more. 'So I ask again: Anthony, what went wrong?'

'Somebody in the Vauxhall must have seen the lads heading their way, and figured out somehow that they were coming for them. As

I say, the traffic was at a standstill, but from what I hear, this Bliss bloke used his car like a battering ram and bludgeoned his way out, went up onto the verge and floored it. Turned off into some woods, the ARV right up its jacksie. Our guys followed, gave chase. But by the time they got close, the Insignia had stopped and everyone was legging it into the trees. The ARV was parked up behind it, its crew out and in defensive positions.'

'I hear one or two of our men rode back out of there as quickly as they came.'

'That's what I understand, too.'

'Get me their names. I have no use for them anymore. In fact, bring them over here and let's see what they have to say for themselves in this room.'

Anthony was chilled by the implied threat in the man's words, but he also found them comforting. If he was being asked to carry out this task for Eric, then he must be walking out of here, intact or not; he warmed beneath the fresh flush of hope.

'Whatever you say, Eric.'

'But not before you explain to me how our team of armed muscle was unable to overcome their targets, only two of whom carried weapons.'

'I don't have that information. Three, perhaps four of ours followed the group from the lead vehicle into the woods, while the others had a bit of a standoff with the firearms cops. It's possible that one of those coppers made their way into the woods after our men, but the other one popped off a few rounds, so our blokes had their heads down at the time. After a few minutes, they heard the sound of backup on its way and scarpered.'

'And the three who went into the woods?'

Anthony shrugged. 'No word as yet. I think we have to assume they were either arrested or put down.'

Eric sniffed and snarled, 'So now, in addition to Ryan Endicott, plus two of his crew and this Molly bitch, the filth have another three of our men in custody.'

'That's about the strength of it, yes.'

'Well, that's a pickle we find ourselves in, Anthony. A massive, fucked-up fucker of a pickle.'

'No doubt. But to be fair to myself, I arrived here in the early hours, so it's only the latest cock-up that's down to me. Even then, the plan was solid enough – I mean, I'd had no time to think about it from all sides, but it was sound. And I wasn't around to make sure it went off as we'd expected because I'd never have got there in time. But yeah, I guess I took on the responsibility of snatching Molly back for you, Eric, so I hold my hands up.'

'I wouldn't hold them up too high, Anthony. You can never predict what might come along to chop them off.'

Anthony was prepared for the threat. 'I'm not sure Leroy would see it that way, man. Disabling his top enforcer doesn't seem like good business sense to me. Especially not for *his* business, if you know what I mean. Look, I take the rap on the knuckles, yeah, and I realise the situation is now worse and not better. But I had to think fast and it was only the execution of the plan that went sideways, nothing to do with the strategy itself. If nobody in that car clocks our blokes on their bikes as early as they did, then we're talking about a whole different result, you know?'

McManus fixed a solitary baleful eye on him. 'So what are you saying? You want a fucking medal? You want a pat on the back for coming up with a great plan that fell apart because… because these people we're after had eyes in their fucking heads?'

Some reflex sent Anthony's gaze momentarily to the empty socket. He held up his hands, fingers splayed. 'That's not what I'm saying at all. I've already copped for the fuck-up, yeah? My plan, so I'm accountable. I get that. But it's not terminal. Forget about your guys in custody for the moment, many of whom were banged up while I was still balls-deep inside a woman in London, yeah? If they're a mixture of your men and Leroy's men, then they are all solid. They won't say a word. The contract you gave me was to get Molly back. Well, either back or gone for good. She's still out there, and I'm still out here. So let me do my job. Let me find out where she is, and this time I'll figure out a way to end it.'

'Tell me why I should give you a second chance, Anthony. Especially when your first attempt cost me dearly.' The man shuffled from foot to foot, hugely irritated but clearly anxious about how the cause of his problems would be dealt with. His heavy overcoat warded off the worst of the cold, but his breath escaped in a dense fog.

Anthony took a beat. McManus's animosity flowed towards him in waves, but he also sensed the man's reluctance to make yet another wrong choice. He decided to use that hesitation to calm things down. 'I already told you, Eric. I'm Leroy's man, remember? So only Leroy has the final say when it comes to me. This shit is every bit as important to him as it is to you, so let me and him have a conversation, and then I'll make this right.'

Eric turned that single eye on him again. 'You're putting an awful lot of faith in how many fucks I give about Leroy Kelly.'

Shaking his head, Anthony shrugged and said, 'No, Eric. You're wrong about that. I'm putting my faith in you being the kind of man who knows how to conduct business. One who values long-term success over short-term failure. A boss who sees the wider implications of his decisions. Be that man, Eric. Allow me to make this right. Just think about how much I will owe you still.'

Eric ran a hand across his face. Silence hung in the air, punctuated every so often by the squeak of a meat hook swaying on the steel rail above. The next breath he blew out was long and heavy. 'Make your call, Anthony. Arrange whatever you need with Leroy. Then feed me those wankers who ran away from those woods, and when you're done with them you find me that girl and you make sure she goes away. And this time I do mean for good. We clear on that?'

'Crystal, Eric,' Anthony said, oozing the kind of confidence he was not feeling. This was his last chance. One more failure, and he'd be swinging from one of these hooks with his intestines spilling out of his carved-open stomach like a human piñata.

FORTY-EIGHT

It was more like a war than a conference, which was why Bliss focussed on thinking of it as a meeting with a side order of aggression and accusation thrown in. On one flank, Marie Collins and Kim Parker snarled and spat their way through a vitriolic diatribe aimed at the incompetence of the police in general, and Bliss in particular. In direct opposition, Bliss defended himself with a surprisingly alacrity, citing the ignorance of the social services when it came to operational decisions taken within the police service. Chandler endorsed everything he said, which was nothing less than he expected. Somewhere in the middle, DCI Warburton and DSI Fletcher attempted to mediate and find some common ground upon which they could all agree.

'I've heard both sides of the argument,' Fletcher said in her most earnest and reasonable tone. 'And I find no cause to sanction Detective Inspector Bliss, irrespective of how badly the operation went awry.'

'Well, of course you would say that,' Collins snapped, puffing herself up. 'He's one of your own. I demand an inquiry into what took place. An independent one.'

For the first time since the meeting had opened, Fletcher showed signs of irritation. 'I'd be grateful if you would not impugn my integrity, Marie.'

'I did no such thing,' Collins spluttered.

'Indeed you did. What you appear to be implying is that I would back my Inspector no matter what, and that is not the case. I can show you many examples to prove my point, with this same specific member of my team. The fact is, DI Bliss was the ranking officer on the ground. He had to react swiftly to unusual and unforeseen circumstances. What's more, events suggest he was right to be fearful. Also, you're in no position to *demand* anything.'

She cleared her throat and took a sip of water before continuing to speak. Earlier she had complained of feeling unwell, and her voice was becoming increasingly brittle.

'Having raided the home of Mr Endicott and secured the young girl known as Molly once more, the team initially brought her back here to Thorpe Wood. My understanding is that a phone call took place between Inspector Bliss and yourself, during which you agreed that – owing to the failure to secure Molly with her emergency foster carer – a valid temporary solution would be for DI Bliss, members of his team, armed personnel, and an appropriate adult of your own choosing to keep the child safe inside the Inspector's own home. That is correct, yes?'

Collins nodded, her throat flushing red. 'Yes, it is. Which brings me back to the main thrust of my complaint, which is that your Inspector failed to adhere to that agreement when he later decided to relocate Molly without informing me of her immediate destination.'

Fletcher gave a weary sigh. 'Marie, when it comes to securing people, our officers have to remain flexible at all times. They have to be able to react to changes in circumstances as and when they occur. I know you know that, so I'm wondering why you're now… posturing. In this instance, DI Bliss believed there was a significant risk of you being compromised to the point where you would give up the location to ensure the safety of your own family. I should add that the Inspector kept Ms Parker here informed at every stage. Now, given that information, given those extremely specific conditions, I believe DI Bliss did precisely the right thing. Unfortunately – and I do understand why your reasoning is off at the moment – Bliss's suspicions were proven to be correct. You *were* compromised, and you understandably did what you had to do in order to protect yourself and your family. So while I have every sympathy for what you went through, Marie, I see no justification for taking this complaint any further.'

The social services team leader turned bright red. She chewed on her lower lip, inwardly fuming. At around the same time as Bliss had driven into the woods, Collins was being released. Blindfolded since being handed over to the two men who spoke not one word of English the entire time she was with them, when she removed the heavy scarf that had been wrapped around her eyes, she realised she was on Princes Gate, outside the entrance to Central Park. As Bliss understood it, Collins had no phone, no money and no ID on her, so she had walked into the city centre where she eventually came across two PCSOs. She had endured no real hardship other than humiliation, and whilst Bliss was sympathetic, her attack on his methods came across as petty and vindictive. He was about to add his own comment when he noticed a change come over the woman.

As Collins processed everything Fletcher had said, she visibly relaxed and eventually nodded. 'I take your point, Superintendent. I'm still not certain I agree with it, but I do understand why Inspector Bliss took that decision. Upon reflection, moving Molly out of the city to a location nobody other than those travelling to it, in addition to the property's owner, of course, was a reasonable enough solution. Especially given the time constraints.'

'Good. Then we are agreed?'

'On that specific point, yes. But I don't think your side can escape further scrutiny as to how these men discovered where you were taking her. I also wonder whether sufficient provisions were made in respect of firearms protection.'

'I'd like to answer that if I may,' Bliss said, sick of listening to others talking around him and about him as if he were not in the same room. He did not wait to be told to continue. 'I'm not convinced they knew our destination. Had they been aware of that information, they surely would have attempted the snatch once our journey was at its end. Stopping us and tracking us the way they did was fraught with all kinds of adverse possibilities, and I don't see them making that choice willingly. Far more likely, I believe, is that we were followed from my home. I suspect that the moment they realised which route we were taking, they contacted whoever is running the show now that Endicott's out of the game, and they set up the vehicle collision ahead of us, at which point they also involved a number of willing bikers.'

There were nods from around the table. 'That seems like a reasonable theory,' Fletcher said. 'Even so, it still calls into question our operational procedures. Did it not occur to you, Inspector, that Endicott's bosses might have either realised or been informed of Molly's presence inside your own home?'

Bliss shook his head with conviction. 'Not in the slightest, ma'am. There were so few people involved, and no official record. When I made the decision to relocate in case Mrs Collins was compromised, I had no idea she already had been; I couldn't possibly have known that while I was talking to her she was already being threatened. In hindsight, I probably ought to have had people outside the house as well, but even if I'd done so, I suspect our watchers would have set up camp further away. I'm sure we'll rip this entire sorry episode apart when we have our post-operation meeting, but I don't see how we could have avoided this outcome.'

Fletcher glanced around the table, gave a single firm nod and rapped her knuckles on its wooden surface. 'Agreed. This will all be scrutinised at a later date, so for now I think it best we concentrate on what happens next. Marie, your thoughts, please.'

Bliss mentally thanked his boss. So far Collins had been judging everything with the benefit of hindsight. Now she was being offered the opportunity of spending some time in the driving seat.

Collins allowed herself a moment or two to consider the situation. Bliss felt some sympathy towards her. The threats made against her were bad enough, but being removed from her home by two men and being kept locked up in a cold, windowless room, prior to her eventual release, was enough to tip anybody over the edge. He knew he did not have to remind her how fortunate she had been, as not everyone abducted in such a fashion made it home safely again afterwards. Though she had not been ill-treated, the emotional impact could not be discounted. That she had immediately made herself available for this meeting was a credit to the woman.

'I wish I had answers,' she said. Her lips thinned; she was plainly perplexed and out of her depth. 'Or even a single bulb of inspiration lighting up above my head. So far we've tried placing Molly with a carer, securing her with one of your senior detectives, and relocating her out of the county. None of these options has panned out. Taking her to your ex-colleague's place of business was an idea with a lot of merit, I admit, but of course that is now entirely out of the question.'

'Which is why the boss and I believe there's only one way left open to us,' Chandler said. 'We keep Molly here, and at the same time we double the efforts to find her an ultimate secure home, far away from this city. I do appreciate the complications, especially in terms of contacting relevant people over the weekend, but these are unusual circumstances to say the least, and I think they deserve our every effort.'

'The first part of that is unarguable,' Bliss said. 'I realise keeping Molly here goes against procedure and protocol, given she was not arrested, but then the rules were constructed having never imagined an incident such as this. I freely admit to being against the idea before, because the longer we kept her here the more predictable it became as to when we would eventually relocate her.'

Bliss shook his head, exhausted after everything that had taken place over the past few days. If he had made errors of judgement, he would eventually have to answer for them. His fate would take care of itself. For the time being, this was all about the girl.

'What happened out there in those woods shook Molly up, and I think it finally sank in that not only are the people she worked for determined to silence her, but that we are equally resolute when it comes to ensuring her safety. I'm absolutely certain that if we put our heads together, we and social services are capable of devising an acceptable one-off agreement whereby we keep Molly behind secure doors in this police station until such time as she can be moved on in safety. If that ultimate goal requires five moves or even ten moves to filter out the number of people who know where she ends up, then we keep hold of her until all of the necessary arrangements are put in place.'

Marie Collins blinked rapidly and exchanged looks with her colleague. 'I have to think we're looking at Tuesday at the very earliest for us to physically undertake that first move. But only if we can make the majority of the arrangements over what's left of the weekend. There are some people we won't be able to reach until Monday, of that I am certain. So I'm guessing you'd need to keep Molly here until Tuesday.'

'I realise that goes against the grain,' Bliss acknowledged. 'But Molly will agree to it, provided she's surrounded by people she knows and trusts. The last thing we can afford is for her to become disillusioned and start thinking she'd be better off out there alone.' He pointed out of the window, dark grey skies beyond.

'May I make a suggestion?' DCI Warburton said. It was her first meaningful contribution to the debate.

'Of course, Diane,' Fletcher replied, sweeping a hand out across the table. 'Please go ahead. There are no bad ideas here in this room today.'

'I have no desire to trample on social services' toes, but if I'm hearing this right, the aim will be to arrange a series of transfers from area to area, with each area limiting the number of people who know where Molly came from. Ensuring multiple degrees of separation, in other words.'

'That's the general idea, yes,' Collins concurred. 'I don't know if it's been done that way before, but I see no reason why it can't happen.'

'Then I have two things in mind. One thing I'd like to ask, followed by my suggestion.'

'Fire away.'

'Are you planning to change Molly's identity along the way? Actually, perhaps the proper way of putting that is to ask if there is any intention to provide Molly with new ID at some point, considering she currently has none that we've been able to locate?'

Fletcher looked across at Collins. 'Marie?'

'The short answer is no. That is something I don't believe we'll be able to negotiate. Certainly not immediately. As things stand, Molly is in our care as a juvenile. While admittedly she is at risk, she is neither a witness for the prosecution nor a vulnerable parolee whose identity needs to be protected.'

'What a bloody joke,' Bliss said, turning his head to one side and cursing beneath his breath. 'Some sick bastard commits an abhorrent crime and when they get released, we hand them a new

ID and a home, find them work, set them up for the rest of their lives and do so until their dying day. But a young kid whose life is being threatened by a criminal gang? No, that's fine. That, we can live with.'

Collins reacted defensively. 'I'm not saying we couldn't make a claim to do so on Molly's behalf, only that she doesn't meet the current criteria and it would all use up a great deal of time that we don't have on our side.'

'Of course not. She's not a bloody paedo or a sexual deviant.'

Warburton jumped in before the disagreement got out of hand. 'I'm sure Marie is merely relaying information to us, not defending the principle,' she said, turning her weak smile on them all. 'And perhaps it's something we can investigate further down the line. For now, I would suggest putting a hold on making all of those arrangements you spoke about beyond the very next area you're thinking of moving Molly to.'

The frown on Collins's face intensified. 'I'm not sure what you're getting at. How will reducing the number of moves improve the girl's chances?'

'No, what I'm suggesting is that you make each individual area responsible for their own arrangements. So, for argument's sake, say you hand Molly over to Norfolk. They pass her over to Suffolk. Suffolk pass her over to Kent… and so on. That way you still get your degrees of separation, only they are absolute. Looking at my example, Kent would never know she went through Norfolk, Suffolk would never know she came from Cambridgeshire. It seems to me that by making the location changes that way, we eliminate the risk factor significantly.'

Bliss followed the DCI's train of thought; the idea was brilliant. It also had the distinct advantage of taking up far less time here in Peterborough, because Marie Collins would be responsible for agreeing the first stage only, in addition to drawing up the documentation outlining the procedure other counties would then follow. After a brief silence during which everyone at the table looked to be running the process through in their heads, they all started speaking at once.

Chuckling at the cacophony, Superintendent Fletcher raised a hand to call for quiet. She regarded Warburton warmly. 'Diane, I have to say that is a stroke of genius. It will slow down the procedure as a whole if each area has to make its own arrangements, but the way you describe it would appear to offer far more security, and a much appreciated improvement on our immediate timescale.'

'I can't think of a single reason not to go ahead with that idea right now,' Collins said, seemingly keen to draw the meeting to a conclusion.

Kim Parker nodded her head in agreement, even raising a smile. 'Me neither,' she said. 'It's a gem of a plan.'

'Bliss? Chandler?' Fletcher said, glancing at each of them in turn.

'It's a cracking idea,' he replied. 'I don't see any way of improving on it.'

Chandler was already nodding by his side. 'I'm with the boss, ma'am. Anything that both adds layers of security and gets Molly away from this city sooner is all right by me.'

The way his partner phrased her response provoked Bliss to realise the full meaning of the new procedure for the first time. He was all for Molly being safe and secure, far away and out of reach of those who sought to harm or even kill her. But, dammit, he liked the kid. He enjoyed her company, such as it was. He didn't often meet a person who reminded him of who and what he used to be; certainly never a girl. But he saw so much of his fifteen-year-old self in Molly that he was already feeling an emotional loss at the very idea of her no longer being around.

FORTY-NINE

After the meeting, Bliss took care of matters back down in Major Crimes. The rest of the team were shocked by what had taken place on the A11 and in the woods. Bliss allowed Chandler to relate their tale of woe, while he kept an eye on his colleagues to see how they were handling it. The strain showed most of all in Olly Bishop's face, and it came as no surprise to Bliss when he was the first to respond.

'This is getting ridiculous,' Bishop snapped. His nostrils flared and his flesh became pinched around his cheekbones. 'Needing yet another firearms callout is taking the piss. Where the hell does it all end?'

'It's a reflection of the times we live in, Bish,' Chandler said casually. 'On a day like today, tasers wouldn't have been enough. That more aggressive response was essential.'

'I understand all that, Penny. I'm not blind to what's happening. But am I the only one who thinks it's getting too bloody dangerous out there on the streets?'

'No, you're not,' DC Ansari responded. 'What with that and the threats made against Marie Collins, I'm also concerned about the level of violence and hostility out there right now.'

Bliss sat patiently as the team batted it back and forth. There was some venting to be done, and he did not wish to interfere. It was interesting listening to the differing points of view; the dynamics of the discussion providing an insight into the way his team thought and expressed themselves. He also considered the differences from previous post-incident discussions. Bishop concerned him, he had to admit. What he had experienced just a few months ago was enough to have shaken even the most iron-willed officer, but Bliss asked himself if his DS was wound too tight and too often these days. He decided to wait for a quieter moment rather than raise it now while everyone else was around, fuses lit. Fortunately, DC Gratton entered the room and snagged his attention.

'What are you doing here on your day off, Phil?' he asked. 'I thought you and John were making the most of your time away from this place, girding the loins ahead of your meeting with Craig Ball.'

'Actually, I have some news on that,' Gratton said, taking a seat behind his desk. 'I was at a bit of a loose end this morning, so I decided to do a bit more work on the case.'

'That's what I like to hear, though in reality I should be telling you to rest for the sake of your mental wellbeing. Wellness, I think we're supposed to call it these days. If anybody asks, that's precisely what I insisted you do, okay? But, since you're here, tell us what you've got.'

Barely able to conceal his excitement, Gratton told the team about his visit to the Antifa-UK gathering at the community centre in Fletton, and how he had managed to squeeze information out of Craig Ball's wife.

'Once I got her started, she couldn't get it out quick enough,' Gratton said, his eyes gleaming at the memory. 'And she remembered Lisa Pepperdine, all right – well, the name, at least. Told me Craig's father hated the woman, especially for the way she tried to expose the far-right movement. She remembered Maureen,

Jason's wife, sniggering when telling family and friends they'd been approached by the police looking for help in encouraging Pepperdine to leave the city. After years of clashes with us, both Jason and his wife thought it was hysterical that we had come to them for help.'

'Did she happen to mention who approached them?' Bliss asked.

Gratton nodded, a wide grin splitting his pale features. 'Chief Inspector Robert Marsh.'

Bliss punched the air. 'Yes! I bloody well knew it.' That put both Joe Flynn and Stuart Sykes in the clear as far as he was concerned. His excitement dissipated rapidly when he realised that it didn't matter so much which of his colleagues had been involved in the journalist's disappearance; the point was that the force was implicated. 'So what did Marsh want of them?' he prompted.

'Apparently he wasn't entirely specific. He told the Ball family that the police were not exactly thrilled with Pepperdine for pointing fingers at them. Knowing they wouldn't be happy with her stance against right-wingers, and in the absolute certainty that she'd be going after the force next, Marsh suggested Jason and his fellow NCM members do them all a favour.'

'Sounds like an incitement to violence to me,' Chandler said. A tight frown lined her face.

'That's exactly how they saw it, too. According to Maureen Ball, Marsh implied a blind eye would be turned to the behaviour of the group in future incidents should Pepperdine decide to move on there and then.'

'So Jason Ball saw a way to kill two birds,' Bishop said, huffing his dissatisfaction. 'But since he's no longer with us, there's bugger all we can do about it.'

'Ah, but here's where it falls apart,' Gratton said. He milked his grip on the audience with a lengthy pause. 'See, Maureen insists her husband chose not to go along with it at all. Told Marsh to take care of his own business. Said if the journalist came after him or his group, then they would step in and do whatever was necessary, but no way was he going to get his hands dirty on behalf of the police.'

'And yet Pepperdine went missing before laying a glove on those responsible for the arsons and murders,' Bliss said.

'She did. What's more, Debbie Ball is one hundred percent confident that when he was refused help, Chief Inspector Marsh told Jason he'd put his own house in order.'

Whatever Bliss had been tasting in his mouth earlier, it turned sour in an instant. If both Maureen Ball and her daughter-in-law were correct, Marsh was now firmly back in the frame for the journalist's murder. He closed his eyes and let it sink in. Just at that moment, DCI Warburton came through the doors; she had held back after the meeting to discuss approaches with the Superintendent. She wore a grim look, and Bliss was immediately suspicious.

Warburton sat, as she usually did, on the edge of a desk, arms folded across her chest. She listened intently as, between them, Bishop, Chandler and Gratton brought her up to date with operation Survival. Bliss never took his eyes off her face; while she was taking it in, it was also clear to him that she was preoccupied. Moments later, she revealed her own news.

'A couple of the bikers from earlier on are talking,' she said. CID had led the interviews, given the trail's source had begun with their raid on Ryan Endicott's flat on Wednesday morning. Bliss had agreed to let them take first crack, provided he and his team were allowed to scoop up the sloppy seconds. Bewildered by the discussion, Gratton had to be brought up to speed before the conversation continued.

'Talking bollocks or business?' Chandler asked, drawing laughs from every corner of the room, the DCI included.

'Business,' she replied. 'Intelligence has them usually doing odd jobs for Eric McManus. These jobs arise when he requires additional muscle, and the biker gang are not averse to earning extra pocket money that way. However, both men separately provided similar information when interviewed. Evidently, today's orders were passed down from a London enforcer, sent up here to knock some heads together. The name Leroy Kelly was mentioned.'

Nobody had heard of the man. Bliss assumed he was at the supply end of the drugs chain and suggested as much.

'That's the word we now have on him,' Warburton said. 'And if Kelly is involved, then this enforcer is most likely a face by the name of Anthony Clarke. Early doors, we're told this man Clarke is not exceptional to look at in terms of what you'd expect from an enforcer, but has a reputation for lacking any conscience whatsoever. When he decides to hurt people, they stay hurt.'

'And this animal is now on our turf?' Bishop said, his face creased into a snarl.

'That would appear to be the case, yes.'

'It's not unexpected,' Bliss said. 'Endicott was always the middle man. The far ends of the chain were bound to step up eventually. But we're the ones who have Endicott banged up, and we're the ones with Molly tucked away safe and secure. Thanks to the new boss lady, we also now have a terrific way of moving Molly on and ensuring she remains safe and secure, and out of the reach of these scumbags. If this Clarke geezer drove up here looking to settle scores and take Molly off the map, then he's failed at one of those things. I suspect he may also be responsible for the threat to Marie Collins. But if he takes out a few of Endicott's crew before he heads back south, then I'm not losing any sleep over it.'

'That's where we have a problem,' Warburton said. Bliss felt his muscles tense. The DCI was clearly about to reveal why she had looked so glum when entering the room.

'We always have problems to deal with,' he said, trying to sound calm.

'True, but as soon as we learned all this, the word went out on the street. Intelligence got even more involved.'

'And? We about to see a drugs war played out in the city?'

'That may yet happen,' Warburton said with a shrug. 'But what we're hearing now is that this London enforcer isn't going away empty-handed with his tail between his legs. Mr Clarke has made it clear that he's getting to both Endicott and Molly one way or another.'

'Then he'll have to come through us to do it,' Bliss said.

'Quite so. But evidently, Anthony Clarke is telling anyone who cares to listen that he's fully prepared to do precisely that.'

FIFTY

Molly was all set up in a quiet room on the ground floor that was more commonly used for interviewing witnesses. A fold-out camping bed stood upright against the far wall, beneath a pile of sheets, blankets and pillows. Bliss had fetched her a couple of cheeseburgers from Five Guys, and she devoured them while he ate his own. Afterwards, they washed the food down with milkshakes. He had sent his team home, so it was just the two of them.

'You're looking a lot better than you did on Wednesday morning,' Bliss told her. 'I hope you're feeling better, too?'

Nodding, Molly said, 'Physically, yeah, I'm doing okay. Bit sore under the stitches, but it could've been a lot worse. Not sure what's going on inside my head, though. It's been a fucked-up few days.'

'You've definitely been through the mill.'

'Yeah, you could say that. Abducted, snatched back in a police raid, chased, almost taken again at gunpoint.'

'Doesn't look to have spoiled your appetite,' he said, nodding at the discarded burger wrappers, melted cheese still clinging to them.

Molly shrugged. 'The way I live my life, you learn to eat as often and as much as you can, no matter what. Never know when your next meal will be.'

'All of which is about to change.' Over their late dinner, Bliss had explained the arrangement being made for moving the girl into care. 'By the end of the week you'll be with a foster family who want you, who will look after you, feed you and keep you warm. That's not the worst of Christmas presents, right?'

Her smile was genuine but fragile. There was still no light shining in her eyes. 'I know you mean well,' she said. 'You all do. I've seen a different side to you lot over the past few days, and I appreciate everything you're doing for me. But… you know, I've heard this kind of stuff before. I've been promised a brighter future more times than I can count. It's just never turned out that way for me.'

Bliss knew then what he had only previously suspected: Molly had been in the system. He sighed. 'I can't imagine what life has been like for you. I only ever had loving parents, and that made all the difference growing up in the east end of London. I could easily have gone down the wrong path, but my old man was a copper and he and my mum instilled values in me. The world can be harsh, and for whatever reason it seems to have been particularly severe on you. But there are other couples like the Paxtons out there for you, Molly. The family you wind up with will have been placed under the kind of scrutiny even I wouldn't pass. You won't be a project to them, and they won't be waiting with open arms in order to feel good about themselves, either. I promise you that. Anybody who takes you in at this point does so because they want you. You treat them well, they'll treat you like a princess.'

Molly rolled her eyes as she sucked up the dregs of her shake. 'Bloody hell, are you always this sappy?'

'Not so's you'd notice. And don't you go telling anyone else. Wouldn't want to ruin my lousy reputation.'

The girl regarded him thoughtfully, her narrow gaze drilling into him. She eventually shook her head and said, 'Nah, you're not as fucked up as you like to make out. Those people you work with, they think a lot of you. I can tell by the way they respond around you, and by how they speak. There's respect there.'

Bliss chuckled. 'How old are you? Fifteen going on fifty?'

Molly groaned. 'I feel flipping ancient today, that's for sure. I've got bumps and bruises all over me after that car chase, and I ache everywhere. You threw that bloody motor of yours around like a stunt driver.'

He winced. With everything that had happened subsequently, he hadn't even thought about what state his car would be in having shunted other vehicles out of the way and off-roaded on the grass verge. He had ridden back to Thorpe Wood with Molly in a marked SUV, Chandler and Kim Parker in a separate vehicle. His Insignia was making the journey on the back of a transporter, along with the ARV. He'd already signed out a pool car.

'I know you got tossed around a fair bit,' he said, 'but it was better than the alternative.'

'That's for sure.' Molly looked down at the floor for a few seconds before her head came back up. 'So, I'll be out of your hair on Monday, then.'

He ran a hand self-consciously over his head. 'What's left of it, yes.'

'I've been nothing but a pain in the arse to you since you stopped me jumping off that roof. I bet you wish you hadn't now.'

Bliss shook his head. 'Whatever's happened as a result of my actions comes with the job I choose to do. It's a rough-with-the-smooth kind of deal. But whether you like it or not, Molly, I'll always look back on Wednesday morning as one of my better days at work.'

'You're so sure, aren't you?'

'About what?'

'That I'm worth it.' Molly's eyes held his, and began to swell as emotion poured out of them for the first time. 'What if you're wrong, though? What if I find myself the perfect family and still manage to screw it up?' Her voice broke as she finished talking.

'That's not going to happen,' he said firmly. 'Look, Molly – if that really is your name – social services won't rest when it comes to digging into your background. Eventually they'll discover who you are. They'll trace whatever family you do have, your flesh and blood, and then the legal procedures will kick in. If you're not sixteen, then your family will be allowed to make a claim for you to be returned to them. You have a right to fight it. But to do so, you're going to have to be honest. You'll need to tell somebody the truth about who you are and where you came from.'

After a moment, the girl said in a hushed voice, 'I'd tell you. You and Penny. You two are the first decent couple I've met in such a long time.'

'Don't dismiss the Paxtons so readily,' Bliss said, then laughed. 'And besides, Pen and I are not a couple.'

'Well, you certainly act like you are. I get that you're a bit too old for her, but you could do worse.'

'You're right. On both counts.'

'Mind you, she could do a lot better for herself.'

His laughter increased, but after a while he grew serious again. 'Molly, my sincere hope is that you will be cared for by a family so ideal that you'll want to open up to them about everything you've endured in your short life. And it's not a case of "out of sight, out of mind" on my part. I want you to find a family you trust enough to tell them all the good, bad and ugly. Believe me, people like that will not think any less of you, no matter what you tell them. That said, if for some reason you decide to tell me first – or me and Pen together – then arrangements can be made.'

'What do you mean by that? What kind of arrangements?'

'Only that once we have completed the first stage of your relocation, the idea is for you to be immediately whisked away again elsewhere. We won't be told where, nor when you are moved on again. It's for your safety, and that of your eventual foster parents. However, we can still arrange a meeting with you on neutral territory at some point in the future, because your new details will sit on a flagged database. That means a few people at the very top of the organisation will have access to your records. If you put in a request to meet with us, they'll make it happen.'

Molly's look of heartfelt relief touched him deeply. He found it difficult to understand why she had become anchored to him, but he also had to make the transition away as easy as possible. For all concerned.

'So, sure, if you decide you want to tell your side of the story, or if social services come calling about your real family and you want somebody else in your corner other than your foster parents, all you have to do is ask. I'll be there for you. I promise.'

'You will, won't you?' she said, as if in awe of such a commitment. 'You'll actually keep to your word.'

'I'm nothing without that,' Bliss said. 'And going back to what you said earlier – yes, you're worth it. I knew that from the moment I laid eyes on you.'

***

Bliss thought about that conversation as he pottered around his home later that evening. It was cold and damp out, so he ignored the garden. Music held no immediate allure for him, and neither did he have the concentration necessary to immerse himself in a film or a box set. Instead, his thoughts flicked between Molly and the chat he had just finished with Sandra Bannister, who had called to ask how everything was progressing.

'I wish I knew,' he'd told her honestly. Bliss fed her as much information as he felt comfortable in relaying about Lisa Pepperdine, keeping any thoughts he had about Flynn, Sykes and Marsh to himself.

'So you're thinking Jason Ball had something to do with her murder?' Bannister said. It was the logical conclusion, based on everything he had told her.

'It's a line of inquiry,' he admitted. 'But I'd hold off on posting that up if I were you. We have fingers pointing in several directions at the moment, and I don't want to lead you astray.' Any other journalist and he would not have applied the caveat, but Bliss thought he owed her that much.

'Good grief, Jimmy – you and I certainly have made progress.'

'It's beginning to look that way.'

'There was a time not so long ago that you would have been overjoyed at the prospect of feeding me fake news.'

Bliss smiled to himself. 'It's a sport we at HQ enjoy playing. Baiting the press is worth a gold star, getting them to run a dodgy story an extra three.'

'But not any more, it seems.'

'Well, I can't vouch for others. Let's just say that you and I have strayed across the fuzzy lines.'

'So, when should I expect to be able to call in my dinner for two chit?'

He heard the amusement in her voice. She was partially baiting him now, but he also sensed genuine interest there. 'Not until this is over,' he told her. 'I need to put a few things behind me before I can relax.'

This time there was a pause. When she spoke next, Bliss picked up on some caution. 'Jimmy, I wouldn't normally ask, but I don't want to go into this thinking one thing, only to be embarrassed when it turns out to be something entirely different. So I'm just going to come out with it and be straight with you. This dinner invitation… it's more than just an opportunity to ingratiate yourself with me so that I'll keep providing you with intelligence, right? I mean, tell me I'm not wrong in thinking it's a proper date.'

And there it was. The question Bliss had feared having to answer ever since he'd first mentioned it. A knot of anxiety pulled tighter still, but he found himself smiling and nodding as he replied, 'You're not wrong. And I'm not trying to wriggle out of it, believe me. But I have a lot on my plate right now, and I can't spare any part of me for something so personal.'

'Fair enough. I accept that. And thank you for being honest with me. Okay, so back to being professional. If I'm hearing you correctly, you're looking at Ball and his group in respect of Lisa, but you have yet to rule out someone within your own organisation.'

Briefly he toyed with the notion of mentioning Chief Inspector Marsh. Introducing his name into the mix would help steer her thoughts away from Flynn and Sykes, but it was a gamble because it might also renew her interest in the police as a whole. He opted to keep it to himself for now, but allowed for the possibility of dropping the name on her if he believed it would improve their chances of getting the man to speak to them again. Talk to us or answer to the media, was the way Bliss planned to steer that idea.

'Nothing is closed off right now,' he told Bannister. 'We're making headway, but of a kind I can't possibly discuss with you at this stage.'

She understood. Over the past year, Bliss had begun to get a better read on her. Each of them regarded the other as being on the opposing side of a divide drawn up before they were born, yet Bannister was not after a leg-up on the back of an exploitive, sensational piece of journalism. She was the genuine article, and for the first time in as long as he could remember, had provided him with a media contact he was able to trust. It had worked out well for both of them, and he hoped to continue that arrangement, irrespective of what happened between them personally.

Still scratching aimlessly around the house and finding himself unable to settle, Bliss took the pool car out for a spin. He headed west past Alwalton and Chesterton, then hung a left and drove slowly up the uneven track towards Hill Farm. It was a bit of a climb, but the Mondeo handled it easily. He didn't like communal vehicles, but with his off the road it was better than paying for cabs.

At the top of the hill he did a three-point turn, came to a halt and switched off the engine. The night immediately became dark and silent, and Bliss appreciated both. He recalled driving Chandler up there late one evening, hoping she would enjoy looking down at the city beneath them as much as he did. The glow was brighter these days, the council having swapped sodium bulbs for LED lighting, but his eyes generally focussed on the cathedral, and the river of lights encircling the city as they always seemed to do no matter what time of night he drove up there. Red and white pinpoints flowed both ways, like blood cells pumping through the city's heart.

'I was born and raised in this area,' Chandler had told him on that first visit. 'Lived most of my adult life in Peterborough, but I never even knew this place existed.'

'You clearly need to get out more.'

She had given him one of her looks, which quickly became a frown. 'How on earth do you know about it?' she'd asked.

'I came up here to do some strawberry picking,' he said. 'I saw a board advertising it one day and decided to give it a whirl.'

'You?' Chandler said, incredulous. 'Picked strawberries?'

'Yeah, me. What, it's news to you that I like strawberries?'

'No, Jimmy. It's news to me that you would volunteer for manual labour.'

Bliss laughed at the memory, though tonight the view was a disappointment. Low cloud and misty rain obscured much of the landscape; they were well into winter now, with Christmas just around the corner. He gave it a few more minutes before driving home again, feeling frustrated. He made himself a cup of tea and stood sipping it while he stared out into the back garden.

After a minute or so he exhaled a deep breath and asked himself why he was on edge. There were plenty of reasons – from the possible involvement of a police officer in Lisa Pepperdine's murder, to Molly's entangled life and the fact that she would be moving on within the next day or so. From being the target of a gangland enforcer, to the continuing aftermath of losing a good friend and colleague. Yet he believed there was something lying beneath and separate from these issues. Related, yet set apart. After a few minutes more, with both his breath and the heat escaping his mug misting the glass sliding doors that led out to the garden, Bliss realised what was causing his unease.

Personal complications seldom intruded into his working life, but right now his thinking was woolly and the reason was clear. Without delaying to second-guess himself, Bliss took out his mobile and dialled a number.

'Hi, Emily,' he said when the call was connected. 'It's Jimmy. I think we need to talk.'

FIFTY-ONE

He had visited many towns and cities over the past few years, and they had all begun to blur into one, to the point where it was sometimes impossible to differentiate between them. The saving grace of a city was usually its cathedral, occasionally a central park. Just as often, the high streets were riddled with betting shops, charity stores, coffee bars, and the kind of jewellers who both bought and sold precious metals. Peterborough, as far as he could discern, was no different.

Sunday morning was a time for reflection, and Anthony understood he had one final chance in Eric's solitary eye. Even Leroy would be inclined to turn his back if another failure left them all with a sour taste in their mouths and the police crawling up their backsides. Eric didn't frighten him. Sure, this was the man's manor, and that deserved some respect – but Anthony had seen nothing so far to cause him anything more than a bit of indigestion. Losing Leroy's business, however, would be an entirely different matter. That was a lot of wedge to drop, and his boss could be a vengeful bastard when he wanted.

As he drove around the city, becoming familiar with its nuances, Anthony considered how best to rectify his own errors. Ryan

Endicott, as he had made abundantly clear to Eric, was not an issue of his or Leroy's making. He'd throw in a solution to the problem as a freebie, but would accept no blame for the mid-level dealer. Word had come down that Endicott had been charged and was being held on remand. He was, therefore, the easy fix. There were half a dozen blokes on the inside who would take care of that fool in exchange for a weekly bag of groceries for their dear old mums.

Molly, on the other hand, posed a genuine problem. Information on her was hard to come by, which meant the police had compartmentalised further. Anthony's guess, one on which he was staking his entire reputation and perhaps even his life, was that after the failed attempt to move the girl, she would now be under lock and key inside the local main nick. If so, she couldn't stay there forever. Nor could she remain hidden afterwards. For people like Eric and Leroy, there were ways of finding out the things they needed to know.

Already that morning he had put calls in to a few contacts they had provided. A guy who knew a guy who knew a copper at Thorpe Wood accepted the task of acting as a liaison between Anthony and whatever the police were doing to protect the girl. First job was to confirm Molly's precise location – a simple enough ask. A police station was like any other workplace, in that rumour and gossip spread as quickly as the legs on an Amsterdam whore, especially if you flashed the cash around. Once he had the answer to that, Anthony had two more questions: was Molly being moved on any time soon? And was it possible to get to her while she was still inside the station?

Ignoring his wider surroundings but taking great care with his wheels in white van man territory, Anthony worked on ideas for those answers when they came. When the police eventually moved Molly, would they make a song and dance about it? A major convoy escort, armed to the teeth? Or keep it low key and smuggle her out in the back of somebody's daily ride? If it was the latter, that left Anthony with far fewer options available to him.

Fuck Eric, and fuck Leroy. I'm only human, after all.

Anthony sucked air through his teeth and his lips curled into a sneer. He couldn't allow himself to be distracted. It was a tough enough ask without losing focus. It occurred to him that getting to the girl before she was shipped out was by far the better option. They had to feed Molly, talk to her, let her get some exercise. All of which meant she'd be escorted by uniformed coppers. How easy would it be to make sure one of them was his man on the inside?

His mind drifted across to the woman from social services. Collins. He'd slipped into her life easily enough yesterday, and he knew exactly how to bend her to his will. She would have to know when Molly was moving, where to, and how. Having his guys set her free so soon in the game had been a big mistake, but this wasn't the time for regrets. Working her a second time could be a good approach. Which was precisely why he wasn't about to do it. No way the police weren't going to have her under observation, probably with a firearms unit close by. No, that was too risky. This time, using an insider was clearly the best way forward.

Those bastards from this shithole of a city's Major Crimes team were due some pain, too. He was in this mess largely because of them, and that was something no enforcer worthy of the name would ever let slip by. Inspector Bliss had become his own personal bogeyman, and as the detective had defeated yesterday's snatch-up plan, he had to be the first to suffer after the Molly problem had been taken care of.

Anthony was slowing down at the lights by the railway station when a vehicle slammed into his rear end. The collision snapped his head forward and back again, sending it thudding into the headrest with a fierce jolt. Immediately his eyes blazed.

My wheels.

My fucking wheels.

So enraged was he at the incompetence of the driver behind him, it took four attempts to unbuckle his seat belt; eventually he had to consciously calm himself and revert to a smooth single movement. He threw up his door and climbed out, ready to tear the other driver limb from motherfucking limb. As he placed one smooth leather sole on the road surface, a man with brown skin and jet-black hair leaned in and waggled a pistol in his face.

'Not just yet, matey,' the man said. He wore a confident smile and his manner was completely relaxed. 'Slide yourself back in and let's take a ride.'

Anthony remained motionless. He dipped his eyes to take in the weapon one more time before raising them to stare at the man pointing it at him. 'Is this your idea of a joke?' he snarled. 'Some kind of wind up? Did Eric send you to threaten me or something?'

Anthony felt his car rock as the passenger door was yanked open and someone climbed into the Audi alongside him. He glanced over his shoulder. Another bloke with brown skin and black hair. 'Eric who?' the newcomer asked. 'We don't know no Eric.'

'Then who the fuck are you and what the fuck is going on?'

The unknown passenger drew his own pistol. Aimed it at the centre of Anthony's face. 'Get yourself back behind the wheel. The three of us are going for a ride. And… be careful. I hear these guns can be a bit lively and sensitive. We don't want no *Pulp Fiction* shit going down here, do we? There ain't no Mr Wolf around to manage the clean-up.'

'Do you have any idea who I am?' Anthony asked, the moment he was driving again. Anger hung off him like a concrete weight bound by heavy chains. He felt the pull of it dragging him down, and wrestled to find a counterbalance.

The first man, who was now sitting directly behind him with the barrel of the gun so close to Anthony's head that every so often it bumped against his neck, said, 'Not a scooby, mate. Nor do I give a shit. You want to drive around here in a motor like this, you deserve everything you get, yeah?'

'I will punish you,' Anthony said, his teeth virtually clamped together. He realised his eyes were bulging, and he imagined blood vessels bursting inside them. 'Both of you motherfuckers. When we're done with whatever this is, I will make you both scream.'

'Big words for a guy with two guns pointing at him.'

'And I am a man of my word. You pair of chancers want to live, you'd better kill me.'

The man in the passenger seat laughed. 'Hear that, Ejaz? He's gagging for it!'

The pair enjoyed the moment, then fell into silence, their talk limited to directing Anthony. He didn't recognise where he was once he was off the main road, but after a series of roundabouts they approached an industrial estate. He swallowed. These places were never a good thing in this kind of situation. He couldn't make out who these jokers were. They weren't acting like Eric's hired muscle, and genuinely hadn't seemed to recognise the name. But unless Leroy had shot his wad too early, he was left to wonder why this was happening.

Rear-seat man – Ejaz, Anthony thought the other had said – had him pause outside a wide steel gate, which swung open a few seconds later. Passenger-seat man used a wave of the gun to indicate that he should carry on through. The driveway curved right, and as they approached a large unit its shutter doors rattled upwards. He nosed into the building's gaping mouth and on into the gloom of its interior.

'Kill the engine and get out,' rear-seat man said.

This time Anthony did as he was told without uttering a response. These two walking dead men had no idea how little time they had left to live, nor how long he would make that time feel for them.

Given the race of the two men who'd jacked his car, he was surprised to see four white people standing in the open bay of what was clearly a working garage. The jackers walked across to one of them – a woman – and handed over their weapons.

'The replicas worked a charm, I see,' she said, slotting the pistols into individual plastic bags.

Front-seat man nodded. 'They had him fooled,' he replied, grinning and shooting a thumb back over his shoulder.

Anthony realised then that the motherfuckers had duped him. Their shooters were not real, and he'd been taken for a fool. He didn't have time to dwell on his mistake or make threats against the pair, because one of the men who'd been waiting inside the garage took a step forward. His tight grin was one of satisfaction, and he had a casual toughness in his expression that Anthony did not like at all. This was a man to be reckoned with.

'Good morning, Mr Clarke,' the man said. Their eyes locked. Anthony knew he was in trouble. 'My name is Bliss. Detective Inspector Bliss from Thorpe Wood nick. I hear you're looking for somebody I know.'

***

The timing was crucial. In most circumstances, Bliss would rather have had Anthony Clarke and Eric McManus scooped up at the same prearranged time, but he'd chosen to take Clarke off the streets first in order to sow the seeds of doubt in McManus's head later on. The emphasis in Clarke's interview was to make him think he'd been given up by the man he was here to do a job for. In the old days, a rolled-up telephone book often forced suspects to squawk. Now it was all about mind games, and people's minds these days were so fragile.

The moment Bliss had become aware of Clarke's intentions, he'd pooled all his resources and drilled down deep into the enforcer's life. Information came in from detectives down in Homerton and Hackney, together with everything Peterborough CID knew about McManus's operation and the goons he employed. It wasn't long before a mental image appeared in Bliss's mind of the man he now had in his sights.

Sharp suits, expensive shoes; swagger, but no bling. A man of the people, for his people. Clarke lived outside the area in which he mostly plied his trade. His flat in one of the Chamberlin, Powell and Bon-designed tower blocks at the Barbican in central London must have set him back a hefty sum of money. Considered either a brutal or a beautiful piece of architecture, the skyscrapers were now approaching fifty years old, yet the residential properties within remained much sought after. An enforcer would have to have a lot of blood on his hands to afford one, and Bliss couldn't imagine how the man had avoided having his collar felt until now.

It was while he'd been reading all about Clarke's lifestyle that Bliss happened upon a piece of information that caused him first to pay closer attention, and then to summon up a wry smile. Was it mere serendipity, he wondered, that he'd stumbled on the fact that Anthony Clarke was a man who enjoyed flaunting a flash and expensive set of wheels, at the same time as the Baqri brothers were running scared? Bliss thought not. Sometimes the cast die fell the way of the good guy.

Catching the Baqris in the act of turning over jacked cars had always been problematic, but locating them had never been an issue. One call to Rashid Baqri's solicitor was all it took to get the brothers into a room with Bliss and Chandler. While they chatted, DS Bishop was finding out more about Clarke's motor.

When his sergeant beckoned him out of the meeting, Bliss knew they had something. As expected, Clarke had the Audi protected, and Bliss thumped the desk in excitement when Bishop told him it was covered by Tracker. The company worked closely with the police; its technology could bypass GPS jamming devices and locate vehicles parked underground, stored in a shipping container, or anywhere within Europe, but this time they had no need of its bells and whistles, just its ability to relay real-time information on the car's precise location. Bliss had reentered the room and put the Baqri brothers to work, doing what they did best.

Next up was the man of the hour.

Clarke was a striking figure up close. His looks matched his attire, and his eyes caught everything. Bliss recognised a worthy opponent, and after a minor recalculation of his tactics, he got down to business.

'For your information,' he began, 'Ryan Endicott has been moved into a single cell, where he will be kept separated from the general population. You should also know that we are running forensic financial checks on all prison workers, just in case you have one or more of them on your payroll.'

'I have no idea what you're talking about,' Clarke said. His features remained impassive.

'Furthermore, the girl you know as Molly is being guarded as if she's the Queen right now, so whoever you hired to get to her will not be successful.'

'Again, I don't know these people. What do they have to do with my being carjacked?'

Ignoring the man's unruffled responses, Bliss continued without pause. 'Whatever you came up here to do, Anthony, you need to know you've been unsuccessful. I can't help but worry about what that means for you. Your bosses won't be happy. I'm sure they also realise that the kind of protection we are providing for Endicott and Molly will not be afforded to you. Behind bars, you will be exposed and vulnerable. I doubt that's the future you'd envisaged for yourself.' Bliss grunted. 'Such as it is.'

Clarke sighed, maintaining his easy posture. 'You have me mistaken for somebody else. Being a black man, I'm entirely used to being pulled over because I'm driving a nice motor. I get that you're under the impression I stole a car of such rare quality, but I have proof of ownership and insurance, if only you'd care to check. Maybe then you'll move my assailants in here instead of me.'

'Do you imagine we're relying on you to cough, Anthony?' Chandler said. She sniffed and shook her head. 'If that's why you're acting so laid back, then I suggest you think again. See, you were sent up here to rid your bosses of a problem. Only, now you *are* the problem. You're the one being detained and questioned. You're the one Leroy Kelly and Eric McManus will have doubts about. And as you well know, when you give doubts a little while to fester, they soon become fears. Both of those men have a lot to lose if you start talking. They may have regarded you as a stand-up bloke, Anthony. The sort of employee who will happily do time and keep his mouth shut – but why take chances? I, for one, don't see them as the kind of men to sleep easy in their beds fretting about you blabbing to us. And they will most definitely be aware of just how much you have to blab about.'

Bliss nodded, pleased with his partner's contribution. He had zeroed in on Clarke's eyes throughout, but was disappointed by what he had seen there. No give at all so far. Time to bear down on the weight of any gathering pressure.

'In many ways, it doesn't matter if you talk to us,' he said. 'All we need in order for this to work in our favour is for one of those two men to believe you capable of it. Kelly understands you best, and he might be inclined to give you the benefit of the doubt. But the way I hear it, he's also a practical man. He can earn back in an hour the kind of money it would take to silence you for good. So I have to wonder how loyal he is to you, Anthony. Especially if McManus decides you have to go. And McManus barely knows you; he owes you absolutely nothing.'

Clarke threw his head back and laughed at the back of his throat. When he spoke, he did so with the same degree of calmness he had demonstrated since his arrival. 'This is all very entertaining,' he said. 'Clearly you people have me mixed up with somebody else. Sounds like a pretty disturbed man to me. Whereas I am not. I'm merely the victim of a carjacking and some police discrimination and casual racism. Now, I have been patient with you, but it's time to put up or shut up. So, either let me go or arrest me and allow me to call my brief. You two are done.'

Bliss arrested him on the spot.

They put Clarke on ice as they waited for his solicitor to travel up from London. By this time, DCI Warburton was on site and asking for details. She wanted to know why they were not sending teams over to arrest Eric McManus.

'He's going nowhere,' Bliss told her. He was unconcerned about the way the interview had gone down. At no point had he expected Clarke to break. He hoped that would come later, after McManus had been spoken to here at Thorpe Wood, and Leroy Kelly down in Homerton. However little was said, something generally cropped up. Snippets of information to feed back to make Clarke believe he'd been thrown to the wolves. And if it didn't go their way with him, they could always convince McManus and Kelly that Clarke was spilling his guts.

'How can you be so sure about that?' Warburton asked.

'DI Bentley tells me McManus considers himself to be the Teflon man. Nothing sticks. Nothing ever will, as far as he's concerned. His arrogance and lack of awareness are about to be his downfall. When we eventually pay him a visit, I want him to know we've had plenty of time to sweat Clarke. I don't just want him to believe us when we tell him Clarke gave him up – I want him to be convinced of it within seconds of us ringing his doorbell.'

'You think one of them will rat the other out,' Warburton said. It wasn't a question.

'No.' Bliss shook his head. 'I don't see that happening. But we'll get something from each of them. Enough scraps to make a whole meal, if we do our jobs properly. Plus it buys us time to bring in a few of McManus's minions again, only this time they'll know their boss is in an interview room right alongside them. They'll also be aware that Ryan Endicott is being held on remand, and that Leroy Kelly is being squeezed down in London. They'll start to feel as if it's all coming apart, and they'll be rudderless. It's those low-level scumbags I'm really after. Because it's them who will eventually crumble and give us McManus and Clarke. If either of those two breaks, it'll be a bonus.'

'Are you certain of this strategy, Inspector?'

'I'm rarely certain of anything, ma'am. But at least give me the opportunity to see if I can get enough to present a case to the CPS. Bagging McManus, Endicott and this Clarke bloke would be quite a coup.'

Bliss was still thinking about that conversation when he sent Bishop and Ansari to pick up McManus, and another team to arrest the man's crew. What had remained unsaid was the issue uppermost in Bliss's mind: that with these specific men trapped inside the walls of Thorpe Wood nick, none of them would be on the outside when Molly was driven away the following day. He did not care about any coup. Somebody was going to flip, and the justice system would slip into gear and grind its way through to some sort of result. It mattered, because taking bad people off the board always did, but not as much as clearing secure passage for Molly. For him, that was everything.

FIFTY-TWO

When in doubt, if Bliss had to grab a bite to eat while remaining close to work, he did so either in the lounge at the Holiday Inn or at the Woodman pub. It was mid-afternoon by the time all of his team were free, but Bliss accepted no refusals when asking them to join him at the hotel restaurant. Only DCI Warburton declined, insisting that as the most senior rank she ought to remain on site in the event an immediate response was required to any issue arising from the multiple arrests.

The food and drinks were on him, and his only stipulation in return was that his colleagues did not discuss work. This was down time, he insisted, and his team deserved both the break and his gratitude. Once again they had come through for him. Nothing was settled in respect of the drugs gang, yet Bliss was comforted by the fact that his main concern, Molly, would now not only be safe but also feel secure when she finally left Thorpe Wood. As for Lisa Pepperdine… the moment Molly was gone, he intended to push all of his attention onto Robert Marsh and Craig Ball.

As he sat back and listened to his team laughing and joking, the stresses of the past few days evaporating amidst the ribald chatter, a shadow appeared over his shoulder. When he turned, he was surprised to see Joe Flynn standing there. After a brief exchange of introductions and greetings with everyone at the table, Flynn asked Bliss if he had a few minutes to spare. The two walked into the bar at the front of the hotel and found a table, where Bliss waited for his old boss to open up. Given the burden Flynn looked to be carrying on his shoulders, he suspected he would not like what he was about to hear.

'The first thing you have to understand, Jimmy, is that I never imagined the decision I took back in the spring of 2005 would end up with that young woman losing her life.' Flynn shook his head miserably as he spoke, eyes dark and a haunted expression on his face.

'What decision was that, Joe?' Bliss asked. His tone was gentle, but his thoughts raced ahead of the conversation.

'It was me Pepperdine wished to speak with. She was insistent, but I was equally determined it was never going to happen. She threatened to expose us as being systemically racist, offering so-called evidence of our inattention and lack of care concerning the spate of arson attacks. She dangled a baited hook, but I wasn't about to bite, because I knew we were clean on that score. I was absolutely confident that we were doing everything within our power to find the perpetrators and stop the assaults. I also don't like giving in to despotic tactics. That said, I have to admit that her passion got to me. It nagged away inside my head, despite my disinclination to talk. Even so, I had no intention of serving up exactly what she wanted. In the end, I tasked Stuart to first hear her out, but then send her off with a flea in her ear.'

'Sykes?' Bliss hissed. 'You're telling me he's responsible for what happened to Pepperdine?'

Flynn abruptly shook his head. 'No, no. Not alone, at least. No, Stuart put his mind to the problem I'd dumped in his lap, and decided to deal with it in the exact same way as me.'

Bliss blew out some air, fearing he knew what came next. 'He gave it to Chief Inspector Marsh to deal with.'

'He did.'

'So it was Marsh. Marsh killed Pepperdine and then buried her. Was it an accident? Did he just snap? What happened, Joe? You've come this far. You have to tell me everything now.'

Flynn stared back at him through flat, lifeless eyes. Torment scarred his face with creases of pressure and neglect. After a moment he shook his head, and in a hoarse voice that trembled with shame, he said, 'I wish it was as easy as blaming Robert. I really do, Jimmy. When I first heard Pepperdine had moved on, I was naturally delighted, but I asked no questions of Stuart. Truth is, I didn't want to know what had been said or done. He tells me he felt exactly the same way after passing the shitty end of the stick to Robert.'

'If Marsh killed her, then he's the one to blame. You and Sykes may be complicit having avoided responsibility for resolving the problem yourselves, but if it was Marsh who choked the life out of her then he's the one we're going after.'

'No.' Flynn shook his head again. 'No – Robert Marsh never even met the woman. That's why the three of us should all be held to account. We each failed in our duty, Jimmy. We passed the problem along the line until Chief Inspector Marsh had nobody to turn to. At least, nobody in the job. Which was why he turned to an adversary.'

'Jason Ball?'

Flynn blinked his surprise as Bliss pressed on.

'I already know about that shady deal, Joe. One of my DCs poked around and came up with the goods. Marsh asked Jason Ball to take care of the problem for him – without much caring how, I might add. And Marsh knew precisely what he was passing off and the way things were likely to turn out. Thing is, so did Jason.

He smelled it coming a mile off, so he refused, told Marsh to stick the job where the sun doesn't shine.'

This time it was Flynn's turn to nod. 'Sadly, Jimmy, I'm equally aware of that. I know about it because before coming here I met with Robert. The old soak is nowhere near as delightful as he once was… Irascible, is how I'd describe him. He didn't want to talk, but I got him there. Enough to reveal what took place. Had he done the deed himself, I doubt he would ever have broken down and confessed. But the thing is, I believed Robert when he told me he did not murder Lisa Pepperdine.'

'Then who did? And if he told you it was Ball, then he's lying.'

'He did tell me it was Ball, Jimmy. And he was bloody convincing.'

Bliss shook his head, furious now with his old boss. 'I don't care what you think. I've heard what Debbie Ball had to say to my DC, and I'm telling you now I believed every word. Why bother spinning us a tale, when Jason is long gone?'

'Because it wasn't Jason who murdered her.'

'But you just said…' Bliss stopped speaking. His train of thought had caught up with the trail of words, the conversation in its entirety. He took a deep breath and let it go, emptying his lungs.

'It wasn't Jason Ball,' Flynn muttered, turning away.

'No,' Bliss said with a single nod of understanding. 'It was his son, Craig.'

FIFTY-THREE

When Bliss walked into the room where Molly waited alongside Marie Collins and Kim Parker, an immediate charge jolted him as the girl's eyes zeroed in on his. It was surely impossible that she had only entered his life a little over four days ago. She had seldom wandered free of the corridors inside his mind since, and what he felt now was a gnawing sensation in his stomach that threatened to eat its way through to his heart. It devastated him to be saying goodbye, but he offered up his best shot at a smile and held out the bags he had been carrying.

'Here,' he said to the girl. 'These are for you. Just a few bits and bobs. If you don't like them, blame Pen. She's the one with the feeble fashion sense.'

Chandler rolled her eyes. 'Take no notice, Molly. And believe me when I tell you Jimmy chose virtually everything you'll find in these bags. He's as much of a control freak when shopping as he is in the office.'

Molly said nothing, but a warm smile lit up her face as she opened up the packages. She withdrew a scarlet winter coat and raised her eyes.

'If you don't want that,' Chandler said, 'then I'll snap your hands off for it. I may not be able to squeeze into it, but I'll give it my best shot.'

Molly hugged the coat to her chest. 'Nah, you're all right. You look as if you can afford your own, anyway.'

'You reckon? I'm surprised my boss can. Mind you, I don't think I've seen him open up his wallet before, so what do I know?'

Bliss ignored her. He could see that Molly adored the coat, which had been one of his choices. 'Take them with our best wishes,' he said. 'I'm sure your eventual foster parents will lavish clothes and all kinds of goodies on you, but that'll take a few days, so in the meantime I hope these will do.'

Molly stared up at him. He saw her eyes flicker, moments before tears sprang from them. She threw down the bags and the coat on top of them, crossed the room in two long strides, flung her arms around Bliss and clung to him as if she never wanted to let go. He smiled and cupped the side of her head with one hand. Her hair felt soft and tangle-free. She smelled clean and fresh. No longer the wild, unkempt urchin from the rooftop.

'I wish it was you,' Molly said, gulping in air through her sobs. 'I wish you were going to be my foster dad.'

'You know something,' he whispered, her words having just about broken him, 'I wish I was, too.' To his complete amazement, Bliss realised he meant every word. This kid had gripped his life in a way he could never possibly have imagined. He knew then it would never be the same again.

'Can I call you from time to time? Can I? Please?' Molly beseeched him with every fibre of her being.

Bliss's throat felt tight. He shook his head and said, 'You know that's not possible, Molly. As I told you before, if at some point in the future you decide you want to see me, then it can be arranged. But it can't be a regular thing, and we can't exchange phone calls or chat online. You're not even allowed to use social media or have your own phone, remember? But sure, we can arrange to meet at a neutral location one day. It's just not something we can do every few weeks. But don't worry about that, don't even think about it. The only thing that matters right now is making you safe and keeping you safe, and the fewer people who know where you are the better. That includes me and Pen. You understand that, right?'

She nodded and blew her nose into a tissue Chandler had given her. 'I know. I know what I'm supposed to do and what I'm not allowed to do. It's just… so hard. For the first time I have somebody in my life who cares about me and stands up for me, and now that's being taken away again.'

'Molly, your foster parents will care for you, they will stand up for you. You may find that hard to believe, but you have to trust me on that. And the rules are in place for your own benefit and welfare. You'll be fine. You'll see. Give it a few weeks and you won't even remember my name.'

'It's Jimbo. And I'll never forget it.' She gave him a determined look that, if anything, pulled Bliss closer.

He let the nickname slide this time. 'Listen to me, Molly. If you still feel the same way when you're sixteen, then you and I can talk as much as you like. But you still have to be safe and guarded. That's never going to go away.'

Molly glanced down at her wringing hands and became quiet. When she looked up again, her expression was thoughtful. 'We've come a long way from that rooftop, haven't we?' she said.

He nodded but struggled to find the right words to express just how far.

'Then I'm glad you did what you did,' she told him. 'And I'll see you in April, if not before.'

Bliss frowned. 'What does that mean?' he asked.

She smiled at him. 'That's when I turn sixteen. Second of April. I used to say I missed out on being a fool by a single day. My mother always told me I was a fool anyway.'

'Then she knew nothing about you. You're the wisest fifteen-year-old I've ever met – wiser than many adults I know. And thank you.'

'For what?' It was Molly's turn to look puzzled.

'For being truthful. For telling us something real about you.'

'I'll tell you more than that. My real name is Molly – Molly Henderson – but the only relative you'll find when you look it up is my drugged-up whore of a mother. My dad died when I was little. I'm sure I had grandparents, but I never knew them. Never even met them. I never had any brothers or sisters, or whatever it was you called them the other day.'

'Siblings.'

'Yeah, that's it. Nah, didn't have either. My mother said she and my dad took one look at me and decided children were a huge mistake.'

'Like I said: she can't have known you at all.'

Molly shrugged and leaked a shy smile. 'I guess.'

Bliss brushed a hand through her hair, never taking his eyes off hers. 'Molly Henderson, eh?' He nodded. 'It suits you.'

'Yeah. Better than Molly Bliss, anyway. That would just be so fucked up.'

Molly was still weeping as Marie Collins led her out of the door. As they listened to the sound of a young girl in pain echoing along the corridor, Chandler barely managed to contain her own tears, and an ache spread through Bliss's insides. The sense of loss was as unbearable as it was startling.

FIFTY-FOUR

Two hours after Molly's departure from Thorpe Wood, Bliss and Chandler pulled into Stansted Airport, their conversation revolving around the impending arrest of Craig Ball and the state of play with Eric McManus and Anthony Clarke.

Ball was proof, if ever it were needed, that apples seldom fell far from their trees. He had swapped one violent extremist group for another, but he was nothing if not his father's son. Bliss had also openly reflected on the role Flynn, Sykes and Marsh had played in the final outcome. None of the senior police officers was directly responsible for the death of Lisa Pepperdine, but their reputations would be tarnished all the same if the whole truth eventually emerged into the public arena. That was something else for him to ponder, but it would wait a day or two.

As for McManus and Clarke, they were going down. The collapse of their empire had already begun with cracks appearing in the minds of their worker bees, exactly as Bliss had prophesised. There was no way back for Ryan Endicott, either, and in London Leroy Kelly sat in a cell worrying about what was happening beyond the four walls that closed in on him further with every passing hour. Scores would undoubtedly be settled at a later date, but Bliss did not care about who was left standing when the predictable bloodletting was over. As far as he was concerned, nobody he had come into contact with during the case was worthy of rehabilitation. They were barely human to his mind.

Except for Molly, of course. The thought of her forced a grin. Another time, in another place, he would have dismissed her as collateral damage and never considered her again. Had she remained inside Endicott's home rather than seeking answers from a cold, wet hotel roof, he would most likely never have encountered her at all. It was this most capricious aspect of life that intrigued Bliss most of all – the way people bounced off one another in unpredictable patterns. In little more than four days, Molly had gone from being a girl he didn't know debating her choices on a rooftop, to someone he cared a great deal about and somehow knew would both inhabit and influence his life in whatever future he still had. Thinking about her caused the dull ache inside to grow more intense, bringing with it some comfort because it meant a permanent connection – perhaps even a life-altering one – had been made.

Bliss, Chandler, and two uniformed officers met and detained Craig Ball in the arrivals lounge. The man's fresh tan appeared to fade in an instant. Bliss politely asked Ball to accompany them into the side room Chandler had arranged with airport security for the interview. He did so without needing to be cautioned or arrested, either of which Bliss was prepared to do if the man changed his mind.

'I remember Robert Marsh visiting my father,' Ball responded without pause when challenged to explain his connection to Pepperdine. 'I heard them discussing how to deal with her and the aggravation she was causing. My dad turned him down. And I mean flat. No argument. But I had a shrewd idea about how my dad would handle matters if she poked her nose into his business, and I also saw the look on Marsh's face when he refused. So yes,

I admit I spoke with Marsh afterwards, and agreed to have words with Pepperdine myself. I assured him I'd take care of the situation.'

'And what exactly did you mean by that?' Bliss asked. 'How did you intend to take care of it?'

Ball snorted and shook his head. 'Not the way you're thinking, that's for sure. All I intended to do was what I thought everybody else wanted. At least, from everything I'd overheard. They wanted her moved on, away from the city. Marsh because she was coming up with a story that would hurt the police, and my dad because he knew the NCM were in the crosshairs as well.'

'So what happened? What did you have in mind?'

'Well, first of all, I had to make sure it never came back to bite us on the arse. I wanted to help my dad, not make things worse.'

Closing his eyes for a moment, Bliss thought about how this case had unravelled so far. Lisa Pepperdine was like a parcel being passed around from one person to another. Craig Ball had stepped up because he wanted to resolve the situation for his father's sake. He didn't want Pepperdine to pry into his father's activities, nor did he want his old man to buckle and do something stupid. Bliss shook his head at the memory of the man whose despicable ideals had destroyed so many lives.

'What did you do, Craig? Did you hand it off to someone else?'

Ball nodded. 'I wasn't a fan of the things my father was involved in – though I never believed him capable of hiring young kids to do his dirty work like you said.' When Bliss raised his eyebrows in surprise, Ball continued. 'Yeah, I remember you. I know who you are. And I still hold you responsible for what happened to my dad.'

Bliss leaned forward across the table, lowering his voice. 'Your father was a monster. Pure and simple. If I'd had my way, he would have spent the rest of his miserable life in prison. I'm more sorry than you will ever know that Anthony Cox killed him, but only because of what it ultimately did to Cox, who clearly felt life wasn't worth living without his son. And no matter what you believe, Craig, your father murdered that boy with his own bare hands.'

Pain bled from Craig Ball's eyes. Bliss understood that, in many ways, he was also a victim of his father's despicable urges. When he spoke next, he blunted the edge in his voice. 'Craig, we're not here to debate any of that. We're here to discuss your role in the murder of Lisa Pepperdine.'

'And as I told you out there in arrivals, I had fuck all to do with that. I wasn't anywhere near the city at the time, and I can prove it.'

'So you were elsewhere when it went down, providing yourself with a nice little alibi.'

'That's not how it was.'

'Then tell me how it was, Craig. Because so far I've heard nothing to persuade me that you're not responsible.'

'Look, I'll never believe half the things that get said about my dad. That's just the way it is. But I wasn't blind to his hatred towards foreigners. I heard what people said about him and how he was behind those arsons, and what my family didn't need was for some bitch from London writing shit about him. Neither did I want her getting hurt, knowing that would blow back on us as well. So I decided to end it tactfully, and take it outside the family.'

'Go on,' Bliss said, nodding encouragingly. 'You've come this far, Craig. You might as well give it all up.'

'I can only share what I know. There was somebody in my father's organisation who had a natural way to get close to Pepperdine. Someone with a lot to lose if she found out about his membership of a far-right group like NCM. So I had a word with him, and eventually he agreed to apply pressure on Pepperdine and ensure she moved on. He assured me she would never bother my father again. And of course, she never did.'

'Did he ever tell you how he intended to apply this "pressure" he mentioned?'

'Those were not his words, they were mine. I was the one who said he should apply pressure.'

'But you never discussed what form that might take?'

'No.'

'You never asked?'

'No.'

'Because you didn't care. Just so long as she was out of your father's hair, right?'

'The fact that I never asked doesn't mean I wanted her killed. I didn't ask because I didn't need to know. If you don't know, you can't tell, right? Also, there's no way anybody can prove collusion if you have no clue what the other person has planned.'

Bliss's mind was working overtime, thoughts colliding inside his head. During the operation, the finger of blame had alighted on several people, yet each time it had picked out the wrong one. Until now, he hoped. He scrolled back through the investigation – all of the interviews, each of the suspects in turn, the many conversations and decisions made, the people who might have had ways to connect naturally with Pepperdine. One by one he discounted them. Until he was left with only two names.

Andrew Regis and Mark Southern.

Both reporters had worked with or around the freelancer. It was Southern who had enjoyed the closer relationship with her. Yet it was also Southern who had been the more willing to discuss their time together, while Regis had sat there with a look of apparent disinterest while he chewed away on his gum. And of course it was Regis to whom Lisa Pepperdine had supposedly mentioned her forthcoming meeting with a police officer. A conversation Bliss now realised had probably never occurred, the man using the invention to deflect attention elsewhere. A lie had been fed into the maelstrom of information, taking root as an accepted truth. A searing hot rage welled inside him, but he damped it down just as swiftly.

'It was Andrew Regis,' he virtually whispered.

Ball's eyes flickered in surprise. He nodded. 'Yeah, Regis. We knew he was in regular contact with her, that he could easily arrange to meet with her away from the newspaper offices. All he had to do was tell her he had an exclusive for her. According to him, she was desperate for a move up to the big time, so she'd be easy to reel in.'

'And you had every confidence in him because he had a lot to lose. His journalistic reputation was everything, and being exposed as a far-right militant would cost him it all. Now you want us to believe that you didn't think about how volatile a situation like that could be? How easily it could get out of hand?'

'Didn't think about it. Didn't want to think about it. Regis knew what we expected of him.'

'Yeah – I bet he did.'

Shrugging, Ball said, 'I can't be held accountable for another person's actions.'

Bliss squinted at him for several long seconds. 'We'll see what the CPS has to say about that, Craig. If I can find a way to charge you, I will.'

'Good luck with that. If all else fails, I guess you can always have someone else do your dirty work like you did with my dad.'

There was no point in arguing further. Craig Ball would always believe in his father's innocence, just as he would always believe that the DI running the case back then was the man responsible for winding up Anthony Cox and pointing him in the direction of Jason Ball. To Bliss's mind, though, it was all ancient history. Right now, Andrew Regis was his target.

FIFTY-FIVE

By the time they returned to Thorpe Wood, their once-fragmented operation was looking more complete. Even so, Bliss worried about the lack of evidence. He desperately wanted a good solid case, to bring closure for Lisa Pepperdine's family.

As he often did when seeking inspiration, he brought up the case file and went back over the investigation in chronological order. Suspects had come and gone over the past few days, but the only solid leads had materialised from the damp Fengate soil. Bliss realised that his knowledge of the crime scene investigators' findings – beyond the remains and jewellery – was lacking.

He pulled up the forensic report and followed a link to the itemised list of bagged and tagged discoveries. His eyes moved down the page, noting the usual array of zips and fasteners that had survived along with the bones. A few coins, too. But it was the final two items that brought a smile to his face.

'Gotcha, Mr Juicy Fruit,' he said to nobody in particular.

He called Bishop, who was heading up to Stamford to arrest Andrew Regis. When he told his DS what he'd discovered, Bishop was initially cautious.

'Chewing gum?' he said. 'Will it even retain DNA after all these years?'

Bliss was prepared for the question, having already looked it up. 'There was a case in Birmingham in 2016 where DNA was found on a piece of gum left behind thirty-five years earlier. It was viable enough to secure a manslaughter conviction. I'm not saying what we have will produce results, but Andrew Regis doesn't have to know that.'

Following a brief consultation with the CPS, Bliss had given his sergeant the go-ahead to arrest Regis at home. They had Craig Ball's testimony as well as hard evidence proving Regis had once been a member of the NCM and now attended regular gatherings of Britain For The British. They also had every chance of securing the main prize with the man's DNA from the gum he'd spat into the shallow grave of the woman he'd just strangled. A man as addicted to chewing gum as Regis wasn't likely to have neglected his fix while digging a hole and burying a still-warm body. It was, after all, hard and thirsty work. He'd need all the moisture he could pull into his mouth. All Bliss had wanted to find listed on the evidence sheet was a single piece. Instead he found two.

Bishop was ecstatic. He paused for a moment to relay the information to DC Ansari who was driving the pool car. When he came back to Bliss, his mood was euphoric. 'When we arrive at HQ, I'll walk him through all the custodial procedures and ask if he's willing to be interviewed by you without a brief.'

Bliss was in a sanguine state of mind, and he believed his sergeant deserved to see the case through. Where once Mia Short's star had shone, now Bishop was more than ready to reignite the flame. 'No, you stick with him. He's all yours, Bish,' he said. 'Yours and Gul's. Take your time and make him squirm before you put the hammer down. He's going nowhere.'

'Are you sure, boss? I mean, I appreciate the vote of confidence, but this is your case, and it's a major one given the circumstances.'

'And you're a top DS who will be moving up the ladder as soon as you decide you want it. If you work him the right way, he'll go. These people always slip up, and Regis is no exception. The more his story changes, the more you can apply pressure. By the time you get around to telling him about the gum and the high probability of finding his DNA all over it, he'll be ready to fold.'

Still Bishop sounded hesitant. 'I know all this, boss, and I've been there before on numerous occasions, yet somehow on this one I'm doubting myself.'

Bliss thought he knew why. 'That's probably because it's my case, and in the back of your mind you think I'm going to be sitting there watching the interview and judging you.' When Bishop failed to respond, Bliss continued. 'Well, the truth is, I *will* be judging you. Both you and Gul. But I'll be doing so in retrospect because I already know I'm going to like what I see and hear.'

'That's good to know, boss. I appreciate your faith in us.'

'You've earned my trust on any number of occasions, Bish. And to prove it, I'm going to leave you to it. I'm off home. You and Gul have this bloke on toast and I'll assess your performance by watching the recordings. Reel him in, Bish. Make us proud.'

Bliss knew he had laid it on a bit thick, but he was also convinced they would get a result. If the DNA bluff did not elicit a confession, there was still sufficient interview-based evidence from Craig Ball to ensure the CPS took the case seriously. With a bit of luck and a fair wind, they would receive the results of the DNA testing before they had to charge Regis. But Bliss had a feeling they would not have to rely on good fortune.

Content with the way the operation had gone, Bliss put on his coat and left the Major Crimes area. On his way out of the station he bumped into Chandler, who was also heading home. They discussed the case for a few minutes as they walked out to the car park together.

'Will you be satisfied provided we get Regis into court?' Chandler asked.

Bliss scowled. 'You know me, Pen. I'm never entirely happy if we don't get the result we want. But at the moment I'm relieved not to be arresting a fellow cop and having the media chew us up over it.'

'That's true. Though we hardly covered ourselves in glory back then. Almost from the top down we passed that woman's fate around, handling it like a hot coal. It might have been Andrew Regis who ended up strangling her to death, but I can't help feeling we helped steer the two of them together.'

'I agree. Some morally questionable decisions were made, especially by Chief Inspector Marsh. At least Joe and Stuart passed it down the blue line. But let's deal with one thing at a time. Nailing Regis is our sole focus right now.'

'Do we have enough for a conviction without forensics?'

'Not yet we don't. Circumstantial at best. But we know from our experience on Friday that the man's a talker and he's bright, so he'll think he can run rings around us dozy cops. People like that invariably come a cropper at some point. But if not, I'm quietly confident the gum will give us our man.'

Chandler's hair was being disturbed by a cold breeze, and she used a hand to try to control it. She shivered and folded her arms. 'Why do you think he killed her? Motive could be key.'

'It will be, and we're weak there,' Bliss admitted. 'My best guess is that he feared how much she'd find out about him. Her interest in bringing down far-right agitators was well known, and he must have worried about her delving deeper into the NCM and exposing him as a member.'

'That's a pretty decent motive. One we can push.'

'Who knows?' Bliss said. 'Regis may have been considering something like that the whole time Pepperdine was here in the city. Perhaps all he needed was a nudge in the right direction. Getting rid of her would only make Craig Ball appreciate him more… maybe he hoped Jason Ball would bring him into the inner circle by way of a reward.'

'Plenty there for us to explore, then.'

'I suppose. Delving into the mind of another killer.' Bliss scratched at the scar on his forehead. 'What a way to earn a crust.'

'Speaking of which, fancy stopping off somewhere and getting some grub?' Chandler said.

'I bought you dinner earlier,' he said, as if appalled.

'That was lunch. And though this may come as a surprise to you, every now and then we normal folk eat more than once a day.'

Bliss laughed, but shook his head. 'No, not tonight, Pen. Thanks for the offer, but I have a couple of things I need to sort out.'

'You sure?' Chandler screwed up her face, scrutinising him. 'You're not going to sit alone in the dark and mope about Molly, are you?'

'I'm positive. I admit I'll have a hard job shaking her from my thoughts, but I feel a lot better now knowing she's out of this place and on her way to a better life.'

'Okay. So what do you need to sort out, and do you want any help with it?'

Taking a second or two to consider, Bliss finally said, 'Actually, if you have a moment, I'd like to run something by you.'

Chandler nodded. 'Fire away.'

They had reached her Ford Focus. Bliss calmed his nerves and set his mind on what he had to say. 'Pen, that business between us in the summer – that was just two colleagues who work closely together getting carried away when emotions were running high and they were both drunk out of their skulls, yes?'

She frowned, her brain ticking over as curiosity got the better of her. 'You mean the… the kiss we shared when we both thought you were in danger of not surviving the weekend?'

He nodded. 'Yes. That.'

Shaking her head, Chandler said, 'Then no. That's not all it was.'

'Oh,' he said, taken aback by her response.

'Jimmy, you must know by now that I love you to bits. And no, I don't mean in that way. You and I are never going down that path. I love you like a brother, like family. I care for you. That snog was about the moment and the booze, but it was also about how I feel about you. And, I hope, how you feel about me.'

Bliss studied her for a moment. Then he tilted his head to one side. 'So you love me like a brother,' he said.

'I do.'

'Do you kiss your real brother like that?'

Chandler bellowed a laugh and slapped his arm. 'You can't do it, can you?' she said. 'You can't have one lovely conversation without ruining it with a bad joke.'

He held his hands up defensively. 'Hey, I'm just asking, is all. We hear these rumours about you Fenland hillbillies.'

'You daft bugger. And why exactly did you ask? About us, I mean. You sounded as if you were trying to get something straight in your head.'

He nodded. 'I think I was.'

Her eyes sprang open wide. Her mouth, too, until she spoke. 'You're moving on. You had to make sure there was nothing between us, because you've decided it's time for you to move on. Is it Sandra Bannister? Are you *that* interested in our very own Lois Lane?'

Bliss let go a long sigh. 'Pen, what if I said you were right about me moving on? What if I told you I've finally come to the conclusion there's a void in my life beyond work, and I've decided the time is right to do something about it?'

Bliss squirmed as he received his second massive hug of the day, then met Chandler's gaze as she pulled away. He saw only joy in her eyes, twinkling in the cold moonlight. 'I'd say it's about bloody time,' she told him, barely able to speak around her wide grin. 'And I'd also say I'm so chuffed for you I could well up all over again.'

'Don't do that. Please.'

'Why not?'

'Because you're so bloody ugly when you cry.'

'There you go again. Touching moment, bad joke.'

Bliss shrugged. 'It's my way of coping. I don't do emotions, Pen.'

'That's not what I saw when you were saying goodbye to Molly.'

There was no denying that. Bliss considered the warm sensation that overcame him every time he thought about the girl. 'She's just a kid. Kids have that awful knack of burrowing beneath your skin.'

'So you're saying you don't do *adult* emotions.'

He thought about that, and decided she was right again. 'I think that's a fair comment.'

Chandler eyed him with all the affection she had alluded to only moments earlier. 'Then that's something you're going to have to overcome if you're seriously intent on moving forwards,' she told him. 'Whoever the unfortunate woman happens to be.'

Bliss was grateful for his friend's understanding. He pulled her towards him once more, pecked her on the forehead. 'In case I've never made it clear,' he said, 'I love you to bits, too.'

Chandler nudged him with her elbow. 'There you go. See. You *can* do adult emotions.'

'Oh, Pen. That would presuppose I regard you as an adult.' Bliss chuckled as Chandler groaned and rolled her eyes. 'Yeah, I know,' he said, smiling affectionately. 'Touching moment, bad joke.'

FIFTY-SIX

Stepping into a dark, empty house was something he'd grown accustomed to. In the early months following his wife's murder, it had bothered him enormously. Before long, however, he had come to welcome the seclusion. If Hazel was no longer there to share his life, then he had no desire to share it with anyone else, and the emptiness of whatever dwelling he inhabited acted as a reminder of that every single day.

Something about his connection with Molly had changed all that, however. It was as if she had brought his guard down; having first opened his mind to wonder what life would have been like had he and Hazel been lucky enough to have children, it had then expanded to accept the possibility of not being alone for the rest of his life.

During the short drive home, the memory of a wailing, sobbing Molly continued to disturb his thought processes. Irrespective of how she had entered his life, the girl had seeped into his pores and somehow managed to make him care about her. If he had been the only person available to look after her, he would have put his life on hold to do so. And it wasn't only the knowledge that his heart had been prised open that tugged at strings inside him, but also the realisation that he had finally felt comfortable enough to welcome someone else beyond the formidable barriers he had erected.

Bliss realised this confluence of events was telling him something. Something he had been resisting for far too long. He understood now that, however many years he had left to roll around on this tiny rock drifting in space and time, doing so on his own would be a terrible waste. Life was meant to be enjoyed. It was also meant to be shared with others. His mother was not enough, nor Chandler, and not his team, either. As for his memories, they would move forward with him, intact and secure, his brain becoming a natural bubble-wrap. He had been willing to open up his home, his heart, and the rest of his life to a fifteen-year-old kid whom he had known for only a few days. Surely now the time had come to consider doing so with another.

He was still contemplating this in his recliner when a phone call disturbed his reverie. The curse of his job was never truly being off duty. 'What's up, Bish?' he asked.

'You're not going to believe this, boss.' DS Bishop sounded breathless. 'Regis took the bait.'

'What?' Bliss checked the time on the phone. 'You've only had him in the room for five minutes!' That was an exaggeration, but he doubted the interview had been running an hour.

'I know. At first he didn't believe we could get a positive DNA sample from gum that old, but after he conferred with his brief I swear he went as white as a ghost. He's admitting nothing as yet, but they've asked what, in theory, might happen in court if he confessed now to involuntary manslaughter.'

Bliss took time to consider the question. If the lab was able to pull DNA off the gum and it matched Regis, that was a strong indication of him having been there when Lisa Pepperdine was buried. It did not, however, offer conclusive proof that he had murdered her. If he wangled a decent barrister, then a jury could be persuaded that Regis had merely been at the scene of the burial, not the murder itself. The only reason the man's solicitor was even considering a confession at this stage was because confessing to an involuntary manslaughter charge would result in a good deal less time served than a conviction for voluntary manslaughter or premeditated murder after a full trial. Accepting the confession did not amount to the best result, but it was still a hot win.

'Tell them they have a deal,' he told Bishop. 'Clear it with the CPS before you do and make sure they agree on the language. We want this prick to do as much time as we can get, with no wriggle room further down the road.'

A win was a win, Bliss decided. What's more, it would bring about an early closure to yet another dreadful incident from that most awful of years. 2005: the gift that kept on giving. The worst year of his professional life by some distance, and one that repeatedly came back to the well for more. The thought lingered, returning him to the decision he had made shortly before Bishop's call. He had been knocked off course, but now it was time to take a risk.

After helping himself to a cold beer and a couple of fingers of whiskey to calm his nerves, he would call both Emily Grant and Sandra Bannister. To one he would apologise and explain his decision. The other he would ask over to his place for a drink and a discussion about a possible future together. If the alcohol injected enough courage, he would also suggest she bring an overnight bag.

As Bliss heaved himself up out of the chair to get the drinks, the room turned on its axis and started spinning. He had never accurately been able to describe the sensation to other people, except to suggest they remember their most drunken moment and consider how they felt at the time. That was pretty much how it caught him now. Instinctively he took two quick steps; right foot further to the side, left foot a pace forward. Though his mind lurched and his stomach rolled over, the double movement and wider stance stabilised him. His condition made falls a genuine possibility, but with experience he had learned to combat the body's natural reaction when one of its senses issued distress signals.

Spreading his arms out to recentre himself, Bliss blinked a couple of times to clear his vision. Rippling shudders coursed through his entire body, as if deliberately adding a new level of difficulty to his quest to regain an even keel. Nausea took hold, and Bliss felt bile scorching the back of his throat. He fought it off, focussing his eyes on a distant point which helped him overcome his disequilibrium. Swaying as if buffeted by a stiff breeze, he made minute adjustments while slowly backpedalling towards his recliner. When he felt it brush up against his calf, Bliss allowed his legs to buckle at the knees and he fell into the chair with a loud whump, sending it back several inches on the floor.

For a few minutes he sat and caught his breath, quelling the urge to vomit, eyes fixating on a solid object until it stopped wavering. Sweat gathered at his brow, and his mouth felt as it were stuffed with cotton wool balls. When he was eventually realigned, Bliss closed his eyes and repeated a pattern of breathing in through his nose, then expelling air between rounded lips for ten seconds. This had the dual effect of calming both his mind and body.

When the vertigo attack was over and his balance restored, his first thought was not for his own sorry state, but for Molly. What use would he have been to her as a substitute parent when he couldn't even take care of himself? Uncertainty over his own future was enough of a burden, without worrying about how it might impact on others.

Which brought his thoughts full circle to the phone calls he'd intended making. Doing so now would be a sick joke. He'd allowed his heart to overrule his head where Molly was concerned, but at the time he'd been caught up in an emotional whirlwind. He had seen in her the daughter he'd never had, and he knew now it had been a mistake. Reality always found a way to keep you in check.

Bliss worked his mind over his life: the condition he'd lived with for many years, its debilitating effects and uncertain prognosis; the pain he felt in his hands, knees and ankles every morning, an arthritic legacy of the many sports he'd played when he was younger; the solitary lifestyle and work demands he brought with him into any kind of relationship. When he was at home he never truly switched off from work, and just about the only thing that successfully slowed him down was the damned illness. All in all, he presented a most unappealing package.

Was that the future he had been about to offer a woman he had feelings for? To take on the burden of sharing her life with such a crumbling ruin of a man? What on earth had he been thinking? It was an act of pure selfish folly to have even considered it.

From time to time, life threw you in at the deep end, handed you a challenge, and Bliss believed that when you had no choice but to react, that was when the genuine inner person emerged. Something about Molly had blinded him to the harsher realities of life, momentarily prising ajar a door that led to hope. Had he been thinking clearly, he would never have even considered nudging it open further.

One of his favourite quotes by TS Eliot talked about the echoing of footsteps never taken along a corridor which led to a door never opened. To Bliss the quote was poignant, a sad reference to what might have been if only risks had been taken. Yet if you knew there was no light beyond the door, with only darkness and melancholy waiting for you on the other side, why would you ever take that walk along the corridor and hear the echo of those footsteps?

A sad, reflective smile of acceptance on his face, Bliss pushed himself deeper into the recliner and, for the first time in as long as he could remember, switched off his phone. As he had told Jennifer

Howey on numerous occasions, being alone did not mean he was lonely. Loneliness was a state of mind, one to which you did not necessarily have to succumb even if you chose to live on your own. He had forgotten that fact over the past couple of days, and it was time to get his head back on straight. The comfort he found in solitude was not to everyone's taste, but for Bliss it was the rock to which he found himself still clinging by his fingertips.

He had no inclination to release his grip and let himself fall, especially if doing so resulted in him taking somebody else with him. It could be a long way down, and there was no sure way of knowing what lay in wait at the bottom. Bliss had not allowed Molly to take her own leap of faith. As for his own, it would have to wait. There was still time, he thought. There was still time.

ACKNOWLEDGEMENTS

No book gets written – certainly not mine – without a hugely impressive and invaluable team working feverishly in the background to make me look good.

First up, a massive shout out to a bunch of fellow authors whose support, advice and help steered me through the murky waters of publication – to my 'Awesome Authors' friends, THANK YOU!!

This time around I am also happy to offer my deepest gratitude to Alison Birch for the deep and challenging edit, Cherie Foxley for the magnificent cover, Sarah Hardy for putting together an amazing list of bloggers for the tour, and to Caroline Vincent for the wonderful promotions.

To my beta and ARC readers, members of my 'Forder and Friends' online group, bloggers, reviewers and supporters everywhere, please know that this book has a piece of all of you in it – inspired by your kindness and generosity.

A special mention to Rachel Speechley, Senior Youth Offending Officer, Cambridge Youth Offending Team, for holding my hand through the quagmire of procedures and officialdom involved in juvenile social care associated with the criminal justice system. Any relevant errors are mine alone.

2019 was quite a year, and 2020 is already shaping up to be even better and more demanding. Quite how I've managed to bluff my way through nine books is beyond my wit or wisdom, but I hope you enjoyed this one enough to want more, because Jimmy Bliss and his wonderful Major Crimes team will be back later in the year with *Slow Slicing*. I especially hope you loved spending time with Molly – a character who certainly captured my heart. Look out for more of her in the future.

Finally, thank you all for making sense of how I spend my days. It's a curious way of life, but one I wouldn't change for anything – except, perhaps, for the opportunity to play *that* final solo from Pink Floyd's *Comfortably Numb*.

Cheers.

Printed in Great Britain
by Amazon